IN

DEFENSE

OF

MURDER

A Novel

by

TOM DENNARD

Tom Dennard

ISBN-13: 978-1983415647

ISBN-10: 1983415642

Cover photo:

Brunswick, Georgia, Courthouse

Cover photo and design:

Jonathan Doster

JONATHAN DOSTER PHOTOGRAPHY

Photography, Film, Education

Sharon. Connecticut 06069

FOREWORD BY AUTHOR

The story I'm about to tell you concerns my early years of law practice during a time when there was an epic shakeup of culture and politics during the late '60s and early '70s.

With no public defender, the judge appointed the young lawyers in our area to represent those accused of a crime who could not afford to hire someone to represent them. As a neophyte, I'd been assigned a murder case with a sordid background of facts that required me to attempt to balance professional duty versus moral justice. It had a profound effect not only on me, but also my family.

I first wrote the book in 1989 on my old Royal typewriter as a true story, then put the draft on the shelf, knowing it could never be published during the lifetime of my elder family members. I would've been excommunicated, banned from future reunions and only spoken of in whispers for publishing a "sex book," a subject totally forbidden to be discussed in our household.

Now that my elders have gone on to their reward, I felt empowered to take the dusty manuscript from the shelf and not only rewrite it, but also publish it. From the time of the trial until now, the subject matter has radically changed from scandalous and shameful to merely ho-hum.

My previous books have all been non-fiction, except one, and while this is based on true events, I'd forgotten how much latitude fiction permits, allowing me to embellish the story as much as I pleased.

ABOUT THE AUTHOR

Like five generations of my ancestors, I was born in Pineview, a small farming community in the heart of Georgia. I attended Davidson College in North Carolina and graduated from law school at the University of Georgia, where I met my wife, Marie. We live on St. Simons Island, Georgia, have three children and eleven grandchildren.

I practice law in Brunswick and am the founder of The Hostel in the Forest. As an avid hiker, I taught backpacking skills to hundreds of students and have hiked mountains on six continents.

TOM'S OTHER PUBLISHED BOOKS:

Discovering Life's Trails, (1993) a non-fiction book about some of his hikes, travels and experiences

Buzzards Roost, (1996) a novel based on his mother's struggle with Alzheimer's disease

Born a Ramblin' Man, (2007) a non-fiction book about his travels and experiences

Letters to Henry, (2010) a non-fiction book about growing up in the small town of Pineview, told through letters to his dog in heaven

Daily Words to Inspire You, (2011) a book of inspirational words written by many different authors, one for each day of the year

Still Ramblin', (2015) a non-fiction book about his travels and experiences with over 100 color photographs

Daily Words to Inspire You, Volume II, (2016) his second book of inspirational words written by many different authors, one for each day of the year

ACKNOWLEDGMENTS

I benefitted from the talents of so many people to help me put this book together. My two friends, Papillon DeBoer and Robert Peter Jacoby, Licensed Professional Counselors, both well-versed in adolescent behavioral problems, helped me greatly with the molestation scenes. Judge Anthony Harrison assisted me with the trial. R. B. Gentry, a former Marine Drill Sergeant, narrated the things a Marine recruit experiences. Bonni Smith, provided me with an anecdote I used very effectively. Jingle Davis, June Alexander, Mary Lewis, Stephen Doster, Jeffrey Rieger, Luisa Perkins, Peter G. Vaughn and Jason Frye gave me valuable suggestions and assisted with the editing. A special thanks to my son-in-law, Hunt Dunlap for his detailed review and cogent suggestions and saving me from embarrassing myself. My good friend, Jonathan Doster, who photographed the old courthouse where the trial took place, designed the cover and spent untold hours in making helpful suggestions. Bob Drury deserves an abundance of kudos for being my go-to person, who carefully and tediously placed the myriad of time consuming editorial changes in the format required by the publisher. And last, but not least, my wife, Marie, who puts up with me on a daily basis, stands by my side and acts as a cheerleader, encouraging me to never give up when I have a goal I'm trying to attain. Her comment, "The best thing you've ever written."

DEDICATION

This book is dedicated to the people of the world who've been persecuted, in one way or another, for "being different."

·   Tom Dennard

CONTENTS

Brunswick, Georgia
1973

On the day after Thanksgiving, I performed my usual task of stopping by the post office on Gloucester Street to get the mail and driving to my favorite parking spot behind the Dunwoody Building. Up one flight of stairs, I unlocked the door to my office, being the first to arrive. As usual, I went directly to my desk, flipped up the calendar to check appointments and found nothing until 11:00. That suited me fine. I had plenty of files left on my desk from Wednesday that'd been left untouched.

The phone was ringing and neither Bailey nor Bonds had arrived, so I answered, "Greene and Parker Law Firm."

The voice on the other end said, "Is this Tyler?"

"Yes. What can I do for you?"

"This is Judge Fletcher."

"Oh, how are you today Judge?"

"I was wondering if you'd have time to drop by my office."

"Sure Judge. When would you like to see me?"

"Now, if you can."

"Of course. I'll be right over."

I'd never had a call like that from the judge since the time he'd rescheduled a case I was supposed to try earlier than I'd expected, but the notice never got to me. When the time arrived, the judge called me at the office and told me in a gruff voice to get over to the court immediately. I walked in, red-faced, with the courtroom filled with prospective jurors. The judge tapped his gavel and said, "Mr. Tucker, I'll see you in my office."

I could never remember being that nervous. After following the judge into his chambers, I explained the predicament and apologized profusely.

"Don't worry about it," the judge laughed. "I had to make an example out of you before all those jurors to keep them from coming in late. Just walk back into the courtroom and act like I've really scolded you."

I saw to it that I'd never be late again. I knew the judge liked me. His son and I played on the same basketball team in the city league.

Bailey came walking into the office and over to her desk where I was standing. "Did you have a nice Thanksgiving?"

"Yeah, we had a good one," I said. "Sort of quiet – just Laura, the kids and me. How 'bout you?"

"I wish mine had been quiet. Too much family to cook for," she laughed as she picked up her schedule of reminders. "You know Mr. Sawter is coming in at 11:00 to talk about buying some property."

"Yeah, I know."

"Mrs. Jack Norton wants to know if she can see you this afternoon to talk about her Will."

"Do I have time?"

"I'm not sure. You have depositions at 3:00 in that power company case."

"Maybe you could put Mrs. Norton down at 2:00. I think I can squeeze her in. I just got a call from the judge. He wants to see me in his office."

"When?"

"Right now."

"What about?"

"Don't know," I responded.

"Is this all the mail?" Bailey asked.

"I dumped it all on your desk."

I walked back to my office to get my coat, picked up the picture of Laura and stared at it for a moment. We'd gotten into an argument before leaving home. It was probably my fault. I'd been feeling guilty for being spread so thin, trying to be a good husband, a good father, a competent lawyer at the office, my regular basketball games every Monday and Thursday nights, and, in addition, I taught the young-adult Sunday school class at church. Laura had been complaining about being cooped up in the house all the time with the kids. She needed an outlet. I was aware of her frustrations, because I'd go nuts being inside all the time. Spending my weekends with our three children and doing the cooking to try to give her some spare time wasn't enough. We'd been discussing whether or not we could afford to hire someone at least once a week to come in and take care of the kids to give Laura a chance to get out. That was the plan we agreed to talk about when I got home. I grabbed my coat and took off for the courthouse.

It seemed that the three blocks were longer than usual, as thoughts rushed through my head about why the judge would be calling me like that.

When I walked into his office, he had his feet propped on the desk, reading the morning paper. He stood up and slapped me on the back. "You still hitting those jump shots on the basketball court?"

I laughed. "The back of the key is my sweet spot if I can ever get open."

"My son tells me what a good player you are."

The judge, a balding, short man, a bit stocky, with bushy eyebrows had the reputation of being a no-nonsense type. As the only Superior Court Judge for five counties, he was usually in a big hurry but seemed more relaxed that day.

He sat down and motioned for me to sit in the chair in front of his desk. "How long you been practicing law?"

"About a year and a half, I think."

"How old are you, Tyler?" He asked with a serious expression.

"I'm 27."

"I know you have a wife and kids."

"Yes sir. I have three children."

"I guess you know you're with two of the best lawyers in the state?"

"Yes sir. I certainly wouldn't argue about that."

"Tyler, I've watched you in the courtroom, and I'm impressed with the way you handle yourself."

"Thank you sir."

"You research your cases and are always well-prepared. I like that about you."

Still completely in the dark what he might be leading up to, I thanked him for the compliment.

"As you know, I've appointed you to a few criminal cases, and it's my opinion you really do a good job for your client, even though you're young and haven't been practicing all that long."

"Thank you sir."

"I know you law-clerked for a judge in Atlanta and had a good opportunity to see some of the best trial lawyers in the state."

I nodded, still wondering where he was going with this.

The judge leaned over his desk with his glasses on the tip end of his nose.

"Did you hear what happened last night?"

"No sir."

"Some people were here in my office just a little while ago. Apparently, their son got into some trouble, and they're not financially able to hire a big-time criminal lawyer. They wanted me to appoint someone to represent him who'd be qualified to put up the best defense possible. I thought you might be the one."

"Thank you sir. I appreciate your confidence." I leaned back in my chair. "What kind of case are we talking about Judge?"

"I've been trying to reach the sheriff's office to find out some of the details, but they seem to be late coming in after the holiday yesterday. The only thing I know is that it involves two boys, where one killed the other."

He stared into my eyes with a serious expression, then said the words that rang in my ears for days, "Tyler, it appears I'm appointing you to your first murder case."

Davidson College
1968

On a cold, January night, my roommate, JT, and I labored over our text books, studying for semester exams. I'd become lost in the theory of the earth's history and how events of the past might influence the future when JT broke the prevailing silence. He, a red-haired, renowned lady's man, leaned back in his squeaky chair and turned toward me. "You know what I was just thinking?"

"No telling," I mumbled.

"Man you haven't done a damn thing in the four years I've known you except study, play basketball and head off to Georgia to see the only girl you've ever dated. And she won't even give you any, for God's sake."

I shot back sarcastically, "So?"

He raised his voice. "You need to get the hell out of this place and do something wild and crazy."

"Is that right?"

"After graduation, what you need to do is take off for Europe all by yourself. And I'd bet my left nut you'd be the only 22 year-old male virgin on the continent."

I offered up my best defense, "I can't help it if Laura doesn't want to have sex until we get married."

"Do what I tell you man. Run away, get drunk, get stoned and get laid. It'd do you a world of good."

Those scholarly words of advice resonated with me much more than I ever expected.

My name is Tyler Tucker, born in Macon, Georgia, in 1946, to Darlene and Tyler Edwin Tucker. My father's name was bestowed upon me. They called him Ed and me, Tyler. I idolized him, a tall, good-looking, successful lawyer who became a Superior Court Judge. His good name and distinction naturally seemed to trickle down to me. My little brother, Vern, born three years later, received the name of my mother's father, Robert Vernon. Not that his name was unacceptable. It wasn't. But it never carried the allure and esteem of my father's.

My parents referred to me as their normal child, the one who always wanted to be outside shooting hoops or playing in my treehouse, while Vern seemed perfectly content to stay at home reading books and helping Mom prepare meals. I shouldn't say it, but, no doubt, I was the favored son. I suppose that gave me a sense of confidence and a feeling of self-assurance.

My dad, at six-feet-three, played basketball for Lanier High. I followed suit, though one inch shorter. We both were captains of our teams. Upon graduation from high school, Davidson College, a Presbyterian school located about a half-hour north of Charlotte, North Carolina, granted me a basketball scholarship. The college had an enrollment of a thousand male students, no women, not even a female professor. That was tough for me. I felt deprived of feminine companionship.

A demanding curriculum, as a philosophy major, caused me to study more than ever before, but I still found time to play basketball all four years. Being point guard and a fast runner, I had the responsibility of getting the ball across center line and earned my good reputation for stripping the net from the back of the key.

Once a month, I'd hop on a south-bound Greyhound for the six-hour trip to Macon, where my girlfriend, Laura, attended Wesleyan College, an all-girls' school. While there, we'd visit friends, but much preferred being alone, eating barbeque at Miss Piggy's and walking on the trail next to the river, especially at sunset.

When Laura and I broke up during our senior year in college, I felt crushed, groundless and hopeless. My world seemed to be caving in, but, on the other hand, it gave me the realization that JT was right. My entire life had been lived in a prison.

Davidson required students for the entire four years of college to sign a pledge agreeing to refrain from using any alcoholic beverage, either on or off campus or even at home. It was also compulsory to attend church services each Sunday with only three cuts allowed per semester. While the school might've been ranked among the top colleges in America academically, to some, it was more like a monastery. Even so, I'll admit I enjoyed Davidson, except for being away from Laura.

Sunday after the break-up, I picked up a New York Times that some student had thrown in the trash. When I got to the Travel Section, an advertisement jumped out at me – a roundtrip flight for $200 from New York to London. JT had his head buried in a book when I interrupted him.

"What if I told you I'm going to Europe this summer?"

He took off his glasses, looked up at me shaking his head, and said, "It's about time! I can't think of anybody in the world who needs to go more than you."

With three months left before graduation in May of '68, I could feel myself becoming more rebellious. I stopped cutting my hair in order to mimic the rock stars, quit shaving, occasionally slipped out of the dorm at night and hitched up to Mooresville to drink a couple of beers, thinking surely they wouldn't kick me out of school that close to graduation.

During that spring, college students all over the country were protesting with sit-ins, occupations and marches, spurred on by their opposition to America's war in Vietnam. Martin Luther King's assassination provoked two nights of rioting in many cities. It was a time of turbulence and conflict throughout the country. The Beatles, Stones, Zeppelin, Pink Floyd and The Doors spoke to me and made me want to become a part of what was going on.

After getting my diploma in May, I booked that roundtrip flight to London, leaving June 1st and returning August 1st. My father gave his approval, only on the condition I'd honor my commitment to return in time to enter law school at the University of Georgia in September.

He drove me to the Atlanta airport, constantly imparting sage advice and telling me about some of his experiences in Europe during the war. It sounded like he and his buddies had quite a time. When he dropped me off, I grabbed my backpack from the backseat and shook his hand.

"Wait a minute," he stopped me. "I'm about to forget that I bought a gift for you."

"Really?"

He handed me a small paper sack. I opened it and looked inside – a box of condoms.

"Dad!" I shouted. I don't think I'd ever been that shocked. Had it taken him 22 years to teach me about sex? He'd never mentioned the subject during my entire life.

"You know son, when I was a GI in Europe, they used to pass these things out to us," he said in a fatherly tone. "You never know. You might find a need for them. So, just remember your Boy Scout motto."

Sowing Wild Oats

"Make sure you have your seatbelts fastened for takeoff. This BOAC flight number 367 is bound for London's Gatwick Airport. If you're not going to London, please exit immediately," the attendant said in jest.

That announcement made my body buzz all over, filled with as much anxiety as excitement. I'd never travelled outside the U.S., much less solo. Attempting to calm myself, I turned to the guy sitting next to me. He seemed to be about my age. "Hi, I'm Tyler."

"Seth," he nodded.

We were both college students headed to Europe for the summer. Seth had earned a studies-abroad program from Boston University to spend three months at Oxford. I had no interest in anything involving scholastics, only pleasure on my mind. Armed with a Eurail Pass, Frommer's Guide Book, *Europe on $5 a Day* and a thousand bucks my father gave me for graduation, I was all set – no itinerary, no reservations, no plans, just bum around Western Europe for a couple of months.

Arriving in London at 7:00 a.m. would've been 2:00 a.m. in Georgia, but my excitement kept me sleepless on the plane. After getting my backpack from baggage claim, I went inside the terminal to Tourist Bookings to find a place to stay.

A middle-aged woman, with a frown on her face as if she didn't like her job, welcomed me. Her red hair, tied in a bun, matched her red-rimmed glasses. The expression on her face was one of "all-business."

"So, I suppose you want an inexpensive hotel, do you?"

I found her cockney accent hard to understand, but fascinating.

"Yes ma'am. I want a cheap hotel."

"Oh dear, you sound like an American," she said.

"Yes ma'am."

"You don't have to ma'am me. I'm not your mother."

Still fascinated by her dialect, I grinned, "OK."

"First time in the UK?" she asked, as if I knew what the "UK" was.

I nodded my head and mumbled, "Yes."

"You look so young. Are you traveling alone?"

"Yes, and I'm 22."

"You don't look that old, but you probably think that's old, don't you?"

I became a little more defensive. "I've graduated from college."

"Sorry. I didn't mean to offend you, dear."

"You didn't."

She flipped her glasses down from the top of her hair. "Let me see what I have here on the cheap side." She thumbed through her list of hotels. "Do you know anything about London?"

"No. I don't know a thing."

"OK. Well, let's see. Here's one I can get you for seven-and-a-half quid. Is that in your price range?"

"Do you know what that is in dollars?"

"It's about ten U.S."

"Yeah. I guess I can handle that."

"The Cranbrook Hotel is in Croydon."

Disappointed, I asked, "Do you have anything like that in London?"

"Love, Croydon is in London. It's one of the boroughs of south London, right near Valentine's Park, about a five-minute walk from Ilford station. By train, you can get from that station to Central London in 20 minutes. Do you think that'd be OK?"

"Sure," I said. Any hotel within my budget suited me fine. I didn't care what it was like. All I wanted was a bed.

The Cranbrook appeared to be at least 300 years old, and, although I'd never seen an English building before, it looked like what I'd expect – three stories, ivy-covered, a red front door, with a restaurant and pharmacy adjacent.

I slept around the clock until the next morning. Breakfast was free. In addition to the eggs and toast with orange marmalade, they served half-cooked bacon, not at all brown, and broiled, sliced tomatoes with grated cheese. My eyes were beginning to open to the different customs I was about to experience.

Like all tourists, I made my way to the Tower of London, Buckingham Palace, Westminster Abby and Trafalgar Square, but I found my greatest fascination at Speakers' Corner in Hyde Park. I must've stood around for at least a couple of hours listening to one after another, a tradition that dates back to the mid-1800s. At least a hundred spectators were gathered around the speaker, who stood on a "soap box," an old wooden crate traditionally used for shipment of soap to a retail store.

Under a sun-drenched sky, unusual for London I was told, one bloke, as they referred to him, went on and on about his opposition to the Vietnam War. He claimed to be a member of the International Socialist Trotskyite group. A woman on crutches barged her way through the crowd heckling him and actually swinging her crutches at him yelling, "Get away with you. Look at you. You've never done a day's work in your life." Another speaker raged about how the young people had become so rebellious, disobedient and defiant. "They've not been properly trained at home," he avowed. "These unruly hooligans should be jailed and put away until they can learn how to act in a more respectful way."

The hecklers were actually more fun to watch than the speaker. They'd yell out, interrupting them, calling them derogatory names and arguing with whatever he or she was espousing.

Afterwards, I hopped a bus to Hampton Court to see Henry VIII's palace and how decadently royalty lived in those days. Later while walking in the maze next to the palace, I rounded a blind curve and literally ran head on into a girl. I apologized and introduced myself to Sylvia from Chicago. We chatted for a while. Something about her, a pretty, brown-eyed brunette, caused me to raise my antennas. She wore jeans and a tight red sweater that emphasized her femininity.

We agreed to splurge and walk across the street for a drink at the Mitre Hotel on the Thames River. While sitting at a table with a couple from Australia in a garden bordered by weeping willows and a multitude of roses, I asked them about the red drink they were sipping.

"It's Campari," the woman said. "Have you never tried it?"

Neither of us had, so we decided to experiment. When the waiter brought the order, I took a small sip and turned up my nose, and so did Sylvia when she had a taste. It was bitter and weird tasting.

"What's it made of?" Sylvia asked.

"It's an Italian liqueur made from pomegranate. It's considered to be an aperitif," the Australian woman said.

Afterwards, the couple excused themselves to go inside for dinner.

Sylvia and I stayed outdoors and laughed about our attempts at drinking this strange drink. Good vibes flowed between us, giving me the impression I might be working something up. Finally, after finishing our drinks, I asked her if she'd like to go out for the evening. Let's face it, I didn't know how to pick up a girl. I'd never hit on anyone in my life except Laura.

"I'd love to," she sighed, as she pushed her chair back and stood up. "I like you because you're tall and cute and mysterious." She reached down and twisted a lock of my hair around her finger. "I love the way your black curls cover your ears."

I almost melted into my chair, remembering how Laura used to do the same thing.

"You remind me so much of my brother," she smiled.

"Is that good or bad?"

"He's good looking like you." She smiled and then her expression changed. "Look, Tyler, I'm sorry. I've enjoyed being with you. It's been a lot of fun. But I have to meet my boyfriend. We're traveling together. He wanted to go to a cricket match, and I told him I'd rather see Henry VIII's Palace. It never occurred to me that I'd meet someone like you. I'd like to go out with you, but I can't."

"Sure, I understand," quickly realizing what a basket case I was at handling rejection. It hurts, but what can you say? Since she's traveling with her boyfriend, chalk it up to strike one, JT.

She leaned over and kissed me on the forehead then dashed off. I watched her until she was completely out of sight, realizing how much I needed someone to love me after losing Laura.

That evening, I found an old pub, dating back to the late 1600s, called The Cat and The Mouse, a couple of blocks from my hotel. I sat at the bar and noticed everyone drinking beer and eating food. I'd never seen anyone eat a meal at a bar, so I decided to order the special of the day, along with a Guinness, my first. When the bartender, with a bushy-black beard, sat the mug down, it had about a two-inch head. After taking a big swallow, the mirror reflected my large foam mustache.

The special of the day turned out to be a shallow bowl with something underneath a brown crust. Digging my fork in, revealed onions, meat and gravy. While it looked enticing, when the fork reached my mouth, the odor, similar to a men's urinal, made me gag. I forced myself to eat it but knew for a certainty it would never happen again. The guy sitting next to me told me I was dining on kidney pie.

I began to chat with him, Martin from Cornwall, a nice-looking guy, who appeared to be about mid-40s, and physically fit, as if he might be an athlete. Among other means of earning a living, he led hikes along the coastal footpath. As he explained the beauty of the Cornish coast, the more inviting it became.

I told him of my hiking adventure with some of my college buddies. We'd backpacked for a week on the Appalachian Trail in western North Carolina. We hiked about ten miles a day and pitched our tents each night next to a waterfall or stream. That experience turned me on to hiking and made me crave for more.

Before leaving, he gave me his phone number, encouraging me to visit Cornwall for a hike.

When the antique clock behind the bar struck midnight, I

decided it was time for me to hit the sack. As I walked out, I became aware of being followed. The guy, who appeared to be in his early 30s, came up beside me and said, "Hi."

Having been warned of pick-pockets in London caused me to be suspicious, although the guy didn't fit the mold. He looked decent, with an expression of sincerity.

"I've been staring at you in the pub. You're a handsome young man," he said.

I kept walking without looking at him.

"Would you like to go to my flat? Rest assured you won't regret it."

I turned my face toward him, but kept walking. "No, I'm really tired – need to get back to my hotel."

"You sound like an American. Come with me, American boy, and I'll give you the best blow job you've ever had."

I'd never had anything like that happen to me. "No. Not interested," I said, somewhat frightened.

"You don't have to do anything. Just sit there and let me pleasure you."

"Gotta go." After picking up the pace, I turned and watched the guy walking back toward the pub. I chuckled, thinking it would have to be the best one, since I'd never had one.

I decided to take Martin up on his offer to visit him in Cornwall. I called, and he said, "Sure, come on. I may put you to work," he laughed.

Chills of excitement came over me as I walked into Paddington Station and showed my Eurail Pass to the ticket agent. It surprised me to learn that it entitled me to sit in first class. Martin had agreed to meet me in Truro.

Being all alone in a foreign country gave me a sense of freedom I'd never experienced. There I was, boarding a train for the first time in my life in a place I'd never been and heading for an unfamiliar location – a novel adventure for me. JT was right when he said I needed to get away and do something different. But I didn't expect that it would feel so good.

The train began moving out of the station at 3:00 p.m. sharp for the five and a half hour trip. An older couple from Nottingham and a girl, who appeared to be college-age from Penzance, were my mates in the compartment. The older man wore a navy-blue suit and tie, and the woman had on something my mother would wear to church. The coed wore more casual clothes like a typical college girl would wear.

A little small-talk helped us get acquainted. The couple were headed to Cornwall for a week's vacation. The pretty brunette, named Tilly, was on her way back home from visiting her grandparents in London. Sitting by the window and acting like a little kid going to the fair, I checked out the alluring countryside and the interesting towns we passed through – Reading, Taunton and Exeter, where I fell asleep and didn't come back into consciousness until we pulled into the station at St. Austell, the first stop in the county of Cornwall.

I saw the sign for Truro, grabbed my backpack from the rack above the seats and bid farewell to my three new friends, who'd all given me their addresses if I'd like to visit.

Martin, who stood by the train wearing a pair of jeans, a jacket and a knit hat, came to greet me with a hug and a welcome to his beloved Cornwall, where he'd been born and lived his entire 48 years. We drove about a half-hour to his home where he told me a little about Cornwall and its history of tin-mining. His wife, Alice, greeted me, "You must be famished!" she exclaimed. "We've eaten already, but I have your dinner in the oven."

They put me up in their son's bedroom. Being the same age, he was away for the summer working in Italy, like his father, leading hikes in the Dolomites.

Alice, a strikingly good-looking strawberry blonde, began taking food from the oven and placing it on the table. Like Martin, she seemed physically-fit to be middle-aged.

"Don't worry," Martin chuckled. "It's not kidney pie."

I laughed.

They sat at the table watching me as I ate unknown

things. I thought it might be impolite to ask what I was eating, but finally Martin came to the rescue. "That's a Cornish pastry with beef, onion, potato and turnip. And those fishes are Pilchards, something like a sardine." I actually liked sardines and used to eat them regularly when I visited my grandparents in Pineview, a small town about an hour south of Macon.

After I finished, Alice brought a dessert. "We call this cream tea."

"It looks delicious," I said.

"It's a sliced scone with strawberry jam and a dollop of clotted cream."

I lapped it up and not just to be polite – very tasty. Martin then brought over a bottle of mead and poured a glass for each of us. We drank the remainder of the bottle. Soon afterwards, being a little tipsy, I excused myself, fell in bed and went to sleep with a big smile on my face.

A tap at the door early the next morning brought me out of a deep sleep. Martin had asked me to join him with a group coming in from America. I jumped up, put on jeans and my black Converse high tops, since I didn't bring hiking boots.

Alice prepared baked eggs with halloumi, a goat cheese with a hard texture, which I quickly found out when I tried to slice it.

We were to meet the group who were arriving by chartered bus from London to Truro. I watched and counted 22 excited tourists step out to arrive in Cornwall for their hiking trip. That's when it hit me that I'd not seen an American since arriving in England. Martin greeted each one, then introduced me as his assistant. They seemed to be all ages from maybe 25 to 65. I introduced myself and found they were from Asheville, North Carolina. Their southern accent gave me a few moments of homesickness. They liked me since I was southern and a Davidson grad.

We waited as they checked into the Alverton Hotel surrounded by gardens. According to Martin, the building had been built in 1830 as a convent then recently renovated into a hotel.

During the day I marveled at Martin's knowledge as he covered the history and description of the dramatic Cornish coastline. The weather had cooperated perfectly and produced sunshine and temperatures in the low sixties.

Martin elaborated over the bus microphone, "When you leave here at the end of the week, you'll probably be like other groups who say that Cornwall is one of the most beautiful places you've ever seen. The Cornish peninsula juts out about 100 miles into the Atlantic Ocean on Britain's southwest coast. The Gulf Stream sweeps the coastline making it the mildest climate in all of Great Britain. A hiking trail runs along the coastline all around Cornwall, and there are huts where you can sleep. It's called the Coastal Footpath, so, one day you should return and enjoy that trail."

After hiking for about five hours, we dipped down to remote coves then to a beach where we had lunch. Some of the guys shed their clothes and jumped into the clear, blue water discreetly wearing their undies. We explored sea caves then walked to the cliff top, where we took a break lying on the ground in a sea of wildflowers. Martin's enthusiasm, without a doubt, added to the charm of the scenery.

At the end of the day the bus dropped the group at the hotel, and we began our drive back home. That's when Martin broke the news. "Tyler, I have to be away for about a month to lead a hike in Morocco. Groups are coming in every week for the month of June to Cornwall while I'm away, and I need for you to take over if you're willing."

Overwhelmed, I didn't respond immediately. Then I said, "Do you think I'm capable?"

"I know you are, and I'll pay you well."

"I don't know what to say, Martin. I'd definitely have a lot to learn."

"I'll be here the rest of this week, so just listen carefully to what I'm saying, and I'll make a list of the hikes each day and how to get there. I'm sure you can do it."

"My flight home is on August 1st."

"No problem. I'll be home the first week of July, and my last group scheduled here finishes the last of June."

At the end of the week, Martin flew to Marrakesh, leaving Alice and me at home, and me alone with the task of leading trips for the next three weeks. He'd given me a whopping £500 before he left, the equivalent of $750.

I grew to love being the leader, enjoyed the groups, and gained additional confidence with each one. When I said goodbye to the last group of hikers, I began to plot my next move.

That evening, the weather had cooled and Alice and I sat at the kitchen table as we'd done every night since Martin left. She wore tight jeans and a red sweater with her hair pulled forward over her ears that gave her a more relaxed appearance. "Are you warm enough?" she asked.

"Sure, I'm fine," as I zipped up my Davidson basketball hoodie. We each sipped a glass of mead.

"Alice, would you mind taking me to Truro tomorrow morning."

"Are you leaving?"

"Yeah. I'm going to take a train to Liverpool."

"Sure, I'll take you."

After finishing dinner, we polished off the rest of the mead, and I told her how much I appreciated all she'd done, especially preparing scrumptious meals each night. She stared into my eyes a little too long and put her hand on top of mine. "Tyler, it's cold. Would you sleep with me tonight?"

That comment hit me like a tsunami. It scared me so much, I didn't know what to say. I blurted out, "Don't you think we've had a little too much to drink?"

She returned the sweetest smile I'd ever seen from her.

"I think we'd regret it tomorrow. Don't you?" I mumbled.

"You're 22. I'm 48. Am I too old for you?"

"Alice, you're Martin's wife. I can't do that to him." My heart was beating 100 miles an hour.

She took her hand away and dropped her head.

I tried to think of something to say, but nothing that made any sense would come out.

18

The next day, I took the train to Liverpool to see the birthplace of the Beatles and went directly to the Cavern Club where they began their career. A brick vaulted cellar underneath had been covered in Beatles memorabilia. Afterwards, I took a walk through the woods of Birkenhead Park with its two fishing lakes, then on to Strawberry Field, the old Salvation Army Children's Home, where the Beatles spent time and wrote a song about it.

On leaving there, I crossed the Irish Sea to Dublin on a ferry, about an eight hour trip, then traveled throughout Ireland and Scotland, but went back into England to Newcastle to take another ferry ride bound for Amsterdam.

While in Scotland I'd had my first drink of Scotch by going out of my way to the Dewars Distillery in Aberfeldy, where I learned that a true Scotch drinker orders it with no ice or "neat," as they call it. Unaccustomed to hard liquor, I drank more than I should have, not because I liked the taste, which I didn't, but I was sitting with some other young guys who knew what they were doing. When I started walking out, I realized I'd accomplished the first of JT's advice to get drunk. I quickly found a room nearby and slept it off.

After arriving in Amsterdam, I found that a boat ride through some of the canals was the best way to see the city. Chatting with a guy sitting next to me, he suggested checking out a bar next to a park that had been opened for centuries.

Pretending to be a seasoned drinker, I sat on a stool at the bar and whipped out a cheat sheet that a Dutch guy on the ferry wrote down. "Mag ik een Scotch neat alstublieft?" It seemed so cool to say that, but, instead, the bartender, about mid-twenties, laughed. "Sure. I'll get you a Scotch neat," he said in perfect English.

Almost everyone in the bar seemed to be smoking, but it didn't smell like cigarettes. Soon, the bartender picked up on my questioning glances.

"You want a smoke?"

Showing my ignorance, "What is it?"

He smirked at my stupidity. "It's pot. Have you never smoked it?"

I felt naïve to say 'no,' but any other answer would be a lie.

"Wanna' try?"

I shrugged my shoulders. "Is it legal?"

"It is here. No worries, if you'd like to buy one."

"How much?"

"Guilders or dollars?"

I didn't have any guilders, so I said, "Dollars."

"Five bucks."

My budget for a day – a bit steep for a cigarette, I thought. But why not? This trip seemed to be shaping up as "the sowing my wild oats tour." How could I not say "yes?"

Being a dedicated jock in high school and college, I'd never smoked cigarettes. So, not surprisingly, some anxiety persisted to start out with pot. The bartender leaned over and lit it for me. I took my first hit, got strangled and started coughing uncontrollably. I looked around to catch other customers who might be staring at me and getting a good laugh. My reaction would've been a dead-give-away that I was a novice. I took a few sips of Dewars to clear my throat. After a couple more hits, I'd become emboldened to go over and plop down at a table, uninvited, with a group about my age. Steppenwolf's "Born to Be Wild" blared from the speakers adjacent to the bar.

A girl at the table asked, "Where you from?"

When I opened my mouth to tell her, I started laughing wildly, as if she'd just told me the funniest joke I'd ever heard. I couldn't stop laughing. She seemed mildly amused.

"Your first joint?" she smiled. "You look like an American."

I got my composure. "How did you know?"

"The way you're dressed," she then added, "First joint, first time in Europe, right?"

"You know me like a book," I tried to be hip.

Instead, she turned back, ignoring me and began talking with her friends. That's when it hit me just how un-cool I really was.

None of them appeared to care as I stood up to leave their table. I wandered outside and sprawled out on a patch of grass surrounding the bar, took another toke, laid my head down and stared at the sky. The laughter of children playing formed the background sounds for a continual parade of cirrus clouds drifting by. Some figures seemed familiar – a barking dog with its tail upward, an old man with a long nose, a white rabbit with ears sticking up, a feather and a kite.

A sense of disconnection with my body came over me. It seemed as though I might be watching a movie or staring at a painting that was mobile and ever-changing. Colors were brighter than ever. My face felt warmer than normal, breath got thicker and heart beat faster. Suddenly a new cloud drifted by with middle finger sticking out as if God were shooting a bird at me. Could the Master be making fun of this poor soul? "Where is my life going? What lies ahead for me? Has the imaginary cord been severed by my parents and my girlfriend, leaving me to drift in a sea of doubt?"

The next thing I remembered was a guy shaking me saying, "Hey! Hey! Hey! Get up. You can't sleep here."

I raised up to see the bartender leaning down, staring into my face.

"OK. OK. I'm getting up." I raised to a sitting position with no idea how long I'd been there. The sun had begun to descend below the trees. "OK. I'm sorry. I'll get up."

"It doesn't look good for our customers," he added.

"Yeah. I understand." I sat up and staggered to my feet, feeling woozy and thinking I'd accomplished two of JT's recommendations.

I'd booked a bed at a rooming house in a residential neighborhood. Looking at the map, it appeared to be only about a mile away from the bar, so I threw on my backpack and started walking. On arrival at the two-story house with double-red doors, I rang the bell. An older woman wearing a blue bathrobe, tangled hair that appeared not to have been brushed in days, who spoke no English, directed me to the stairs that led to my bedroom on the second floor. I'd never seen a stairwell that narrow, making it impossible to walk up wearing my backpack, so I dragged it up the steps to my room that contained a bed and a chest. I didn't care. Like always, I only wanted a bed.

After napping about an hour, I decided to go out on the town. I grabbed my wallet and passport, put on a jacket and went out. The night air seemed cool but refreshing. I looked at my watch – 10:15 – at least another couple of hours in me before bedtime. Walking along the sidewalk next to one of the canals, still in somewhat of a daze from my afternoon experience, I came upon something I never knew existed. A pretty girl sat behind a plate glass window. I thought at first it might be a mannequin until she smiled and cut her eyes toward me. She wore a pink mini-skirt and a scant white top that exposed most of her body. I realized she was for sale with no price tag. As I slowly walked along, a different girl sat behind each succeeding window, all good-looking and enticing – at least fifteen girls in all. No matter how tempting they may've seemed, that was not my idea of how I wanted to lose my virginity.

After a day of rest, I caught a train to Koblenz, Germany, to meet an American, who lived there and had served in the military with my father. The uneventful ride didn't spark my enthusiasm, but I knew I owed it to my dad to make the call to Joseph Ackerman. It suited me fine when he told me he was tied up for the evening, but would like to meet me at a bar for a drink, sitting at the confluence of the Rhine and Mosel Rivers. Tall, like my father, but not nearly as good-looking, he wore blue cord pants and an untucked, yellow shirt, drooped below his hips, that didn't match his outfit. He told me tales of the two of them going to Germany when the war ended, and how they celebrated, got drunk and did all kinds of wild and crazy things. It seemed strange to hear of my father being carefree and fun-loving, not exactly the man I'd known. He, for me, had been loving, yet stern and strict. My mother used to say when he'd come home, he acted as if he were still sitting on the bench like a judge.

To be like other tourists, I was told to order a glass of Rhine wine along with a Mosel and experience the difference. The wines were OK, not great, but a little sweet for my taste. For a teetotaler, this trip had introduced me to scotch, beer, cannabis and wine, and I was beginning to consider myself sophisticated in my tastes – Ha!

My Eurail pass, in addition to train rides anywhere in Europe, allowed me to hop on a river cruiser to head up the Rhine River to Bingen. A six-hour trip would give me a chance to lie back in the sun and think my thoughts.

Spread out on a lounge chair with my head slightly elevated, I watched the spectacular scenery with castles dotted along the Rhine Gorge, about a four-mile stretch between Koblenz and Bingen, carved along banks that are over 600 feet high, the most famous feature being the Lorelei, a tall slate of rock on the right bank of the river.

But what caught my eye, and even more spectacular, were the two girls across from me reading books. I left my pack leaning against the chair on a trip to the WC, which I'd learned earlier meant "water closet." I interrupted the girls. "Hi. Would you mind watching my pack for me?"

"Sure," one of them said.

When I came back, I made an attempt at starting a conversation. "I'm Tyler."

They seemed remotely interested, but obviously not overwhelmed.

One of them pointed to herself, "Sofia," then to the other, "Mila." The blonde hair on both girls, long and stringy, blew in the wind. Sofia's piercing blue eyes were hypnotic as she gazed up at me. She wore a maroon leather jacket and a low-cut blouse. Mila's beauty seemed more subtle than her older sister. Her hoodie covered her upper body, and she wore white jeans.

"Would you care for something to drink?" I asked.

"Sure," Sofia spoke up. "Maybe a beer."

I went to the bar and ordered three Löwenbräus. As we drank, we chatted. They were sisters from Hamburg heading to Spain. They'd never cruised on the Rhine and had stopped off to do this short stretch before boarding the train for Barcelona. Mila was 17, Sofia 19. When they asked my destination, I responded, trying to appear more mysterious, "Wherever the spirit moves me."

At first, they didn't seem impressed, but later asked me to come along with them, an eighteen-hour overnight trip. Why not?

The train had open-seating, and we found a vacant compartment – three seats facing three seats that could be pulled together to make a bed. Before boarding, we split the cost of a bottle of Chianti Classico, a relatively cheap Italian wine that we drank in short order. This loosened our tongues to the extent that we began telling things we normally would not have said to a stranger. I told them about how my girlfriend had shafted me for missing a date with her, and that I was really having a hard time dealing with it.

Shedding tears, they told me about their uncle, who'd sexually molested them as teenagers. He gave them money and all kinds of favors to stay in their good graces, even bought a car for them when Sofia turned sixteen. They were afraid to tell their mother, since he was her brother, and if their father had found out, he would've killed him. Basically, they'd gotten up the nerve to run away from home, not telling anyone they were leaving, and had found employment at a resort hotel in Palma de Mallorca, an island in the Mediterranean, which can be reached by ferry from Barcelona.

"I wish there were some way I could help you," I said, as my eyes filled with tears too, while listening to their heart-wrenching story."

Sofia spoke first, "You have. You don't even know how much it helps to talk with someone else about this. You are the first person we've ever told."

That gave me an overwhelming feeling to want to reach out and help them deal with this tragedy in their lives.

We talked until after eleven, then pulled the seats together and made a bed. I'd chosen to be next to the window, which put me beside Sofia with Mila on the other side. As we stretched out, I was on my back, and Sofia had turned toward Mila. At some point, a jolt of the train woke me out of a sound sleep. I found my body turned toward Sofia with my arm around her. I quickly removed it in hopes she wouldn't wake up and think I was trying to hit on her. I think I'd been dreaming of Laura.

Before reaching Barcelona, I developed a raging case of diarrhea and had to shove the girls next to the window so I could be near the door, trotting back and forth to the toilet for the remainder of the evening.

We arrived in the bustling metropolis of Barcelona about mid-day and found a Tourist Information bureau that located accommodations for travelers. A room with a double bed and a single was all they had. Sofia, who spoke enough Spanish to get by, went out and found Imodium for me. After taking it, I felt drowsy and passed out for the rest of the afternoon.

Coming out of a deep sleep, I felt fine and ready to go out on the town with the girls. They'd learned, from the woman who runs the rooming house, the best place for eating paella. I'd never heard of it, but learned that it was the national dish of Spain. I loved it. The waiter told Sofia, which she interpreted for Mila and me, the ingredients in the dish: shrimp, mussels, chicken, sausage and ham on a bed of saffron rice, topped with sautéed onions, tomatoes and green peas. I knew when we left, I'd never forget that meal, and I'd order it again the next time I saw it on a menu.

Walking along the sidewalk, we heard music coming from behind a wall. A DJ played American music, while the three of us drank a couple of beers and danced along with about 50 other people to songs like "Can't Take My Eyes Off of You;" The Monkees' "I'm a Believer;" The Doors' "Light my Fire;" Jefferson Airplane's "Somebody to Love;" "This Girl's in Love with You," by Dionne Warwick; and many other pop songs of the day.

By 1:00 a.m., I was wasted. We went back to the room. I took the single bed and was zonked out in minutes.

My next knowledge of existence came the next morning when I raised up. The girls and their packs were gone. I saw a note on the table, turned on the light and read: "You don't know how much it meant for us to meet a guy like you who listened to our story with a sympathetic ear. We both wish you much luck and hope you and your girlfriend will find a way to get back together," signed Sofia & Mila, with a picture of a heart next to their name.

I took a train to Nice and found a hostel. I'd never heard of hostels, but a couple of guys on the train told me that would be the most inexpensive place to stay.

After eating a couple of croissants and having my first espresso coffee, I went walking on the beach, staring at the sea, not paying attention to where I was walking, and accidentally brushed beside a girl. We laughed and started talking. Her name was Celia, who'd just graduated from Yale. We hit it off. I think her blonde hair and engaging smile reminded me of Laura.

She told me my swim suit looked like something out of the '20s. "Please go and buy another one," she insisted. "Everyone will know immediately you're an American. You know we're such prudes when it comes to exposing our bodies." She'd obviously shed her Americanism since the pink bikini she wore exposed almost every ounce of her flesh.

"Buy a new bathing suit?" I thought to myself. I really didn't want to get one of those banana hammocks that the European guys wear.

Then she added, "I tell you what. You don't even have to buy one. I'll take you to a nude beach."

"Oh my God!" I thought. A newbie from Georgia, I didn't know if I was ready for that! But I agreed to go along with her. Why not get everything I could out of this trip? The only time I'd ever been skinny-dipping was at my grandfather's farm near the little town of Pineview. They called it Pappy Jack Springs, where all males swam in the nude.

Celia knew of a small boat taking passengers over to this little island. "Have you ever been to a nude beach before?"

"Me. No. Not hardly." I didn't feel it worthy to tell her about Pappy Jack.

"I can't remember the name of the island," she said. "But there's a beach where a lot of people go to sun in the nude."

Within the hour, we found ourselves traveling in what I'd call a bateau, not much bigger than my father's fishing boat on the Ocmulgee River. No way could this boat be certified to carry all these people! But somehow, someway, we made it. We stepped out of the boat and scrambled over a wall of rocks along a well-worn path to the other side of the island. That's where I began to see people sunbathing in the nude. My expectation of being titillated were doused when I saw old men who looked like dead walruses washed up on shore and some of the women didn't look much better.

Celia quickly slithered out of her pink bikini without a care. Shedding my clothes seemed more on the awkward side. Unaccustomed to being nude in front of a crowd, I blurted out, "If I'd only known I was going to be naked in front of all these people, I'd have worn my big dick today," the first time I'd had a chance to use JT's favorite expression.

She laughed.

As we strolled on the sugary, white sand toward the water, it reminded me of some of my nightmarish dreams where I'd found myself wandering around a crowded airport without a stitch.

I can't say it felt comfortable showing off all my wares, but then the thought hit me that anyone who looks at me will never see me again, and even if they did, I'm sure I'd be easy to forget.

Celia had a towel spread out on the sand where we sat, looking out over the unusually blue water. Her blonde hair, draped over her shoulders, became airborne when the wind began to blow. She had a picture-perfect face, her body a bit on the plump side, but still attractive. We talked about our lives and what we had to look forward to after college. We built sand castles and had a great time laughing like little kids.

She broke the news that she had to get back soon to meet her boyfriend.

"You know, I like you Celia," I said. "You remind me of my girlfriend."

"I figured a guy like you would have a favorite girl."

We walked slowly back to the boat. She talked about her boyfriend. I talked about Laura but didn't tell her the sad details of our breakup.

Later that afternoon, another first occurred on entering a gambling casino in Monaco, something I'd only seen in movies. Within fifteen minutes, I'd put one franc in a slot machine and got eighty back. What a great way to make some money! That is, until it'd all been lost within an hour – a good lesson to be learned.

Regrettably, I'd reached the time when this trip of awakening would come to an end – only five days left before flying back home from London. I hopped on an overnight train from Nice to Paris, a fifteen-hour trip.

I found a seat in a compartment, occupied by an older French couple, who spoke no English. Leaning back in my seat, I closed my eyes while reviewing the past few weeks. I laughed about my roommate, JT, telling me I needed to get drunk, get stoned and get laid. I'd accomplished the first two, but it looked like I'd have to wait until another trip to accomplish number three. However, JT should give me a few points for doing a nude beach.

Before leaving school, he'd handed me the book, *One Hundred Years of Solitude*, inscribed with this statement, "Take this with you and read it. It's a 448-page masterpiece." After a couple of hours of reading, something I'd taken no time to do on the entire trip, I began to really get into the Buendia family, who founded a small village in the swamps of Colombia, but then was overcome by hunger pangs.

The dining car was three cars ahead, and the aroma of food aroused my taste buds. I didn't care what I ate – just wanted to fill my stomach. While sitting at a table, I caught a glimpse of a girl in front of me with a gorgeous face, long blonde hair, dreamy blue eyes, dressed in a white blouse, tight jeans and long, dangling earrings. Her lips looked like they needed to be kissed – preferably by me. That's when I realized how much I yearned for love from a female companion. I wanted to experience that same sensation I used to have with Laura when we walked along the river at sunset.

After a few minutes of staring at her, our eyes locked on each other's. My body began to grow weaker and my breath more rapid. The good news – she stared back at me with the same intensity. Neither of us changed facial expressions, but the vibrations between us were overwhelming.

A French waiter with a thin mustache interrupted our interlude by handing me a menu and asking, "Qu'aimerais-tu manger?" Of course, I didn't understand him.

"Do you speak English?" I asked.

"A little," he said with a heavy accent.

He pointed to something on the menu I'd never heard of, croque-monsieur, avec pomme frites. I shrugged my shoulders and said, "Sure." I didn't care. I thought it'd have to be edible. Thinking I'd ordered something exotic, I was surprised when he brought a ham and cheese sandwich with french fries. I motioned for him to come back with a beer. He brought a Kronenbourg, my first try at a French beer.

While eating, I returned to gazing at the breathtaking female, and again, she returned the gaze. I could sense my body becoming more vulnerable. Somehow, I had to meet her.

Our eyes locked for what seemed like a long time, as if neither one of us wanted to let go.

Almost choking on the ham and cheese, I had to redirect my eyes to find my beer to wash it down. Hunger for food had dissipated and had been transformed into a desperate craving to experience the love I'd been missing from Laura.

As if I'd been hypnotized, I walked slowly to her table, still staring, and said, "Hi, I'm Tyler."

The smile she gave dissolved all fears. Without speaking, she pushed her chair back, grabbed her coat and followed me out to the space between the railway cars. When the doors to the restaurant car closed, it was as if we were in a private closet. I reached out to her. She grabbed me in, what I'd call, a tight romantic embrace. Our breath became short and labored, until someone opened the door to the restaurant car, exposing, as well as interrupting, our magic interval.

She followed me to my compartment. I opened the door and motioned for her to go in first. She slid down onto the three seats on her back across from the elderly couple. We hugged and kissed for quite a while until the French lady across spoke up with undetectable words.

She'd broken the spell, so we sat upright.

"What was that about?" I asked the girl, whose name I didn't know.

She spoke the first words since we'd met. "She wanted to know if we'd like for them to leave. I told her, 'No, it was OK. We just hadn't seen each other in a very long time.'"

I laughed. In addition to all of her other qualities, her accent intrigued me. "Where are you from?"

"Sweden, but I'm living and working in Paris."

"I love the way you talk. It's so soft and smooth." I paused for a moment to again study her face. "You haven't told me you name."

"Lina," she smiled.

"Hmm, that's a pretty name. I'm Tyler."

"Obviously, you're American," she paused. "From the South, maybe?"

"How'd you know that?"

"I don't know," she said. "I feel like we've known each other before."

"Yeah, right, I know what you mean."

She placed her palm on my cheek and spoke softly, "Maybe in a past life we were lovers."

"And I guess we picked this spot to meet again," I said clumsily, with no skill or finesse.

We spent the rest of the trip talking and sleeping in each other's arms. But somehow I felt restrained as if I were cheating on Laura.

The train arrived at the Gare de Lyon Station in Paris about 8:00 a.m. She'd checked her bag. I put on my backpack, and we walked to the railway car where the bags were being unloaded. She suggested we take the Metro. "It'd be so much quicker than a taxi at this time of day."

We walked down the steps and caught the train. She said we'd get off at Saint-Germain-des-Prés. "It's in the sixth arrondissement." I had no idea what she was talking about.

The excitement of walking along a sidewalk in Paris with a good-looking girl seemed unreal, as was the anticipation of what might happen next. Her apartment was only a couple of blocks away from the stop but up four flights of stairs without an elevator. Wanting to appear manly, I insisted on carrying her heavy bag along with the pack on my back, the best workout I'd had on the entire trip.

She had one of those old 45 rpm record players. I watched her load one on the spindle – "Ain't Nothing Like the Real Thing" by Marvin Gaye and Tammy Terrell. I always loved that song, but it began to get monotonous when it continued to play over and over and over again.

She made coffee, brought two cups then walked away. While she was gone, I hurried over to my backpack and slipped the box of condoms to the pocket of my jeans, just in case. But what if it did happen? Would I know how to do it? I'd never read any instructions. I guess it's the type of thing where you just do what comes naturally.

Wearing only see-through panties and a sexy bra, she returned and sat next to me on a large sofa. We began again staring into each other's eyes with a more intense perception, interrupted occasionally to take a sip of coffee.

Finally, she leapt on top of me, and we began ripping off our clothes. As she was kissing me, the ringing of the phone interrupted our embrace. She jumped up to answer it. In a few moments she rushed back into the room.

"Tyler! You have to get up now!"

I leaned up trying to make some sense out of what was happening.

"Get up, Tyler! My husband is on his way home!"

Those words were sufficient to rev my motor and get me moving. I quickly jumped up, threw on my clothes and shoes. As I snatched up my backpack to run out the door, I turned around and saw the box of condoms I'd left on the floor beside the sofa unopened. I picked up the box and stuck it in my pocket.

Lina grabbed me. "Look, I'm sorry, Tyler," she hugged me tightly. "Oh, God! Why does life have to be so complicated?"

I didn't know what to say. I'd just had all the stuffing knocked out of me. The only thing I knew for certain was I needed to get the hell out of there in a big hurry.

Disheveled and spent, I stumbled out onto a busy sidewalk with a sigh of relief that I'd not been murdered. In Georgia, killing a man in a situation like that is considered justifiable homicide.

A world of thoughts bulleted through my head. Did the past few hours really happen or was it all a prodigal dream? I couldn't help but feel guilty knowing there's no love for me except from Laura?

The walk along the Boulevard Saint-Germain to Boulevard Saint Michel and all the way to the River Seine provided me with a chance to begin getting my head back together. Admiring the beauty of the river with the Cathedral of Notre Dame in the background, I wandered toward the front of the famed church and decided to go inside. Several people for hire approached me to be my guide. At that point, I only wanted refuge, to absorb the solace of the church and seek answers to my questions.

How could anyone walk into this great cathedral without being overwhelmed by its splendor? I took off my pack, sat in an empty pew, pulled down the kneeler and dropped to my knees to pray. Nothing came forth. My mind was filled with endless thoughts, but none of them could be formulated into words. I was speechless, for the events of the previous night and morning were hard for me to comprehend. It all happened in such rapid succession. My heart had been filled with so much love and longing from a stranger, only to come crashing down like an unexpected avalanche. Was there a hidden meaning? I asked for a sign to help navigate through the stormy waters.

While sitting there all alone, a short, thin man, bald on top with a bushy gray beard, came up next to me and leaned down. Dressed in all white, he wore large-rimmed glasses and a serious expression on his face. "Can we talk?" he asked.

There're no words to say how much that offended me. I wanted to be left alone to think my thoughts. He should've sensed my displeasure.

"Please talk to me," he said in understandable English as he sat down beside me.

"What do you want?" My tone was enough to offend anyone.

"I want to talk."

"About what?"

"About you."

The thought of another guy trying to put the make on me made me angry. "What do you want to talk about?

He handed me a book. The cover read *Be Here Now.*

"I'm sorry. I have no interest in buying your book."

"Will you listen to me for just a minute?" he pleaded.

"What!"

"The book is not for sale," he paused, and in a velvety, smooth voice said, "I felt you calling me, and I answered."

What is this guy talking about? He's obviously been doing too much acid. I felt offended that he encroached on my space, yet, somehow, became captivated by his eyes, clear blue and penetrating. For the first time, I began to drop my defenses and started to listen.

"You're a young man, and you have much goodness in you – a warm heart. You have potential to take your talents and use them to benefit mankind."

"How do you know that?"

He didn't answer. He only glared into my eyes, then said, "If you listen to your inner voice, it will tell you where you are now and which method will work best for you in your evolution towards the light."

That went right over my head, but I had to concede the man spoke as if he had wisdom.

"You, my dear friend, are going to experience an event in your life that will cause you great conflict. When it happens, try to remember what I'm saying. Separate your ego from this experience and do the right thing."

He rose from the pew. "Keep the book," he smiled and slowly wandered off. I turned to watch him exit the church, but he'd disappeared – not a sign of him anywhere. Was I hallucinating?

I slumped in my seat and pondered what that was all about, then knelt to pray. Now my mind churned more than ever – I had so much baggage that paralyzed me and made me powerless. My overwhelming thought was to get myself in order and get Laura back into my life.

I spent the next couple of days working my way toward London. Two things dominated my thoughts. One, was Laura. Her smiling face kept staring at me. I could hear her laugh and feel her kiss. I'd been captivated by a force that kept saying, "No matter what it takes, get her back into your life."

The other was the book the stranger had given me at Notre Dame, *Be Here Now*, by Ram Dass. I read the words over and over that had real meaning for me, like,

"You play many roles in the course of a day. Who you are changes from moment to moment."

"There is the angry you, the kind you, the lazy you, the lustful you—and so on. Sometimes one 'you' does something for which all the other 'you's' must pay for a long time afterwards."

"You don't need to go anywhere else to find what you are seeking. If you listen to your own inner voice, it will tell you where you are now, and which method will work best for you in your evolution towards the light."

"Every time you work on yourself, you get calmer, you hear more, you sense more, and you are more."

Memories of our first date paraded through my mind. At the age of sixteen, after I'd begun paying more attention to girls, I was leaving a matinee at the Rialto Theater in Macon one summer afternoon. A good-looking girl about the same age came into view, wearing tight jeans and a pale blue shirt. I began to think of some scheme to meet her. She was walking out, so it had to be quick. Grabbing my sunglasses, I tapped her on the shoulder and asked, "Did you drop these?" When she turned around, our eyes met, and that's when I knew this girl had to be a part of my life. Laura was the same name as my grandmother. I asked her if she might consider catching a movie sometime. It would be my first date. She had a hard time convincing her father since it was also her first date. "He's the son of a judge," she pleaded my case. But that didn't cut any ice with him. He wanted references. I gave Laura some names to call and received scant approval, "He's a pretty good boy."

She later said he wanted her to describe how I looked. "He's tall, good-looking, black, curly hair, physically fit and looks like a nice guy to be around."

My dad said he'd let me drive his big, black Cadillac de Ville. That should really impress her. I spent hours washing and polishing the outside, scrubbing tires and cleaning the inside, even sprinkled some of my father's English Leather aftershave lotion on the seats to try to calm down the pungent odor of his cigar smoke.

On our first date we went to see *To Kill a Mockingbird*. Some thirty minutes or so into the movie, I cautiously edged my hand over on top of hers – a really bold move! She never removed it for the entire movie, emboldening me even more than I'd ever dreamed. Taking the long way home, we listened to the Shirelles sing "Baby It's You," and I became mesmerized watching her mouth move as she spoke. I didn't hear a word she said. My only thoughts were how much I wanted to kiss her lips. I walked her to the door, and leaned down for that first kiss that sent electrical charges throughout my body as if I'd stuck my finger in a light socket. In a couple of weeks and a few more dates, I gave her my ID bracelet, so all the world would know we were going steady.

During Christmas holidays of our senior year of high school, Laura asked me to escort her to the Bon Hommes Debutante Ball. That was a big deal to introduce young girls into society. I boasted to some of my buddies that I had the best-looking girl of anybody. "You see that girl over there with the long, curly, blonde hair, beautiful face, good figure and sexy smile? She's mine."

We continued to date while I was in school at Davidson, and she was at Wesleyan College in Macon. Unfortunately, a storm occurred in our relationship during February of our senior year. A couple of classmates convinced me to skip classes for a few days and head south to New Orleans for Mardi Gras. Up until that point, I'd pretty much walked a straight line, obeyed the rules, and did what I was supposed to do. When I accepted their invitation, it somewhat shocked them and surprised me, as well.

"Hell yeah!" I'd never been to the Crescent City, much less to what is known as "the greatest festival on the planet." The only drawback – I'd told Laura I'd go to Macon for the weekend to take her to an informal dance at school. I tried to call and couldn't reach her. But I'd gotten it in my head that I wanted to do something wild and crazy, so, four of us took off in a friend's Oldsmobile.

Each time we stopped for gas, I'd head directly for a payphone to call Laura, but to no avail. Once we arrived in New Orleans, we were blown away. That place was unreal! To say we had a blast at Mardi Gras would've been a classic understatement. We cut loose and partied like we'd never done before.

We laughed as we talked about what the Dean of Students would do if he'd seen us drinking beer, watching good-looking girls sitting on top of floats, being introduced to strip-shows, and catching beads being thrown by topless girls from balconies over Bourbon Street. By the time we left, we'd definitely had our eyes opened.

On the drive home, my calls to Laura at Wesleyan went unanswered. When we got back to school, I called her parents. Her father picked up the phone. "She doesn't want to talk to you, Tyler. You stood her up."

I tried desperately to explain what happened.

"Listen," he interrupted, "if you don't know Laura by now, it's time you learn that she's stubborn, hard-headed and has a temper just like her mother."

By the time I reached the Cranbrook Hotel back in London, my thoughts of Laura had turned into an obsession. I hurried to the pay phone on the wall in the lobby of the hotel. I'd converted some pound notes into shillings and pence to feed the phone and finally reached an international operator. Within minutes, I heard the magic of her voice when she said, "Hello."

"Laura!"

Her mood changed to somber. "What do you want?"

"I'm in London."

"So?"

"Laura, I want to see you when I get home."

"Tyler, I'm dating someone now."

I paused for a moment to collect my thoughts. "Do I know him?"

"I doubt it. He's at Mercer."

"Laura, how many times have we told each other we are soulmates – meant for each other?"

She didn't respond.

"I'm flying out tomorrow morning and should be back in Macon by tomorrow night," I pleaded.

"I can't see you. We have plans."

"Laura, you don't understand. What I'm trying to say is 'I want to marry you!'"

"Are you drunk?"

"No. I haven't had a thing to drink. I'm serious."

"Has Europe made you crazy?"

"Yes. It made me crazy enough to know for certain what I want in my life, and you have to be a part of it."

"So, I'm supposed to fit into your plans, is that it?"

"Laura, damn it! I love you. I want you to be my wife. I want us to settle down and have children."

"I thought you were going to law school."

"I am, and I want you to go with me as my wife. I need

you, Laura. Please listen to me. We've got to get back together."

"You haven't even apologized for what you did to me."

"Laura, I'm very sorry. I didn't mean to hurt you. Please accept my apology."

"You'd rather go out with your friends than me."

"Look, I told you I was sorry. Can't you forgive me?"

That comment was met by silence.

"I've traveled around Europe and had a lot of time to think about things. Think about my life. Think about what I want my future to be. And, you've got to be a part of it. Laura, I love you."

A dial tone could be heard from the other end.

My body slumped to the floor, back against the wall, face in hands. I tried to focus on what Laura had just told me, knowing there would be no way for me to have a happy life without her.

I raised my knees and put my arms and head on them. Tears filled my eyes as I thought about Laura, about myself and the need for us to get back together.

I felt a tapping on my shoulder. Looking up, I saw an older woman wearing glasses and a black hat staring at me.

"Are you all right?" she asked. "Is there something I can do to help you?"

"No, thanks," I said. "I'll be all right.'

Back Home

It surprised no one, not our families or friends, when Laura and I married a few weeks after my return from Europe. I'd used every persuasive power in my arsenal to get her to consent and hoped that I could, in the future, apply those same convincing powers to sway a jury when trying some famous case.

Our wedding took place in Christ Church Episcopal in Macon with my father as best man and a slew of groomsmen and bridesmaids. At the reception, JT congratulated me on accomplishing two out of three of his admonitions and gave me some credit for the nude beach. Then he began shaking his head, "Two virgins getting married – ain't gonna be no sleep for you guys tonight!"

I laughed, then remembered something I'd almost forgotten. I reached in my pocket with a sly grin and pulled out the unopened box of condoms my dad had given me. "Here, JT, you might find a good use for these. I don't need them."

A few days afterward, we moved to Athens in order for me to enroll in law school at the University of Georgia.

One night, while pouring over my notes on contract law, a disturbing phone call came from my mother, who seemed to be in deep distress. She couldn't stop crying.

"Mama, what is it?"

"It's just so horrible, I don't know how to tell you."

"Has something happened to Dad?"

"No, no. It's not like anybody dying," she said, but she didn't go any further.

"Well, what is it?" I pressed her.

"It's just so hard for me to talk about. It's so terrible," she continued to cry.

"Mama, please tell me!" I insisted.

"It's your brother, Vernon," she whimpered.

"Oh my God! What's wrong? What did he do now?"

"Your father and I almost collapsed onto the floor when he came over to the house tonight and broke the news to us."

"About what?"

"It's hard for me to speak to you about things like this and your father refuses to talk about it."

"Mama, please tell me what it is."

She lowered the tone of her voice almost to a whisper. "Your brother said he likes men."

"What?"

"I can't believe it," she cried. "And we just can't accept something like that. Think of what it would do to your father's reputation if people were to find out?"

"My God, Mama. I'm sorry," then I said something I probably shouldn't have. "I can't say it surprises me, because it doesn't. He certainly fits the pattern."

"Well, I just don't know what to do about it, honey. I thought maybe you'd know what we should do."

"You want me to come home and talk with him?"

"I don't know if that'd do any good. You think there may be some possibility you could talk him out of it? What do you think? Should we send him off some place?"

"I don't know. I don't think it's anything I can talk him out of, but I'll do whatever you want, Mama."

After I hung up, Laura wanted to know, "What was that all about?"

"Vern told the folks that he's queer."

"Oh, my God," she sighed. "I feel so sorry for him."

"Why do you feel sorry for him? He's always been weird."

"Tyler Tucker, look at me! No, Tyler, turn your head toward me and look straight into my eyes! Can you comprehend what it must've been like for him growing up having you as an older brother?"

I sat down beside her. "Now what do you mean by that?"

"Tyler, you've always been Mr. Perfect in their eyes. You

did everything right – everything your parents wanted you to do that made them proud. He couldn't compete with that. No wonder he became introverted and shy. He's a good person. He's just different, and you and your parents need to accept it."

"I can still hear his words ringing in my ears, 'I'm telling Mom,'" I exaggerated in baby-talk.

Then I began to think that, more often than not, Laura was usually right about things. She seemed to have a better insight and manner of analyzing a situation than I did, and I guess that's why I'm not shy in seeking her advice. "So, what do you think I should do?"

"What do I think you should do?" She repeated. "I think you should call your brother right now and tell him you're proud of him for telling your parents about who he is."

"Are you kidding? I'm not proud of him for trying to ruin my parents' lives."

"Tyler, I'm surprised at you. I thought you were more open-minded than that."

"Well, I am about most things, but I don't like him hurting my parents."

"Your parents?" She raised her voice. "They're not just your parents. They're his parents, too."

"Look, I've got to study. Let's just forget about it. I'll try to think of something later to help mom and dad."

Time passed, and nothing more was said. My family seemed to let it go, but I know they certainly didn't forget.

By the end of the first year of law school, we had our first child, a daughter, named Hannah. She lit up our life – very independent and strong-willed. She had beautiful ringlets of blonde hair and a pretty face like her mother.

By the time I graduated from law school in 1971, we had our second child, a son named Tyler Edwin Tucker, III. We thought Wynn would be a good name for him – an alteration of my middle name, Edwin. He seemed to grow taller every time I saw him. He had big feet and long arms like mine. I was convinced that he'd be my basketball player.

After graduation, the law school helped me get a job as a

law clerk for a prominent Superior Court Judge in Atlanta. While clerking for the judge, I had the good fortune to watch the best trial lawyers in Atlanta display their talents in the courtroom. In addition to doing legal research for the judge, I assisted in writing legal opinions.

Laura, having learned journalism skills at Wesleyan, was quite a good writer. She wrote pieces for the Atlanta Journal involving famous women in Georgia, such as Martha Berry, Coretta Scott King, Celestine Sibley, Margaret Mitchell, Flannery O'Connor, Carson McCullers and Joann Woodward.

We lived in a two-bedroom apartment on Roswell Road. Having a three-year-old girl and a one-year-old boy didn't give Laura much time to write, only on occasions when the children were napping.

Clerkships normally lasted only one year, so at the end of my term, I began looking for a job in a law firm. I'd gotten to know many of the trial lawyers in the courtroom, and, as a result, received a number of offers from the best firms in Atlanta. Laura pleaded with me to leave the city, which had recently reached one million population, the largest city in the south. She wanted to raise our children in a smaller town, plus we were expecting our third child. She did a lot of arm twisting in convincing me to leave the city. My argument, "I love Atlanta, playing basketball in the City League, teaching at John Marshall night law school and coaching their basketball team."

"With all its traffic and congestion, our kids need to grow up in a small town atmosphere," she pleaded. "This place is getting too big."

When Laura sets her mind to something, there's no changing it. So, like a good husband, I bowed to her wishes.

Going back to Macon, would always make me Judge Tucker's son. I wanted to be my own man.

A cousin of my dad's in Brunswick, a coastal town in Georgia, heard of my dilemma and called to tell me she knew a good law firm there looking for a young lawyer. I called them and made an appointment for an interview. The firm consisted of two older lawyers who'd formed their partnership in the 1930s. Both of them were rated "A" by Martindale-Hubbell, the standard-bearer for rating lawyers all over the country. The older one, James Greene, was 65 and represented the City of Brunswick, while the younger one, Davis Parker, 62, represented Glynn County. Being only 26, I relished the idea of working with lawyers who could train me with their experience and skills.

When I arrived in Brunswick, I looked at my watch – 11:30. I'd been instructed to meet Mr. Greene and Mr. Parker at noon at Cody's Restaurant. I knew a smattering about the town. J.T. and I had a summer job lifeguarding on the beach at nearby Jekyll Island after our freshman year at Davidson.

The restaurant, located directly across Gloucester Street from their office in the two-story Dunwoody Building, was filled with customers. I wore my only suit, navy blue, with a red and gold striped tie.

Cody's had an aroma that ran the gamut from collard greens to fried chicken and lots of noise from talkative patrons. A slightly plump gentleman, about four inches shorter than I, with a receding hairline and wearing a tweed sport coat, stood up from a table and walked toward me.

"Are you Tyler?" he asked with a friendly smile.

"Yes sir."

He stuck out his hand, "I'm Davis."

"Nice to meet you, Mr. Parker."

"Please call me Davis, OK?"

"Sure."

I followed him back to the table, feeling a bit nervous for my first interview. I stood and waited for Davis to sit first, as I'd been schooled by my mama with a set of good manners in how to be a southern gentleman.

He appeared to be about five feet nine or ten, had a friendly smile and engaging personality that made me feel comfortable. His short cut, gray hair had receded halfway back from the top of his head making him seem casual, but distinguished.

"James will be here shortly," Davis explained. "He got tied up at the office."

An overly friendly waitress, with dyed black hair, heavy lipstick, dangling earrings and a short skirt strutted over, introduced herself as Hazel, and handed us both a menu.

"Hazel, why are you giving me a menu? You know what I want," Davis joshed.

"Oh," Hazel smiled. "I guess I was just a little bit nervous with this fine looking young man you have with you."

Davis smiled and turned toward me. "This is Tyler Tucker. He's talking to us about joining the law firm."

"Well, I sure hope he does," she patted me on the shoulder. "Are you single, honey?"

"Afraid not. Gotta wife, two children and one on the way."

"Oh, my!" she laughed, "You've really been busy, haven't you?" Then added, "I sure hope you go to work with them. You won't find two better gentlemen anywhere in the world to work for."

I nodded my head and smiled.

Soon Mr. Greene arrived. About five feet eight, he wore thick, wire-rimmed glasses and had a decidedly intellectual air about him. His gray hair and wrinkled face made him appear older than he was. In our later discussion, I learned that Mr. Greene had finished both undergraduate and law school at the University of Virginia.

Davis laughed and said, "He thinks if you didn't go to UVA you don't know anything."

Davis grew up in South Carolina and had graduated from George Washington University. He worked for a few years in the Commerce Department during the Roosevelt administration in the '30s. That's where he met his wife, Betty, who'd been born in Brunswick and was the daughter of the First National Bank president. After they married, she brought him back to her hometown to practice law. Her father and James Greene were close friends, and that's how Greene and Parker got together.

James had lived in Brunswick all his life, as did his father. In fact, his great-great-grandfather, Nathaniel Greene, was a Revolutionary War hero and, at one time, owned

Cumberland Island, just to the south of Brunswick. I later noticed a large portrait of General Greene hanging in his office.

While eating a fine southern meal at Cody's, the three of us had a lively discussion about current events, the law and what the two older lawyers would expect from me. I had a favorable impression of both gentlemen, and even though the population of Brunswick was only 20,000, the law firm of Greene and Parker had a thriving practice. James seemed to be inundated with legal work having to do with the city, and Davis was bogged down with the county. They needed a general practitioner who could handle the rest of the legal work. So, when the offer came, I agreed to give it a try and become an associate of the firm. The three of us shook hands and that solidified the deal.

Davis commented afterwards, "I knew you were someone I could get along with when I saw you lapping up those greens and fried chicken." We all laughed.

With the help of Davis and James, I found a house to rent for $100 a month on Fourth Street near Brunswick College. After settling in for a couple of weeks alone, I was joined by my two kids and Laura, eight months pregnant. The firm had offered me a salary of $400 a month, which I thought was reasonable and adequate to take care of our needs.

It surprised and delighted me that the law firm turned out to be more like a close-knit family. The two lawyers and two secretaries, Susan Bailey and Claire Bonds, referred to by all as Bailey and Bonds, had been working there together for decades. Born and raised in Duluth, Minnesota, Bailey's parents were Swedes. She was slim, average height with an attractive face even without makeup. Her blue eyes and wavy, blonde hair made her look much younger than her age of 49.

Bonds was older, closer to sixty, wore glasses and had a wit about her that made us all laugh. One of her sayings went like this:

"I like my bifocals,
my dentures fit me fine,

my hearing aids are perfect,
but I sure do miss my mind."

Anytime we forgot something, we'd refer to her rhyme.

Not only did the four of them work with each other during the day, but often would socialize together on a weekend night. They welcomed my family as one of their own. After our third child was born, a boy we named Miles, the firm expected Laura to bring our children to all social events.

Each working day at 10:30, business at the law office came to a screeching halt. No matter what urgent legal work needed to be done, we met together in the library to sit around the table and have coffee. Frequently, Laura would stop by with the children and bring cookies or, on special occasions, a cake. I never imagined in my wildest dreams that working conditions could possibly be that warm and pleasant.

My practice mostly involved real estate transactions. I spent a lot of time at the courthouse checking property titles and handling closings for people, who were borrowing money to purchase a house. I took on a few divorces but later tried to shy away from them as much as possible. The people were too demanding, clients calling me at home at night, and no matter the results, the client was always disappointed and blamed me for not doing a good job.

Criminal law was another part of my practice but not by choice. Glynn County didn't have a public defender system in place, so all the young lawyers in the county were expected to take our share of criminal case appointments from the judge without compensation. There were eight lawyers in Brunswick who'd practiced less than five years. We were all required to attend the opening of each term of court on the first Monday in January, May, and September. If the case load became too heavy, a special term would be added in December. The sheriff would bring the prisoners from the jail to a holding cell next to the courtroom. One at a time, the accused men were brought before the judge for what was known as arraignment. The judge would ask them, "How do you plead, guilty or not guilty?" If they replied, "not guilty," which most of them did, the judge would assign one of us to represent them.

Believe me, I had a lot to learn about criminal law. I'd taken only one course in school involving that field, and my judge in Atlanta never tried a criminal case.

One appointed case that had to be tried involved a burglar who broke into St. Mark's Episcopal Church, where we attended services each Sunday. My client had stolen all the previous Sunday's offering. It was not a comfortable feeling having to cross examine my minister, Father Morris, in an effort to properly represent my client. Justice had been served when the jury found the man guilty.

I had several other criminal jury trials at each of the terms of court during the first year of my practice, but most of them were misdemeanors, and I never found a comfort level in trying any of them.

Wes and Agnes

Times were tough in the deep piney woods of southern Georgia where no industries existed to provide work. The downtrodden, who owned no land, became sharecroppers, a harsh system whereby landowners allowed a tenant to farm their land in return for a share of the crops produced. Those of color, who didn't migrate to the North, worked on farms along with uneducated whites, scathingly referred to as "poor white trash."

The Jennings family could easily be identified among the latter group. None had ever traveled more than 50 miles from their home, nor did they own a vehicle other than a horse and wagon. However, that changed for Luther Jennings when he, along with many other men from the area, was drafted to serve on the Western Front in World War I.

After the war ended on November 11, 1918, Luther returned to his father's farm in Atkinson County, Georgia, near the town of Willacoochee. He never attended school, was unable to read and could barely write his name. After settling down on the farm, he married a girl a few years older, who lived about five miles away. They had two sons: Wesley Jennings, born in 1921, and Andrew Jackson Jennings, born in 1923. They called him Andy (and later on he became Duck.)

The oldest child seems to always be filled with more guilt than younger siblings. The eldest is expected to be responsible, more disciplined and is often leaned upon by the parents, who expect him or her to help manage little brothers and sisters. This sometimes brings about a domineering attitude that the older one has over the younger ones, and that certainly held true in the Jennings family.

From the time the boys were little, a fist fight between Wes and Andy occurred once a day if not twice. Their father, remembering how rough he'd been treated in his training for the Great War, had mandatory chores for both of them starting at the age of three or four. Being a tough disciplinarian, he believed strongly in the adage of "spare the rod and spoil the child," and the boys were dealt sound whippings for mischievous deeds. In fact, during drunken rages, whippings became more like beatings. He would hit the boys in the face, bloodying noses, bruising cheek bones and shouting obscenities at them.

Wes had to learn responsibility from a very young age, since on occasion his father was sent off to some place, unknown to the children, to be "dried out." That subject could never be discussed by any member of the family. While his father was away, Wes undertook the obligation to become man of the house and assumed the role of authority figure over the younger two children.

Times became increasingly difficult during the Depression. Skimping on everything, including food, convinced the boys that they had no desire to be farmers, and that they needed to get away from that place, especially their father, as soon as possible.

Wes stuck it out until he finished high school at the age of sixteen, which most everyone did at that time, given there were only ten grades to complete. By working two jobs, he managed to put himself through South Georgia College in nearby Douglas. While not the smartest boy in the class, he did manage to graduate with a few Bs and some Cs.

One of his part-time jobs involved hauling wood from the farm into Douglas for city folks who lived in nice homes with fireplaces. That's how he became acquainted with Colonel Smith, a generous lawyer in his late sixties, who often gave Wes an extra quarter for placing firewood in a large box on the back porch. Wes naturally assumed that Colonel Smith had been an officer in the military during World War 1, until one day he asked and was told that older lawyers are often referred to as "Colonel."

Colonel Smith took a liking to Wes and asked him if he'd run errands for him at his law office. Wes jumped at the opportunity, working full-time after he graduated from the two-year junior college at age eighteen. That's where he met Agnes Duckworth, a pretty girl with a sweet face and long, red curls that hung down to her shoulders. She could type faster than any secretary Colonel Smith had ever employed. She was a year older than Wes.

Wes, who barely made enough money to do anything other than eat and sleep, luckily found a space at Ma Hull's Boarding House. She let him rent a windowless back room for 50 cents a day.

For some time, Wes had been trying to get Agnes to make eye contact, but she'd always quickly look away from his glances. Wes, six feet tall, had black, wavy hair like his father and a good physique. He wasn't the best-looking boy in Douglas but looked good enough not to be ashamed of his appearance.

One Friday, Wes tried to muster up the nerve to ask Agnes to go to the picture show with him that night. *Stage Coach* was playing, starring John Wayne, his favorite, along with Claire Trevor. He'd stopped drinking Cokes and eating ice cream for an entire week in order to have the money to take her out, maybe even enough to buy a bag of popcorn and a Coke. He'd put aside a dollar and a half in the drawer where he kept his underwear, tucking the money all the way to the toe inside one of the socks. The movie cost twelve cents, popcorn and a Coke were a nickel each, so he felt confident he'd have enough to buy a burger for each of them at Joe's after the movie, if he could just talk Agnes into going out with him.

When Colonel Smith left the office to go to the courthouse, the two of them were alone. Wes jumped at the opportunity, walked up to her desk and blurted out, "Agnes, would you like to go with me to the picture show tonight?"

She looked up at him after a moment of silence, and nonchalantly shrugged her shoulders, "I guess so."

Even though she didn't sound very enthusiastic, it was enough. "I'll walk over to your place about 6:30. The show starts at 7:00."

He wore his best clothes: a pair of black pants, an open-collared blue shirt, a clean pair of socks and his only pair of shoes, brown loafers.

About twenty or so people formed a line to buy tickets. Plunking down a quarter for the two tickets, he took his penny change, then, with his other money, bought each of them a coke and a bag of popcorn. All totaled 44 cents. He then had a dollar and six cents left to go to Joe's, more than enough for both of them to have a fifteen-cent hamburger.

This became a regular occurrence every Friday night, an event Wes enthusiastically looked forward to all week long. He wanted to ask her to marry him, but he hadn't been able to save any money yet.

Then the infamous day arrived, Sunday, December 7, 1941, when hundreds of Japanese fighter planes attacked the American naval base at Pearl Harbor near Honolulu, Hawaii. It happened just before three o'clock in the afternoon, Georgia time, and everyone hung around the radio for the rest of the day listening to frightening news of what had happened. The entire country was in turmoil.

Andy, who'd turned eighteen in May, drove the old family pickup to Douglas to talk with Wes about them joining the Army together. Agnes cried when Wes told her that he and his brother needed to do their patriotic duty to fight the enemy. Preacher Roscoe Evans married them in his living room the afternoon before they left, with Andy standing in as a witness. They only had one night to consummate the marriage, so Colonel Smith kindly loaned them his cabin on the Ocmulgee River for this momentous occasion. Wes would never forget that evening until his dying day. To say that their sexual experience proved sensational is not sufficient to do it justice. He lost count of the number of times it occurred.

On that magical night, one of the legions of sperm found its way to unite with an egg, and on September 10, 1942, while Wes fought the Nazis somewhere in Europe, a son was born. Agnes named him John Wesley Jennings and decided to call him Wesley, knowing that a nickname would eventually surface sometime later. Southerners are loath to raise a child without a nickname, so he became Buddy rather than Junior when he was about two or three years old. Wes never saw his son until his first furlough. By then Buddy was almost four.

In 1945, the GI's who were lucky enough to come home were accorded a hero's welcome. It's well known that people grow up in a hurry when the angel of death constantly looms over their shoulder. The Colonel, having recognized increased maturity in Wes, invited him to "read law" while working in his office. Under Georgia law at that time, after two years of studying law under the supervision of an attorney, the candidate could take a written examination from a Superior Court Judge and, upon passing the exam, he or she would become a full-fledged lawyer.

Agnes continued to work as a prized secretary for the Colonel, and Wes learned law better than either one of them expected. He passed his bar exam and their future appeared to be bright.

But things seemed to go sour. After Agnes's third miscarriage, Wes realized that he had to get them away from Douglas and find new scenery. They hated to leave Colonel Smith after all he'd done for them over the years, but a change had to be made. They chose to move to Palatka, Florida, where Agnes's cousin practiced law. Paul Reynolds, a sole-practitioner, invited Wes to join him, assuring him that he'd have no problem at all passing the Florida Bar Exam.

The firm of Reynolds and Jennings struggled. It was hard to make a decent living. A lawyer could only charge $15 for preparing a deed or $25 for a will, clearly printed on the minimum fee schedule which all lawyers in Palatka meticulously adhered to. But often clients only wanted free advice.

The move, however, seemed to be a motivating factor, for in 1955, Agnes gave birth to their second child, a son they named Thomas Smith Jennings and true to fashion, everyone called him Tommy. His middle name came from Colonel Smith, Agnes's first employer and Wes' devoted mentor.

With a thirteen-year-old son and a new baby boy, Agnes could no longer manage the task of being the secretary in the law office. The demands at home were much more than she could accommodate. Diminished income caused by the loss of her salary, however, made it tough, so they had to be extremely careful with their expenses.

The firm hired Miss Carolyn Burns a spinster lady who wore long skirts and high-top shoes, to take Agnes's place. She had experience with typing and bookkeeping at a law firm in Jacksonville.

Wes learned that in order to build his practice, he should acquaint himself with as many waitresses as possible. They always seemed to be looking for a good, inexpensive lawyer to handle their divorces. As a result, Wes' domestic practice soared. Of course, very few had any means to speak of, so he managed to get most of his fee from their husbands. When that failed, he took his fee out in trade. After all, barter is the oldest method of compensation known to man, and, furthermore, it never gets reported on an income tax return – just one favor for another.

In 1951, Wes' partner, Mr. Reynolds, died suddenly from a heart attack, so Wes and Miss Carolyn, a staunch, pinch-lipped woman, albeit an exceptional secretary, had to carry on the law practice. Her poor eyesight caused her to wear thick glasses and her appearance posed no temptation for Wes. But she looked out for him, told him what to do and what not to do as if he were her son. And he listened to some of what she said and paid no attention whatsoever to the rest. The most important quality, however, was to cover for him when needed.

Since getting out of the military, Wes had problems with his eyesight, too, and also wore glasses, which he seemed to continually misplace. His black, wavy hair had become sprinkled with a smattering of gray. Each day he wore baggy, pleated pants held up by suspenders, wing-tip shoes, long silk socks with garters, a white shirt and tie and a panama straw hat that had become his uniform. He had no interest whatsoever in the Ivy League look that many of the younger fellows had begun to wear.

Most everyone suspected that Wes ran around on his wife, a practice which began several years after moving to Palatka. "Variety is the spice of life," he'd laughingly say to his male friends. Agnes heard the rumors about these escapades from various sources. But like so many devoted, southern women, she carried the hurt in her heart, escaping her sadness and disappointment by relentlessly delving into the work of the church, the institution that has been the salvation for so many housewives, who've had to put up with their whiskey-drinking, philandering husbands. Where else could a woman find refuge and solace other than in the safe haven of a church? Most southern ladies with children would never undertake the humiliation of divorce unless the situation at home became totally unbearable. That was not the case. Wes had reached the stage where he made enough money to get by, as long as they lived within their means. Generally respected in the community, he attended church regularly with Agnes and had no desire to get out of the marriage. She, on the other hand, paid her penance like a martyr, an act of self-abasement which normally results in incurable piety.

They would celebrate their 32nd wedding anniversary within a couple of weeks, and both of them seemed relatively secure in their marriage of convenience. Wes rose early each morning and, after coffee and a piece of toast with jam, headed for the sanctuary of his office. Golf every Wednesday afternoon and Saturdays, followed by a gin rummy game in the clubhouse kept him relatively happy and gave him something to look forward to. After a couple of whiskey sours or some other spirituous libation while playing cards, he'd drive home to have dinner with his dependable wife.

Wes' law office was in a one-story frame house, built as a residence in the early 1900s, directly across from the Putnam County Courthouse. The front room, formerly the living room, had been converted into a reception area for Miss Carolyn's desk. The sofa and two stuffed chairs sat so low to the floor that some clients, who'd been sitting there, had problems trying to stand.

Buddy, having reached the age of 31 on September 10, 1973, had followed too many of the vices and desires of his father's and grandfather's heart. The following spring. after his second DUI, he'd been sent off to a rehabilitation clinic in the Blue Ridge Mountains of North Georgia. Wes had been able to persuade the district attorney to drop the charges for possession of marijuana, provided Buddy agreed to seek medical help.

Wes pretty much abandoned Buddy as an incurable drunk, who'd dropped out of high school and never made a go of it. His relationship with Tommy never developed either, due to a lack of time spent together. Wes had his own agenda and left the children for Agnes to raise.

The secret he'd kept from his family for years was the amount of money he'd lost gambling from his gin rummy games at the Country Club. Not even Miss Carolyn knew. It took every penny he could get his hands on to pay the mortgage on his home and office and the expense of food, insurance, taxes and the like.

The Wednesday afternoon before Thanksgiving of '73, Miss Carolyn was typing a deed to be signed by Bill Dawkins, who operated the local dry cleaners. Wes looked at his watch – almost 2:00 – the time for Bill's appointment. Of course, Wes had forgotten to tell Miss Carolyn about the need to prepare the deed until after 1:30.

She knocked softly on the door then walked into Wes's office and saw him reared back in his chair with his feet on the desk reading the newspaper. "There's a gentleman here to see you."

"Is it Bill?"

"No. He wouldn't tell me his name," she said.

"Well, who the hell is it?" he acted perturbed.

"I've never seen him before," she responded.

Wes walked out to the reception room and exclaimed, "Well, I'll be damned! Jimbo Martin! What the hell you doing here? I ain't seen you in a coon's age."

"Wes, you old son of a bitch, you look the same as you always did – ugly as hell."

Jimbo didn't look all that good either, much too stocky with thinning hair and a red face.

"What brings you to these parts?"

"Well, I was driving down to south Florida and thought I'd stop by here and see if I could find you. It must've been 20 years since I've seen you."

"Probably longer than that," Wes laughed. "Jimbo, this is Miss Carolyn. She's the best damn secretary in the state of Florida. Me and Jimbo grew up together back in Willacoochee, Georgia, a hundred years ago. He lived on a farm about a mile from our place."

"Pleased to meet you ma'am," he said politely.

Miss Carolyn smiled, nodded her head and continued right on typing the deed, trying not to be offended by the unbridled profanity being used by Wes and his friend.

Jimbo and Wes walked back into his office and closed the door. Wes didn't sit behind his desk, which might indicate a separation between them. He pulled a chair up next to Jimbo.

"You wouldn't turn down a drink, would you?" Wes smiled.

"It's a little bit early, but I guess a little snort wouldn't hurt anything."

Wes got up, reached in his desk and pulled out a half-empty bottle of Jack Daniels, Black Label. "You wouldn't object to a little Tennessee sour mash, would you?"

"Damn, Wes! You drink good stuff. You must be making a heap of money."

"Hell, you can't make no money in this town," he shook his head. "I represent a man who owns a liquor store, and this is how I get paid."

He poured them both a small glass and sat back down.

"Tell me 'bout yourself, Jimbo. Where you living?"

"I'm up in the big city of 'Hotlanta.'"

"Oh yeah. You a big shot, ain't you?

"Hell, Wes, you know you can't take the country out of the boy."

"What your do up there?"

"I work for Co' Cola."

"The hell you say!"

"Yeah, I've been working with 'em since '46 when I got out of the army. Started off as a taster, traveling all over the southeast to make sure the fountain cokes at the lunch counters tasted like a Coke. I finally made it up into management and now I'm working in public relations."

There was a knock on the door. Miss Carolyn opened it and stuck her head in. "Mr. Dawkins is here to sign the deed."

"Tell him I'll be right there," Wes got up. "Excuse me, Jimbo. This won't take more than a couple of minutes."

"You go right ahead, Wes. You gotta make a living."

"Hell, I don't get no money outta him either. Just get my

dry cleaning done for free."

Wes went into the waiting room and chatted with Bill Dawkins, who signed the deed.

"Is our arrangement still good?" Bill asked.

"It is with me," Wes agreed.

He shook Bill's hand and walked back into the office, sat down and took another sip of whiskey.

"Wes, you ever hear from Andy?"

"Funny you ask. He's due in here today to spend Thanksgiving with us," Wes leaned back in his chair. "You know everybody calls him Duck now, 'cause he tried to fix his hair in the shape of a duck's tail like Elvis."

Jimbo laughed. "That sounds just like him. I ain't seen that sorry rascal since we all joined the army back in '41. How many years ago was that?"

"Let's see," Wes began to count aloud. "'41, '51, '61, '71. That's 30 plus 2 to get to '73. So, 32 years ago."

"Well, how's he doing?"

"Truthfully, don't think he's changed a damn bit. He's just like he ever was. Never married. I'm sure he couldn't find a woman who'd have him."

"Yep. There'll never be another one like him."

"He's had so many jobs," Wes added. "I don't know how many, and I don't know if he's workin' now or not. I guess I'll find out tonight."

"How's your wife?" Jimbo apologized. "Damn! I'm sorry. I can't remember her name."

"Agnes," Wes responded. "We still hanging on the side of the cliff by our finger nails."

"Is that right?"

"Hell, Jimbo. Everything's a tradeoff, you know. If I had me a passionate woman who wanted to make love every night, she probably wouldn't be worth a damn around the house. Wouldn't cook, keep the house clean and I'd have to worry about her running around on me. So, in exchange, I got one who's a good cook, keeps the house clean, and I know she ain't giving none to nobody and that includes me. The only concern in her life is the Baptist Church. The doors can't open without her being Johnny on the spot. There's Sunday School, Church in the morning, Church in the evening, Prayer Meeting on Wednesday nights, Missionary Society and I don't know what all else. I mean it's going on all the time."

"Well," Jimbo chided. "I guess there're worse places she could go."

"Talking 'bout Duck. I ain't seen him in a while myself," Wes said. "When he was driving a truck, he'd stop by every so often in that big semi, blowing his horn. You could hear him a damn block away. But since he lost that job, I don't hear much of him."

Duck

Wes had called his brother to invite him to spend Thanksgiving with their family because his favorite nephew, Tommy, would be home from boot camp. The call had been a pleasant surprise since Duck had not been welcome in their house since Tommy's graduation six months earlier. To offend the preacher was a cardinal sin in that household, but most of all to insult your sister-in-law was not to be taken lightly. But, what the hell, Duck thought the whole episode was pretty funny after Wes told him the next morning what he'd said at the dinner table the night before. Naturally, he had no recollection of the fact that he'd called the preacher an asshole, but he did remember he'd been quite accurate in his assessment.

He'd had a string of jobs, moving from one place to another. A steady job was not Duck's bag, but he'd been clerking at Jobbers Hardware in Tallahassee, Florida, for the past few years. The boss had done him a great favor by giving him three days off to have Thanksgiving with his brother's family.

Truck driving had always been his favorite occupation and shooting pool his favorite pastime. He bragged to everyone how he'd traveled in every state in the lower 48. Unfortunately his license had been revoked after he received his second DUI. He justified all weaknesses by telling himself that he'd sacrificed for his country by fighting in World War II. He never forgot how the Japanese tried to lure the Americans into battle at Midway Island, but as he many times said, "Our guys ambushed those Japs and sunk four of their best ships." That was a turning point in the war, and Duck always prided himself in being a part of it.

Duck had reached the time in his life when his hair was rampantly receding. No longer could he mimic Elvis. His ruddy face carried a smile, for he seemed to find most things funny. He had a tendency to be loud and raucous when drinking too much, yet he had a surprisingly good physique, disrupted only by a protruding beer gut over his belt. Most people who knew Duck couldn't help but like the guy. But admire him – no. Yet he was the sort of man who'd return your wallet with the money still in it if he found it on the street, and he'd stop and help an old lady change her flat tire if he saw her car beside the road.

After throwing a few clothes and a bottle of Early Times in a ragged, worn-out suitcase, he walked out to his pickup to find, much to his surprise, that his truck was parked in the center of his landlady's flower bed. Not having remembered much about coming home the previous evening, he walked around the truck to assess the damage.

He heard the front door slam at Mrs. Harper's house next door as she came rushing out at a fast pace, shaking her finger, "Do you see what you did?" she shouted. A small, wiry lady, who didn't pull any punches, she'd just about had enough of Duck.

At first, he pretended he didn't hear her, but when she persisted, he hung his head in shame then looked up like a little boy who'd been caught with his hand in the cookie jar. "I'm sorry. I'll make it right."

"How're you gonna make it right when you've crushed my chrysanthemums? And, besides that, you know you haven't given me this month's rent!"

"I get paid this Saturday, Mrs. Harper. I promise you'll have your rent when I get my check, and I'll get your flower bed fixed, I promise."

"How do you think you're gonna fix those crushed chrysanthemums that have been so pretty? Just tell me, how're you gonna to do that?"

"Do you think I could prop 'em up with a stick? Or do you want me to buy you some more?"

She put her hands on her hip and disgustedly walked back in, slamming the door so hard, it sounded like a shotgun.

Bonnie Sue

Bonnie Sue Atwater had lived all her life in Tallahassee. She stopped by to see her mother the day before Thanksgiving. She'd arrived around eight in the morning and found her mother still in bed.

"You ain't working today?" Bonnie asked.

"Don't have to be there 'til noon. Boss gave me a half-day off."

"Mama, I need to get away for a long weekend. I've decided to go to Jacksonville Beach right by myself."

Her mama stared at her for a few moments then asked, "Honey, don't you want somebody to go with you?"

"Nope. Just me, myself and I."

"You gotta be careful when you're out there by yourself. You're too pretty, and you know how men are. They might try to take advantage of you."

She laughed at that comment. "Mama, you know I've been taking care of myself a long time. I wasn't born yesterday. I'm almost 40 years old."

Bonnie Sue, Mrs. Atwater's only child, had been the center of her mother's attention ever since her daughter had been born out of wedlock. It wasn't easy raising a child all alone without financial support from anyone. She worked six days a week at J. C. Penny and, to make ends meet, sewed at night for many women who had dresses to hem.

Bonnie had never married. Every time she found a boyfriend, it seemed that something always happened to cause them to break up. When she was 31, she'd had an abortion, a really difficult decision for her and her mother.

"Honey, why don't you ask Betty Jean to go with you?"

"I told you before, Mama, I want to go by myself. Ain't nothing gonna happen to me. I have Jesus to protect me."

Bonnie walked over to her mother's dresser, looked in the mirror, rubbed her cheeks and patted her hair.

"Well, what about HIM?" Mama questioned.

"HIM? I'm not telling HIM anything," she said emphatically.

"What do I say if he calls me looking for you?"

"I don't think he'll call. Besides, I think he's taking his wife to some highfalutin' dance or ball or something like that."

Mama thought for a minute then said, "I'll just tell him you've gone on a church retreat."

Bonnie sat on the bed beside her mother and patted her on the hand. "No, don't do that," she said in a soft voice. "I haven't told him anything about me being saved. It's just been a week ago tomorrow, and I ain't seen him since. I need to get away and think this whole thing out."

"Well, if you break up with him, are you gonna have to give back that new car he gave you?"

Bonnie laughed. "Mama, you know I wouldn't be a man for nothing in this world. They think they're so smart, but they're all so downright stupid. I can make a man do anything I want him to and have him beg for more."

Her mama laughed.

"I don't know, "Bonnie said. "I've just got to get away from everybody for a little while and talk to the Lord about what He wants me to do."

"Heavens to Betsy, child, there ain't no reason to have to drive all the way to Jacksonville Beach to talk to the Lord. Can't you talk to Him right here in Tallahassee?"

"I just want to sit down on a sandy beach by the ocean and watch the waves come crashing in. I'll probably have my Thanksgiving dinner right there – maybe eating a turkey sandwich," she laughed.

It hadn't been easy for Bonnie growing up without ever knowing anything about her father. Her mother refused to talk about him. Every time Bonnie would broach the subject, her questions would be met by silence. Bonnie had been in and out of so many relationships, but she'd now been cast in a new role; the other woman. She needed money and gave him everything he wanted in exchange for the lavish gifts he provided. She could make him whine like a baby, moan like a tiger, whimper like a kitty cat then howl like a banshee as he cut loose from reality to float on a sea of ecstasy. To experience that addictive sensation provoked untold generosity on his part. His socialite wife provided him with the dignity he needed for a man in his position. But intimate times in their bedroom, compared to a fling with Bonnie Sue, was akin to listening to a child playing Yankee Doodle on a toy piano versus the New York Philharmonic's stirring rendition of Beethoven's Ninth Symphony.

He held the position of CEO of one of the major insurance companies, and received a healthy commission for every policy sold in the state of Florida. He'd also held the position as president of the Chamber of Commerce of Tallahassee and was well-respected by his peers.

Mama sat up in bed while sipping the cup of coffee Bonnie had dutifully prepared. "Honey, I want you to promise me you'll be careful," she said.

"Can't you see, Mama, I've got to go off and be alone to work out what I must do with my life. I can't go on sinning no more. I've got to start living by the Word. That's what the preacher told me I had to do."

"But what's going to happen to you, honey? You got that fancy new car, that swishy apartment and cash to burn. What you gonna do if you lose all that?"

"I'll just get a job like everybody else." At first, she questioned whether or not to make the next statement, but on second thought, decided to say it anyway. "I'm getting a job selling life insurance. I can even start now, but they said that later on, they'll send me off to a school to train me."

"Sell life insurance!" Mama raised her voice in disbelief.

"They say I can make a lot of money. I'll get a percentage of every policy I sell."

"But what if you don't sell none?"

"I know, Mama, I'm thinking all those same things you're thinking, and that's the reason I'm gonna go to Jacksonville Beach to work out all these questions in my life."

As Mama got out of bed to put on her bedroom slippers, she said, "I'm going in the kitchen to fix you some breakfast before you go."

"No, Mama. Get back in bed. I've already decided, I'm fixing to stop by Al's Chat and Chew."

Al's Chat and Chew

Duck pulled his truck into the parking lot of Al's Chat and Chew, the best greasy spoon café in Tallahassee. The customers not only loved the food, but they also had the added attraction of listening to Al talk about most every subject imaginable. The early breakfast crowd had finished eating and left, so Al was not too busy when Duck walked in. Al's big, burly frame was adorned with a long apron that once had been white but the multitude of stains made it appear brown. Of Greek descent, he had a generous amount of curly black hair and a bushy beard.

"How's it going, Duck?" he said, while picking his teeth.

"Pretty good, Al. You OK?"

"I've been worse."

Duck sat on a bar stool closest to Al and the cash register, where one could become mesmerized by the aroma of coffee perking and bacon frying. Al walked over to the kitchen window and yelled to the cook, "Duck's here," the signal to fix scrambled eggs with cheddar cheese, sausage patties, grits with lots of butter and a hot biscuit. The sounds of dishes clanging together rang out as Al handed him a cup of black coffee while Duck perused the morning newspaper he'd found on the counter.

He sniffed the cup before taking a sip and wondered why the first one always tasted best.

Shortly, the cook placed Duck's breakfast on the counter and slammed the bell so hard he almost knocked it off the window onto the floor.

"I'm gonna kill that son of a bitch one day," Al exclaimed as he put the breakfast plate in front of Duck.

"You know you couldn't do without him," Duck laughed.

Al's full name was Alex Antonopoulos. He'd inherited the Chat and Chew from his father, known by all as "Big Al." It seemed customary at the time that many Greek immigrants gravitated toward operating a restaurant. So, when Little Al came back from the war, he never gave it a second thought. The only right thing for him to do was to help out his aging father. The café, a well-known eating establishment in that part of Florida, appeared to be frequented mostly by Florida rednecks and displaced Georgia crackers.

Just as he was finishing his breakfast, Duck exclaimed, "God Almighty, Al! Do you see what's getting out of that Caddy convertible?"

Al walked to the window and looked out. "I've seen her in here before, but I don't know who she is."

"Man, oh man! Wonder whose bed she's been sleeping in to get those wheels."

Duck watched closely as Bonnie stepped out of a brand new '73 Cadillac Coupe de Ville convertible, maroon in color, white cloth top, white side-wall tires and white leather interior – a real sight to behold.

Bonnie's bleached hair had been teased in the shape of a bee hive, heavy eye makeup, rosy-red lipstick and long dangly earrings adorned her head. She wore a tight baby-blue sweater over her voluptuous bosom and a short navy-blue skirt, cut about four inches above her knees. The matching spike heeled shoes made treading on Al's brick walkway somewhat challenging. But then again, her grand entrance into the café mimicked a scene from Mame, as if to say, "Life is a banquet, and most poor suckers are starving to death."

Only three customers remained inside the café, all males. Needless to say, their eyes were glued on her. Even the cook came out of the kitchen to catch a glimpse of this phenomenon until Al gave him the evil eye, signaling him to get back to work.

As she strolled past Al and Duck, who were still standing next to the cash register, she never gave them a passing glance. The whiff of her perfume seemed strong enough to light a fire, and she was giving that Juicy Fruit chewing gum a real workout.

After she sat down in a booth, Essie Mae, the waitress, walked out of the kitchen, checked her out, and with hands on hips, marched over and slapped a menu down.

Duck, like a quail-sniffing bird dog, eased away from Al

and sauntered over to her table. Intoxicated by her good looks, he leaned down and asked, "Well, how're you doing, Sugar?"

"I'm just fine, honey," she said in an exaggerated southern accent. "How're you?"

"Well, I'd be a whole lot better if you'd let me sit down in front of you and feast my eyes on your good looks."

"Just have your little self a seat and feast away all you please," she said with a coy expression.

Duck positioned himself directly across from her, propped his elbows on the table and rested his head on his hands. "The Lord shore has been good to you," an expression he'd used many times before in trying to pick up a woman. For Duck, this situation was more like a Basset Hound trying to leap up for the doggy bone held just out of reach.

Essie Mae, the short, stout waitress with graying hair, sized up the encounter perfectly, placed a glass of water in front of Bonnie, and asked with a surly attitude, "Do you know what you want?"

Bonnie took her chewing gum out of her mouth with her thumb and forefinger and placed it in the ash tray. She then took a small drink of ice water, exposing her lengthy, artificial, fuchsia nails as if she were sipping champagne. She looked up at Essie Mae and said with a drawl, "Could I have just a little more time, honey?"

"You can have all the time you want," Essie Mae contracted her eyebrows and walked away.

Bonnie, looking at Duck with large cow eyes and sugar dripping from her lips, said in an exaggerated sexy voice, "I bet I got something you want, honey," she lured him like a decoy.

"Hell yeah, baby, you shore do."

"Well, I think I'm gonna let you have it, and you'll be my first one," she teased. "What I'm talking about, my friend, who I don't even know your name, is something much more important than sex."

"I don't get it," Duck shook his head. "There ain't nothing more important than sex."

Tom Dennard

"Oh, yes there is," she smiled.

"OK. What is it?" Duck insisted

"Life insurance."

"Life insurance? What the hell!"

Bonnie leaned back and pressed her body against the booth, "That's right, honey. There ain't no getting around it. You're gonna die sometime, so the money won't be wasted."

Having the wind sucked from his sails, Duck murmured, "Are you really a life insurance salesman?"

"I am now. Except I'm not a salesman. I'm a sales person."

Duck shook his head. "Why in hell do I need life insurance? I ain't got nobody to leave it to."

Unable to take "No" for an answer, Bonnie pressed him further. "You got to have enough money to bury you, and then you could give the rest to somebody in your family."

"Girl, I thought you and me were 'bout to get something going. I didn't know you were a damn life insurance salesman."

"Sales-person," she corrected him.

Essie Mae arrived at the table, a little bit disgusted, "Have you decided what you want to eat?"

"I'll have pancakes and sausage, and please Sugar, bring me a cup of black coffee."

Essie Mae did a military about-face and briskly walked away.

Duck lit a cigarette, took a long draw then turned from Bonnie to blow the smoke. "I think me and you need to get to know each other better. We don't even know each other's name? Everybody calls me Duck."

"That's a funny name," she smiled. "Everybody calls me Bonnie. Bonnie Sue Atwater."

They shook hands over the table.

"I'm glad to meet you, Mr. Duck," she said.

"Yeah. I'm glad to meet you too," he smiled.

68

"OK, Mr. Duck. Tell me how old you are, so I can look up the premium in my big black book out there in my car?"

"Me? I'm 45," his typical answer to women he pursued. Actually, he was 50.

"And when will you be 46?" she probed.

"Next May 29th."

"So, you're a Gemini just like me. My birthday is June 3rd."

"And how old will you be?" Duck asked without thinking.

"Don't you know, honey?" she scolded. "You never ask a woman her age or how much she weighs. That's impolite."

They laughed aloud, as Essie Mae abruptly shoved the plate of pancakes in front of Bonnie.

"I had sausage, too," she reminded her.

"And you'll get them if you'll just be patient," she snarled.

After finishing her breakfast, Bonnie pushed her plate aside. "You going somewhere?" Duck asked.

"Yeah, I gotta go. I'm heading to Jacksonville Beach."

"Really. Well, I'm going to Palatka to visit my brother for Thanksgiving and I'll get to see my nephew, Tommy, before he's shipped out to 'Nam."

"Oh yeah?" Bonnie said. "How old is he?"

"He ain't but 18," Duck paused, then turned serious. "You know, Bonnie, I've been having some bad dreams about him that I can't figure out."

"What kind of dreams?"

"I don't know. Just some crazy dreams that something went wrong with Tommy."

"Aw, you're just worried about him going to 'Nam."

"Yeah. You're probably right."

"You say you're going to Palatka. I've heard of it, but I ain't never been there," Bonnie said.

Duck thought for a moment. "It's about 50 miles south of Jacksonville."

Bonnie picked up the check, grabbed her pocket book,

and they walked over to the counter where Al was standing. Bonnie paid her check, adding a very small tip for Essie Mae.

"Al, I'll be seeing you in a few days when I get back," Duck said.

Al cracked a big smile as Duck and Bonnie walked out together.

"You gonna give me your phone number?" Duck pleaded.

"No, but I'm gonna give you the premium for your life insurance policy," she said.

"I tell you what, Bonnie," Duck smiled. "I'll give you my phone number, and you call me when you get back. We can talk some more about life insurance and other more serious matters."

Disappointed by the brushoff, which, of course, had occurred many times before, Duck flung open the door and jumped in his old Ford pickup. He tried to start it, but nothing happened. He watched Bonnie walking back into the café. He let the window down and yelled out, "Everything OK?"

"I left my pocketbook by the cash register, or, at least, I hope I did."

Duck raised the hood on the truck and wiggled the battery cables. He got back in and tried to start it, but nothing happened. "Damn it to hell," he said under his breath. He saw Bonnie walking toward her car holding on to her pocketbook. He yelled out, "Hey Bonnie!"

She turned toward him and saw the hood up on his truck. "You got problems?" she asked.

"I think the damn battery is dead."

"I can drop you off at a service station if you want me to."

Realizing he didn't have enough money for a new battery, he knew he would have to throw himself on Bonnie's mercy.

"You takin' Highway 90 over to Jacksonville?"

"I don't know highway numbers, honey. I just look for road signs to Jacksonville."

"If you don't mind, I could ride with you to the other side of Lake City, and you could drop me off. I'll hitch from there to Palatka."

"How're you gonna get back?"

"I'll just hitch. I've done it plenty of times before. My thumb has carried me more places than you can imagine. Don't have any mechanical problems – just trim my thumb nail every now and then."

"Well, I guess you're old enough to know what you're doing."

"So, is it OK for me to go with you?" Duck pressed her.

"Well, I guess so, but you cuss too much. I don't like nobody cussin' around me."

"I promise I won't say a damn word. Ah, hell. I can't help it. It's just the way I talk. But I'll do my best not to say no cuss words."

Duck ran back in to tell Al he was leaving his truck in the parking lot. Al laughed and agreed. He came back out, closed the hood on the truck, grabbed his bag and jumped in the Caddy convertible with a big smile on his face.

Tom Dennard

East on Highway 90

"Turn here on East Tennessee," Duck directed. "That'll get us on Highway 90."

"Whatever you say," Bonnie agreed. She thought she had a pretty good first impression or an intuitive sense of this man in her car. She'd known so many guys just like him – what she'd describe as "good ol' boys." They were all pretty much alike: wanted sex with a woman any time they could get it, favorite food and drink would be barbeque and an ice cold Bud, usually drove an old pickup truck – either a Ford or Chevy, favorite pastime, other than chasing women, would be huntin' and fishin', only listened to country music, right-wing conservative in their politics, liked to tell dirty jokes, never missed watching a football game on TV and wouldn't be caught dead letting another person see them shed a tear.

For a while, Bonnie and Duck rode along Highway 90 without talking, just thinking their thoughts and wondering what might happen next. Duck saw a roadside park up ahead and interrupted the silence. "Pull over, Bonnie. I gotta take a leak."

She drove the car under a big shade tree, as he reached in the back seat for his suitcase.

"You need your suitcase to take a pee?"

"Ah yeah, I need to get my medicine out."

He walked a few yards away into the woods, put his suitcase down, and stood beside a large pine tree. He then reached into his suitcase, pulled out the Early Times and took a couple of slugs.

When he got back into the car, he said, "Hey, Bonnie, let's get wild and crazy and let the top down, whatcha' say?" The weather had warmed enough so his suggestion wasn't completely insane.

"Are you crazy?" she said. "I paid fifteen dollars for this hairdo, and I ain't 'bout to mess it up."

"Aw, come on. Ain't you got something you can wrap around your head?"

"Yeah. I guess." She reached into her pocketbook, pulled out a scarf and wrapped it over her hair, tying it as tightly as possible underneath her chin.

She drove back onto the highway into a stiff breeze that had her scarf flapping in the wind and Duck's hair standing straight up. Had you seen them, you'd think they were a couple in love. They talked, laughed and really seemed to enjoy each other's company.

"You know, it ain't fair that guys can pee so easy anywhere they want. Sometimes I wish I had one of them things so I could stand up next to a tree like you did. Girls have it harder. Don't you think?"

"Maybe. But I'm glad you got what you got."

"See," Bonnie added. "I gotta wait 'til we get to the next service station for me to pee. It ain't fair."

Just before the city limits of Monticello, she saw a Gulf station and drove to the side of the building where the restrooms were located. There were four doors with signs above each one. "Men," "Women," "Colored Men," and "Colored Women." She thought things like that didn't exist anymore, but in some small towns, Jim Crow still existed. She went inside to get the key.

The eager young attendant asked, "Ma'am, you want me to pump you some gas?"

"No, I think I've got enough, thank you."

When she got back in the car, she said, "That was the nastiest restroom I've ever seen. I wouldn't take my pig in there if I had one."

After cruising through Monticello, Bonnie asked, "How far is it to Jacksonville anyway?"

"From Tallahassee, it's 'bout three hours, but to git to the beach, it's probably another thirty minutes," Duck replied.

Bonnie began to increase the speed exponentially. Whisking through the pine forests of the panhandle of Florida, she loved the excitement of driving fast and passing every car she approached on the two-lane road. Duck noticed, but didn't say a word, as he watched the speedometer move past 75 in a 55 mph speed zone. She'd been stopped twice for speeding in the previous two months, but, armed with the confidence that she'd mastered the art of getting most anything she wanted out of a man, she'd always been able to talk her way out of getting a ticket. She even knew how to make the cop feel guilty for having stopped her.

Bonnie broke the silence. "Duck, we been together for almost two hours, and I don't hardly know a thing about you. I tell you what..."

"What?"

"Let's play a game. I get to ask you three questions about anything in the whole world, and then you can do the same with me." She looked over at him with a sort of eagerness that excited him. "Whatcha' say?"

"Hell, it's all right with me. I ain't got nothing to hide," Duck laughed and relaxed back in his seat.

"I tell you what," Bonnie said. "I'll let you go first, OK."

"Yeah, if you say so," Duck smiled. "Let me see. What would I like to know about you?" He pondered for a moment. "How'd you like for me to give you a good roll in the sack?"

"Duck!" she screamed.

"Well, you said I could ask you anything."

"But, damn," she said. "Oh my God! I can't believe what I just said. I promised the Lord I would never again say another cuss word. I just can't believe I said that. I have sinned."

Duck paused then turned toward her with a serious expression, "I don't really think one 'damn' is gonna send you to hell."

"It's all your fault for asking me a dirty question like that. It just shocked me so much. I didn't know what I was doing."

"You mean that's the first time you've ever been asked that question?"

Bonnie chose to ignore him. "You talk nasty," Bonnie said. "I've a good mind to stop this car and put you out."

"Why?"

"You're a bad influence on me." She jerked her head around and stared with a stiff jaw straight ahead at the road.

After a moment of silence, Duck said, "You never did answer the question I asked you."

"What do you think the answer is?" She raised her voice, still peeved. "The answer is NO!"

Duck thought for a moment, then said, "Religion shore does take a lot of fun out of life."

"Well," she paused. "When you have religion, you only have sex when you're married. That's what the Bible says. At least, I think it does."

"How many times you been married honey?" Duck asked.

She waited a long time before responding, then admitted the truth, "Never."

"You ain't never been married? You mean you're telling me you're still a virgin at your age?"

"After a long pause, Bonnie broke the silence. "I know what you gonna' say before you even say it. Yes, I've sinned in the past, but I've quit sinning. Anyway, let's change the subject, because it's obvious you have a one-track mind."

Bonnie turned on the radio and tried to find some music she liked; but in between all those small towns, she couldn't find a station. She took off at an even faster rate of speed. They cruised along the highway lined by pine trees on both sides with not much scenery other than that.

"Bonnie!" Duck raised his voice. "There's a car with flashing lights coming up behind us. Damn, it looks like the fuzz has got us."

She slowed down and drove the car onto the shoulder of the road, while the highway patrol pulled right up next to her rear bumper. The nice-looking young officer, with black, curly hair, and a dark complexion, appearing to be in his early twenties, sauntered up to the side of the car. He leaned his six-foot frame over toward Bonnie.

"Lady, you going to a fire or something? Let me see your license."

She fumbled through her pocket book and handed it to him, then took off her scarf, brushed her hair with her hands and looked in the rearview mirror to make sure she looked her best. "Honey," she said in an exaggerated southern accent, "was I going too fast?"

He didn't answer but studied the license thoroughly. "Bonnie Sue Atwater. Is this your correct address in Tallahassee?"

"Yes sir, it is."

"Do you realize I clocked you at 78 miles an hour, and this is a 55 zone?" He seemed stern and serious.

She gazed at him and batted her eye lashes with a flirty expression. "Well, sugar, you must be mistaken, because I don't ever drive that fast."

The officer looked over at Duck. "Are you Mr. Atwater?"

"No. This good-looking lady wouldn't marry nobody like me. I'm just a hitchhiker."

"A hitchhiker? You got any identification?"

Duck pulled his license out of his wallet and handed it to Bonnie to give to the officer.

He studied it. "Andrew Jackson Jennings."

"Yep, that's my name," Duck said.

"Is that your name?" Bonnie seemed surprised. She then looked up to the officer. "Honey, everything here is legal."

"Don't you know better than to pick up a hitchhiker?" the officer lectured her.

Bonnie explained, "His truck was broke down, so I offered him a ride since I was going to Jacksonville Beach, and he was going to Palatka. Now, if you don't mind, Sugar Doll, could you tell me if you're married?"

He looked at her with a curious expression, then said, "No."

"You're as good-looking as a movie star, Darling. I bet I got something you want," she said, as if honey were dripping from her lips.

"What you getting at?" he said with an unforgiving expression.

"You need some life insurance. You never know what might happen to you, running up and down this road like you have to do. You might turn over and kill your handsome self."

"Look lady."

She interrupted, "At your young age, a $10,000 policy wouldn't cost much at all. You can pay for it by the month, and when you do find that sweet little wife and have a house full of young'uns, you're gonna be proud you met me."

"I don't make much money," he said in a more mellow tone. "It's all I can do to pay the rent."

"Well, honey, you could probably get anything you wanted. You know you look like a Greek god."

Becoming less official, he snickered, then said, "I am Greek."

"Really?" She smiled. "What's your name, Sweetie?"

"Dimitris Antonopoulos."

"What?" Duck raised his voice. "Do you know Al who runs Al's Chat and Chew in Tallahassee?"

"Yeah. He's my uncle."

"Oh, my God," Duck laughed. "Can you get on your phone and call him right now. He's one of my best friends."

He shuffled his feet, looked left then right and said, "OK. I'm gonna let you folks go, but lady, you gotta' slow down and quit driving so fast."

"I promise you I will, honey," as she batted her eyes. "Could I give you my phone number? You're such a good-looking man, I'd like to see you again."

"No ma'am, I have a steady girlfriend."

"I bet you do. That lucky girl! But I want you to call me when you feel you can afford some life insurance."

"I got your name. I can look you up."

He hurried back to his patrol car and took off so fast that his back wheels were spinning on the grassy shoulder of the road. They watched him fly off in the distance. Duck couldn't control his laughter.

"What are you laughing at?" Bonnie asked disgustedly.

"I'm laughing at you."

"Why you laughing at me?"

"Because you're so full of shit. You do know that, don't you?"

"And what do you mean by that?" She emphasized each utterance emphatically with anger dripping from each word.

"OK. You blow smoke up people's ass, and I happen to think it's funny."

"Well, I'll tell you what you can do. You can get your ass out of my car right now!"

It was obvious to Duck she was really mad.

"Look, baby. You know I was just kidding you, don't you?" he apologized.

"I said 'GET OUT OF THIS CAR RIGHT NOW' AND I MEAN IT! NOW!"

"Come on, Bonnie. Can't you take a joke?"

She reached in the back seat, grabbed his suitcase and slung it out of the car onto the ground. She started the motor and shouted again, "GET OUT! OUT! I MEAN IT! GET OUT NOW!"

"OK. OK. OK." Duck opened the door, got out of the car and stood forlornly as she scratched off onto the highway, floor-boarding the accelerator. He watched in a daze as the maroon Cadillac convertible moved swiftly off into the distance. In only a few seconds, the car had passed completely out of sight.

Back at Wes'

While Wes and Jimbo chatted in the office drinking Jack Daniels, they were interrupted by a tap on the door.

"Come in," Wes said.

The door opened partially, but they couldn't see who was on the other side.

"This is the police," a loud voice called out.

The door flung open, and there stood Duck, laughing.

When he saw Jimbo, he blurted out, "Who is that fat shit sitting over there?"

"Who you calling fat, you sorry bastard?" Jimbo laughed.

"Looks like to me, you two are getting drunk here in the middle of the afternoon," Duck said.

They all shook hands and slapped each other's backs.

"You probably wouldn't turn down a drink, would you?" Wes asked with a smirk.

"Has a cat got an ass?"

Wes poured him a glass of Jack Daniels.

"You drink the good stuff, brother."

"I guess you're still drinking that rot gut stuff you used to drink?" Wes kidded.

"Excuse me, Mr. Hot Shit, but I got plenty of class. If you don't believe it, just walk over there to the window and check out what I'm driving."

Wes and Jimbo got up, walked to the window and Wes pulled back the curtain.

"Damn! Did you steal that Caddy?" Wes sneered

"I want you to know I got class," Duck chided.

Wes said, "I just remembered, I need to go tell Miss Carolyn she can leave early."

He walked out, stayed a few minutes, then came back into the office where Duck and Jimbo were talking, laughing and still kidding each other.

"Well, brother," Wes interrupted. "I was thinking about getting you fixed up with some hot stuff tonight, but I see you brought your pussy with you."

Tommy

The phone rang as Agnes put the finishing touches on the cake. She licked her fingers, grabbed the dish cloth, wiped the rest of the chocolate off her hands and picked up the phone.

"Hello."

"Mama, this is Tommy."

"Tommy!" she shouted. "Oh my God! Where are you?"

"I'm at the bus station."

"I'll be there in five minutes," she said with so much enthusiasm and excitement, the phone dropped out of her hand onto the floor. Grabbing her pocketbook, she rushed out the front door, jumped in the car and headed for the bus station with her heart beating so fast.

From a block away, she could see him standing on the sidewalk in front of the station with the setting sun beaming on him like a spotlight. He was wearing his dress uniform – white hat with black bill, dark blue coat with white belt, a yellow private first class pyramid-shaped stripe on his right arm, white gloves, medium blue pants with a red stripe down the side and shiny black shoes. Pride engulfed her like a tidal wave, as she thought to herself, "That good-looking boy standing there is my son. Look at him. It's like seeing an angel from heaven. He is so beautiful, and to think I birthed him, and he's my child."

In haste and numb with excitement, the front tires of her car hit the curb. She flung open the door, jumped out, grabbed him in her arms and hugged him for a very long time. He hugged her back just as hard. He loved his mother. She'd always been the bright spot in his life, the one who taught him the right way to live and the person whom he looked up to the most.

"Tommy, I can't believe how good you look! You look so distinguished in your uniform," she smiled excitedly with tears flowing down her cheeks. "I'm so glad you came home for Thanksgiving. I can't wait to show you off."

He looked at her and smiled. "I'm glad to be home for a few days."

She knew he would be shipped out to Vietnam as soon as he returned, a thought hard for any mother to comprehend. The unbridled pride she had for her beloved son being a Marine and serving his country did not extend to sacrificing the love of her life in some foreign country halfway around the world.

She drove away from the station, but continued to turn her head toward him rather than keeping her eyes on the road. Up ahead, she saw a friend of hers working in the flower bed outside her house. She pulled the car next to the curb, this time without hitting it, blew the horn, let the window down and yelled out "Sally, come over here and see who I have in my car!"

Nothing in the world makes a son more uncomfortable than to have his mother gushing over him to her friends. He looked down at his feet, as his mother went on and on to Sally about how excited she was to have her son at home. He tolerated this outpouring as much as he possibly could, but finally looked over at his mother with an expression that said, "Enough is enough."

Being thirteen years younger than Buddy, they were never very close like brothers who played together. They had vast differences in personality that prevented them from spending much time with each other. Tommy didn't feel as if he really knew his brother at all.

Tommy graduated near the top of his class in high school. His mother wanted desperately for him to go to college, but he was well aware they couldn't afford to send him. He'd hoped to get an academic scholarship, but when that fell through, he felt it his duty to serve his country in a time of war in the same way his father and Uncle Duck had done some thirty years earlier.

He'd been told by his recruiting officer that after he served his time, he'd be entitled to certain VA benefits including pension, education and training, health care, home loans, insurance, employment and burial. At 18, he had plenty of time to go to college after the military. Anyway, at his young age, he had no idea what would be his major even if he went to college. Maybe after service, he'd have a better feel for what he wanted to do with his life.

His closest buddy was Michael Goodman, known as Mikey. His parents had insisted Mikey go to the University of Florida and wouldn't hear of him joining the military at his young age. But he knew he had to make good grades or else he'd be subject to the draft.

Tommy had a girlfriend in high school named Angela. Mostly they went to movies together. They'd kissed, but had not gone much beyond that. He liked her a lot, but during their senior year, she'd given him the shaft for the captain of the football team. Tommy took it pretty hard, but it made leaving for the military upon graduation a lot easier.

Tommy and Mikey were in the same class in school and went to the same church as dedicated members, not just because their parents made them go. They sincerely believed in the teachings of Jesus.

They were on the track team together. Tommy had broken the school record by running the 100-yard dash in 10.5 seconds. He prided himself in this accomplishment and felt he might want to pursue track after graduation. But in October, 1968, he watched Jim Hines of the U.S. on TV win the 100 meters in 9.9 seconds at the Olympics in Mexico City, and he realized he was not in that category.

As Agnes drove toward home, Tommy asked if Mikey had come home from school.

"I'm sure he'll be coming home for Thanksgiving," she replied.

"Yeah, I guess so. I'd sure like to see him."

In addition to school and church and track, he and Mikey played backyard basketball and card games like gin rummy, black jack and canasta.

Their appearances were in stark contrast. Mikey was 5' 9", had a light complexion, blondish-red hair and wore glasses.

Tommy, on the other hand, was tall, like all the Jennings males, good looking, with dark skin color and curly, black hair like his Uncle Duck. Many girls wanted to date him but he had been dating Angela.

Graduation Present

The night of their graduation from high school in May of '73, proved to be a memorable one. Wes and Duck had made plans for Duck to take Tommy and Mikey on a little coming of age road trip. The boys sat together in the back seat.

"Where're we going, Duck?" Tommy asked.

He was non-committal for he had a surprise in store. "Don't worry, Mikey, I got permission from your parents," he said, as he drove away heading north from the high school auditorium after the ceremony. Actually, he'd told Mikey's parents that the boys were going to ride up to Jacksonville with him to visit a sick friend.

Duck remained mute each time Tommy would question what he was up to. He drove the car out of Palatka toward Jacksonville. He'd iced down some beers, put them on the floor of the back seat and tried to coax the boys into drinking one. After his continued insistence, they each picked up a can of Bud and began to take a few sips. They'd both drunk a few beers before, but not much. As for hard liquor, Tommy had only had his father's eggnog at Christmas time. Mikey, on the other hand, was from a very strict religious family. He'd never tasted anything stronger than beer.

"Hey, Duck," Mikey pleaded. "Please don't say anything to my parents about me drinking a beer. They'd kill me."

"Don't worry. My lips are sealed," then he added, "My old man started me and Wes off drinking moonshine when we were about 14 or 15. He believed to be a man, you needed to know how to hold your liquor. It was a lesson he thought a boy needed to learn early in life." Duck paused to chug the rest of his beer.

"You think a boy can't become a man unless he drinks?" Tommy asked.

"You're a Jennings, Tommy, and there ain't no denying it."

After about an hour's drive, they arrived on the south side of Jacksonville and came to a stop light. Duck broke a long silence by turning around toward the boys and saying,

"You boys gotta learn what it's like to be a man. You're not little boys anymore. You gotta know what to do when you get out in this world."

"Why won't you tell us where you're taking us?" Tommy asked. It was obvious his uncle was up to something. He just didn't know what it was.

"Finish drinking your beers. We're almost there." Duck said.

The summer night was warm with the smell of sea-life saturating the air from the shrimp boats in the nearby St. Johns River. The lights of the city glistened on the water as they crossed over the bridge.

Both boys turned up their beers and gulped them down, creating a slight numbing effect on their brains. They looked out the window and checked out the neighborhood. The houses looked run-down with unkempt front yards, a few junk cars on concrete blocks, some windows broken out, screen-doors ajar, old appliances sitting in a few of the front yards, a number of "For Rent" signs, and beer cans on the sidewalk. Suddenly Duck pulled the car over to the curb of a two-story frame house, probably built in the early 1900s, with a sofa sitting in the front yard where two men were sitting. This house seemed to be a little nicer than the others surrounding it. Several cars were parked there and some of them were new. The house had green shutters and a large magnolia tree in bloom in the front.

"Just get out and come on in with me," Duck ordered.

They proceeded along the walkway through the fragrance of magnolias until they heard music coming from the front of the house. Duck nodded to the men sitting on the sofa, "How y'all doing?"

He rang the doorbell. No one opened the door for a few minutes, so he rang it again. Finally, a woman, who appeared to be much older than Duck, opened the door. He turned to Tommy, "You boys sit over there in the swing and wait out here on the porch while I go inside."

It seemed like a long time before Duck came back to get them. When the two boys walked through the front door, they could see scantily clad girls sitting about in a multitude of positions, a couple had their legs hanging over the arms of the chairs. Some of them started giggling when Tommy and Mikey walked in. The boys had their suspicions confirmed when they saw the interior of the room. One guy was holding one of the girls in his lap while kissing on her arm. A flood of emotions ran through them. They were stunned, embarrassed and frightened by a cloud of fear of the unknown.

"Come on over hear, honey, and sit with me," one of the girls said to Tommy.

Tommy looked at Duck.

"This is your graduation present, Tommy. I hope you enjoy it." Then he turned toward Mikey. "Go on over there son, and pick one out for you."

The older woman knew Duck, who'd been there with Wes on several occasions. "Hell, Duck, you gonna scare those poor kids to death! Are you sure they're ready for this?"

"Hell, Gladys, I had my first piece when I was 15," Duck responded. "These boys are 18-year-old virgins."

"You were 15?" Gladys acted surprised.

"Yep, she was my English teacher in high school. She always made me stay in after school to tutor me. That's what she called it. She tutored me all right. She had the biggest tits I'd ever seen and wore the tightest sweaters and a tight skirt to boot. She was supposed to be teaching me Shakespeare, so we wound up playing Romeo and Juliet in the coat closet."

"You sound just like your brother. You can't believe a word he says," Gladys laughed. "You know all lawyers are liars."

She then turned to the boys. "What would y'all like to drink?"

Duck responded for them. "Fix them a Shirley Temple, except put a little fire water in it," he laughed.

Gladys turned toward the redhead sitting on the table, "Go fix these boys a little smile." The girl was young, not much older than Tommy and Mikey, and her red hair matched the color of Mikey's.

Gladys, the madam, probably in her mid-sixties, had seen better days. Her beauty had faded into oblivion. You could look at her and tell she had high-mileage, but she tried to camouflage it with dyed black hair and lots of makeup.

Soon the redhead returned with two Shirley Temples, traditionally a non-alcoholic drink made of ginger ale, a splash of grenadine and garnished with a maraschino cherry, but she further enhanced the drinks with a jigger of vodka in each one.

The boys were sitting on the sofa obviously scared shitless. When she handed them the drinks, she sat down beside Mikey and grabbed his hand. He took a deep breath as his heart was beating like a snare drum. "Do you like me?" she asked.

"I don't even know you," he responded.

"Would you like to get to know me better?" She said in a sultry, seductive voice like melted butter.

"Could you tell me where the bathroom is?" Mikey asked.

"Sure." She got up and walked toward the back of the house. Both boys followed.

After the door was shut, the two of them stood there looking at each other. "What are we going to do?" Tommy asked.

Mikey looked at Tommy with great sincerity, then blurted out, "I'm going to kill your uncle!"

Tommy came right back at him, "No, you're not, because I'm going to kill him first!"

Mikey held up his glass. "Are you gonna drink this shit?"

"I tasted it. It's not too bad."

"I don't know," Mikey said. "I just know one thing, and that is if I go home with alcohol on my breath, I'm a dead man."

"They'll probably be asleep, won't they?"

"I can tell you for a one hundred percent certainty that my mama will be waiting at the door when I get home." He looked down at the floor then back up at Tommy. "Your old man wouldn't care."

"Yeah, I guess you're right about that."

When they walked back to the front room, Duck sounded off in a loud voice, "What you boys been doing back there?"

They both sat down on the sofa holding their drinks. The redhead, whose nickname was Rosy, grabbed Mikey by the hand and led him trembling up the stairs.

An older blonde, about mid-twenties sat down by Tommy.

"Hi, good looking. You know who you look like?"

Tommy shook his head.

"You look just like Tony Curtis would've looked when he was eighteen with that head full of curly, black hair. You know you're a real dreamboat. I bet the girls are all over you."

Tommy looked away embarrassed.

"They call me Blondie. Come on and go with me so we can get to know each other better," she said as she tugged at his hand.

They both got up and walked up the stairs.

"I sure would like to be a fly on the wall and watch what's going on up there," Duck chuckled.

"Awe, let 'em be," Gladys scolded him. "My girls are pretty good teachers."

No more than ten minutes had passed before Mikey came running down the stairs.

"Well, that was quick!" Duck kidded.

Mikey never slowed down. He scooted out the front door without acknowledging anybody.

Duck looked at Rosy with a questioning glace. She shrugged her shoulders and smiled.

"He must be pretty quick on the trigger," Duck kidded with Gladys.

Gladys asked him. "You want to know what happened."

"Of course, you know I do.

Gladys called out to Rosy, "Honey, would you come over here just a minute?"

The girls had hovered around the TV to watch

Gunsmoke. They thought Marshall Dillon was good looking and sexy in his effort to prevent lawlessness from overtaking Dodge City with the help of Miss Kitty and Doc. They hoped that clients wouldn't come calling during that 30-minute segment.

"Would you like a drink, Rosy?"

"No ma'am, Miss Gladys, I'm OK."

"Sugar, you want to tell me what happened between you and the little boy?"

She pointed to Duck. "You really want me to tell you, Miss Gladys in front of him?"

"Yeah, honey. He's one of us."

"Well," she paused. "He wouldn't take off his clothes. It's kinda hard for me to wash a boy's thing with his clothes on."

"Yeah," Gladys said as she winked at Duck.

"So, I just let him keep his clothes on, but I told him I couldn't do anything until I washed his thing with our special soap."

Gladys smiled.

"Then he said he'd rather wash it off by himself. I told him he'd be missing out on all the fun. I could tell he was scared. So, I soaped up my hand and put it on his thing, and when I did, he shot his wad right there in the sink like a streak of lightning. Then his face turned as red as a tomato."

"Oh, my goodness!" Gladys laughed.

"I told him it was OK. We could still get in the bed and play around a little if he wanted to, but he just zipped up his pants and went running out the door."

Gladys snickered. "OK, honey. Thank you for telling me."

"Yes ma'am. Can I go back now and watch Gunsmoke?"

"Sure."

Duck smiled and said, "I hope my nephew is doing better than that. Hell, Gladys, he's going to be a Marine. We gotta make him tough. He needs to work hard, drink hard, and play hard. That's what a Jennings boy needs to do."

"Well, honey, I hate to tell you, but he's gonna be

whatever he's gonna be, and your wants ain't got a damn thing to do with it."

Duck pulled out his pack of Camels and offered one to her. She took it, put it between her lips as he flipped on his lighter.

Duck and Gladys talked for a few minutes. He became more and more anxious about what was taking Tommy so long. Shortly afterwards, Tommy came running down the steps and rushed out the front door, slamming it behind him.

"Well, at least he's got enough energy to run," Duck kidded.

When Blondie came down the steps, Gladys got up and walked over to her at a distance so that Duck couldn't hear. They talked for a few minutes, then she went in with the rest of the girls to watch Gunsmoke. She obviously said something to the other girls that caused them to erupt in laughter, until one of them hushed the rest and admonished them to watch Miss Kitty making eyes at Matt Dillon.

"How did it go?" Duck questioned Gladys with a bit of anxiety in his voice.

"I think the boy is gonna be all right," she patronized him.

"You mean he's gonna be a stud horse like his old uncle?"

"I don't think you have anything to worry about, Duck."

He paused for a minute with his thoughts then said, "OK, Gladys, total up my bill. We got to get on back to Palatka."

Silence prevailed in the car like a tomb as Duck drove back home. He could see in the mirror that the boys were asleep. He turned on the radio and listened to music with a sense of pride for what he'd just done for those two boys.

When they arrived at Mikey's house, the lights were still on inside. He walked up the steps slowly and went in through the unlocked door.

On the way home, Tommy said to Duck, "You seemed to be pretty well-known up there. I guess my old man introduced you to the place."

"Don't be too hard on him," Duck grew more serious.

"There's a lot you don't understand, Tommy. Maybe one day you will when you get married. But going up there beats the hell outta' doing without." No other words were spoken after that.

Wes and Tommy

A couple of days later after the Jacksonville trip and the night before Tommy had to report for boot camp at Camp Lejeune, Wes came home from work and asked Agnes, "Where's Tommy?"

"He's in the shower."

Wes walked into the bathroom to find Tommy towel-drying his body. He looked up in surprise to see his father bursting in on his privacy without knocking.

"Get dressed," Wes ordered. "We're going out for little bit."

"Where?" Tommy asked without much enthusiasm, since he had plans to go with Mikey to the movies.

"Just get dressed and come with me," Wes showed off his usual authority and impatience.

Having been hijacked after his high school graduation two nights previously, he wondered what his father might be up to.

As Tommy got into the car, Wes explained, "I'd like for me and you to spend a little time together before you leave."

Tommy never remembered hearing him say anything like that before, but it pleased him that his father was paying some attention to him.

Wes drove the car about a mile outside of town and pulled in to the parking lot of the Tried and True bar, where a lot of locals gathered after work to have a couple of drinks before going home. When they walked in, several men spoke to Wes. He introduced Tommy, "This is my boy. He joined the Marines. Leaving tomorrow for boot camp at Camp Lejeune," he said with pride.

Wes led Tommy over to a booth and motioned to one of the waitresses, "Give us a couple of Buds."

"Gotcha," she said. Before walking away, she added, "Who's that good-looking boy you got with you, Wes? Is that your son?"

"Yeah, that's my boy. He's gonna be a Marine," he

boasted.

"I sure wish I was a little bit younger," she laughed. "I'd like to take him home with me."

The waitress was a pretty girl in her early twenties and Tommy cut his eyes toward her with a conspicuous smile. She returned with the beers, set them on the table and gave a seductive smile back to Tommy. He acknowledged it and looked back at his father.

"Let's have a toast," Wes said. "To your good health and safety."

They both raised their bottles and clinked them against each other.

Tommy, for the first time, felt a sense of affection for his father. Never had they sat down together for a man-to-man talk.

Wanting to contribute to the conversation, Tommy began telling his father about what it felt like to graduate from high school. Wes told him about some of his school days, which were not all that pleasant. As soon as he came home from school, the hard work really began in the fields of tobacco or cotton or corn. There seemed to always be something that his father made him do. As he remembered it, he really put in some hard, physical labor, and there were no excuses like "I don't feel good" or "I've got homework to do" or "Can't I just have one day off?" He did have one day off, and that was Sunday. His mother wouldn't allow his father to work the boys on Sunday.

Wes finished his beer and Tommy had drunk about half. Wes called the waitress back over. "Give us another round."

Tommy gave him a look that expressed his doubt about whether or not he could drink a second one. Soon, the waitress returned with two more Buds.

"Tommy, I'm going to tell you something I've never told anyone else other than your Uncle Duck."

Tommy took another sip and stared into his father's eyes.

"I think I've told you how my father was mean to me and

Duck. He used to beat us up pretty bad. He'd tell us he wanted to make us tough, but we were still young boys when he would sock us in the face if we even acted like we disagreed with him. He'd get drunk, and that's when he'd get on a tear and start breaking furniture or plates or glasses, and believe me, that's when me and Duck would hide. Sometimes he'd hit my mama, and one time he knocked her down on the floor. Me and Duck were watching from behind a curtain that separated the kitchen from the dining room."

Wes picked up his beer, took a large slug, then continued, "But one night when I was about 15, my old man was all drunked up on moonshine, and I saw him hit my mama. She fell down on the floor like she'd been shot. I saw the expression on her face when she got up crying. She ran out the front door, and I did something I'd never done before. I ran over and grabbed that son of a bitch by his shirt. I shoved him up against the wall as hard as I could. I couldn't believe I had the guts to do it. He swung at me and hit me on the side of my head pretty hard. I grabbed him and got him in a headlock and choked him around his neck and said, 'You sorry bastard, if you ever lay a hand on my mama again, I'll kill you.'"

Tommy picked up the bottle and chugged the rest of his beer down in one swallow. He saw a different person sitting across from him than he'd ever seen before. He sensed an admiration for his father for the first time ever.

After another large gulp, Wes said, "I'm telling you this, and I don't ever want you tell anyone else what I'm saying to you, do you hear me?"

"Yes sir," Tommy agreed.

"After I married your mama, and we moved to Palatka, I got a call from my cousin one evening that my old man was in the hospital in Douglas, and they didn't expect him to live. I hadn't seen him since me and your mama got married. I jumped in my car, didn't tell anybody where I was going and drove up to Douglas by myself, about a three-hour drive. It was after dark when I got there. I went in the hospital and up to his room. He was lying there in the bed hooked up to all kinds of stuff, and nobody else was anywhere around. I grabbed that bastard with both hands and beat the ever-loving shit out of him. I hit him just as hard as he used to hit me and Duck. I didn't care. I just wanted to give him a dose of what he used to give us before he died. I walked out of that hospital like nothing ever happened. No one saw me. I don't know if I killed him or not and I don't care. I got in my car and drove back to Palatka with a smile on my face, and I never regretted for one minute what I did to this day."

Thanksgiving Eve

As Agnes busied herself around the kitchen, she looked at the clock. It was almost six. She'd completed all the finishing touches on the food and had arranged yellow chrysanthemums for the center of the table.

She saw Tommy coming through the door, and thought, "Well, at least one Jennings male is here on time!"

Tommy walked into the kitchen and hugged his mother. "Something smells good," he said.

"Do you have any idea where your father is?"

"No, I haven't seen him."

"I'm sure that brother of his has arrived in town, and they're at the Country Club getting drunk."

"You want me to call out there and find out?"

Agitated, Agnes paced around the kitchen, then said, "No, I don't want you to have to deal with it." After stirring the pot of turnip greens, she asked, "Did you see Mikey?"

"No, he's coming in later tonight."

When the telephone rang, Tommy answered. "Where are you? Who? What's her name? Is she Uncle Duck's girlfriend?" He paused. "Who else? What's his name? Have I ever met him? So they're all coming for supper tonight? When will y'all get here? Yeah, she's got it ready now."

"Tell me what he said," Agnes asked in disgust, knowing that she was about to have to set extra plates on the table.

"You were right. They've been at the Country Club, and it sounds like they stayed too long."

"And who's with him?"

"Uncle Duck and his girlfriend and some other guy that Daddy said was a friend of his."

Agnes swelled with anger, "I will not let that brother of his bring some sleazy woman into my house. I told Wes to let him know, under no uncertain terms, his brother was not allowed to come for more than one night, and I certainly didn't expect him to bring anybody with him – especially some floozy. She

97

is not coming into this house, and I mean it."

"Mama, you better calm down," Tommy tried to unruffle her. "You already know what kind of condition they'll be in."

"How am I supposed to feed all these people?" She exclaimed. "I don't have enough food. I was just counting on the three of us and your uncle. Why does your father have to do me like this? I'm sure he has known all afternoon that they were coming, but does he bother to call me? NO! Of course not. All I am is a door mat." She walked back into the kitchen with her blood pressure sky high, mumbling to herself, "So, that means six people instead of four. If I don't have enough, that's just too bad. And to think I have to serve one of his brother's sluts!"

"How do you know she's a slut?" Tommy tried to calm her down.

"Do you know of any reason in this world why any woman of decency would go anywhere with him? He has no money and probably no job."

The ringing of the doorbell interrupted their discussion., ma'am

"Who could that be?" Agnes asked. "Tommy, go to the door and see who it is."

He opened the door. "Oh, hey, Preacher."

They shook hands. "So glad to see you son. We've been praying for you."

Agnes saw him walk in and scurried toward him, changing her demeanor. "Preacher Wraggs, what brings you here?"

"I hope I'm not coming at a bad time," he said. "Smells mighty good, sister Agnes. I bet you've been cooking up a storm for that boy of yours." He looked back at Tommy. "Son, I'm so glad you've come home to see your mama before you leave for duty. She's been so worried about you."

"Yes sir," Tommy said.

"Have you got time to sit down?" Agnes asked, hoping that he would say no. She was so afraid that Wes and the other three drunks would come storming into the house any minute, and she didn't want to suffer that embarrassment.

Tommy excused himself to go to his room, leaving his mother and the preacher time to be alone.

"You know I was just across the street visiting poor old Mrs. Thomas, and I saw all your lights on. I wanted to see if Tommy was here so I could speak to him."

"Well, I'm so glad you did stop by," Agnes said with a bit of dishonesty.

"Have you seen Mrs. Thomas lately?" the preacher asked.

"I took lunch over to her yesterday."

"Well, that was nice of you. When we were having prayer, she just broke down and cried. She looks so bad. I can't help but feel sorry for her."

"I do know. She's in bad shape."

There was a pause in the conversation as each of them seemed to be thinking about what to say next.

"You know, Bessie Ruth will be coming back tomorrow. She has been on a mission study," he said.

"Oh, my goodness. I'd completely forgotten all about her being gone. How's her mother doing?"

"Not all that good."

"You poor thing. I should've had you come over for dinner while she was gone."

"Well, I will have to admit, sister Agnes, there's nobody in my congregation who can cook as good as you can."

"Oh, Preacher. You're just saying that," she blushed.

"No. I'm serious. I've told Bessie Ruth there is no one in our church who is as faithful as you are."

"Oh, Preacher."

"No, Sister. I'm serious. You're always there when you're needed. You love the Lord and you serve the Lord. You do exactly what you're supposed to do."

The front door was thrown open with such force, it banged against the wall as if a tornado had blown through.

"We're home," Wes yelled in a loud voice.

With much revelry, Jimbo, along with Duck and Bonnie Sue, came bursting into the room. The men were laughing and joking and slapping each other on the back.

"Is Tommy here?" Wes asked.

"Wes, would you come into the kitchen with me this minute," Agnes said with a stern look on her face.

"Don't you want to greet the guests?" His voice slurred, giving away his condition, just as she'd expected.

"Just come in here with me first," she ordered.

He tagged along behind her, knowing what he was about to get into.

As she closed the kitchen door, she scowled, "Just what do you mean doing this to me?" She tried to hold her voice down.

"What are you talking about?"

"You didn't tell me one thing about anyone else coming to dinner other than that brother of yours. You come in here, smelling of strong drink, and humiliating me in front of the preacher."

"Hell, woman, just serve the damn dinner and let's get it over with," he raised his voice. "I want to know where Tommy is!"

"He's in his room," she said but continued her argument. "And you know I didn't fix enough dinner for all these people."

"Let's just go the hell out to dinner," he shouted.

"You know I'm sick and tired of the way you treat me," she argued.

"If you're sick, go get in the damn bed. We can eat without you!"

"This dinner is for Tommy – not for you and your drunk friends."

"I'll go tell everybody not to eat much," his words filled with sarcasm.

"I only fried one chicken," she said. "I thought we were having four people to eat."

"Well, why did you ask the damn preacher?"

"I didn't know he was coming. Just go get in your car, if you're not too drunk to drive it, and get another chicken. And one other thing. I hope you don't think that all those people are going to sleep in my house tonight."

"Your house?" Wes yelled. "When did it get to be your house?"

"If you're not too drunk to remember, the money for this house came from the Duckworths, my family."

"Will you just shut up? They'll sleep here if I say so."

"I'll ask Tommy to go get some more fried chicken," she said with all the intonations necessary to try to make him feel guilty.

"Hell, woman, I told you I'd go get the damn chicken."

"But you know you're too drunk to drive," she continued her tone of voice, but making Wes feel guilty was a total waste of time.

Disgusted with her, Wes walked out of the kitchen into the living room and called out to Jimbo. "Come over here. You remember Agnes, don't you?"

"Of course. How're you doing, Agnes?"

"I'm fine, Jimbo. It's good to see you."

Then Wes called Bonnie Sue, "Come here Sugar. I want you to meet my sweet wife."

Bonnie Sue walked with him back into the kitchen to face a frustrated Agnes, who wheeled around and surveyed her from head to toe without speaking – bleached blonde hair, tight black sweater with "Jesus Saves" in sequins and a short black skirt that was so tight you could see the outline of her panties.

Wes excused himself, so the two women could get acquainted.

"Hi, Miss Agnes," she smiled. "I'm Bonnie Sue Atwater."

"Is it Miss or Mrs?"

"It's Miss. I've never been married."

"Well, I certainly hope you're not planning to marry Andy," she said.

101

"Oh no ma'am. I just met him today."

"Today?"

"It's a long story, but we met this morning eating breakfast in Tallahassee. His truck wouldn't start, so he wanted to catch a ride with me over here."

"Oh, I see," she sounded somewhat relieved. Then her eyes fell back upon the wording across her chest. "Tell me about your sweater."

She cleared her throat nervously. "It's a long story, but I found the Lord, and I'm doing my best to live by His teachings."

"Well, my advice to you if you want to be a Christian is to get rid of Andy as soon as possible."

"He does talk ugly," she agreed. "In fact, I got so mad with him, I stopped and put him out of my car while we were driving over here today because of his nasty talk."

Agnes nodded her head in complete agreement and understanding.

"But then after I left him, I started feeling sorry for him," she paused for a moment and then continued, "I began to wonder about what Jesus would do in a situation like this. He would never leave someone stranded out on the side of the road like that, so I turned around and went back to pick him up. Don't you think that's what Jesus would've done?"

Agnes thought for a moment. "Well, I suppose so," she said very slowly and deliberately. "But with Andy, Jesus would probably have to think twice."

Bonnie Sue added, "I let him talk me in to coming down here to Palatka to drop him off. I was supposed to be going to Jacksonville Beach for Thanksgiving, but when I took him to the law office, your sweet husband just insisted that I stay here and have Thanksgiving with y'all."

"Yes, I'm sure he did," Agnes sighed.

"What can I do to help you with the supper, Miss Agnes?"

"There's nothing to do. It's all ready," she said.

Jimbo and Duck were out on the front porch talking and having a couple of snorts. Wes had gotten Tommy to drive him to the store for more chicken. When Wes and Tommy returned, the four men walked in the living room together where they saw the preacher sitting on the sofa.

"Well, I'll be damned if it ain't the preacher," Duck said. "Ain't seen you for a long time," He stuck out his hand. "How you doing, Preacher? Been getting any?"

"Mr. Jennings, you have a very filthy mouth," the preacher responded.

Agnes walked in the room just in time to hear the preacher's comment. She quickly interrupted, "Oh, Preacher, I'm so sorry. I didn't realize that you were in here with HIM!"

"That's all right sister. I can take care of myself."

She looked sternly at Duck. "You promised you'd watch your tongue in this house!"

"Honey, I've been just as sweet as an angel. Ain't that right, Preacher?"

Agnes announced that dinner was ready, so they all walked into the dining room where the table was filled with a luscious meal.

Duck said, "I'm hungry as a billy goat, myself."

"OK, let's see, Preacher, you sit here by me. Miss Atwater can sit over there. We'll let HIM sit over there by Tommy. I'll sit here and Wes and Jimbo can sit over there. I think that's everybody, right?"

At that point, the front door opened with a bang. Everyone looked around. Agnes's face turned pale, as she yelled out, "Buddy!" He was standing there holding a suitcase in his hand, looking around at everyone and the food on the table. His face appeared flushed and puffy and his body much overweight. He looked like a lush, who'd spent too much time at the bar.

"Well, I'll be damned," he said in a loud voice. "Y'all started the party without me."

Wes and Duck stood up and shook his hand. Agnes hugged him, and everyone else remained seated. He had not been home since he received his first furlough from the Blue Ridge Home for Alcoholics.

Buddy was introduced to Jimbo and Bonnie Sue. "Where'd you find her, Duck?" he blurted out.

"They just met today," Agnes said.

Buddy then looked over at the preacher and said sarcastically, "So Preacher, you still hanging around town trying to save everybody from sinning?"

"I do my best," he replied.

"To me you always acted like you were trying to make people feel guilty for having a little fun."

Duck laughed.

"Buddy, mind your manners," Agnes said with a stern look that he'd seen many times before.

Agnes tried squeezing in another chair and an eighth place at the table.

"OK Buddy. You sit here," she then added, "Let's please eat before all the food gets stone cold. Preacher, would you bless the food for us?"

"Let us bow our heads in prayer." All of them complied except Buddy. The Preacher stared at him; but, realizing it was useless, began, "Lord, make us truly thankful for this food which has been prepared by our faithful servant. Lord, you know better than any of us what a good cook sister Agnes is. She can beat anybody I know of when it comes to cooking. Let her delicious food nourish our bodies, nourish our spirits and nourish our souls." His voice grew louder. "Forgive the sinners of their sins, and save them from eternal damnation." Duck raised his head and winked at Buddy. The preacher continued, "You know who they are, Lord, even better than we do. We ask that you right their souls within their wretched bodies and make them see the truth and turn from their wicked ways." Buddy snickered loud enough for everyone to hear. "As we enter into this Thanksgiving season, let the name of Jesus be on every lip as we praise Him for the many blessings he has bestowed upon us. He has given us all bountiful gifts, which we are very thankful for. And more especially we ask you, O Jesus, for your special blessings on young Tommy as he goes off to fight for our country. Please protect him from any harm that might come upon him. Be with him every hour of every day and every minute of every hour, and let him come back home safely to be reunited with his family. Now give us grace for this evening, and all of these things we ask in the precious name of Jesus Christ, our Savior. Amen."

Buddy blurted out, "Damn, Preacher, you prayed so long, all the food got cold."

Duck chimed in, "He shore did."

Wes spoke up in a stern voice, "OK, let's eat and cut the crap!"

Before they ate their first mouthful, a dog barked at the back door. Wes jumped up and let their aging black dog, of no definable type or breed, into the dining room. He was so fat, he could hardly walk. Buddy leaned over to pet him. "Jambone, you're getting old and fat, too." The dog wagged his tail in rapid motions and licked Buddy's hand. "You come over here and lay down by me." The dog did as he was told and sat underneath Buddy's chair. "Now you be a good ol' boy." He patted him on the head.

Jimbo reached out to get some pear relish and turned over his ice tea glass.

Duck yelled out, "Jimbo, you clumsy bastard!"

All of this banter back and forth did not add to the glamour of the family reunion. Agnes had given up trying to control the situation. What was the use? She had endured ill-bred, dirty-talking Jennings males for much too long, and now they were making a mockery of southern custom, which demands that a man must be on his best behavior at the dinner table, especially in the presence of the preacher, with no discussion of politics or sex.

When Tommy asked that the biscuits be passed to him, Duck said, "That reminds me of a joke."

Wes quickly spoke up with authority, "None of your jokes at the table tonight, Duck."

Buddy and Duck couldn't help but notice that the preacher was staring at Bonnie Sue's sweater. Jimbo had already commented to Duck about "his girlfriend with the big knockers."

"Where did you get that nice sweater?" The preacher asked her.

Buddy jumped into the act. "Shame on you, Preacher! She does fill it out pretty good, don't you think?"

Duck laughed longer than he should have.

"I'll have you know I was looking at the nice writing on her sweater," the preacher tried to explain.

Bonnie Sue smiled, "I just bought this sweater. I'm so glad I found Jesus. I just want everybody to know about it."

"I'm so happy about that," the preacher said.

While most were gnawing on their fried chicken, Bonnie Sue spoke up and batted her false eyelashes rapidly, "Preacher, I was just wondering if you're married."

He smiled and responded, "My wife has been away on a mission study for the past two weeks."

Bonnie Sue came right back with "I think I may have something you might want?"

"Holy Jesus!" Buddy exclaimed. "You shore ain't shy, are you, girl?

Bonnie Sue paid no attention to him. "This is something I think the preacher needs."

"Hell, baby, we all need it," Buddy laughed.

"Will you please stop it, Buddy," Agnes shouted.

"I didn't mean to start a ruckus," Bonnie Sue said. "I just thought the preacher might need some life insurance."

"Life insurance?" Wes exclaimed.

"You probably didn't know that I'm a life insurance sales lady, and I would think that somebody at this table might need some."

All of a sudden, Jambone inappropriately cut a rather loud fart. Buddy shoved his chair backward so fast, it fell to the floor. He ran out of the room gagging. Duck followed, then Wes, then Tommy, and all the rest.

Buddy shouted out, "My God! Jambone. That's the worst thing I've ever smelt in my life."

Wes led Jambone out the door then hurried to the back

of the house to get an electric fan. He placed the fan under the table in hopes of blowing away the stench. In an attempt to retrieve order out of chaos, Wes stated with authority, "As soon as it clears out, let's all get back in our places."

When they all returned, Agnes, in a futile attempt to raise the level to a higher plane, asked the preacher, "Could you tell us something about the mission study your wife is attending?"

He began relating in unnecessary, lengthy detail about his wife's mission study, which no one, including Agnes, wanted to hear. After a much-too-long dissertation, Bonnie Sue broke into the conversation again. "I think we should all sing to Tommy, 'For He's a Jolly Good Fellow,' don't you think?"

When she started singing, the rest of them chimed in. She stopped and said, "No, no, I think we should all stand."

With that command, everyone stood, except Tommy, and sang.

Tommy sat there, embarrassed and humiliated by the shameful lack of respect for his mother at the dinner table. When they finished singing and Tommy got the congratulatory slaps on the back by Duck and Jimbo, he announced that he'd made plans to meet Mikey. This was not exactly true since Mikey wasn't coming into town until the next morning.

"But you haven't eaten any of the pecan pie I made for you," Agnes pleaded.

"I know. I'm so full right now, Mama. Just save me a piece, and I'll eat it when I get home."

Tommy quickly told them all goodbye and ran out the door, much to his relief. His family was on the verge of driving him crazy. He'd earlier gotten permission to drive his mother's car, so he went to the movies alone to see *American Graffiti.*

Tom Dennard

Thanksgiving Morning

Before the sun came up, Jimbo took off early to get back to Atlanta to be with his family. Wes and Duck decided they'd like to spend the morning fishing. Buddy thought he might as well go along to keep them company, knowing they'd take a bottle with them. The three of them convinced Tommy to join so they'd have an all-male Jennings adventure.

"Somebody told me they're catching largemouths up at Spring Lake," Wes said, as he walked into the garage, pawing around through massive disorganization to scrape up four fishing poles. Wes and Duck decided to skip the live bait and go with fishing lures. Neither of them really knew all that much about fishing anyway, and it'd been a long time since they'd wet a hook.

It was a short drive up to the lake, and when they pulled into the parking lot, they saw a guy getting out of his pickup, towing a boat with an outboard motor. He was dressed like you'd expect a fisherman should look, unlike the four of them, who were rag-tags in comparison. Wes didn't recognize him but asked him if he'd been fishing at the lake before.

"Yeah, I fish up here a pretty good bit," he said with a southern drawl.

"I heard the largemouths are biting," Wes said, pretending to know a lot about fishing.

"Yeah, I caught a couple last time I was here, but what I really got into was the bream and blue gill and crappie," he said.

That remark whetted their appetite with visions of filling up the cooler with enough for a big fish-fry. Wes passed around the bottle of Early Times for each of them to take a swig.

They watched the guy back his truck, with boat attached, down to the edge of the water, then wade out about knee deep to float it off the trailer. He anchored it, then pulled the truck and trailer up to park it. He jumped in the boat, waved to the Jennings and took off.

Without saying a word, they all had the thought that

they'd just observed a real fisherman, and realized they were a bunch of bumbling amateurs.

Carrying their fishing gear, they marched single-file up an embankment about three feet above the water level. Each of them carried a pole, and Wes had the tackle box. Wes wanted Tommy to have the best rig and gave Duck the one that appeared to be the oldest.

"Brother, this reel is so damn rusty, it looks like something you brought back from the Civil War," Duck laughed.

"Here's some WD-40," Wes said, reaching into his tackle box then handing it to Duck. "Squirt some on it. When you finish, you might want to squirt some on your pecker, too. It's probably about as rusty as the reel."

Buddy and Tommy laughed at how the two brothers still kidded each other.

Duck chided, "You're so funny, you almost made me laugh, but not quite." Wes made the first cast and sent it out about 50 feet into the water. Buddy made a good cast, too, that dropped about ten feet from Wes' bobber.

"How deep you fishing, brother?" Duck asked.

"I'm not sure how deep the water is. About three or four feet, I'd guess. Why don't you swim out there and see if you can stand up?"

"You know what you can do, asshole?"

"Which reminds me, I haven't whipped yours in a long time," Wes joked. "And I think it's getting about that time."

"You and whose army?" Duck responded.

Reverting to childhood, they both joshed each other just like they'd always done, much to the amusement of Buddy and Tommy.

Tommy was the first one to see his float go under. He pulled it in only to find a small crappie struggling to get off the hook.

"Hell, you need to send that thing back home to his mama." Buddy, like his father, also got great pleasure in yanking his little brother's chain.

After about 40 or 50 minutes with no action other than Tommy's throw-back, Duck's bobber suddenly plunged under the water with a force that bent his pole over. He'd hooked something big and had no idea what it was. He struggled to pull it in, but it was giving him a fight for its life. All eyes were on Duck's line with anticipation of what he was about to pull in. As it got closer, Duck could see something long and thin. "It looks like a damn eel," Duck said.

As he lifted the fighting creature out of the water, their mouths dropped open. "What the shit!" Wes shouted. "It's a damn cottonmouth moccasin!"

"Son of a bitch!" Buddy shouted. "I never heard of nobody catching a damn snake!"

"Cut the line!" Wes shouted. "And let's get the hell outta here. Those bastards will chase you!"

The other three scampered back to the car as Duck snipped the line and watched the large creature slither back into the water.

The four of them laughed all the way back home and unmercifully kidded Duck about his catch. "Why didn't you reach down there and grab the back of its head and take the hook out of its mouth?" Wes joked.

Thanksgiving night

The dinner was comprised of turkey baked in the oven, oyster dressing with gravy from drippings, green bean casserole, creamed corn, macaroni and cheese, sweet potato soufflé, cranberry sauce, homemade sweet pickles and sweet iced tea. After eating so much food, Agnes brought out a pumpkin pie, which later had the men staggering into the living room and collapsing into various chairs. Wes turned on the TV to watch football for the rest of the afternoon. Most of them fell asleep in short order and some were even snoring,

Late in the afternoon after Agnes had finished a long nap, Tommy asked his mother if he could borrow her car to go spend some time with Mikey.

"Of course, honey. You can use my car."

He put on a pair of jeans and a Palatka football jersey that Buddy had given him years ago. He drove to Mikey's house and went to the door. They'd not seen each other since Duck had driven them to the brothel in Jacksonville for their graduation present.

"How's it going?" Tommy greeted him.

They shook hands.

"Doing OK," Mikey smiled. "How you doing?"

"Lot of water over the dam since we last saw each other."

"Yeah, it seems like a lifetime," Mikey replied.

"First of June to last of November. Longest we've ever been apart."

"Yeah, I guess so."

"A lot has changed. For me, Boot Camp at Parris Island, making PFC, now being shipped out to Nam. How 'bout you?"

"Not much to tell," Mikey sighed. "Gainesville is an OK place. Been studying more than I ever studied before. It's not bad though. Made some new friends. A few good-looking coeds."

"Yeah," Tommy chuckled. "That's something we don't

111

have."

They laughed.

"What you want to do?" Tommy asked, as he drove toward the downtown area.

"I don't care. Let's just hang out and talk. I'll leave it up to you, Mister Marine Man."

"You wanna get a six-pack and go out to our old hangout at Horseshoe Point?"

"Sounds good to me," Mikey laughed. "I remember the last beers we drank together when your Uncle Duck took us to Jacksonville after graduation."

"Yeah, I can't believe he did that. He's crazier than hell."

"So, how're we gonna get a six-pack since we're both under age?"

"Just watch me," Tommy smirked.

He drove just out of town to The Shed, a package store where most of the younger set went to get their beer. He pulled his mother's Chevy into the parking lot. No other cars were there, so they sat for a few minutes. Shortly, a Ford pickup came driving up and parked nearby. The guy who got out was Rocky McFadden, a classmate of Buddy's. He'd been a star football player at Palatka High, but that had been thirteen years earlier. He had lost any trace of athleticism with a beer gut that protruded over his belt.

"Hey, Rocky," Tommy yelled.

He turned around and looked to see who'd called him. Tommy walked up to him. "I'm Tommy Jennings. You remember me?"

"Yeah. Ain't you Buddy's little brother?"

"Yep. That's me. You think you might get me a six pack of Bud?"

"Sure. I'll get it for you."

Tommy handed him a five-dollar bill.

Armed with a six-pack and a night with perfectly cool Thanksgiving weather, they drove past the New Zion Baptist Church out Lundy Road until they arrived at a dirt path that led to Horseshoe Point, a spot overlooking the St. Johns River toward the city of Palatka.

When they pulled into their old hangout spot, no other cars could be seen. "Looks like we got it all to ourselves," Tommy said.

It was 5:15, and the sun had begun to set. They got out of the car and spent a few moments staring in silence at the lights of Palatka flickering on the surface of the river, reflecting the golden hue of the sun.

Tommy picked up a small flat rock and sailed it toward the water, watching it skip four or five times along the surface before it sank to the bottom.

"So you like Gainesville OK?" Tommy broke the silence.

"Let's crack a beer, and I'll tell you all I know in ten words or less," Mikey said.

They sat on a log of a fallen tree. Each of them took a large gulp, then Mikey said, "What can I say? It's a college town – good pizza. I met a girl I like a lot. There's not much else to talk about."

"No shit! You got a girlfriend!"

"Aw, we've had a few dates. Nothing serious."

"Tell me about her."

"She's in a sorority. I didn't go out for rush myself. Guys in fraternities seem to think they're better than anybody else. But she's an OK girl. She pledged A D Pi."

"What does that stand for?"

"Alpha Delta Pi. It's one of the good sororities on campus." Mikey took another swallow of beer. "We went out to a couple of parties and things. It's not like we're gonna get married."

"Well, that's good. I guess I won't be getting a girlfriend until I get back from 'Nam."

"Come on. Tell me about going through basic training."

"It'd take me days to tell it all," Tommy paused. "But first, it's not called basic training. That's the damn army. Marines call it 'boot camp'."

"Sorry. I didn't know that," he said with a bit of sarcasm.

Tommy took another sip of beer. "You wouldn't believe what all they did to us. It lasted for eight weeks and you talk about a hot place to be in July and August. It was a killer!"

"Your mama told my mama you were in North Carolina."

"I did my boot camp at Parris Island in South Carolina. Then they sent me to Camp Geiger. That's a part of Camp Lejeune in North Carolina. I did four weeks of infantry training up there. Then they sent me back to Parris Island for my first duty station.

"You must be scared shitless going to Vietnam," Mikey said.

"They told us 100 percent of us would go and 10 percent would not come home. So, I guess that's not bad odds."

"It's still one out of ten."

"I did things I thought I'd never be able to do, Mikey. I pushed myself harder than you can imagine, but I made it, and I'm a Marine now. 'Once a Marine, always a Marine,' they say."

Mikey stared at Tommy for a moment, realizing how much he'd changed. From a physical standpoint, his short haircut was most obvious and his upper body was more muscular. But, otherwise, he seemed more confident and self-assured, not shy like he used to be.

Tommy continued, "When I left home the first of June, I went by bus up to Charleston with a whole bunch of other recruits. We were all scared. Some of the guys were telling horror stories about what they do to you. There was this one black guy on the bus named Roosevelt. He was huge, like a linebacker for the Steelers, and a big talker, too. He told us a story about a drill instructor who marched his entire platoon through a tidal stream called Ribbon Creek. The tide started coming in, and he said that fifty recruits drowned. We heard later it was only eight, but the story was no lie. It did happen.

"We pulled up to the receiving barracks at Parris Island about 1:00 a.m. I kept thinking how good it would feel to get in a bed. I hadn't eaten anything since lunch, and I was starved. This big, mean-actin' guy, who looked like he might eat nails, got on the bus. I thought he'd come to welcome us to Parris Island and assign us a bunk, so we could hit the sack and get some sleep.

"When he stepped up in the bus, he yelled out at the top of his voice, 'You goddamn sons of bitches, get your asses off this bus right now!

"We were all so tired, we just kinda looked at each other and didn't say anything. So, he reached up and grabbed one of the guys sitting in the front seat, dragged him down the steps and slammed him up against the side of the bus like he was a sack of flour."

"What the heck!" Mikey said.

"Yeah, that's the first thing I thought – what the hell have I gotten myself into? Guys started jumping off that bus like it was on fire. When we got out, there were footprints painted in yellow on the street, and we all had to stand on those footprints. This big drill instructor started chewing us out, up one side and down the other, calling us yellow-bellied scum and every other thing he could think of. Then the worst that possibly could've happened – I jumped out of that bus in such a big hurry, I left my shaving kit in my seat. That was the only thing we were allowed to bring – just the clothes on our back and a shaving kit. The bus driver came walking up to the DI with my kit in his hand and said, 'One of the boys left this on the bus.' The DI said, 'Who does this belong to?' I raised my hand and said, 'It's mine.' That DI looked at me like he was going to kill me. He ran over and put his face right up in mine and yelled at me, 'Did I say you could speak?' I said, 'No sir.' He grabbed the front of my shirt and wadded it up in his fist. Buttons were popping off everywhere. He yelled at me again, 'Don't you ever open your mouth and speak to me until you get permission!' He took my shaving kit and threw it as hard as he could against the side of the barracks. I was shaking all over. Then he said, 'You sorry shit, go over there and pick it up.' When I started walking over there, he said, 'You better run, you lazy bastard!' So, I started running, and all I could smell was my Old Spice shaving lotion my mama had given me. It'd broken into a million pieces."

Mikey laughed. "Man, I bet you crapped your pants."

"Yeah," Tommy laughed, then continued, "Most all of us had been up without any sleep for over 24 hours, and we were dead. The DI marched us into the barracks. We thought, 'Hell yeah, we're now going to bed.' But then we found out they were about to give us a written test. It lasted for about three hours. Everybody was nodding off, but if we did, it was the kiss of death. Some PFC was carrying a stick about ten-feet long, and anyone who went to sleep got slapped on the head with it."

"Did you go to sleep?"

"Are you kidding? I was too scared. Adrenalin was pumping through my body about 90 miles an hour.

"Then they marched us over to the mess hall to eat. We had to get our metal trays and hold them in front of us. We were not allowed to look to the left or the right and you better not say a word. They dumped some powdered eggs on my plate and some other slop. Roosevelt had told us on the bus coming up that powdered eggs is what they put the saltpeter in to keep you from jackin' off."

"Does that stuff work?"

"Naw, it didn't work for me," Tommy laughed.

After a pause, he started again.

"I started eating the other crap and not touching my eggs. The DI walked over to me, grabbed the back of my head and smashed my face right into the eggs. He held it there so long, I could hardly breathe. He finally took his hand off my head when I started gasping for air. He yelled out so that everybody in there could hear him, 'You sorry scum bag, you get down there and lick those eggs so I don't see a trace of them on your tray!' I did what he said and started licking my tray, and everybody else got the message. They started eating those eggs like crazy.

"After that, they marched us down to meet our senior drill instructor, Staff Sergeant McDonald. I was expecting some really big guy, but when he walked out, he was a squat, bald-headed man who looked like Elmer Fudd. But the fact that he was short would fool you. He was the toughest son of a bitch I'd ever met.

"When we got to the barracks, the DI said, 'OK, when we go inside, we're going to meet the junior drill Instructor. I need to warn you that this man just got back from the penitentiary for killing two privates. He's a mean son-of-a-bitch, and we're hoping like hell he won't kill any of you.

"When we went in, we didn't see anybody, so the DI walked all the way to the back to where the wall lockers were. He said, 'I bet he's hiding in here.'

"Roosevelt was standing right behind me, and I heard him say real soft so the DI couldn't hear him, 'This ain't shit, man.' About that time the DI hit one of the wall lockers really hard and out jumped this big bastard foaming at the mouth. We found out later he'd eaten some Alka Seltzers. But when he jumped out, he started screaming like a hyena. When he did, Roosevelt fell flat as a pancake right next to me. I grabbed him just in time before his head hit the floor. That crazy guy started screaming, 'You hog-bodied, worm-eating, slimy fucking puke headed douche bags, I'm gonna kill every one of you.'"

Mikey started laughing. "I can just see you right now."

"You're right. I've never been so scared in my life. Anyway, that night we went into the barracks. When they played taps, we all had to say the Lord's Prayer. I can tell you that prayer took on new meaning, especially when we said, 'Deliver us from evil.' Then after that, we all had to say, 'Goodnight, Chesty Puller, wherever you are.'"

"Who is that?"

"He's the Marine's Marine, a real legend. He was a general who fought guerrillas in Haiti and Nicaragua, fought in World War II and the Korean War. He's the most decorated Marine in American history and even turned down a bunch of honors. He's the one we all want to be like."

"Yeah?"

"We hadn't been asleep more than ten minutes when that little junior DI threw open the doors and tossed a garbage can down the middle of the barracks. He started grabbing people out of the sack and throwing them on the floor like a madman. He yelled out, 'All you little sweet peas, you got 45 seconds to be out on the street.' We were stumbling all over everything trying to get our clothes on and most of us made it out there on time. It'd started raining. I don't think I'd ever been that miserable in my life. This one guy was late getting out there, and that Junior DI threw him down on the ground and started choking him. We all thought he was gonna kill him. He kept slapping him in the face, and the boy started crying. I felt sorry for him, but there was nothing we could do. He finally grabbed the boy and stood him up, then he got out in front of us and started saying stuff in a real loud voice like, 'I'm Jesus Christ, and you better treat me like your savior.' Then he started marching us about five miles all around the base in the rain and part of the time he made us run. You could hear guys cussing that Junior DI for all he was worth. If anybody started dropping back of the group, he'd go back and knock them on the ground then reach down and jerk them back up. We were out there until the sun started coming up. I was determined to stay up with the others so he wouldn't put his slimy hands on me."

"Man, that sounds like torture!"

"Torture is not the word for it. It was the closest thing to hell I'd ever had.

"They finally let us go back to the barracks to get in our bunks again. About an hour after we got to sleep, the senior DI came in, blowing a whistle and throwing guys out of their bunks. He might've been short, but that guy was strong as an ox. After we got dressed, he told us all to get in a circle. Then he asked us how that junior DI was treating us. Nobody said a word. Then he wanted to know if he had hit any of us. Two boys raised their hands. One of them said the Junior DI had choked him. The DI said, 'You mean he choked you?' He said, 'Yes sir.' So, the DI wrote his name down. Then he went over to the other guy who raised his hand, and he told the DI that he had been beat up by the Junior DI. Nobody else admitted anything, although practically all of us had been hit some kind of way. The DI asked if any of us had seen it happen to those two guys. One boy raised his hand. The next day all three of those guys were gone and never heard from since."

Mikey was shaking his head in disbelief.

"I'm not saying anything about this to anyone else but

you," Tommy insisted.

"Don't worry. I'm not going to tell anybody."

"I feel different about it now looking back on it, but going through it was pure hell on earth. They drilled in us 'The more you sweat in peace, the less you bleed in war. And in order to really live, you have to nearly die.'" Tommy's words were growing more emotional, with a strong sense of pride.

"You really have become a Marine," Mikey said, as he stared at Tommy with disbelief at how much he'd changed.

"You damn right!" Tommy said, emphasizing each word. "I'm a Marine down to the core," then added, "I paid the price, and I'm glad I did."

Tommy stood up and walked over to the nearest tree to take a leak, then came back and sat on the log. He took another sip of beer and continued. "You know what, Mikey? You could be a Marine, too. But you'd have to really get in good shape first."

"Why would I want to go through all that?" Mikey chuckled. "You know me. That's not who I am."

"But you could if you wanted to," Tommy paused for a few moments where no words were spoken, then started back. "Another thing, we had to keep our footlockers ready for inspection at all times. The DI would come walking into the barracks and surprise us. He'd start throwing footlockers open, and if it wasn't perfect, he'd flip them upside down and give the guy 20 seconds to put it back together. If you didn't do it right in 20 seconds, he'd say, 'Drop down and give me 50 pushups.'

"They made us run with our M14 rifles for three miles, and you had to make it in 36 minutes, or else. That's where my track came in handy. I could do that with no problem. I was in pretty good shape compared to some of those other guys.

"Another thing they made us do was something called fireman's carry, where you had to run 40 yards and pick up a wounded Marine and carry him off the field as fast as you could. And some of those guys you had to carry were pretty big guys. Then they'd run us on the parade field and every 30 yards, you had to drop to the ground and act like you were firing your weapon. We used to call it 'the grinder.'"

Mikey piped up, "Did you know I've never shot a gun in my life?"

Tommy stood up and grabbed a stick about three feet long from off the ground and faced Mikey as if he were holding a rifle and said, "This is my rifle," then Tommy reached down and grabbed his crotch. "This is my gun." Holding the stick toward Mikey. "This one's for killing," then back down to his crotch, "And this one's for fun."

Mikey laughed.

"Just remember you never call your rifle a gun."

"I'm glad you told me."

"Yeah. It took me awhile to learn the lingo. I really sort of surprised myself. I'd never shot any kind of weapon either. But I did pretty good. If you shot less than 190, they called you an "Unq" for unqualified. They wrote it on your forehead with a magic marker and those poor guys went around for days with their heads down so no one could see their face."

Mikey said, "Some of that stuff sounds cruel to me."

"Maybe so. But it's necessary to beat us down to nothing and then mold us into Marines."

"And you want me to join something like that?"

"As I look back on it, I can see it was necessary. It made me feel good to know that I could go through hell and back without dying. It made me tough!"

Tommy stood up. "Come on, man, hit me!"

"What?"

"Come on and hit me as hard as you can in the chest or the stomach."

"But I don't want to hit you."

Tommy stood erect with his chest poked out. Mikey stood up and slugged him in the chest.

"Hit me again. I didn't even feel that."

This time Mikey hit him pretty hard.

"See, I can take it. You want me to hit you?"

"No thanks. I'm not into pain."

"You know I could kill you right now with my bare hands."

"Please spare me, OK?" Mikey laughed.

"A Marine has to have that killer instinct if he expects to survive in combat. If he hesitates at that moment of truth, he'll be a dead Marine. They would say to us, 'The Marine Corps wants killers, who are indestructible men without fear.' That's what they drilled into us."

"But how do you feel about killing somebody you don't even know? It's not like you're mad with them."

"It's either kill or be killed."

"Do you feel it's really necessary to give your life?"

"They used to tell us 'Marines sometimes die, but the Marine Corps will live forever, and that means that all Marines will live forever.'"

"And you don't think that's bullshit? Does that mean you go to some big Marine Corps heaven up in the sky when you die?"

"It's not bullshit." Tommy seemed upset with Mikey for making fun of it. "It's not funny either."

There was a long period of dead silence when Tommy finished talking. Only crickets and tree frogs could be heard. The two of them looked at each other, both painfully aware that they were observing the sundown of their long friendship. Tommy had taken off in a totally different direction and had turned into a person Mikey didn't know. During their awkward years of struggling to grow up and trying to be accepted by their peers, they adopted each other, because of their lack of concern for being social. Neither of them wanted to be or ever considered themselves to be one of the guys or a good-ol'-boy. Because they always felt different from the others, it brought them together as a shelter from the storms of a society that demanded conformity. But now Tommy had turned into someone completely different. He'd become a member of a group that obviously excluded others, somewhat like the fraternities at the University of Florida that Mikey had shunned because of their exclusivity. Tommy seemed to have found his niche. He no longer felt the scars of being a shy kid and an outsider. He'd successfully suppressed his shyness and had performed a miraculous role reversal that was far beyond Mikey's understanding.

Tommy walked out toward the river and began throwing bigger stones into the water causing large ripples to march in an orderly manner toward the shore. A sense of uneasiness seemed to prevail in the air surrounding them.

"Well, what do you think?" Tommy asked.

"Think about what?"

"About what I just told you."

"I think you've changed a whole lot. You're not the same person I used to know."

Tommy didn't respond, because he knew it was true. He gazed out over the river. His presence provoked an eerie feeling in Mikey. Then Tommy turned around facing him. The moonlight revealed a dreadful look in Tommy's eyes. "You damn right, Mikey. I've changed a lot!" Tommy said proudly, as if it were rehearsed. "I'm a leatherneck! By God, I'm a Marine!"

That statement brought about another period of awkward silence between them that lasted for what seemed like a long time.

Finally, Mikey broke the silence. "You remember Mr. Lawson, our shop teacher?"

"Yeah, what about him?" Tommy raised his voice and responded much quicker than Mikey expected.

"He was killed."

"How was he killed?" Tommy spoke as if it took his breath away.

"Motorcycle accident is what I heard," Mikey said, with a bit of sadness in his voice.

Tommy became more introspective and didn't say anything more.

"I always liked him," Mikey added, as he walked out toward the river and sailed a rock, skipping it across the water. "I never did understand why you quit shop when we were freshmen. You never would tell me."

"I told you a long time ago it was nothing," Tommy acted aggravated as he brushed it off. "We just had a misunderstanding."

"OK. It's all right. You don't need to tell me." He stared into the river with the lights of the city flickering on the surface of the water. "My daddy said the funeral was about two weeks ago," Mikey added. "If I'd been here, I would've gone. They said there were a bunch of people there, a lot of former students."

"Did they bury him here?"

"Yeah. I think it was that cemetery out there on Reid Street. You know, the one next to the river."

"Yeah, I know," Tommy acted troubled. "You about ready to go? I'm getting tired. It's been a long day."

"Sure, I'm ready."

Tommy drove quietly for several minutes down the dirt road through a thicket of pine trees and turned right on Lundy Street.

Mikey, unaccustomed to the silence between them, asked, "You OK?"

"Yeah, why?"

"You haven't said anything since we got in the car."

"Sorry. I'm just tired."

When they arrived at Mikey's home, Tommy pulled the car into the driveway and quickly got out. Mikey walked around the back to where he was standing. He looked directly into Tommy's eyes. "I hope everything will be all right, Tommy. Are you scared?"

"No, I'm fine. I'll be just fine. It's all gonna be fine," Tommy said in such rapid-fire speed, as if rehearsed and insincere.

"OK. I hope so. You know we've been friends for a long time."

"Yeah, you're right. We have. Practically all our lives."

They shook hands, and Tommy stood still and watched

as Mikey walked to the front door then turned around and threw up his hand. Tommy returned the wave, got into the car, backed it into the street and squealed the tires as he took off.

It was late when Tommy arrived home. The house was dark except for the porch light and a lamp in the living room. He drove his mother's Chevrolet to the spot where she always parked it under a live oak tree, went into the house and down the hallway to the closet where his father kept his personal items. He turned on the closet light but couldn't see what he was looking for. Then he saw the little step ladder leaning against the closet wall. He opened it and climbed up a couple of steps that allowed him to see what he wanted on the top shelf, the Winchester 12-gauge shotgun that his father always called his "corn-sheller."

Next to the gun was a full box of shells with a flashlight standing right beside them. He took all three items, placed the ladder back against the wall, turned out the light, shut the door and tiptoed out of the house so as not to wake anyone. Uncle Duck, sleeping on the sofa in the living room, made deafening sounds coming from his mouth that would drown out any noise that Tommy might make.

While driving his mother's car downtown, no traffic could be seen anywhere at that time of night. The whole town seemed to be asleep. He drove down Reid Street and turned to the left just before getting to the St. Johns River into the City of Palatka Cemetery. Cruising up and down the little alleys separating the gravesites, his eyes searched for what might be a fresh grave. In the distance, one appeared that still had both dead and droopy flowers around the site. After stopping the car, he walked over to the gravesite, shined the flashlight on the grave marker, and there it was: "Michael Jerome Lawson – Born January 18, 1936 – Died November 14, 1973."

He grabbed the last two beers, popped open both cans and chugged them in short order, then filled the pockets of his jacket with shells, loaded three into the gun and cocked it. Standing beside the grave for a few minutes made it easy to recall in vivid detail what had happened between the two of them.

Just after Tommy turned fifteen and in the ninth grade, Mr. Lawson, the shop teacher, one day asked him to stay after class for a little while, because there were some things that needed to be discussed about the class. Tommy had no idea what had brought that about. A good student in other classes, he'd found shop was not one of his talents and regretted having taken it. But maybe things could be learned about construction, a subject which he had no clue.

After all the boys left class, Mr. Lawson, with a cunning smile, said, "Come on back here in the shop with me to my office." Tommy followed him, curious about what this was all about. Mr. Lawson plopped down in his office chair, took his glasses off, ran his fingers through his thick curly hair, and said, "Son, sit over there in that chair," pointing to a straight, wooden chair against the wall.

He looked Tommy up and down, scouring him from head to toe, then said, "You're a good-looking boy. You know that?" He shuffled his feet then asked, "Had you rather make an A in this class or an F?"

Tommy shrugged his shoulders, then stuttered, "I don't know what you mean. Of course, I'd like to make an A, but I know I don't deserve it."

"Good," he smiled. "I've noticed you seem to be a shy type. Would you describe yourself as being shy?"

"I don't know. I guess so."

"Well, I'd like to help educate you in some of the ways of life you may not be familiar with."

Still unaware of Mr. Lawson's intentions, Tommy replied politely, "Yes sir."

Mr. Lawson leaned forward in his chair. "Stand up and walk over here to me."

Tommy obeyed.

Mr. Lawson put his hand on Tommy's belt and unbuckled it. Tommy quickly pushed his hand away.

"I thought you wanted an A in this class, Tommy. That's what you said."

"Yes sir, but…"

"No buts. Just do as you're told," he ordered.

Mr. Lawson proceeded to again unbuckle his belt, then unbuttoned his jeans and pulled down the zipper.

"No," Tommy demanded. "No, Mr. Lawson, I can't do this. It's wrong." Tommy again pushed his hand away.

"Well, let me sweeten the pot a little bit," he cracked a venomous smile. "You do love your mother, don't you?"

"What are you talking about?" Tommy raised his voice.

"Your mother. You do have one, don't you?"

"What's that got to do with anything?" Tommy asked even louder.

"It sounds like to me you need a little coaxing, Tommy. If you don't do what I say, something really bad is going to happen to your mother."

"What are you saying?" Tommy shouted.

"You heard me. Just put your hands down by your side, and remember this is going to really feel good to you. You've never had sex with anyone before, have you?"

"No sir."

"That's what I thought," he smiled. "A virgin. That really turns me on."

Tommy noticed him playing with himself.

"Just stand still," Mr. Lawson ordered. "It's not going to hurt you. In fact, I think you'll enjoy it."

Tommy had never been that afraid in his entire lifetime. His heart was pounding so fast he could hardly catch his breath as Mr. Lawson pulled his jeans and underwear down to the floor, and as much as he tried, Tommy couldn't control the tears from flowing down his cheek.

"Oh, Tommy. You're well hung. Did you know that? You have a real mouthful."

After completing his lecherous act upon Tommy, he smiled like a dragon and leaned back in his chair. "Whoa! That was quick!"

Tommy brushed his arm across his face to wipe away the tears, pulled up his underwear and pants, and buckled his belt. "Can I go now?"

"How was it? How did it feel?"

"Mr. Lawson, let me go now, and please don't harm my mama."

Tommy ran from the shop, vowing that he would never tell anyone what had occurred, because he couldn't stand the thought of any harm happening to his mother.

The next day, when Tommy went to school, he'd become a different person. He acted as if he'd been punched in the stomach or that the rug had been pulled out from under him. As he looked around at his fellow students laughing and kidding each other, dread and horror and shame enveloped him. For days afterward, his entire demeanor was absorbed in humiliation and guilt and downright pain.

One of the girls, a friend of his, asked him if he was sick. "No, just a bad headache." He had terrible nightmares and sometimes his contempt caused him to dream about beating the life out of Mr. Lawson and killing him with a baseball bat. His anxiety had turned into depression to the extent that he was moping around the house and at school, not being himself. All he wanted to do was sleep; he had no motivation to study or do anything else. There were times he felt as if he was not even inside his body, that he was somewhere else in another dimension. His mother wanted to take him to a doctor, but he wouldn't hear of it. "No," he would say. "I'll be all right. Just leave me alone."

After it happened the third time with Mr. Lawson, Tommy never went back to shop class again. He went to the principal and told him that he would have to drop the course. The principal advised him that if he dropped the class, he would get an F.

"That's OK. I'll deal with it."

The principal insisted by saying that if he ever wanted to get into college, he would need to have a good grade point average. But Tommy insisted. "It's OK. I'll take the F."

"Is there some reason you don't want to take the shop class, Tommy?"

"No. I just don't like it. It's not something I want to do."

"Just finish out the term," the principal insisted. "You'll probably get a passing grade, but an F is going to really hurt you."

"I know. But that's OK. That's what I want to do."

He leaned forward in his chair. "Tommy. I hope you know what you're doing. Don't you think I should talk with your parents about this?"

"No sir. I'll explain it to them."

Tommy knew that if he told his father or Uncle Duck what had happened, they would both have to serve the rest of their lives in the penitentiary for killing Mr. Lawson. So Tommy concluded that this was just something he would have to deal with himself.

Tommy took the shotgun, pointed it next to the granite slab over the grave and cried out, "You sorry son of bitch! I hate your guts!" At this, he pulled the trigger, blowing a large hole in the ground next to the slab.

He then backed off far enough to shoot at the engraving on the slab without any of the shots ricocheting back on him. He continued yelling obscenities with each blast of the shotgun until all the shells were gone. He then threw the gun in the backseat of the car, got in the driver's seat and put his head on the steering wheel, panting as if he'd just run a 100-yard-dash.

Finally, pulling himself together enough to start the car, he slowly drove back toward home. His brain did flip-flops, being bombarded with thoughts of the past. Tears filled his eyes so that he could hardly see the street. Pulling in to the driveway, he parked, got out and took the gun from the backseat. The thought flitted across his mind to use it on himself, but there were no shells left.

He walked into the house where Uncle Duck's snoring on the couch sounded more like a growling bear. He shined the flashlight on the grandfather clock that sat on the mantelpiece over the fireplace. Ten minutes past eleven. He went back to the closet, replaced the gun and flashlight and opened the kitchen door. He turned on the light and sat down at the breakfast table where his mother always sat each morning to read her Bible. She kept a writing pad and pen there to make her grocery list. He sat still for a few minutes, trying to collect his thoughts, and began to write:

> Dear Mama,
>
> I feel so sorry for you having to live in this crazy screwed up family. You've always tried so hard to make things right but it just seems hopeless, doesn't it? You deserve the best, and I hope someday you get it.
>
> I know it's Thanksgiving Day, and I had promised you that I'd be here for the weekend, but I've decided to go back to Camp Lejeune. I got so much to do to get ready before I get shipped out on Monday. It will be good for me to have a chance to do all the things I need to do.
>
> I'm sorry I didn't get to spend more time with you, Mama, but I'll be back. I promise. Don't you worry! I'll come back home to you even though it may be a long time.
>
> Tell Daddy and Uncle Duck and Buddy I said goodbye.
>
> I love you, Mama.
>
> Tommy

Before getting up from the table, the slice of pecan pie caught his eye, sitting in a saucer on the counter, covered with a piece of wax paper. A fork was sitting next to the pie, and he devoured it in short order. Knowing how much his mama loved him brought tears to his eyes.

Quickly realizing that real Marines don't cry, he got dressed in his uniform, put the rest of his gear in his duffel bag and walked out of the house feeling guilty for staying such a short time and disappointing his mother.

As he walked along the dark sidewalk toward town, he noticed a police car coming from behind. He watched it pull up beside him. The cop let his window down and yelled out to him, "Where're you going?"

Tommy walked over to the car.

"Ain't you Wes Jennings' son?"

"Yeah. Going back to Camp Lejeune."

"At this time of night?"

"I never have any problem getting a ride with this uniform on."

"Well, come on around and get in son. I'll drive you through town for a ways. Maybe you'll find somebody who'll take you to Jacksonville."

"Thanks," he said as he got into the passenger seat and threw his duffel bag in the backseat.

"You sure you don't want to stay at home tonight and leave early in the morning?"

"No sir, I think I'd rather travel at night."

They drove through town making small talk, then the officer said, "I've known your daddy a long time. Had to help him a few times get home from the Country Club," he chuckled.

"I'm not surprised."

The officer looked vaguely familiar, not unlike most small-town cops, but Tommy didn't know his name and he never introduced himself.

He dropped Tommy off at a service station on Highway 17, north of Palatka that had a lot of lights illuminating the front, easy to be seen by passing vehicles. Tommy jumped out and thanked him for the ride. The officer blew the horn, did a U-turn and headed back into town.

In no more than ten or fifteen minutes a paneled truck pulled into the station to gas-up. A young fellow came running out and asked the driver, "Fill 'er up?"

"Yep," the driver replied and walked into the station to use the rest room. When he came back and got in his truck, he saw Tommy standing next to the highway. He drove up beside him, let his window down and yelled, "Where you going, soldier?"

"North Carolina."

"I'll take you up to Jacksonville. That's as far as I'm going."

"Sure," Tommy ran over and jumped in the front seat next to the driver. The first thing he noticed was a strong odor of shrimp. "What you got in here?"

"This is my shrimp truck. Every night I pick up shrimp from the docks in Jacksonville and haul them to a supplier in Orlando during shrimp season."

"You probably don't even smell them, do you?"

"Naw, not really."

They rode in silence for a few minutes.

"By the way, I'm Jack Overby. Looks like you're a jarhead."

"Yep, just finished boot camp. Heading out Monday for 'Nam."

"No shit. I served my time in the Korean War."

"What branch were you in?"

"Army."

"A grunt," Tommy laughed to get him back for calling him a jarhead.

Jack came across as a nice guy, about mid-40s, tanned skin like most shrimp fishermen. They continued chatting with each other. When they went through Green Cove Springs, Jack said, "You know there used to be a big naval base here durin' World War II?"

"Yeah, I know. My father used to tell me about havin' some fun drinkin' with those guys."

"You're right. Those boys definitely knew how to drink."

When they drove through Orange Park in south Jacksonville, Jack said, "I live off Main Street on West 28th, but I'll take you up 17 far enough to get you out of town. That way, you'll get a longer ride."

"Thanks, 'preciate that."

Jack took him up north of Trout River to a spot he thought would be a good place for Tommy to be seen.

"Thanks Jack," he said as he stepped out of the truck.

"Good luck to you," Jack said. He waved and drove off.

Calvin

Calvin, the only child of Joe and Vivian Livingston, was born in Brunswick, Georgia, in 1953. Joe, like many other men in and around southeast Georgia, left the farm and came to the coastal town of Brunswick to work in the paper mill. The wages were not all that great, but it beat laboring in the tobacco fields, the dominate employment for those in the inland counties. "I'd rather make paper than crop tobacco," was the typical reply one would hear from those farm boys when asked why they moved to Brunswick.

Joe met Vivian, a simple young girl with long, blonde hair and pale white skin. Her parents were poor and uneducated. When she was seventeen, she and Joe had to get married in order to make their child she was expecting legitimate. They named him Calvin after Joe's grandfather.

When Calvin started to school, Vivian felt the need to help support the family. She found an opening at an elementary school lunchroom. They rented a small two-bedroom house on Eighth Street in the Arco area of Brunswick between Palmetto Cemetery and the pulp mill. It took almost all they had to pay the rent and keep food on the table, because rental payments had escalated so much during the war.

Even though times were hard in most places, Brunswick was booming. During the war, a shipbuilding outfit had been commissioned to build 99 Liberty ships adjacent to the Brunswick River. 16,000 workers were employed. In the 1940 census, prior to the war, Brunswick's population was 15,000, so the population had more than doubled during the war. In addition, the Navy had established Glynco Naval Air Station, located in the northern part of Brunswick, which, during the war, became the largest blimp base in the world.

Joe, a large man, weighing over 250 pounds, with reddish hair and of Scottish descent, had been wounded in the Battle of Anzio, Italy, in 1944, by an exploding hand-grenade. Since then, he walked with a permanent limp. But he was more than satisfied to accept that physical defect, since he, unlike many of his buddies, came home alive.

They couldn't afford to buy a car, but that really didn't matter too much. Joe could always catch a ride to the mill, or if necessary he could walk, being only a half-mile away. Weather permitting, Vivian walked in the other direction to the cafeteria at Arco Elementary School.

Since Joe returned home, Vivian became aware that he had more than just a limp as a malady. His personality had changed. He was moody, irritable, and sometimes had nightmares. Other than going to work, he didn't care to leave the house except to go to church on Sundays. Furthermore, Vivian thought he disciplined Calvin much more than he should, not to mention that he physically and mentally abused her as well.

Calvin entered the first grade at Arco Elementary School, a five-minute walk from their house. He usually arrived home from school a couple of hours before his mother and about four hours before his father. He'd made friends with a boy in his class named Steve Russell, who lived only a block and a half away. Steve's father also worked at the mill, and his mother stayed home and made a decent living as a seamstress. She'd told Vivian it would be perfectly all right to let Calvin come over after school to play until she got home.

That worked fine. The boys got along very well with each other and seemed to have a lot in common. They played on Steve's slide in the backyard and with toy cars and trucks, constructing make-believe roads from a house they'd built with sticks to a mill made from concrete blocks. Rafters ran across Steve's bedroom about ten feet above the floor where his father had built a swing. The boys loved to push each other until they reached a height where they could leap from the swing onto the bed. That was the most fun of all.

Steve had a dog named Thunder, a mongrel, white with several black spots, including one over his right eye. Calvin and Steve had measured Thunder's height at nineteen inches. He loved for them to swing, because he'd chase them back and forth before they jumped to the bed. Thunder usually met the two boys when they came home from school, because that meant playtime for him outside.

As the boys grew older, they'd walk down Ross Road to the railroad tracks past Palmetto Cemetery, where only white people could be buried, then past Selden Park, a playground for black kids, then past Greenwood Cemetery, used by blacks exclusively as their burial ground, then over to Reynolds Street, where there was a park that had a large array of playground equipment. Thunder ran along behind them and sometimes would speed up and run ahead, then turn around and wait for them to catch up. They liked to play at that park, because so many other kids were there, both younger and older.

This arrangement for the two boys worked fine so long as Calvin got home before his father returned from work; otherwise it meant a sound whipping. When this occurred, Vivian would cry, but she knew better than to say anything or otherwise he would turn his anger on her. It didn't help matters that most of the time Joe was pretty well intoxicated when he arrived home.

At the age of fourteen, the boys entered Glynn Academy, chartered in 1788, the second oldest public high school in Georgia. After school, they began going down the street to Selden Park. Unlike the Reynolds Street Park, Selden had an indoor basketball court, and sometimes the black kids would allow Calvin and Steve to play if they didn't have enough guys to make a team.

In the summertime, Steve's dad would often take the boys to a baseball game at Lanier Field. Brunswick had a farm club with the Pittsburgh Pirates. Branch Rickey, Jr. managed the team, a part of the Georgia-Florida League. Both the boys were in awe of those professional players and often talked about taking up baseball as a career.

Calvin had grown five inches over the previous year to five feet eleven inches but he only weighed 137 pounds. He had pale skin and thick blond hair, like his mother's, which he wanted so much to groom like Paul McCartney's, but the school had a rule forbidding a boy's hair to touch his ears. In spite of being skinny, most of the girls thought of Calvin as a good-looking guy, although his face seemed much too pretty to be attached to the body of a male. His large, dreamy eyes and long eyelashes made him the envy of girls on the campus. He had an unblemished, milky white complexion and a thin nose that complimented his face. Some girls would've given anything to go out with him because of his good looks, but he was much too shy, so they were aware that was not likely to happen.

Steve, on the other hand, had a stocky frame and measured only five feet eight inches. He had short hair, sort of reddish-brown, and an emerging case of acne.

Toward the end of their junior year, Steve's father took the boys to the Blessing of the Shrimp Fleet, a centuries-old tradition originating in southern Europe among Catholic fishing communities.

When Sundays rolled around, it meant attending Sunday school at 10:00, Church service at 11:00, and Sunday evening service at 6:00. Prayer meeting occurred on Wednesday night at 7:00. In both households, no excuse was good enough to miss any of them – not even sickness. The only time Calvin could remember missing a service was when he had the mumps at about the age of twelve. Even then, Vivian felt he should go, but Joe intervened and insisted, "If the boy gets out of bed, the mumps might go down on him, and then he'd be in a heap of trouble. He could be sterile for the rest of his life."

The white, clapboard church building, adorned with stained-glass windows and a steeple on the top, had a bell to ring to signal the beginning of each of the services. Reverend Mitchell measured six feet two inches and weighed about 220 pounds. He was a nice-looking fellow, in his early forties and never married, a fact that some found a bit unusual. The congregation had never had a minister without a wife. He assured them, however, that he had a girlfriend in Savannah and visited her as often as he could. He'd graduated from Bob Jones University in Greenville, South Carolina, and was the first minister of the church with a college degree. He pleased the congregation with his conservative views and made it his practice to stand out in front of the church building to greet the congregation as they arrived.

The Sunday following the Blessing of the Fleet, Preacher Mitchell gave a stirring sermon that Calvin and Steve would never forget:

"Today my sermon is based on Psalm 104, verse 35, of

the Holy Bible, which reads as follows. He opened his Bible, put on his glasses and turned to the passage. He raised his voice louder, 'Let all sinners vanish from the face of the earth; let the wicked disappear forever. Let all that I am praise the LORD. Praise ye the LORD.'

"I want to talk to you today about sins of the flesh and their consequences. I'm telling you right here and now that it's impossible to ignore those secret sins like self-satisfaction. Many people suffer from this sin, starting at a young age, usually in their early teens. It's unnatural and dangerous, because it's done in secret. It can become such an addictive habit, that some boys and girls, and even men and women, perform self-gratification even when there is no physical need for it. This habit can become so strong that when people do it too much, they become overwhelmed in the power of a satanic force, which they're unable to control. It causes them to become listless and apathetic and is bad for their health.

"So why do the Scriptures warn about the struggles with carnal lust? One reason is because the sin of fornication exhausts the physical strength and health of a person. The apostle Paul warned, 'The fornicator sins against his own body.' It makes sense, because having sex outside of a marriage wears the body out much faster, because sexual life that is not connected with love requires much more power than a normal relationship inside a marriage. And I should add that sex with a stranger could cause the fornicator to contract an awful venereal disease.

"Those who have given themselves to lascivious passion have a decreased ideal for life. They deny themselves the values of having a decent job that benefits society. They prevent themselves from having a happy life with a loved one. A healthy youth who performs self-gratification will gradually fade into oblivion as he watches his ideals evaporate.

"Those who pleasure themselves become cynical, because their conscience becomes filled with dirty pictures and filthy books. The young men who perform this act of self-pleasure begin to look at females as nothing but a plaything. Evil thoughts begin to invade and dim their brains, so that they succumb to only one desire in their hearts, and that is to satisfy their lust.

"God's grace abandons a person who has given in to self-gratification, and, because of this, the faith of that person in God grows weak, and they no longer have spiritual inclinations. They stop hearing the voice of God. They no longer have any conscience, even though the voice of God is pleading with them to repent of their sins. Cold and gloom and rage are established in their souls, and they suffer a spiritual death. And after that, there is nowhere else to fall.

"Because they are unable to turn away from their wicked ways to the path of righteousness, God punishes them with His Holy Judgment. 'My Spirit will not be content with man forever, for he is mortal,' God said.

"As you probably remember from previous Bible studies, God punished the cities of Sodom and Gomorrah for their sins of debauchery, by raining burning sulfur from the heavens. He overthrew those cities, including all those people who lived in the cities – and also the vegetation in the land according to the nineteenth chapter of Genesis, verses twenty-four and twenty-five.

"The apostle Paul said, according to Hebrews, the thirteenth chapter in the fourth verse, 'God will judge all the adulterers and all the sexually immoral people.'

"Think of how many great empires and civilizations have perished and how many people who indulge in any type of sexual behavior outside of marriage, have disappeared from this earth without leaving a trace!

"Having sexual relations before marriage or outside of marriage or self-gratification destroys a proper sexual relationship between spouses. It devastates those who do it, physically, emotionally, and spiritually. Unless you come to God with a contrite heart and confess your sins and beg for forgiveness, then you will be doomed to an eternity of hellfire and damnation.

"Please remember this, my brothers and sisters, and if I have touched anyone's heart with these Holy Words of Wisdom, then I hope and trust that you will turn away from your sinful ways and live a righteous life from here on out and for the rest of your days.

"And now if there are any of you who feel that you have committed sins of the flesh and want forgiveness, then I ask you to get up from your seats and walk down the aisle and we will pray for you – God will wash away all your sins and cleanse you for a new life ahead.

"While Miss Bernice plays that beloved old hymn, "Just As I Am," I ask you to come down to the altar. If there is any lost soul who wants to be saved today, please come down as we sing."

The congregation began singing:

"Just as I am, without one plea
But that Thy blood was shed for me,
And that Thou bid'st me come to Thee,
O Lamb of God, I come! I come!"

Calvin looked at Steve, and Steve looked back at Calvin. As Steve stood up to walk down the aisle, Calvin followed, and the congregation continued to sing.

"Just as I am, though tossed about
With many a conflict, many a doubt;
Fighting and fears within without,
O Lamb of God, I come, I come!"

Preacher Mitchell, standing in front of the altar, reached out and grabbed each boy's hand and shook it, then patted them on the back.

After the hymn had been sung, he said to the congregation, "Let us pray in silence for these two young fellows who want to have their sins washed away."

They both stood still, embarrassed to have silently and by default, confessed their wrong-doings of self-gratification in front of all the people in the church, including their parents. But they both wanted to have their slate wiped clean so that if anything ever happened to them, they would have a clear path to heaven.

When Preacher Mitchell dismissed the congregation with a prayer, he leaned down to Calvin and Steve and told them to remain for a few moments after the church service. After the church had been emptied, with only the three of them remaining, he told the boys that he would like to meet with them privately at the church the following afternoon after school. "Don't mention anything about this to your parents. I'll be waiting for you right here."

They agreed and went outside to join their family. Preacher Mitchell followed. He said to Calvin's mother, "Miss Vivian, these boys are on the right path. Calvin is blessed to have such good parents like you and Joe. There's one thing I know for sure, Miss Vivian, your conscience is clear."

Joe popped right back with, "I always heard that a clear conscience is a good sign of a bad memory."

"Joe Livingston," Vivian said sternly. "I can't believe you said such a thing like that to the preacher."

He laughed and the preacher smiled.

On their walk back home, Vivian seemed terribly upset and began crying. Joe told her to quit worrying about the boys. "They're fifteen years old for God's sake! What do you expect?"

The next day after school, Calvin and Steve took the school bus back home, as usual. When they got off, Thunder met them. Neither of the boys had spoken a word to each other about the preacher's request.

As they walked along, Steve asked Calvin, "What do you think he wants to talk to us about?"

"I don't have any idea. I've been thinking that maybe for punishment, he wants us to clean up the grounds around the church or mow the grass or something like that."

"I thought they had a maintenance guy who did that."

"I don't know," Calvin shook his head. "Let's just go to the church and get it over with."

They could see Preacher Mitchell sitting on the front

steps of the church building as they approached. When they walked to the foot of the steps, he stood up and shook hands with each of them. "How're you boys doing?"

They both said, "Fine," at the same time.

"Your dog will have to stay outside," as he closed the door in Thunder's face. The boys followed him through the sanctuary of the church to his office in the back. As they walked in, he shut the door, locked it and motioned for the boys to sit in the two chairs in front of his desk. He took his seat behind the desk.

"Let's bow our heads in prayer."

Both boys obeyed.

He began, "O Lord, we ask you to bless these two young men as they enter into a time of their life that presents tremendous changes and challenges to their bodies. We ask you to be with them and help them through this period of their lives. Please give them the strength not to be tempted to commit sins with their young bodies, and give me the strength to help them in every way I can to prevent them from partaking of the sins of self-satisfaction and other sins of the flesh, which is an abomination to you, O Lord. And we ask this in your name. Amen."

The boys raised their heads and stared at the preacher in wonder of what he planned to do.

"Now, boys, I need to ask some questions that you must answer as honestly as you know how. You have to be truthful with me, because I'm here to help you from committing any sins. Do you understand?"

"Yes sir," they both responded.

"I believe both of you are fifteen. Is that right?"

"Yes sir," Calvin answered.

"I want you to know that it's a sin to have sex with a female before marriage, and I mean any type of sex whatsoever. You are not allowed to touch each other's private parts until you get married. And, under no circumstances can you have any type of sex with another male. Period! I hope you haven't done that with each other."

He looked first at Calvin and then at Steve, and they both

shook their heads.

"And you can't pleasure yourself. That is a sin before God."

The boys didn't dare look at each other. They only stared at him.

"Has anyone ever explained puberty to you?"

They both shook their heads since neither of them knew the meaning of that word.

"OK. Let's see what I can say to help you with this, because I need to find out for sure whether you have reached puberty."

He looked into the eyes of one of the boys and then the other.

"Have you noticed hair growing on your body where there was no hair before?"

Both boys squirmed in their seats feeling ill at ease about this conversation, but then they both nodded in agreement.

"Have you noticed when you're singing hymns in church that you are having a harder time hitting those high notes?"

Steve shrugged his shoulders. Calvin didn't respond.

"I don't know if you've noticed it or not, but your voices are changing. I've noticed it myself that you're speaking with deeper voices."

"Have you or any of the boys you know started shaving their face?"

They both shook their heads, then Steve spoke up, "Yeah, that guy, James, in our class. Someone told me that he'd started shaving every Sunday."

"Boys, you are going through a transition period from being a boy to becoming an adult. Your bodies are starting to change."

They nervously shifted around a little more in their seats.

"Have you looked under your arms or on your legs to see if hair is growing?"

It was obvious that neither of the boys seemed to have paid any attention to it.

"Take your shirts off," the preacher ordered. "I need to check to see how far along into puberty you are."

They looked at each other, then proceeded to remove their shirts.

The preacher stood up. "Hold your arms up and let me inspect your arm pits."

Both the boys held their arms straight up.

"Steve, I can see a few hairs coming out." Then he put his hand on Steve's chest and moved his head in close. "Yes, you have some hairs on your chest, too.

"Calvin, I don't see any hairs on you yet, but with all that blond hair you have, it may be hard to see."

They reached for their shirts to put them on but were stopped by the preacher, "Just leave your shirts off for a minute, OK?"

"When boys reach puberty, they usually have hairs coming out just above their penis. Let's check that."

Both the boys looked at each other in fear, not wanting to do what the preacher seemed to be getting around to. But they trusted him implicitly to do the right thing and looked upon him as a spokesman for God.

"Just drop your pants and underwear down, and let's have a look."

They reluctantly did as they were told.

"Oh yeah. I can see some pubic hairs coming out on both of you. Have you noticed your penis and your testicles becoming larger? That's a usual sign of reaching puberty, too.

"One of the first signs of puberty is your testicles. Hormones from a special part of the brain cause the testicles to grow bigger. Do you know what testosterone is?"

They both shook their heads.

"Well, your testicles make testosterone, and it starts during puberty. It's what causes your testicles to produce sperm and gives you a sex drive. Here let me check."

He reached out to Steve and grabbed his testicles in his right hand and squeezed ever so gently.

"Yes, I would say they are beginning to grow larger. And I would say your penis is getting larger, too. What do you think, Steve?"

"I guess so."

Then he performed the same ritual on Calvin. "I can see some blond pubic hairs beginning to pop out."

"Calvin, I'll start with you. Look at me in the eye son. Have you ever masturbated?"

Calvin looked away and turned his head toward Steve for help.

"Look back at me, Calvin. I asked you a question, and I need for you to answer me truthfully. Do you hear?"

"Yes sir," he said. "I don't know what that word means."

"OK, I'll use a street term. Have you ever jacked-off?"

Calvin sucked air into his lungs that swelled his chest, then exhaled. He looked down at the floor, "Yes sir."

The preacher then turned toward Steve, "And how about you?"

"Yes sir," he responded with a timid expression.

"You boys remember what I said in my sermon yesterday, don't you? And you do realize that you're sinning each time you do that."

Steve spoke up. "I thought when we went down before you in church last Sunday, you were going to ask forgiveness for us."

"That is true, but I want to keep you from committing any more sins in the future," He shook his head. "Can't you understand that?"

They nodded.

He asked them to pull up their underwear and pants and put their shirts back on, which they did with a sigh of relief, then he told them to sit back down.

"Also, I wonder if you have noticed that your body has started to smell differently, especially when you are sweating or at the end of the day. This is normal when you reach puberty. You may have to start taking a shower more often and maybe use some deodorant.

"Steve, the acne and pimples on your face are another common thing with puberty. It's caused by the skin oil and a particular kind of bacteria that grows inside the pores of your skin. You might want to get some medication at the pharmacy. They can help you with what you should buy.

"Most boys have a lot of emotional ups and downs during puberty. You may find that you feel sad or angry and don't know why. You may feel bad one moment and happy the next. You might feel worried about what other people think about you. And you may feel like you don't want to be as close to your parents as you used to be. These feelings are all a normal part of puberty and come and go in your early teen years. If you feel sad, angry or depressed for more than two weeks or have trouble doing everyday things like going to school, you should talk to your school counselor.

"I want you to remember that puberty is temporary and something that everyone experiences. Those cracks in your voice won't last, and eventually your body will reach a steady size and shape.

"Now before you go, I want to tell you how much I want both of you to go to heaven when you die. And you can't get into heaven if you commit sins. I don't want you to ever jack-off by yourselves, because that's a sin that cannot be forgiven. Any time that you feel the need to do this, you must call me. I will meet you here in my office, and I will take care of it for you. That way it is not a sin. As your preacher, I represent God, and God allows me to do this for you to keep you from sinning. But you cannot tell anyone at all about what you're doing, because if you do, that would also be a sin. Do you understand?"

Calvin immediately spoke up, "Yes sir," because he knew that whatever the preacher said would be right, since he spoke for God.

Steve seemed a little more dubious, but he finally said, "Yes sir."

"And one other thing," the preacher added. "If either of you have a wet dream, do you know what I'm talking about?"

They both nodded.

"I have a paddle here." He picked up a wooden paddle about two feet long. "If that ever happens, you must be punished, because a wet dream is also a sin. That's the reason you should come to see me often so that it will keep you from having those wet dreams. Do you understand?"

They both said, "Yes sir."

"Do either of you have any questions?"

They both shook their heads.

"OK. You may go now."

As if they'd been shell-shocked, the boys and Thunder, who'd been waiting patiently on the front steps of the church, left and walked slowly and deliberately back toward Steve's house without saying a word to each other. In fact, neither of them ever discussed it again. However, they both did as they'd been instructed by Preacher Mitchell by visiting him at least two or three times a week to be relieved of their sexual tension. They also dutifully reported to him when they'd experienced a wet dream. That resulted in him taking his paddle, making them bend over his knees and receive a few whacks on the rear end. And this routine continued through their fifteenth and sixteenth year and even after they'd turned seventeen.

In the early part of May of their junior year, the school routinely held a Sadie Hawkins Day dance for the juniors and seniors, even though historically the date occurred only on February 29th, once every four years. At this dance, the girl had to ask the boy for a date, pick him up at his home and give him a rose bud to wear in the lapel of his coat. This brought about much speculation and anticipation on the part of the male students, wondering whether or not the right girl would ask them. Susan Miles had asked Calvin, and the invitation had to be accepted by the boy, according to the rules. A few days before the dance, Steve had not received an invitation. Calvin became worried he might not be asked, so he pressed Susan to see if she could find a girl for Steve. The day before the dance she came through, and Josephine Crowley, a girl who was no beauty queen, asked Steve.

Calvin, being curious about how this event came to be,

went to the library and did some research. He found it came from a comic strip by Al Capp called Li'l Abner, who lived in Dogpatch. Sadie Hawkins had been deemed to be "the homeliest gal in them thar hills." After she turned 35, her father, Hakzebiah Hawkins, feared he had a spinster on his hands. He, being one of Dogpatch's most prominent citizens, called for a foot race where all the town's eligible bachelors were required to run. The loser of the race had to marry his daughter. It became popular in colleges around America to have these Sadie Hawkins Day dances to switch the dating custom for girls to ask boys to go out, pick them up and pay for the evening.

Calvin had learned that most of the guys were wearing suits. He didn't have one. His mother asked around at the school cafeteria where she worked and found a man about the size of Calvin who agreed to lend him his suit. Steve's parents had purchased one for him.

Both boys were excited but nervous. Neither of them had ever been to a dance, and, furthermore, didn't know how to dance. When the big evening arrived, Susan's father drove his black, four-door Buick to the Livingston home. Susan, a pretty brunette, wore a pink evening dress of tulle, a thin, fine net of rayon, handmade by Miss Cora, a seamstress who lived in south Brunswick. Her high-heel shoes were dyed to match the dress, and she wore long, white leather gloves that came above her elbow. She'd visited a beautician to have her hair done in curls.

When Susan walked up the steps to the front door, Calvin anxiously watched through the window. He wore a blue suit, white shirt, red tie and black shoes, all borrowed from his mother's fellow employee. Neither Joe nor Vivian knew how to tie a necktie, so Vivian asked a neighbor to come over and help Calvin.

She was so proud of her son. "You look so good, honey. I wish I had a camera to take your picture."

When Susan knocked, Calvin ran to the back of the house and asked his mother to answer the door. She walked into the living room and opened the door slowly and politely. "Oh, my!" she gasped. "Don't you look gorgeous! I'm Vivian Livingston. Please come in and let me get

Calvin." Vivian walked to the back of the house where Calvin waited, shaking from fright. "Tell her how nice she looks," Vivian coached.

Calvin walked into the living room where Susan stood and said very awkwardly without any feeling, "Hi. You look nice."

"Thank you," she smiled. "You do, too." She handed him the rose as a boutonnière, which his mother, who'd come in behind him, placed in the lapel of his coat.

Vivian touched both of them on the shoulder, "You'll be the best-looking couple there."

They got into the back seat of the car, and Susan's father chauffeured them to the "wood gym," the basketball stadium at Glynn Academy. When they got out, Mr. Miles said, "I'll be back at this same spot at 10:30 to pick you up, so don't make me have to wait for you."

When they walked in, they stopped and gawked at the hundreds of students milling around on the gym floor. Some were dancing to the music being played by a disc jockey from a Jacksonville radio station, WAPE. Calvin looked around and saw Steve and Josephine coming into the gym. They walked over to greet them.

Josephine, a large girl, taller than Steve and not at all shy, announced, "I want to dance." Steve and Calvin sort of stared at each other, since neither of them had a clue about dancing. In fact, they both were very much aware that some of the members of their church felt it was a sin to dance.

"Come on!" Josephine encouraged them, "Just follow me."

The four of them walked out on the gym floor, a bit shy about attempting to dance in front of their schoolmates, but others were dancing too. As the DJ played "Ain't No Mountain High Enough" by Diana Ross, each couple held hands and began moving to the rhythm, which at first was an awkward feeling for the boys. When the song finished, Steve wanted to go back and sit down, but Josephine wouldn't hear of it. They danced to Three Dog Night's "Mama Told Me Not to Come," followed with "Everything Is Beautiful" by Ray Stevens, a slow dance, where the boys felt the sensation, for the first time, of what it was like holding a girl up close against their bodies. Then they held hands and danced to "American Woman" by The Guess Who. Josephine knew the words to each of the songs and sang them out loud as she danced with a flair. When the DJ played "My Sweet Lord" by George Harrison, she sang even louder, for this was her favorite song. And she threw her arms up and danced like crazy to "Signed, Sealed, Delivered, I'm Yours" by Stevie Wonder.

After that, Steve insisted he needed to rest. They sauntered over to the punch-bowl to have a drink. Little did they know that some of the senior boys, prone to mischief, had spiked the punch. The four of them had never tasted alcohol before, so they were completely unable to detect it.

Afterwards, they danced with more enthusiasm, until Susan looked at her watch and noticed it was past 10:30. She grabbed Calvin's arm and rushed out of the gym to the car where her father was waiting.

"Sorry, Dad," she apologized. "We were having so much fun, we let the time slip by."

Mr. Miles, remembering his own teenage years, understood, and no words of reprimand were spoken. However, he became more than a little bit curious and concerned about the giggling coming from the backseat. He constantly checked his rearview mirror to see what was going on back there and was relieved that he didn't see them touching each other.

When Susan walked Calvin to the door to carry out the tradition, he shuffled his feet awkwardly, not knowing what to say, then blurted out, "I had fun."

"I did too," she smiled.

Calvin opened the door, went inside and watched through the window as they drove away.

Vivian, who'd waited up, tried to pry answers from him. "Well, did you have a good time? Did you dance with her? Were there a lot of people there? What did you think of Susan?" And on and on and on with more motherly-like questions, all of which were answered with "Uh-huh."

Toward the latter part of May, a few days before the end

of their junior year, Calvin noticed that Steve seemed quieter. "You OK?" Calvin asked as they left school walking toward the school bus. Steve looked like he was in another world and didn't respond. Calvin suggested they walk home and not ride the bus. Steve agreed. Calvin, holding his biology book, and Steve, empty-handed, walked in silence for a while along Newcastle Street through downtown Brunswick. As they passed through the business area, Calvin asked, "What's wrong?"

Steve shrugged his shoulders.

"No, come on. Something's bothering you."

Steve turned his back to Calvin and said, "No."

"Steve, we're best friends. You can tell me anything."

"I don't know. Nothing really." He ignored Calvin's plea.

"You're making good grades in school," Calvin urged. "Is something wrong at home?"

Then Steve blurted out, "I can't keep on doing this!"

"Doing what?"

He dropped his head. "I can't keep going to the preacher!"

"But, Steve, you remember what he told us."

"It's just not right!" He shouted out so loud, it startled Calvin. "I dread having to go there. It makes me sick to my stomach."

"I know. I don't like having to go there either, but we have to do what he says, Steve. He speaks for God."

Steve raised his voice in anger. "I feel so ashamed of myself! Why do I have to go to him to get a hand-job or a blow-job every time I feel the need?"

Unprepared for that comment since it was a subject they'd never discussed, Calvin gave a weak explanation. "Because he said so."

"But it feels so wrong!" Steve acted irritated by Calvin's feeble response. "I hate it when I have to go see him."

Calvin didn't really know what to say. He believed so strongly that the preacher had to know what was right and what was wrong.

Exasperated and resentful, Steve blurted out, "You must enjoy it! But I don't!"

"It's not that I enjoy it, but when I feel the urge, I have to do something about it. I don't want to commit a sin by doing it by myself."

"Let's don't talk about it anymore. OK?" Steve brushed it off and began walking faster.

Calvin caught up with him. "I want you and me both to go to heaven."

Steve didn't say anything, as he picked up the pace.

Calvin caught up with him in an attempt to change the subject, but nothing came to mind. He then blurted out, "Do you ever see Josephine?"

Steve ignored him and hastened along.

Before going into his house, Calvin broke the silence. "I've got a biology final tomorrow. I need to study for a while, and then I'll come over later. OK?"

It was not like Steve to completely ignore him, but he kept moving along and never acknowledged Calvin's comment.

Calvin ran up the steps to the front porch and turned to watch Steve as he continued walking. When he rounded the corner to go to his house, Calvin walked in and found a platter of cookies his mom had made before she went to work. He ate two or three – peanut butter, his favorite, then drank a glass of milk, a custom he'd been doing for years. He found a paper sack and stuffed three or four cookies inside to take to Steve later on.

Biology was not Calvin's favorite subject, but he'd managed to have a passing grade. He went to his room, crawled in the bed, opened his book and read the first sentence of his notes: "Biology is learning about the interactions and functions of living organisms." That statement seemed so lame compared to the concerns he had for his friend. But he continued reading while struggling to keep from going to sleep. He lost the battle, however, and dozed off. When he woke, he sat up in bed, not knowing how long he'd been asleep. He couldn't stop thinking about what Steve had said, so he decided to take the cookies over and come back later to study for his exam.

He casually walked into Steve's front yard. Thunder was standing on his hind legs pawing at the front door. "What's wrong, Thunder? They lock you out of the house?" He handed him a cookie. Thunder lapped it up, then again started clawing on the side of the porch next to the front door. Calvin gave a couple of taps on the door like he always does, then opened it. Thunder rushed in between his legs and scampered back to Steve's room. "Steve!" Calvin called out. "Hey, Steve, where are you?"

Knowing his mother would probably be in her room sewing on some dresses, he exclaimed, "Mrs. Russell! Mrs. Russell, are you here?" It seemed strange that she wouldn't be there, but, then again, on occasions she had to drive to the grocery or the fabric store.

He ambled back to Steve's room, expecting him to be asleep. He didn't want to wake him, but Thunder was barking, so it'd be hard for him to sleep through that. He gently opened the door to his room then screamed a piercing cry at the top of his voice, "STEVE!" he yelled. "STEVE! OH GOD! STEVE! STEVE! OH MY GOD!"

Steve's body was hanging by a rope tied around his neck from the beam where they used to swing as kids. Thunder was jumping up trying to grab Steve's pants leg to pull him down. In a mad panic, Calvin ran to the kitchen, took a butcher knife, rushed back into Steve's room, grabbed a chair to stand on and frantically cut the rope. Steve's lifeless body dropped to the floor with a thud.

Calvin cried out, "OH NO, STEVE!" Thunder began whining and licking Steve's unconscious face.

Calvin ran out the front door like a madman, not knowing what to do or which way to turn. He stopped the first car that passed by and told them what'd happened. The man driving instructed him to go back in the house, phone the police and then call the hospital to send an ambulance.

The tears gushing down his face made it hard for Calvin to see. He couldn't find a phone directory, so he dialed zero. The operator answered, and he told her to call the police and send them to the Russell house at 1004 Ross Road. Like a zombie, he stumbled down the hallway back to Steve's room. He kneeled beside him and hugged his body. Thunder looked up at Calvin and whined, pleading to explain to him what'd happened to his best friend.

Shortly, two police cars arrived. Three officers rushed into the house. An ambulance pulled into the driveway, retrieved the body, placed it on a stretcher and put it in the back of the ambulance. Thunder ran behind them, trying to leap up on the vehicle. They pushed him back and took off with blue lights flashing.

One of the policemen turned toward Calvin, "We're going to have to take you down to the station to get a statement about what happened."

Still stunned, Calvin got into the backseat. The driver pulled away, leaving the other two officers at the house to inspect the premises. Calvin turned to gaze out the back window and caught a glimpse of Mrs. Russell driving up. He saw her jump out of the car and rush into the house. He could only imagine what would happen when they told her about her only child.

When the policeman interrogated Calvin at headquarters, he told them that Steve had been depressed but didn't mention what the cause of the depression might be. When asked, he shook his head, "I don't know."

After being thoroughly questioned, one of them drove Calvin back home. He ran into the house, where his mother had begun cooking supper. Still in shock and with tears flowing down his face, he told her what'd happened, then ran to his room and locked the door behind him. He got in his bed, put his face in the pillow and wept uncontrollably. Vivian stood outside his door, listening to him sobbing. She had the urge to go in and hug him, but, with better judgment, she knew he needed to be alone.

Not too long afterwards, Joe stumbled into the front door, obviously drunk.

Seeing Vivian cooking in the kitchen, he yelled out at her, "Where's that damn, sorry son of yours?"

She stared at him with hatred in her eyes.

He shouted back at her, "Don't you look at me like that, you bitch!"

"Are you aware of what happened?" she yelled.

"Yeah, I know what happened," was his surly response. "And I want you to go get him right now! We've got some talking to do."

"He's upset, Joe. Can't you at least give him a little time to grieve?"

With this remark, he hit her hard enough to knock her to the floor. When she screamed, Calvin came running out of his room, red-eyed and with a wet face.

"Leave him alone, Joe!" She screamed from the floor.

He then kicked her on her side and yelled, "Shut up!"

When Calvin ran toward him, Joe clobbered him on the side of his face, knocking him to the floor.

"Get your queer ass up, you sorry bastard!"

"What are you talking about?" Calvin shouted.

"You know what I'm talking about!" He snarled at the two of them lying on the floor. "Preacher Mitchell came to the mill to tell me and Steve's old man what'd happened."

"And what?" Vivian snapped.

"We were both pretty broke up about Steve killing himself until we found out our two sons have been queering each other!"

Vivian tried to stand up. "What are you talking about?"

"He told us our sons were queers."

Calvin yelled, "That's a lie. It's not true."

"Are you calling the preacher a liar? Bastard! Get your ass up!" He shouted. "Go get your clothes. I want you out of this house right now. I'm not living in a house with a damn queer."

"Joe, let the boy explain," Vivian cried out.

"It's your damn fault, bitch. You always babied him. And anyway, you're the one with queers in the family – not me!"

he screamed.

"What are you talking about?"

"You know that sissy-ass uncle of yours? He had to be queer."

"He was not! He was married!" she shouted back.

"I want that son of yours out of my house, and I don't ever want to see him again as long as I live!"

Calvin got up, slowly trudged toward his room then turned toward his father. "I want you to know, and I'm telling you the truth, that me and Steve were not queering each other. If you want me to swear on the Bible, I will."

No words were spoken, so Calvin went to his room and sat on the bed for a few moments to get his wits about him, then began filling a laundry bag with clothes. He walked hesitantly out the front door, listening to his mother blubbering as if her heart would break and pleading with Joe to go and get him to come back. As Calvin crossed the street, Joe opened the front door and yelled, "Good riddance, you damn queer! Don't you ever come back to this house again!"

The sun had dipped below the horizon, as he carried his bag of clothes under his arm. Blindsided, he moped along toward Selden Park all the way to the edge of the marsh, collapsed on the ground then leaned back against the bag of clothes. As if he were in another world, he stared at the last glimmer of daylight and watched it fade away. When his day began that morning, he had no remote idea it would end like this.

He had no tears left in his body, so he lay on the grass resting his head on the soft bag. He studied the last glimmer of clouds in the sky, searching for some meaning to the events of the day. Dwelling on the awful tragedy of Steve, his father's ultimatum and how he would spend his future life kept him awake, not to mention the mosquitos that wouldn't leave him alone.

After a miserable night, the sun brought him out of a stupor. He walked over to the outdoor restroom in the park, washed his face in cold water and decided to go to Reynolds Elementary and wait for his mother to come to work.

Tom Dennard

After an hour or so, he saw her walking down the sidewalk, a welcomed sight. He ran to meet her, and they embraced for a long time.

"I've been awake all night," she cried in his ear.

"Me too," he sighed.

"What are you going to do?" She put her arms around him again.

"I don't know."

"I want so bad to give you some money, but I don't know how. I have to account to him for every penny I spend."

"Mama, how can you keep living with him?"

She shook her head. "I can't leave him. It would be wrong – a sin. I took a vow to stay with him until death do us part," she lamented.

Calvin looked down helplessly.

"He told me I'm not allowed to see you," she said.

Calvin gave a blank stare.

"I don't care what he says, he can't keep me away from you, even if he has to kill me. You're my only child, the only person I have in the whole world. I promise I'll see you no matter where you might be."

They hugged for a long time.

"I can't be late for work," she said. "They don't like that."

"OK," Calvin understood.

"Meet me back here today after work," she said. As she walked away then turned back, "Your father forbids you from going to Steve's funeral." She hurried into the cafeteria, not waiting for a response.

"Where do I go? What do I do?" These questions ricocheted through his mind. He wondered whether or not to go to school, but being totally unprepared to take the biology exam, he knew that would be useless. With no plans in mind, he began walking downtown as a homeless person. He wandered down Union Street to Mansfield, where Glynn Academy was located. The First Baptist Church sat on the corner of the two streets.

A man out front, wearing shorts and a T-shirt, spoke to him in a friendly voice. Calvin nodded.

The man could obviously detect from his demeanor that something was wrong. "Are you OK?" He seemed sincere.

"Uh-huh," Calvin mumbled.

"Do you need help?"

"I'm OK," not wanting to lay out his predicament to a stranger.

"Do you need money?"

Calvin hesitated, dropped his head and didn't respond.

The man walked over to him, reached in his pocket and pulled out a twenty-dollar bill. "Here, take this."

Calvin felt bad about taking it, but he'd been feeling pangs of hunger all morning. He stared at the stranger, reached his hand out and took the money. "Thank you sir. I appreciate it."

Calvin hiked a few blocks toward Cody's Restaurant and ordered a big breakfast of scrambled eggs, sausage patties, grits and toast. He'd never acquired a taste for coffee and always drank milk or orange juice instead.

The next two and a half years proved to be a life-changing experience. His mother had found him a job at the Downtown Pharmacy, delivering prescriptions for Mr. Bunkley, the owner. The pharmacy, located on Newcastle Street, used the ground floor of the two-story Dunwoody Building underneath the law office of Greene and Parker that occupied the second floor.

Calvin didn't own a car, but Mr. Bunkley took him under his wing, taught him how to drive and let him use his car for deliveries. Calvin had located a place to live at Herring's Boarding House on Ellis Street next to the courthouse, just a couple of blocks away from the pharmacy.

He never went back home, as his father had ordered, and he never again attended Preacher Mitchell's church. He did, however, walk the few blocks on Sunday mornings to the First Baptist Church, where the man had given him the money and only missed if he didn't feel well. He'd had to drop out of school, which upset him, but he had no choice. He knew he had to make it on his own. Almost every day his mother walked from Reynolds Elementary to the pharmacy to check on him to make sure he was all right.

She'd noticed he still had a sadness about him that he couldn't shake. It had lingered ever since that fateful day. He didn't laugh or smile. With Steve gone, he'd never reached out to meet new friends. Every day except Sunday he worked tirelessly helping around the pharmacy and seeming to have no interest in outside activities. He spent most of his leisure time watching TV in the living room of the boarding house, sometimes went to a movie at the Ritz Theater, and occasionally walked to Palmetto Cemetery to visit Steve's grave.

His condition worried his mother so much that she finally talked him into going with her to the health department to have a doctor check him out. After talking with Calvin for a long time and examining him thoroughly, his diagnosis revealed severe depression. He recommended that he see a psychiatrist in Jacksonville.

"He's the best one for you to see." He wrote his name on the back of a card, "Dr. Aaron Berkowicz, 1648 San Marco Blvd, phone number 904-388-2623."

"But how much does something like that cost?" Vivian asked.

"Fifty dollars an hour," the doctor replied.

"Oh, my goodness! I don't have that kind of money."

"Let me call him and talk to him. Maybe something can be worked out as far as payment is concerned. I'll make the appointment, and Calvin, I'll call the pharmacy tomorrow to let you know what day and what time."

Calvin seemed somewhat frightened by the idea of going to a psychiatrist. He thought only crazy people went to doctors like them. He didn't think of himself as a looney tune, but, then again, maybe he was.

He'd been wanting to find some kind of transportation that he could afford, but with a salary of fifty dollars a week, it didn't seem likely. So, he set out to find a second job. Luckily, he found one as a night clerk at the Holiday Inn at the intersection of Gloucester Street and Highway 17 that would double his income. As a perk for being night clerk, he was given a room in the motel for free. That would save even more money, since he could move out of the boarding house.

Carl, an older guy in his seventies, who lived next door to Calvin at the boarding house, had a car and offered to drive him to several used-car lots around town. After a couple of hours of searching, he found an old '57 Ford Fairlane with high mileage. They were asking $750 and were willing to finance it for him at twelve percent interest for three years. His monthly payments would be $24.91, a figure he felt he could afford. He signed the loan papers, but the car had some transmission problems. They agreed to fix it and have it ready for him in a few days.

The day came for Calvin to visit the psychiatrist in Jacksonville. Since his means of transportation wouldn't be ready for a few more days, Calvin boarded a southbound Greyhound Bus in Brunswick at 6:25 a.m. His appointment was at noon, and the trip only took about an hour and a half. He had to walk over a mile from the Jacksonville Bus Station along the busy, downtown streets to the doctor's office on San Marco Blvd. He seemed a little shaky, not knowing what to expect from a psychiatrist. He arrived at the doctor's office before eleven with over an hour to kill. He'd taken enough money to get some food and something to drink, but no way could he eat. Maybe a Coke would help settle that gurgling feeling.

He entered the office about a quarter of twelve. It appeared to have a homey atmosphere – a nice soft couch, two stuffed chairs, a floor lamp and a smattering of pictures of landscapes on the wall. Magazines filled the entire surface of the coffee table including Better Homes and Gardens, Reader's Digest, National Geographic, Good Housekeeping, Ladies' Home Journal, Time, Cosmopolitan and others. After a few moments of thumbing through the pictures in National Geographic, the opening of a door startled him. He expected someone who looked like Einstein but this man was nice-looking, fairly tall, dark hair with graying sideburns and a friendly smile.

"Hello, I'm Doctor Berkowicz. I suppose you're Calvin."

"Yes sir," he answered nervously.

They shook hands.

"Come on back to my office."

Calvin's knees were shaking as the doctor directed him to a cozy-looking stuffed chair that leaned back at a 45-degree angle. It seemed so comfortable when he sat down, he imagined it would be a great place to take a nap. The doctor sat beside him in a straight chair so that their faces were no more than three feet apart.

"I want you to be relaxed," the doctor smiled.

"Yes sir."

"Let me start by asking you not to say 'yes sir' and 'no sir,' because that makes us too separated from each other. I appreciate the respect, but just say 'yes' or 'no,' OK?

"Yes sir," Calvin stuttered. "I mean yes."

The doctor smiled.

He couldn't help but admire the doctor's teeth. They were so white and even. He wore a pair of khakis and a yellow shirt that portrayed a more casual appearance. This lack of formality helped Calvin to relax.

After they both took their seats, the doctor said, "OK. Tell me about yourself."

Calvin had practiced what he was going to say on the bus ride, so he reeled it off about his growing-up years and how his mother and father didn't have much money. That his father drank too much because he'd been injured in World War II. That he and Steve were best friends. Then with a bit more hesitation told about what happened to Steve, and he felt that Steve's suicide might be the cause of his depression. And that his father got mad with him and kicked him out of the house before he finished his junior year of high school.

"Why do you think Steve did that to himself?"

Calvin stuttered. "I-I don't know." He stared toward the floor.

"Are you sure you don't know?"

Calvin hesitated before answering then blurted out, "Yes, I'm sure."

"What if I told you I think you do know?"

That comment caught Calvin completely off guard. He'd never had anyone question his answers like that. His hesitation to speak or to respond was a dead give-away.

"How old are you, Calvin."

"I'm 20."

"How old were you when Steve did this awful thing to himself?"

Calvin squirmed in his seat, then answered. "We were just finishing our junior year of high school – 17 almost 18."

"So that was a couple of years ago, right?"

"Yes."

"Just how close were you and Steve?"

Calvin took a few moments before responding. "What do you mean?"

"How long had you known him?"

"Since before we started to school. We used to play together. He lived only a few houses away from mine."

"How intimate were you with each other?"

Calvin stammered again. "I-I don't know what you mean."

"Just how much did you care for him?"

That threw Calvin for a loop. He'd never thought about it. He remained speechless for a few moments. "I've never told any person I cared for them except my mama."

"But you could've still had a close feeling about Steve without telling him, right?"

"I don't know. I never really thought about it."

"But he was your closest friend. Is that right?"

"Yes," Calvin said. "I guess he was the only friend I ever had."

"You never had any kind of sexual relation with him?"

"No. Never." Calvin said emphatically.

"Are you uncomfortable discussing sexual things with me?"

Calvin waited a few moments before responding, then snapped back. "It's hard for me to talk about things like that. It's too personal."

"You've got to talk about things that are very personal or else I can't do you any good. You've got to open up and talk to me. Tell me your innermost thoughts. Do you understand?"

Calvin nodded his head.

The doctor realized he'd hit upon a sore subject that Calvin didn't want to talk about.

Calvin never expected to discuss anything like that, especially with a stranger. This was a subject that was totally off limits.

"So," the doctor pressed on. "Have you ever had sex with another person?"

With this question, Calvin clammed up completely.

"Are you going to answer me or not?" he insisted. "Calvin, if you want me to help you, you've got to be honest with me in order for me to find out what's causing your depression."

"But I don't know how to answer it," Calvin said. "I know it's wrong"

The doctor leaned back in his chair. "Who told you it was wrong?"

Calvin hesitated for a few moments. He'd not planned to tell the doctor or anyone else about Preacher Mitchell.

"Are you going to tell me?" the doctor insisted.

"OK," Calvin said, as if he'd been pushed into a corner. "It was the preacher of my church where I went when I was growing up."

"OK. And what did he say?"

Calvin waited for a moment before speaking then admitted, "He said it was a sin to have sex with anyone before you get married."

"And does that mean you can't have sex with yourself?" the doctor questioned.

Calvin remained silent.

"Did Steve go to the same church with you?"

"Yes, his family and my family went to the same church ever since we were little boys."

"So, are you telling me that you are now 20 years old and you've never had sex with another person?"

Calvin nodded, "That's right."

The doctor sat up forward in his chair. "Do you pleasure yourself?"

Calvin hesitated, then admitted, "Sometimes. But that just started after I left home."

"Well, what happened before you left home? You were almost 18 at the time, right?"

Calvin clammed up again. He could sense he was getting boxed in.

"I'm asking you, what did you do for sexual relief before you left home?"

Calvin refused to answer.

After a few moments of silence, the doctor asked, "Did the preacher have anything to do with this?"

Calvin tightened up even more and remained silent and stone-faced.

The doctor raised his voice. "Did the preacher sexually molest you, Calvin?"

Calvin looked out the window for a few moments, as if he didn't hear the question.

"Answer me, Calvin," he demanded. "Did he sexually molest you?"

He shook his head and mumbled, "No."

"Look straight into my eyes, Calvin."

Instead, he ducked his head, because he couldn't bring himself to look at the doctor.

"Please look into my eyes," he insisted.

Calvin faintly raised his head and sheepishly gazed into his eyes.

With a raised voice, the doctor said, "Did he sexually molest you?"

Calvin kept shaking his head, not wanting to answer.

"Please answer me, Calvin."

But he kept shaking his head without responding.

"If you're not going to answer the question, I need to stop this session."

Calvin dropped his head, then stared into the doctor's eyes. With tears streaming down his face, he mumbled, "Yes sir."

The doctor then wheeled around, "And that's the reason Steve killed himself, isn't it?"

At this, the dam broke. Calvin doubled over and began sobbing as if his heart would break forth from his chest. His slender, willowy frame shook all over. Old wounds had been pried open and allowed to drain. Each tear that fell into the lap of his jeans told a story of pain.

The doctor remained quiet and allowed him to have his cry. Then after a few moments, he said in a soothing voice, "Calvin, I know this has hurt you greatly."

He handed him a box of tissues to wipe his eyes and face and waited for a few moments for him to calm down enough to continue talking.

"Would you like some water?" the doctor asked.

"Yes sir," he whimpered.

The doctor went over to a sink in the corner of his office and brought back a large glass of water. Calvin turned it up and drank most of it.

"Thanks," he said.

"Sure. Now, Calvin, I know you don't like to talk about it, but we need to continue pursuing the sexual issue. I believe this is the source of your problem."

Feeling somewhat defeated, Calvin surrendered, "OK."

The doctor pulled his chair up closer and crossed his

legs. "When you pleasure yourself, do you look at pictures or do you fantasize about another person?"

Calvin paused before speaking. "You know, this is really hard for me to talk about."

"You do understand that I'm not allowed to tell anyone what you say to me."

"I can't believe I'm telling you this, but I do think of someone." Again, he stalled, then revealed his secret, "Larry Daniel."

"Who is he?"

"He works at Penny's across the street from the pharmacy. He's a senior at Glynn Academy, and only comes in after school and on Saturdays."

"Have you ever..."

Calvin stopped him immediately. "No. We've never even met each other."

"What does he look like?"

"He plays football. He's strong. Really good-looking. He has a girlfriend, I think."

"How often do you see him?"

"Almost every day, I guess."

"Do you ever dream about him?"

"Sometimes," he shrugged.

The doctor then switched gears, "Are you sexually attracted to girls?"

Without hesitation, he said, "No."

'Why not?"

"It just doesn't seem like the thing you should do to a girl."

"Why do you say that?" The doctor seemed puzzled.

"Mama told me that sex is very dirty and nasty and sinful, and I wouldn't want to do that to a girl unless we're married."

"I see," the doctor shook his head.

In despair, Calvin pleaded, "Please help me. I'm tired of hating myself. I want you to change me and make me into a normal person."

"I'm afraid there's nothing I can do to change you, Calvin. My job is to help you accept yourself for who you are. Society may not agree with me, but it's not a sin or a bad thing to be the person you are. God made you, and God doesn't make mistakes."

"I don't care about me," he uttered. "I want to be normal for my mama. She wants to have grandchildren. She always talks to me about that. Her life is so miserable with my daddy, she needs something in her life to make her happy."

"I understand," he continued on with his questioning. "Do you drink alcohol?"

"Not really. But one of the older men who lived in the boarding house where I lived used to give me a beer every once in a while. And the man I work with at the pharmacy gave me a glass of wine one time when we were closing down the shop."

"And what did you think?"

"I don't know. It tasted sweet. But I need to stop drinking, cause it makes me do things I shouldn't."

"Like what?"

"I can't believe I'm telling you this, but one night the old man at the boarding house sold me a six pack of beer. I drank three of them, then I went outside and started thinking of Larry. I knew where he lived, and it was only about a half-mile away. So, I walked there and stood out in front of his house. I'd carried a beer in my pocket, so I drank it all to get up the nerve to go up and look in the window. I could see him and his sister sitting on the sofa watching TV. He had on a tight pair of jeans and his football jersey. He didn't have any shoes on and his feet were propped up on a stool. It made me want to be with him and touch him," he paused.

"And then what?"

"I don't want to tell you."

"You masturbated?"

"Yes," he said dropping his head in shame.

"What happened after that?"

"I left and went back to the boarding house feeling so guilty. I thought if anyone had seen me, they probably would've killed me. And maybe that would be a good thing."

"Why do you say that?"

"That's the reason I shouldn't drink. It makes me do things I wouldn't do normally."

"Do you feel comfortable talking with me?"

"Yes sir. I do."

"Do your parents know you're gay?"

Calvin looked at him with a curious expression.

"Do you know what I mean?" The doctor asked.

"No sir."

"Oh, I'm sorry. The word "gay" has been popular in the world of homosexuality for a good while and is now beginning to creep out into the outside world."

"No, I've never heard that," Calvin admitted.

"And you've never had any type of sex with another person?"

"The preacher was the only one having sex with us, because he said that would be the only way for us to get sexual relief without committing a sin."

The doctor, shaking his head at that comment, looked down at his watch. "I'm going to have to terminate our session now. We've gone way past the hour allotted. It's almost 1:30."

Calvin apologized. "I'm sorry."

"No, it's not your fault. We need to have another session. I believe I can work with you and help you to understand yourself. Don't feel like you're a bad person. You're not. You're very special. You've had some pretty traumatic events in your life – enough to shake you to the core."

The doctor stood up and Calvin followed, getting out of the most comfortable chair he'd ever sat in. He brushed himself off, reached in his pocket and pulled out two twenties and a ten. "They told me 50 dollars. Is that right?"

"Sure, that's fine. I'll throw in the last half hour," he

laughed.

Calvin reached out to shake the doctor's hand. "Thank you very much." He turned to walk out the door.

"Calvin," the doctor called out. "I feel we really should have a few more sessions. You have some issues we need to work on."

"That'd be fine, but I don't have the money."

"I understand," the doctor conceded. "If money is a factor, I can continue to see you, and we can work out a payment plan that would be suitable to you."

Calvin shrugged his shoulders. "But I don't know when I'd ever be able to pay you."

"Don't worry about it. Let that be my problem," the doctor smiled.

"Well, if you say so," Calvin conceded. "When would you want me to come back?"

"How about every other Thursday at this same time."

Calvin agreed, and the sessions did continue on a regular two week basis. After five additional sessions, Dr. Berkowitz told Calvin, "I can see real progress. You've really come around a great deal in accepting yourself for the person you are and have gained a lot of confidence. I think we're ready to suspend our regular sessions and see how it goes. Maybe you might want to come back every other month just for a checkup."

"Sure. That would be fine," Calvin agreed. He shook the doctor's hand and turned to walk out the door. When he opened it, a man was standing in the waiting room.

"Paul," the doctor called out. "Did you not get my message?"

"No," he said. "I didn't go back to my office after my first class."

"I'm sorry," the doctor said. "I had a conflict come up, and I'm not going to be able to make lunch."

"Well," Paul kidded. "I've been spurned my entire life. By the way, do you treat people who have rejection problems?"

They both laughed. Then the doctor turned toward

Calvin, "Paul, this is Calvin Livingston," then turning toward Calvin, "This is Paul Cohen." They shook hands. The doctor then explained to Calvin that Paul is a good friend who is a professor of English Literature at the University of North Florida. He turned back to Paul, "Calvin is from Brunswick, Georgia."

"Oh, really," Paul said. "I have cousins who live in Brunswick – the Brownsteins. But I don't guess you'd know them. They're pretty old."

Calvin shook his head and smiled.

"Well, Calvin," he paused. "Perhaps you'd be my lunch guest today."

"Thank you. I appreciate it, but I was going to pick up a sandwich before I catch the bus back home."

"What time does it leave?"

"3:25," Calvin said.

"You've got plenty of time. I hope you'll go. I can't stand two rejections in one day," he laughed.

Calvin, somewhat caught off guard, said, "Sure. That'd be fine."

They shook hands with the doctor and walked out to Paul's car – a yellow Chevy Camaro convertible that appeared to be brand new.

"You got a nice car," Calvin commented.

"Thanks. I've only had it a few months. It's a fun car to drive."

Paul appeared to be in his early forties, had brown, curly hair and wore a pale blue V-neck sweater and a tweed jacket.

They drove downtown and parked in a garage next to a twelve-story bank building on Forsyth Street. The elevator let them off on the top floor. When the doors opened, Calvin was shocked to step inside an elegantly decorated foyer where a good-looking young man dressed in a navy blue suit and yellow tie greeted them. Calvin had never seen any place that fancy other than in a movie or a magazine.

The man who was about Calvin's age said, "Welcome to Magnolia's."

He then made a remark that took Calvin aback. "Who's the cutie you got there with you, Paul?" He turned toward Calvin and said, "Billy, this is Calvin. Calvin, this is Billy." They shook hands, and Billy escorted them to a table in the corner. As they sat down, Billy said to Calvin, "You've never been here before, have you?"

Calvin shook his head. "No," he said nervously. As he looked around, the patrons and even the workers were all males. He stared at Paul with the most tension he'd felt all day. He didn't know what to say, except "This is a nice place."

"It's the best food in town," Paul smiled, as he placed the white linen napkin in his lap.

Calvin, not knowing anything about table manners, followed suit.

The décor in the restaurant seemed like a jungle, with hanging baskets of ferns and huge pots of palmetto palms. A man wearing a white coat played easy-listening music on a Steinway grand piano.

Calvin, overwhelmed by such grandeur, tried to make conversation. "I like what he's playing." He was not accustomed to listening to music like that. His favorite tended to be the rock and pop music of the day.

"That's "The Man I Love" by Gershwin," Paul smiled and asked, "Are you familiar with his music?"

"No sir. I'm not."

"Well, Gershwin was a good Jewish boy like I am. He wrote music with his brother, Ira, in the twenties and thirties."

Calvin nodded as if he knew what he was talking about, but, of course, he didn't have a clue. The one thing he knew for sure was that he was totally out of his element and very ill at ease.

A tall, young waiter, dressed in a dark blue suit, red bow tie, and hair slicked back with gel, brought the wine list.

Paul looked toward Calvin. "Do you drink wine?"

"Just once with the man I work for," he shrugged.

"What did it taste like?"

"It was kinda sweet."

Paul smiled. "I rather like French Wines myself. I prefer reds." He looked up at the waiter. "Do you still have the Chateau Coutet?"

The waiter nodded. "Of course, we try to always keep it on hand for you."

"Thank you. Just a glass please, and my friend here would like a bit of something like," he paused then uttered in a very distinguished tone, "Oh, I know. How about the Chateau Sigalas-Rabaud?" He turned to Calvin. "It's a nice Sauterne. I think it's something you'll like."

"Sure," Calvin smiled. "Whatever you say."

The waiter brought the two glasses of wine, and they both took a sip.

Paul looked at Calvin, "What do you think?"

"It's good," he said politely, although he had his doubts whether or not he'd be able to finish the entire glass.

"I'm glad you like it." Paul leaned back in his chair, brushed the right side of his hair with his hand and looked into Calvin's eyes. "Do you mind if I ask if you're gay?"

Startled by the question, Calvin merely shrugged his shoulders without answering.

"You know," Paul said, "Once upon a time I was twenty, and I remember very well how my sexual desire was hard to control. It was a force to be reckoned with, and I found out that sex can also become very addictive."

Calvin, uncomfortable talking about things like that with a stranger, especially in a public place, nodded his head, not knowing what to say.

Paul finished his glass of wine and motioned to the waiter to bring another. "Will you do me a favor, Calvin?"

"Sure. What?"

"Turn all the way around in your chair and look at every person in this room."

Calvin seemed puzzled, but did as he'd been told.

"I don't know this for a certainty, but chances are that

every single person in this room has been curious about his sexuality. You may think that everyone else is normal, but I'm here to tell you that they're definitely not. What these fellows have done is made the necessary compromises in order to live their lives in a socially acceptable manner," Paul paused to take a sip of wine the waiter had just placed in front of him. "And what is normal? Is anyone normal? A lot of these guys are professionals who do good work for their clients, but they are different in their sexual preference. It's a condition that's frowned upon by our society." He took another sip. "This probably is an oversimplification but if we would put sexual preference on a scale of 100, some people would be 90% heterosexual and 10% homosexual, or 80 – 20, or 70 – 30, or whatever. No two people are the same. But there's no such thing as anyone being 100% heterosexual and 0% homosexual or vice-versa. Things can't be all black or all white, they are only different shades of gray. So, people you look at as being what you might call normal are a great deal more complex than you may think. But a word of caution – those guys, who are partly homosexual and try to suppress it, can be dangerous. They hate the homosexuality in themselves and therefore hate the homosexuality in others. As they say, the things you hate most in others are the things you hate most about yourself. They're called homophobic, and they can hurt you."

Calvin seemed uncomfortable with Paul's words.

"It's true. People are very complicated. We all put up a front and let others only see the part of us we're willing to show. But there are worlds of things going on underneath the surface that even psychiatrists don't understand. It sometimes takes a lifetime for us to learn who we really are. And sometimes, a lifetime isn't enough. It's much more comfortable to let the socially acceptable side of ourselves be on display before the public. But, Calvin, I don't want to give you the impression that society will accept you as a homosexual, that is, if you are, because they definitely will not. They will mock you, sneer at you, laugh at you, make fun of you, hurt you, or even kill you. So, you must be careful."

Calvin nodded his head.

Paul continued. "One other thing. If you don't remember

anything else, don't forget this. It's the wounds in our lives that can make us stronger if we're able to overcome them. Some people take their wounds and overindulge in food, alcohol, drugs, work, cigarettes, even sex. But if you can overcome the pain and make peace with your wounds, then you can turn them into strengths."

The waiter came back for their food order.

"What would you like?" Paul asked.

Calvin hadn't even thought about it. "I don't know, just a hamburger, I guess."

"If it's what you want, that's fine." He looked up at the waiter. "How's your seafood quiche today?"

The waiter shrugged his shoulders.

"OK. I get the point. I think I'll have a Reuben, please."

Calvin's eyes had been partially opened to a new world outside the narrow confines of his past life. He wondered for the first time in his life about leaving Brunswick and perhaps moving to Jacksonville, so he could be around other people who felt the same way he did.

When they finished their lunch, Paul drove him to the bus station. He still had 30 minutes to spare before it was scheduled to leave.

As Calvin got out of the car, he thanked Paul profusely and shook his hand.

Paul then offered, "By the way, they're having a big party at Magnolia's next Thursday afternoon. It's Thanksgiving, you know. Why don't you come back down and be my guest?"

Calvin nodded and smiled nervously. He accepted the invitation in hopes he'd have his own car to drive by then. On the bus trip back to Brunswick, he replayed the sessions with the doctor and the experience he had with Paul at the restaurant. It seemed as if a veil was beginning to lift from his eyes.

Calvin had gotten accustomed to his new job at the Holiday Inn. In the beginning, staying up late at night took some adjustment, but the motel furnished a reclining chair where he could catch a few winks. Guests didn't normally come in asking for a room after midnight, so he got more sleep than he'd expected.

The day before Thanksgiving, Carl came by to tell him that he'd been notified by the salesman that his car was ready to be picked up. Calvin had difficulty controlling the excitement of owning his first car. After completing the purchase, he drove it around town, over to St. Simons Island and even over to Jekyll Island, as well. But he didn't want to be too extravagant, because, after all, gas cost 35 cents a gallon, and he had to watch his spending carefully.

As a gesture of goodwill, Mr. Bunkley, a friendly fellow, who'd done his best to help Calvin, gave him a little time off from work one afternoon to take his mother for a ride. They talked about many things, and while Calvin didn't reveal too much about his doctor's visits, he did tell her that he really liked him and that a friend of the doctor had taken him out to lunch. He also told her he was thinking about going back to Jacksonville Thanksgiving afternoon if the manager of the motel would let him off from work for a few hours. He felt he had a good relationship with the manager and seemed confident that it shouldn't be too much of a problem to take Thanksgiving night off.

Like all mothers, she lamented, "Be careful son. You know how much I worry about you."

"I'm feeling much better than I've felt in a long time. I'm not as depressed as I used to be," he said.

Mothers intuitively know their sons much better than sons ever suspect. In many relationships, the mythical umbilical cord is never quite severed. Mothers should be a safe harbor for their sons, and Vivian certainly provided that for Calvin. They laughed, reminisced and had heartfelt talks, something they weren't able to do at home with Joe around. Many boys, who are close to their mothers, tend not to buy into hyper-masculine stereotypes. They don't believe you have to always act tough, go it alone, or fight to prove your manhood. And perhaps that's what happened to Calvin.

When he woke on Thanksgiving morning, he was eager to get on with the day and drive his car to Jacksonville for the party at Magnolia's scheduled to begin at 6:00 p.m. He'd arranged to pick up his mother in front of the Reynolds Street

School at noon to have lunch with her since she had a holiday. They went to Crew's Restaurant on Highway 17, one of the best places to eat good southern food. They talked about many things, and then his mother brought up the subject of Joe. "I don't know what I'm going to do with him. He's meaner than he has ever been. He's so depressed. He has no pleasure in his life. He doesn't want to go anywhere or do anything. It's just pitiful."

Calvin shook his head. "I worry so much about you, Mama. I wish I knew what to do."

"There's nothing to do," she murmured. "Just pray for him."

Calvin nodded his head.

She then added. "If he knew I was having lunch with you, he'd kill me."

"Why don't you leave him?" he insisted.

"I told you, I can't do it. I can't go back on my vow to stay with him."

"I feel so sorry for you, Mama."

He drove to the Reynolds Street School, so she could walk home from there. She'd told Joe she'd be away for a while to visit a sick friend, who'd just gotten out of the hospital.

Calvin leaned over and kissed her on the cheek. "I love you, Mama."

"You have no idea how much I love you, Calvin. You're all I got in the whole world."

After a brief moment of silence, she said, "Can you tell me what you and the psychiatrist are working on?"

He paused to collect his thoughts. "I like him. He makes me look at myself in a good way."

"Calvin, look at me," he turned toward her. "You are different, aren't you?"

"What do you mean?"

"You're not like other boys who like girls."

"Mama, the doctor made me feel like it's OK to be

different."

"Please let me hold both of your hands and let's pray," she pleaded.

They held hands. She squeezed his tightly, and said, "Oh, God. Please watch over my son. I beg you to please change him and make him like other boys. I pray, don't let him be different," she paused for a moment. "Dear God, let him be normal. Let him find a nice girl and get married and have some children. Please, Dear God, I beg you." She began to cry.

"Mama, please don't cry. I have to be who I am. That's how God made me. He wants me to be me. That's what the doctor told me."

"I'll keep praying for you as long as I'm able," she cried. "You know I will. I love you so much, Calvin."

"I love you, too, Mama."

Later that afternoon, Calvin dressed in his nicest clothes. He drove his car south on Highway 17 and into downtown Jacksonville, getting more excited by the minute. He took the elevator to the top floor and got off into the elaborate foyer that had impressed him so much. Billy, the same guy who'd greeted them before, was there. Billy remembered his face, but couldn't recall his name. "Hey, there," he said. "Welcome to Magnolia's Thanksgiving Party. Tell me your name again."

"Calvin."

"Oh yeah, that's right - Calvin," he repeated. "I sure would like to get to know you better."

Calvin smiled and swelled with pride to have his ego salved like that. He'd never been told that by anyone. Calvin walked in, a bit apprehensive, since he didn't know anyone and didn't see Paul. About 25 guys of all ages were standing around talking and holding drinks in their hands. He knew he couldn't buy a drink since he was under 21. He felt awkward and self-conscious until a young man walked up to him and introduced himself as Eric. They exchanged a brief conversation, then Eric offered to buy Calvin a drink. He couldn't remember the name of the wine Paul had gotten for him, so he said, "Just a beer will be fine."

Eric was strikingly good-looking, a well-built young man, probably mid-twenties, originally from St. Augustine, who worked at a sporting goods store. Eric had been hoping to find someone he liked well enough to live with him and help pay the rent.

A small combo of musicians took the stage and began playing some popular songs of the day. Calvin and Eric continued talking and getting better acquainted as they listened to Marvin Gaye's "Let's Get it On" and Elton John's "Crocodile Rock." "That's one of my favorite songs," Eric said. The band then sped up the tempo with "Bad, Bad Leroy Brown" by Jim Croce. Some of the others in the crowd began to dance.

When they played "You're So Vain," by Carly Simon, Eric asked him to dance. At first, Calvin felt awkward dancing with another male, but, as the doctor had told him, he needed to accept who he was. And it especially hit home when the doctor said, "God doesn't make mistakes." After "Me and Mrs. Jones," the band began playing Stevie Wonder's "You Are the Sunshine of my Life." That'd been one of Calvin's favorites for a long time, so they continued to dance. As Calvin danced, he could feel the tension and stress leaving his body.

He and Eric danced and laughed and drank more beer, and he had the best time he'd ever had in his life. When he saw the clock on the wall and realized it was after midnight, he remembered he had to be at work at the pharmacy at 9:00 the next morning. He hated to tell Eric he'd have to leave, because he really wanted to stay.

Eric seemed puzzled, "Aren't you having fun?"

"Yeah, I'm having a blast, but I have to be at work early in the morning."

"I was hoping I could persuade you to spend the night with me," Eric pleaded.

"I'd like that, but I can't tonight. Maybe next time."

Eric walked over to the bar and came back with a brown sack and handed it to Calvin.

"What's this?"

"A little gift from me. It's my favorite wine, a chenin blanc. It's light and a little on the sweet side, but not too much. I think you'll like it."

"Thanks, Eric," Calvin smiled as he took the wine and started walking toward the exit.

Eric followed him. "Here, you forgot something."

Calvin turned around with a questioning glance.

Eric handed him a card. "My phone number."

"Oh yeah. Thanks. I'll call you. I'd like to see you again."

Disappointed he hadn't seen Paul, Calvin walked through the foyer and onto the elevator in a daze. A whole new world had just been opened to him.

When he drove out of the parking lot, he became aware that he felt a little buzz, but not so much he couldn't drive. He turned north on Main Street and began planning his future. He thought maybe he could find a job in Jacksonville that paid enough to afford a room in a boarding house or maybe even a small one-bedroom apartment. He could visit his mama in Brunswick when he wasn't working. There seemed to be plenty of guys like Eric he could meet and make some friends who were like him. His future appeared bright, a sensation he'd never felt.

A dense fog had begun to roll in as he drove out of the city north along Highway 17. He slowed, knowing that he'd been drinking and, with the fog, it would make driving a little more dangerous. He said to himself he wouldn't go over 50. As he carefully drove along, he suddenly glanced to his right and realized he'd just passed a figure that appeared to be a person standing beside the road. He slowed down and looked in his rearview mirror. It seemed to be someone holding a hand out, trying to catch a ride. He pulled the car off the road onto the shoulder and came to a stop. He turned around and through the fog, he could see the figure running toward him. At first, he felt a little uneasy, but, then again, he knew if he were out there trying to catch a ride, he'd want someone to stop for him. As the figure approached the car, Calvin reached over and unlocked the door. The door flung open, revealing a guy carrying a bag. He threw his bag over into the back and plopped down in the passenger seat.

Calvin stuck out his hand toward him. "Hi. I'm Calvin Livingston."

"Tommy Jennings," he nodded.

Tyler

Leaving the judge's office after the appointment, the drive back seemed like a long time. My mind kept wandering somewhere in another galaxy. I'd just been given a full-blown murder case with only a year and a half under my belt – downright scary! The DA screaming for the death penalty made matters even worse! Rumors had already begun circulating about the DA running against the judge in the next election, and the more criminals he could fry would make it look better on his résumé.

As I walked into my office, I noticed four people sitting in the waiting area. Bailey spoke up and said, "These folks are here to see you."

Since there were only two chairs in my office, I asked Bailey to direct them to the library. After she shut the door, I asked her what they wanted.

"I don't really know. Something to do with a criminal case."

"Oh yeah."

In the restroom, I doused my face with cold water, wiped it with a dry cloth then proceeded into the library.

"Hi, I'm Tyler Tucker. What can I do for you folks?"

One of the men stood up, extended his hand and said, "Wes Jennings. I'm a lawyer in Palatka, Florida. This is my wife Agnes. This is my brother, Jack Jennings, better known as Duck. And this is his friend, Bonnie Sue Atwater."

"It's a pleasure to meet y'all," I said, as I pulled a chair up to the table.

Agnes spoke up first. "You look so young. Are you going to be able to help my son get out of this?" She broke down and began to cry.

Bonds always kept tissues in her desk for such occasions, so I quickly grabbed them and handed the box to her. She thanked me and apologized.

"That's quite all right."

Wes spoke up. "I got a call about 4:00 o'clock this

morning from a detective here in Brunswick who said our son was in jail, and that he'd killed somebody. We all jumped in the car and drove directly to the jail, but they wouldn't let us see him, so we went over to the courthouse and waited for the judge to come in. He said he was going to appoint you to represent our son. I'm a lawyer myself. I used to practice in Douglas, but I let my Georgia license expire. I'd like to hire the best lawyer I can find, but the judge convinced us that he had full confidence in you to do a good job for our son."

"Please, Mr. Tucker, find out what happened," Agnes pleaded. "I'm so upset," she whimpered. "I just can't believe this has happened. He was supposed to be shipped off to Vietnam this coming Monday."

"Well, I can understand how upset you must be. I don't know anything about what happened. I just left the judge's office, and the only thing he told me was that a Marine was hitching from Florida and got picked up by a guy from Brunswick. Apparently, they went to where the Brunswick guy lived. They'd been drinking, and when the boy made a sexual advance, the Marine killed him."

"You mean my son killed the man who picked him up?" Agnes whimpered. "I told him not to hitchhike!"

"Just calm down," Wes said.

"Oh my God! I just can't believe this," Agnes began to cry again.

"I'm sure this is quite a shock to you, Mrs. Jennings, and I'll do what I can to find out more."

"Yes, we want you to find out what you can," Wes said. "We're staying out at the Oak Park Motel on Highway 17," he turned toward his brother. "Duck, didn't you get one of them cards?"

Duck reached in his pocket, felt around among coins, chewing gum, keys and what sounded like a bunch of other junk and came up with a wrinkled card. "Yeah, I got it. Give me your glasses, Wes. I can't see the damn numbers. OK. Here it is – 265-2475."

"That's fine," I said. "I have an 11:00 o'clock appointment. So, as soon as I finish, I'll find the detective who investigated the case. After I talk with him, I'll try to see your son at the jail, then I'll call you."

Agnes recovered enough to say, "Oh, please do. We'll be waiting by the phone for your call."

We all shook hands, as they started to leave.

Suddenly Bonnie Sue wheeled around and blurted out, "Are you married, honey?"

That caught me by surprise, but I responded. "I have a wife and three children."

"You know what you need?" She asked in her decidedly southern accent.

I wasn't sure where this was going, so I followed along with her, "No ma'am," I answered.

"What you need is some life insurance."

Later at the Jail

I ran into Bill Beckham, Brunswick's only detective, as he was leaving the jail. I told him I needed to talk to him, so he came back inside to the small conference room in the jail where those arrested are brought for questioning. I'd known Bill, a genuine good ol' boy, from other criminal cases I'd tried. He was easy going and usually investigated the more serious crimes.

We shook hands and exchanged a little small talk. "Looks like the judge gave you a real doozy with this one," he said.

"It seems that way," I groaned. "So, tell me what you know?"

"Well, let's see. The police officers arrested the Marine out on Highway 17. He'd stolen the boy's car."

"Really? So we got theft of a stolen vehicle, too?"

"Yep. When I talked to him, he was all shook up – still had his Marine uniform on. Told me he was hitching from his home in Florida back to Camp Lejeune in North Carolina. Some boy from Brunswick picked him up, and when they got into town, they went to his apartment or wherever it was he lived. They'd been drinking some beer and a bottle of wine. They were sitting next to each other on a sofa, and the Brunswick boy made a move on him. The Marine must've gone berserk – grabbed a lamp and smashed it over the boy's head then messed him up pretty bad. I think when he came to his senses and realized what he'd done, he took the boy's car keys and headed north on 17. That's when the police pulled him over for speeding. He confessed what he'd done. And that's about the size of it."

"What the hell! These guys were pretty young, weren't they?"

"I think the Marine is eighteen – believe the Brunswick boy is twenty."

"Who was the Brunswick boy?"

"Let me see," Bill picked up the report and began perusing it. "His name is Calvin Livingston. Says he worked at the Downtown Pharmacy and lived at the Holiday Inn on Gloucester."

"Yeah. I've seen that guy. You know that pharmacy is in the Dunwoody Building right underneath our law office. I go in there a good bit to fill prescriptions for my kids. I've seen him but never met him."

"Well, good luck," Bill snickered, as if he felt sorry for me.

"Yeah, I know what you mean," I said, feeling somewhat sorry for myself.

"We got a written confession," Bill added.

"Yeah. I guess that's going to be pretty hard to overcome."

"You do know, Old Dillinger will want to fry him. He's already telling everybody about wanting to run against Judge Fletcher next election."

"Yeah. I've heard."

"Even though the boy is guilty as hell, you can't plead him to a death penalty," Bill said. "That means you're gonna' have to try the case if you wanna keep him out of the chair."

We both stood up and stared at each other.

"Well, buddy," Bill said, "All I can say is, I wish you the best." He turned to sit down.

"Thanks, Bill. I'll need it."

"By the way," Bill added. "The medical examiner is going to do an autopsy this afternoon. You wanna be in on it?"

"Thanks, but no thanks. I think I'll pass on that one."

We shook hands, and I left the room to find a jailer who could take me up to Tommy's cell. I saw Old Jim, as he was called, who unlocked the door to the metal steps that led to the third floor, the location of the bullpen. He'd been working at the jail for ages, but never seem to tire of helping out the lawyers when visiting their clients.

The bullpen was where most of the prisoners were held in one large room. It housed about 15 or 20 men with a cot for each one. Every time I'd been up there in the past, the guys inside would always run up and grab the bars like caged monkeys. They'd yell, "Hey, lawyer, I need to talk to you!" No way could I, or anyone else, talk to all those guys. Nothing to do but ignore them. If one happened to be my client, I'd have to shoo the others away like they were a pack of dogs fighting over a bone.

Old Jim apologized, "Tyler, I completely forgot. They put your man on the second floor."

"With the women?"

"No, he has that cell down the hall by itself. You've been there before, ain't you?"

"No, I don't think I have."

After walking down one flight, Old Jim reminded me that women prisoners are kept two to a room. He escorted me past them along the hallway to a place set apart from the rest.

"I'm gonna' leave it with you. You know where to ring the bell next to the door to get you outta' here, don't you?"

"Oh yeah. Done it plenty of times."

As I approached, I could see a figure on a cot wearing a Marine uniform, curled up in the fetal position with his back turned.

"Hey," I yelled out.

There was no movement.

"Hey, buddy. I need you to wake up and talk to me."

Still no movement.

"Look, the court appointed me as your lawyer. I need to speak with you."

He still didn't move.

I was beginning to get a little exasperated. "Your mother and father and your uncle and his girlfriend are here in town. They're not allowed to see you, and they want to hear from you about what happened."

The Marine gradually began straightening his body and turned over on his back with his face toward me. It shocked me. Expecting to see a cold-blooded murderer, I saw a scared, nice-looking boy, who you might imagine singing in a youth choir at church.

185

"Is your name Tommy Jennings?"

Still silence.

"If you don't want to talk with me, then I need to go."

He mumbled something.

"I couldn't hear you. What did you say?"

There was a moment of silence, then he spoke up, "I want a Marine lawyer."

"That's fine with me. But I don't know how you go about getting one."

"Can you check?" he pleaded.

"Sure. I'll see if it's possible."

I still couldn't believe how young he looked. He seemed more like the kids I'd represented in juvenile court.

"You don't want to tell me how this all came about?"

"No. I want a Marine lawyer," he insisted.

"OK. I'll see what I can do."

It was almost time for my two o'clock appointment. My stomach was growling, but no time for lunch. At the office, I found Mrs. Norton waiting for me. I led her to my office and excused myself for a few minutes. "Bailey, could you see if you can get either Mr. or Mrs. Jennings on the phone."

She quickly handed me the phone. "They're anxious to hear from you."

Explaining to Mr. Jennings what'd happened, I asked him to contact the Judge Advocate General at Camp Lejeune to see if there was any possibility to provide a defense for Tommy.

"I doubt very seriously if they would do anything like that, but I'll call to find out," Wes said. "Is there any way they'd allow us to talk to Tommy?"

"I'm afraid not. But you could write him and I'll deliver it."

"I'll do that, and I'm sure my wife will want to write him, too."

No Place Like Home

On leaving the office, I stopped by the florist shop. The bell on the door jingled. No other customers could be seen; only Joseph, the somewhat effeminate owner, standing behind the counter making a flower arrangement. The fragrance always overwhelmed me when I entered his place. A middle-aged man in his fifties, he had the reputation for being the best florist in town. His arrangements were used at weddings, funerals and other special occasions with a flair that stood out from all his competitors.

"And how are you today, Tyler?"

"I'm fine, Joseph, but I'm in trouble again."

He laughed.

"What can I get my wife to get me out of the doghouse?" In the year and a-half I'd been with the firm, I'd found it necessary to stop by every so often. Joseph had become accustomed to my needs.

"Not again," he joked. "How bad is it? Is it roses bad or just carnations bad?"

"Ah, probably somewhere in between," I laughed.

"I have some lovely autumn chrysanthemums that should make her melt in your arms."

"If you say so, Joseph. You always steer me right."

As he busied himself wrapping the bright yellow flowers with green paper and a pretty, yellow ribbon, he said, "Tyler, I don't mean to pry into anything personal, but I heard you're representing the Marine who killed Calvin Livingston last night."

"Good gosh! Word spreads fast around this town."

"Yes, it does. Especially in our little community."

I knew exactly what he was referring to. "Did you know him?" I asked.

"Of course, I did," he shook his head. "Such a sweet boy."

"I didn't know him," I said. "But I'd seen him. You know

he worked in the pharmacy underneath our law office."

"Yes, I know."

"Well, actually, at this point, I don't know if I'm representing him or not. The judge assigned the case to me, but some things are going on that I can't discuss. You know, everything we do is confidential."

"I know. But I just feel so sorry for Calvin's mother. We go to the same church."

"I'm sorry, Joseph. At this point I don't really know very much about what happened."

"Calvin's funeral will be this Sunday – graveside at Palmetto."

"I'm really sorry, Joseph. You know if I'm appointed, I don't have a choice. I'm required to do my best to represent the Marine. The law guarantees every person the right to a fair trial."

"I understand that. But I heard he confessed. Doesn't that mean he's guilty?"

"Look, Joseph. I can't discuss any of this. How much do I owe you?"

"Just take them as a gift from our little community."

"I can't do that. I'm not allowed to take any gifts from anyone that has any connection to the trial. I could be disbarred."

"OK. Give me ten dollars," he conceded.

I handed him a ten, bid him goodbye and left. My mind became troubled that I might be hated for representing a confessed killer.

The little VW Beetle I'd owned since we married, got me home. When I opened the front door, Hannah, who'd recently celebrated her fourth birthday, ran to me and jumped into my arms. Wynn, my two-year-old, pulled at my leg. He wanted my other arm, but that one held the flowers. No thrill in the entire universe could equal that daily welcome from my kids. It's my crowning glory to have them jump into my arms. Little Miles seemed to be growing daily but still hadn't begun to crawl. He was a cute little fellow who definitely loved attention.

I didn't see Laura but heard the shower running in our bathroom. Was she still angry after our argument that morning? I put the kids down, quietly walked into the kitchen, took a vase from one of the cabinets and shoved the flowers into it. The vase needed water, about three-quarters full, and the tips of the stems cut, according to Joseph's instructions. While arranging the chrysanthemums, I heard Laura laughing behind me.

"When did you learn to arrange flowers?" She asked with a tinge of sarcasm.

"I'll have you know my mother taught me," I joked. "She was president of the garden club."

"That's funny. I've never seen you arrange flowers before."

"You have no idea about all my hidden talents."

She came over, grabbed me and planted a juicy kiss on my cheek. The expression on her face spoke a thousand words. I wheeled her toward me and kissed her on the lips for a long time. "You just made my day, honey. You know I love you."

"And I love you, too," she smiled.

"What can I do to help you?" I asked, realizing how much she's cooped up with the kids every day.

"The children have all been fed but if you want to get them to bed."

Standing next to the telephone, the ring startled me. I grabbed the receiver. "Hello."

"Tyler, sorry 'bout calling you at home. This is Wes Jennings, Tommy's old man."

"Oh, yes, Mr. Jennings."

"I wanted to let you know I talked to a number of different offices at Camp Lejeune, including the JAG office. They thanked me for letting them know the circumstances. But they said there's nothing they can do as far as providing a lawyer to defend Tommy. The lawyer has to be licensed in the state of Georgia, and they don't have anyone there who could do it."

"Oh, I see."

"They did say they could send an officer down to testify and tell the jury he'd been a model soldier. I thought you ought to know that."

"Yeah, that would be really good. Thanks for calling."

"So, Tyler," Wes said. "It looks like you got my son's case in your hands."

"Yes sir. I suppose it does."

"I want you to know we'll stop by your office tomorrow to drop off letters we wrote. Sure would appreciate you delivering them to Tommy."

"Of course. I'll be glad to do that."

"I hope you have a good evening. Sorry to disturb you at home."

"That's OK. No problem."

I turned toward Laura.

"What was that all about?" she asked.

"It's a long story. Let me get the children in bed and we'll talk. I think we need to fix a stiff drink for me to give you all the gory details."

Hannah and Wynn slept in twin beds in one of the bedrooms. Miles slept in a crib in a separate bedroom. My normal routine for getting the children to sleep started with Miles. I usually cuddled him next to my chest, wrapped him in a blanket, and sat in the rocking chair next to his crib. After putting the pacifier in his mouth, in almost a whisper, I'd sing songs like:

"Rock-a-bye baby, in the treetop,
When the wind blows, the cradle will rock,
When the bough breaks, the cradle will fall,
And down will come baby, cradle and all."

My mother used to sing that to me when I was little, and I

never realized how stupid and horrifying the lyrics are until I started singing it to my babies. One I liked better was:

"Go to sleep, little baby,

Go to sleep, little baby,

When you wake, I'll give you cake,

And ride the pretty little pony."

Unable to remember the lyrics to Brahm's Lullaby, I, instead, hummed the tune. Before long, Miles stopped sucking on the pacifier and was fast asleep.

I gently laid him in his crib, and then went to Wynn next. Getting him to sleep was a slam dunk. All I had to do was gently stroke him with my finger between his eye brows, the so-called third eye. In no time flat, he'd be off to dreamland.

For Hannah, it meant playing my ukulele and singing songs like "Jesus Loves Me, This I Know," and then her favorite the Peter, Paul and Mary song:

"If you miss the train I'm on, you will know that I am gone

You can hear the whistle blow a hundred miles."

With all the children asleep, I went into the kitchen. "It's a little chilly tonight. You want me to build a fire? I'll turn on some music and we'll get a drink and sit by it."

"Sounds good to me," Laura agreed.

I turned on my Sony reel-to-reel tape deck with my recently purchased KLH high-quality speakers to set the tone for the evening.

When I finished telling her about the case, Laura wanted to know if there was any way to get out of it.

"I don't think so. When the judge appoints a lawyer to handle a case, there's no way out that I know of."

"Why don't you call your dad and ask him?"

"Yeah, I will. I haven't told him about it yet."

"What's it going to do to your reputation? Are people going to hate you for representing a confessed killer?"

"I don't know. I'm sure Joseph at the florist shop and some of his friends aren't exactly going to love me. But, as a lawyer, I won't shirk my duty. I can't shy away from a case because it's unpopular.

"And what's your brother going to say?"

"I haven't even thought about him. You know, we don't communicate all that much. Maybe he won't find out."

After finishing our drinks, sitting on the floor in front of a cozy fire, I leaned over and kissed her. She'd put on a fresh coat of Shalimar, a scent that always stimulated me. As Etta James sang "At Last," Laura lay back on the carpet beside me, my arm around her. We melted into each other's arms and began shedding our clothes. As the power of love began to envelop us, "Ain't Nothing Like the Real Thing" by Marvin Gaye and Tammy Terrell began playing. I jumped up in order to fast forward it to the next song.

Laura leaned up. "What are you doing? I thought you liked that song."

"I do, but I just don't want to hear it right now."

"You're so crazy!"

"Yeah, I know," I conceded. What I'd never tell her was that this was the song that played over and over when I was on Lina's sofa in Paris.

We returned to our former position on the floor and began kissing each other. The spell returned when the Beatles added to the charm by singing:

"When I find myself in times of trouble, Mother Mary
comes to me, speaking words of wisdom, let it be."

I came to the realization that it's worth every minute of a good argument in order to experience the splendor of make-up love.

Monday
December 2, 1973

My father had gained years of experience hearing criminal cases as a Superior Court Judge in Macon. He seemed surprised when I told him I'd been assigned a capital murder case. But, like the good father he'd always been, he encouraged me and made me feel more confident in my ability to tackle it. However, a gnawing thought persisted in the back of my mind I hadn't been able to shake, which I didn't disclose to him – that I'd been set up, the judge knowing it'd be an unwinnable case for a neophyte.

My ability to try the case dominated the conversation at the coffee break the next morning. Davis offered his support. "It'll be good for you to have a capital case under your belt. I'll help you any way I can."

James added, "You'll learn a great deal from it. I'm sure you'll do a good job."

My dependable cheerleaders, Bailey and Bonds, like pandering hucksters, said, "No lawyer in Brunswick could do a better job than you."

After two mugs of black coffee, I felt the need to talk to my client. That's when Bailey handed me three envelopes, "Mr. Jennings brought these by the office earlier before you got here."

Old Jim unlocked the steel door that would require a wrecking crew to penetrate, and handed me a metal folding chair to take with me. Curious about what I might find, I ambled down the hallway armed with a legal pad and letters in hand.

Tommy was sitting on his cot, dressed in an off-white prison uniform like a forlorn little boy. His appearance, however, seemed much different from the way he appeared on Friday. His stare seemed frightened, as if he'd never seen me before.

"Tommy, you remember me," I cleared my throat. "I'm

the lawyer who came to see you last Friday."

Without hesitation, he asked, "Did you get me a Marine lawyer?"

"No. Your father called all around Camp Lejeune on Friday, and they said they couldn't furnish you with a lawyer. So, that means you either have to hire your own or you're stuck with me."

"You mean the Marines can't do anything to help me?" he insisted as if he didn't believe me.

"You committed a crime here in Georgia, and this county has jurisdiction over you and that supersedes the Marines."

Tommy turned his head away in disappointment. He stared at the floor for a few moments, then asked me my name.

"Tyler Tucker."

Tommy took a deep breath then exhaled, as if he didn't know what to say. His disappointment seemed obvious. "I don't know what else to do," he hung his head.

"Tommy, pull that chair beside your cot up here next to me, so we can talk more privately, OK?"

He did what I asked. I unfolded my chair and placed it next to the bars. When he sat down, our faces were no more than three feet apart. His eyes revealed a disillusioned and desperate young boy.

I lowered my voice. "Here're some letters from your parents."

Tommy took the letters, checked out the handwriting on each of them then put them on the floor next to his chair.

"I don't want them to see me here," he mumbled.

"Don't worry. They're not allowed to see you."

"Good. I can't face them."

"Tommy, I'm a lawyer here in Brunswick. I've been practicing about a year and a half. I've tried a few criminal cases, but I've never tried a capital murder case. I need to let you know right now in the beginning that the District Attorney wants you to get the electric chair."

Tommy flinched from the jolt of that statement.

"At this point, the DA's not willing to compromise. I'm hoping that by trying the case, the best I can do for you is get a life sentence, where you'll be eligible for parole in seven years."

Tommy's eyes locked on mine. The fright from my blunt statement was obvious, but I felt he needed to know right off the bat the seriousness of the situation.

"I was hoping the Marines would help me out," he mumbled.

"They did say they'd send an officer down to testify on your behalf."

He brightened a little in hearing that.

"You want to tell me what happened?"

Tommy looked down at the floor and rubbed his face with both hands. After hesitating for a long time, he said, "I went home to Palatka for Thanksgiving. That night I started hitching back to Camp Lejeune. This guy picked me up."

"Where did he pick you up?" I interrupted, meticulously taking notes of what he was saying.

"North of Jacksonville."

"Then what?"

"He told me he lived in Brunswick and he'd take me that far," then Tommy stopped talking, as if he were trying to remember what'd happened.

"Go on."

"We talked. He seemed like a nice enough guy," he paused for a while.

"OK."

"It was really foggy that night, so he had to drive pretty slow," he stopped talking again as if he were trying to piece things together for the first time.

"Then what?"

"He had a bottle of wine. He asked me to open it. I unscrewed the top and handed it to him. He took a drink, and I drank some, too."

"What happened after that?"

"By the time we got to Brunswick, we'd drunk the whole bottle."

"OK."

"He lived at the Holiday Inn," he paused for a few moments to collect his thoughts then started back in a lower tone of voice. "He asked me to go to his room and sleep it off, and he'd get me back on the road the next morning." He had long pauses after each sentence.

"Then what?"

He didn't respond. I waited for a little while for him to get his composure, but when he didn't speak, I asked him, "What happened after that?"

He stared at the floor as if he couldn't bring himself to talk. I waited for a while, then said, "Tommy, you're going to have to tell me what happened when you got to Calvin's room."

He continued staring at the floor and wouldn't lift his head. His upper body shook. I did something I'd never done before. I reached through the bars and patted him on his shoulder in the same way I do for my own children when they cry.

I waited for a long time. Tommy's body continued to shake.

"I know you don't want to talk about it, but I've got to know what happened."

I continued to wait, until he finally raised his head and wiped the tears from his face with his sleeve.

Still whimpering, he said, "We were sitting on a sofa next to each other drinking a beer," he stopped.

"And then what?"

He waited awhile then blurted out, "He tried to put the make on me."

"What did he do that made you think he was putting the make on you? Did he say anything to you?"

Tommy hesitated as if he were ashamed to tell me, "No, he put his hand on my crotch."

"And what happened after that?"

Tommy stared into my eyes with sincerity and said, "I don't remember. I can't remember what I did. That's when I blacked out."

"The detective said you told him that you hit Calvin over the head with a lamp."

"I don't remember telling him that."

"What's the next thing you remember after he tried to put the make on you?"

"Waking up here in this jail."

"You don't recall anything about what you did to the guy?"

"No," he shook his head.

"You took his car and tried to escape. You remember that?"

"No. The cop told me I did."

"They caught you and brought you to the jail?"

"I guess so."

"Do you remember signing a confession that you killed the guy?"

"No."

"Listen, Tommy. You've got to tell me the truth. If you don't tell me the truth, the DA is going to make you and me both look silly. Do you understand?"

"I'm telling you the truth," he insisted. "I don't remember killing anybody," he raised his voice.

"Tommy, I want you to look at me. Have you ever had lapses of memory previous to this?"

"No. Not that I can think of."

"What traumas have you had happen to you in the past?"

"Traumas?"

"Yeah. Bad things that happened to you."

He thought for a minute then said, "I can't think of anything."

"You mean you've never had anything bad happen to

you in your entire life?" I was beginning to get exasperated, doubting his answers.

"I don't know of anything."

Irritated with how this was going, I asked him, "Are you telling me the truth, Tommy? I can't believe that anyone who has lived eighteen years has never had anything bad happen to them."

"When I was about fifteen, I was running a 100 yard dash and fell and broke my arm."

I got the impression that he was hiding something. "Have you had any sadness in your life caused by your family or friends or by anyone?"

He thought for a minute. "Before I went in the Marines, I was a pretty-shy kid. I lost my girlfriend my senior year."

"OK. That's traumatic. Did she shaft you?"

"Yeah. I guess you'd say that. I think she got tired of me. She hooked up with the captain of the football team."

"That should've hurt you. Didn't it?"

"Yeah. I was pretty sad for a while after that. But when I went to boot camp, I got over it."

"OK, Tommy. I want to ask you something very personal. Think really hard and tell me the truth. Has anyone ever tried to have sex with you against your will?"

The silence lasted much too long before Tommy answered, "No."

"Are you sure you're telling me the truth?"

"Yes sir. I am."

I decided to shut it down. "OK. Tommy, I have to get back to my office. I want you to think about all the things you've told me. If you've failed to tell me something I need to know, then remember, it's your life on the line."

I stood up, grabbed the chair and started to walk out, when Tommy called out, "Do you know when the trial will be?"

"No, I don't."

When I returned to my office, Bailey told me the judge

had called. I went to my office to return the call.

"Good morning Judge. How're you today?"

"Fine, Tyler. I hope you are."

"Yes sir. I'm fine."

"I wanted to let you know that we're going to have to go to trial on your case next Monday morning."

"Next Monday morning?" I asked in disbelief.

"Yes. We need to go ahead and get this matter taken care of. You know the case is getting a lot of publicity in the Jacksonville, Savannah and Atlanta papers. Do you think you can be ready?"

"Ah, I'll do my best."

"Well, please do," he insisted.

In shock, I walked out to the reception area where Bailey and Bonds were typing away on legal documents. "I can't believe the judge is making me go to trial next Monday!"

They both were surprised. "That's not much time to get ready!" Bonds said.

"I sure do have a lot of work to do between now and then. You think y'all can cancel my appointments for the rest of the week? I'll have to spend full-time on this case."

Both Bailey and Bonds agreed.

I walked into our law library where James was toiling over a stack of books on the table in front of him, smoking a cigarette. "Excuse me for interrupting," I said, knowing how James could get so absorbed in studying the law he'd blank out everything else.

"That's all right," James said.

"What do you know about a plea of temporary insanity?"

"Are you accusing me?" he joked.

I laughed.

"I don't know much about it," James answered. He'd been working diligently over the past year since the merger of Atlantic Coastline Railroad and the Seaboard Air Line Railroad. He'd represented the ACL for many years and another lawyer in town represented Seaboard. After the merger into the Seaboard Coastline Railroad, the new company gave James the full representation of the newly merged company. Along with his representation of the City of Brunswick, these clients had become a full-time job.

Always eager to help, James walked around the library, the largest space in the entire office, pulling down various books for me.

"Thanks. Do you mind if I sit at the table with you?" I asked. "I promise not to talk."

"Of course," James said, being the most polite southern gentleman I'd ever known.

I began reading:

> *Temporary insanity is an unsoundness of the mind which the law recognizes as freeing one from the responsibility for committing a crime. In legal terms, insanity refers to a disorder of the mind which impairs an individual's ability to know right from wrong, or otherwise prevents him from understanding that his actions are wrong.*

After studying for about an hour, I went back to my office and called Tommy's father at the motel. Wes was glad to hear from me and continually asked questions about Tommy's well-being. I assured him that he was doing as well as could be expected.

Then I hit him with a question he wasn't prepared for. "Mr. Jennings, do you think you have the funds to pay for a psychiatric examination of Tommy?"

After a few moments of silence, he asked, "Do you think that's necessary?" He seemed surprised.

"Yes sir, I do."

"How much are we talking about?"

"Probably around $150. Maybe $200 at the most."

After another moment of silence he said, "I guess between me and my wife and my brother I think I can scrape up that much."

"Good. I'll keep you informed," I said.

I called an older lawyer who'd been practicing about ten years in Brunswick and had handled a lot of criminal cases. He recommended a psychiatrist in Savannah named John Underwood, who occasionally used hypnotism. I had the feeling that the psychiatrist could extract from Tommy things that I'd been unable to. I called him and told him of the urgency. He agreed to come down to the jail the next evening after his last appointment. He told me he'd have to charge $250 for doing me that favor. I thanked him and told him the fee would be OK. If Wes couldn't come up with that much, I knew my father would lend me an extra fifty bucks to kick in.

Tuesday
December 3, 1973

I'd made an appointment with Tommy's parents at 11:00 o'clock, just after coffee break. They arrived a little early, so I told them to wait out front until we finished. Coffee breaks were sacrosanct; much too important to be interfered with by legal business. It seemed to be an unwritten edict that no one spoke about clients or the law during that 30-minute interlude, only about personal things going on in each other's lives. This one ended on a good note with an agreement to have the office Christmas party at James's home, where everyone was expected to bring their spouses and children and a small present for each person that wouldn't cost over a dollar.

When the group left the library and Bailey and Bonds had cleaned the table, I invited the Jennings family to come in. Wes asked me if I would mind if Duck and Bonnie Sue joined them. I'd learned that she'd recently become an accepted item in their family.

"Of course," I agreed.

"How's he doing?" Agnes asked, as if she were about to cry.

"I had a much better talk with him yesterday," I responded. "He seemed to be doing as well as can be expected."

I explained to Wes, knowing as a lawyer he would best understand my idea about using temporary insanity as a defense. Wes admitted he'd tried very few criminal cases and would have to rely on me to make that determination.

"I'm not sure it'll work, but that's my reason for wanting the psychiatrist."

"Well, I'm glad you explained it," Agnes chimed in. "I didn't understand why you felt our son would need a psychiatrist. He's never had any mental problems."

I viewed her remarks as a typical response. Mothers, in general, know more about their sons than anyone when they're younger; however, when it comes to sexual hang-ups, most mothers would be completely in the dark.

"What can we do to help?" Wes asked.

"Well, I was wrong about the charge of the psychiatrist. Since he agreed to come on short notice, it's going to be $250."

"Oh, my!" Agnes exclaimed.

"When do we have to have it?" Wes asked.

"He'll be here tonight after he finishes his last patient in Savannah. He's probably going to expect payment before he begins his examination."

"Let me see how much I can come up with," Wes said with a concerned look. Then changed the subject, "Who do you plan to use as witnesses for Tommy?"

"I'm hoping if the psychiatrist report comes out like I expect, then I'll use him. I'll call Camp Lejeune and see if they can send someone down who'll tell about Tommy's record as a Marine recruit."

"Yeah, that would be good," Wes commented.

"Did Tommy attend a church?" I asked.

Both Wes and Agnes spoke at the same time. "Yes."

"He certainly did. Every Sunday," Agnes said, as if I'd insulted her by asking such a silly question as that.

"Do you think we could get his minister to come up and say a good word for him?"

Agnes immediately took the reins. "Oh yes. Preacher Wraggs will be glad to do that. Tommy never missed going to church and Sunday school unless he was sick."

"And sometimes, even when he was sick," Wes chimed in.

Agnes gave him a dirty look.

"OK. That'd be good," I said. "Those are the only ones I've been able to come up with, so far. Can you think of anyone else?"

Agnes immediately said, "His best friend goes to the University of Florida. I'm sure we could get Mikey to come up and testify."

"I really don't think that would be necessary," I responded. "When you have family and friends testifying, it just doesn't hold all that much weight."

After a lull in the conversation, they excused themselves, but not before Bonnie Sue seized the opportunity to take one more swipe at me. "With three children, if you don't have any life insurance, you're going to need to get some. You may not realize it, but it could cost you up to $10,000 just to educate those children," she insisted.

"You're right," I said. "I'll think about it."

After they left, I went immediately to the phone and called the Adjutant General's office at Camp Lejeune. They agreed to send an officer to the trial to testify for Tommy. I was happy to hear that, because I knew it'd be really persuasive with the jury.

I then went to the jail to make arrangements for having Tommy removed from his cell and brought downstairs to the interview room when the psychiatrist arrived. When I got that accomplished, I grabbed a folding chair and walked upstairs to visit Tommy. He was lying on the cot in his cell.

"Tommy," I called out.

He raised his head.

"I need you to pull your chair up here beside me."

He did as he was told.

I reached through the bars and shook his hand.

"How are you?"

Tommy shrugged his shoulders.

"I want you to know I'm trying my best to help you. You've got to trust me."

Tommy stared into my eyes.

"You've got to cooperate with me," I insisted.

Tommy continued staring at me without responding.

"Listen, Tommy, it's your life on the line."

He still didn't respond.

"I want you to know I've lined up an officer from Camp Lejeune to come to the trial and testify in your behalf."

Tommy brightened for the first time, and said, "That's good. Who is it?"

"I believe his name is Staff Sergeant McDonald."

"Old Elmer Fudd," Tommy grinned for the first time since I'd met him. "If he came down, that'd be great! He could tell them anything they wanted to know about Marine training. He definitely ought to remember me."

"We'll see," I then changed gears. "Tommy, listen to me. I have a psychiatrist coming to see you tonight to talk with you."

"What?"

"You have to cooperate with him. It's really important that you do that. Do you understand?"

"Why?"

"I have to prove a legal theory called temporary insanity. I need the psychiatrist to do that for us."

"What's he gonna' do?"

"He's going to ask you a lot of questions, and you have to answer them truthfully. That's really important, Tommy. Do you understand?"

He didn't respond.

"He may need to hypnotize you."

"Hypnotize me?" Tommy squirmed with a frown on his face.

"Yeah. I think it might be necessary."

"I'm not talking to some quack doctor," he argued.

"Let me tell you something. You've got to trust me. I'm doing everything I can to help you. And you've got to cooperate. Do you hear me?"

"Hypnotize? What's that all about?"

"We need to see what's going on inside you that made you do what you did to Calvin."

"I don't know about that," he slurred and looked away.

"Do you want me to try to save you from the chair?"

Tommy sighed.

"Well, you've got to do what I tell you. I'm on your side. You have to trust me. OK?"

He nodded.

"I'll be here tonight when he arrives. We'll take you down to the interrogation room. Do you remember being there the night it happened?"

"No."

"Well, anyway, I won't be in the room with you. It'll be just you and Dr. Underwood."

Tommy seemed depressed – his lackadaisical movements, sleeping most of the time and showing no interest in helping me with the trial. No doubt, he felt guilty.

I looked into his eyes. "Tommy, if you could have anything you wanted right now, what would it be?"

He didn't hesitate a second in answering that question. "I was supposed to ship out yesterday with my troop to Vietnam. That's where I wanna' be. I want to be with them. For the last six months, that's what I've been training for. I'd rather be killed in 'Nam' fighting for my country than killed in an electric chair."

Those were the most words I'd heard him speak; and, for the first time could only imagine the pain he must be feeling from the sudden transformation of being a macho, leatherneck Marine, trained to fight and kill, into a vulnerable, timid, and scared young boy, who'd made the gravest mistake of his life.

I went back to my office to work for the rest of the day and wait for Dr. Underwood's call that didn't come until about a quarter-to-seven that evening. Wes had earlier brought by an envelope containing $250 in cash.

At that time of year, darkness falls around 5:30, so it seemed much later than it really was. I hurried out to the car, drove to the jail and met the doctor. He appeared to be late-fifties or early-sixties, bald, deep crow's feet between his eyes, wore glasses, and had a dimple in his chin. After telling him what I knew about the case, the doctor said he was ready to examine Tommy. I handed him the envelope with the cash.

The jailer brought Tommy into the interrogation room. I

excused myself to wait outside. When the doctor told me it should take maybe a little over an hour, I decided to run home and eat a quick bite with Laura.

When I walked into the house, she asked, "How's it going?"

"I don't know. I'll know a lot more after the psychiatrist examines him. Where are the kids?"

"I got Miles down about a half hour ago. Wynn is in bed, but I've been hearing talking coming from his room."

"Who is he talking to?"

"Who knows?" She laughed. "Talking to himself, I guess. The last time I saw Hannah, she was playing with her dolls."

"I need to go give them all a kiss," I said as I walked down the hall to their rooms. When I came back, I sat down beside Laura on the sofa and held her hand.

She looked toward me with a questioning expression on her face. "Tyler, what are you hoping to accomplish in this case?"

"I'm trying to keep my client out of the chair."

"You know, the thing that bothers me most about this case is that there's no doubt your client is guilty. He killed someone. And it was not in self-defense. He killed him because the guy made a sexual advance toward him. Why couldn't he have just said, 'No, I'm not into that,' then nothing would've ever happened. You don't kill somebody just because they make a sexual overture toward you. He could've jumped up and run out the door. I don't like the fact that you're working so hard in defending a murderer who is guilty. He needs to be punished. Don't you think?"

I put both my hands on hers and kissed her on the cheek. "I understand what you're saying, honey. And, believe me, I've thought a lot about the things you're talking about. I'm not trying to get him off. But I don't think taking another life accomplishes anything."

"Do you not believe in capital punishment?"

"Good question! I wrote a paper on that subject in law school – a life for a life. I don't think I believe in capital punishment. That's what I stated in the thesis I wrote. And maybe that's why I'm giving it all I got to keep that from happening. Nothing is accomplished by killing another person, even if he is guilty of murder."

"What if the boy who was killed was your brother? How would you feel about it then?"

"Another good question. I honestly don't know. But there are worse punishments than death like living in a miserable prison for the rest of your life."

"But what if all this hard work you're doing for your client were to get him off scot-free? How would you feel about that?"

"Yeah, believe me, I've thought about that, too."

"How is justice served if he were to walk?" Laura demanded.

"You're asking me all these questions, and, frankly, I don't really know how I'd feel."

"This is serious, Tyler. And you need to think about it. You can't set a guilty man free to go back on the streets."

"I told you I'm not trying to set him free," I raised my voice.

"But what if you did?" She responded in a tone louder than mine.

"Look. I gotta go, honey. Don't worry. Whatever happens, justice will be served."

"Ha. Do you really believe that?" she chided.

"I gotta run, honey. I have no idea what time I'll be home."

I walked in the jail, and was told that the doctor was still with Tommy.

When Tommy first arrived in the interrogation room, the doctor had tried to get him to feel as comfortable as possible by making small talk, then gradually moving into the usual questions about his background and life experiences. Tommy seemed reluctant to go into too much detail. The doctor kept pushing him gently, but Tommy seemed to back off, as if he didn't like being interrogated about his life.

The doctor watched him with his head hanging down,

unable to look him in the eye. "Tommy, I want you to know I'm here to help you get to the bottom of why you murdered someone. You need to cooperate with me."

Tommy acted as if he didn't hear him. The doctor didn't find it at all unusual that his demeanor remained sad, dejected and depressed. After all, this eighteen-year-old kid had just murdered someone who'd befriended him. But why? That's what the doctor had to find out.

"Tommy, I need to get your permission to let me put you into a trance state. Are you willing?"

"Why do you need to do that?"

"I understand you don't want to talk, but I believe it's necessary to find out what's going on inside you," the doctor cleared his throat. "Tommy, what I'm doing could save your life. It may not, but we need to explore all avenues to prevent the State of Georgia from putting you to death. Do you understand?"

"I suppose so," he mumbled.

"So, are you willing to go into a trance state?"

"I guess," he repeated.

"You've got to say, 'yes' or 'no,' one or the other."

"Yes," he muttered.

The doctor put a cushion that he'd brought along with him in the back of Tommy's chair to make him more comfortable. The doctor sat across from him and placed his upturned hand on the table between them. "Now put both your hands on my palm."

Tommy did as he was told.

"Sit up as straight as you can, but be comfortable. Now I want you to look into my eyes," the doctor said, knowing he had to have full command over his own eye movements and the ability to maintain eye contact without blinking for as long as possible.

"I'm going to count – one – two – three. Now press down on my hand."

Tommy cooperated.

"Now press down on my hand even harder."

The doctor knew that Tommy would be somewhat aware of the state he was in, because with hypnosis the patient is knowledgeable of his surroundings.

The doctor placed his hand over Tommy's eyes, shading his view then said in a soft, soothing voice, "It's very late. You are so tired. You are feeling drowsy. Now doze off and go to sleep. The doctor then slipped his hand away from Tommy's eyes so that he would have the sensation of falling asleep.

The doctor started counting very slowly and softly – five – four – three – two – one. After each number spoken, he whispered loudly enough for Tommy to hear, "Your eyes are growing heavy and droopy and are now closing," then he added, "Tommy, you are now sleeping, and when I say the word, 'bugle,' you will wake up. I want you to know you are safe and that you will remember everything you tell me when you wake up, so long as your conscious mind can handle it."

He then paid close attention to Tommy's breathing, making sure it was even and normal. "Become aware of your breathing. Focus on slowing down the rhythm of your breathing. Your chest and abdomen will expand outward with each breath, like a balloon gently filling with air."

"Tommy, I want you to pay attention to your toes, and make sure they are relaxed," he waited a moment, then said, "take the tension away from your feet and ankles." He paused, "Slacken the muscles in your legs." A minute later, he said, "Now your calves. Untighten those muscles and make them loose." After a few more moments, he said, "Let your hip muscles relax all the way down the back of your thighs then concentrate on your spine. Make sure it's straight and not curved. Now loosen your shoulders all the way down your arms to your wrists and hands and fingers. Move your attention to your upper back. Feel the relaxation flow down your spine. Let all the muscles give up their hold. Relax your upper back, middle and lower back, allow your entire back to relax completely, and feel the relaxation in your whole body."

After the doctor was confident he was in a hypnotic trance, he began asking questions.

"Tommy, have you ever had sex with a female?"

After a few deep breaths, he answered, "Yes."

"How many different girls."

"Just one."

"You want to tell me about it?"

"My uncle took me and my friend to a whorehouse the night of our high school graduation."

"Oh, really? And that's the only time you've had sex with a female?"

"Yes."

"Tommy, have you ever had sex with a male?"

He noticed Tommy squirming in his chair like he was uncomfortable. Moaning sounds began emanating from him as if he might be in pain.

"It's OK, Tommy. You can tell me. I'm here to help you."

He finally answered. "Yes."

"You want to tell me about it?"

"Mr. Lawson," Tommy answered.

"Who is Mr. Lawson?"

"My shop teacher."

Tommy then revealed to the doctor what he'd never told anyone else about what'd happened between him and Mr. Lawson. He responded in such a way as if it were liberating to share this horrible experience with another person, even though he was unconscious at the time. Tommy even went further to tell the doctor about Thanksgiving night when he went to the cemetery and took shots at Mr. Lawson's grave marker.

The doctor then pursued the evening when he met Calvin while hitchhiking, and going to Calvin's place in Brunswick. "What happened at Calvin's that night, Tommy?"

"We were sitting next to each other on the couch drinking a beer. We'd already finished off a bottle of wine. We were talking about me going off to Vietnam, and that I might never come back," Tommy spoke very slowly and deliberately. "Calvin leaned over toward me like he wanted to kiss me or hug me, so I pushed him back. Then he put his hand down on my leg and then moved it up to my crotch just like Mr. Lawson did to me. I think I went crazy. I lashed out at him, grabbed the lamp off the table and broke it over his head. He started bleeding. Blood was coming out of his mouth. He was gurgling and gagging. It scared me. I jumped up, grabbed his car keys from the table, and took off in his car."

"Then what happened?"

"I got stopped by a cop. I guess I must've been speeding. I was only a couple of blocks from the Holiday Inn where he lived. The cop took me back to Calvin's room. I saw him slumped over with a lot of blood on his shirt. I didn't mean to do it," Tommy said. "I didn't want to kill him. I would never have done anything like that." Tears began to drip down Tommy's face, when the doctor yelled out "Bugle."

The doctor was well aware that Tommy would not remember something he said during hypnosis if he was not ready to handle it.

Tommy began wiping his eyes, blinking them several times, then looked around at his surroundings, as if he were trying to get his wits about him. He then looked toward the doctor.

"How do you feel?" The doctor asked.

Tommy shook his head back and forth. "How long was I asleep?"

"Not long."

"Why are my eyes wet?"

"You were crying."

"I was?"

"What all did I say to you?" Tommy seemed anxious to know.

"You told me about your uncle taking you and your friend to a house of prostitution."

"I did?"

"You told me about Mr. Lawson."

"I did?" Tommy seemed very troubled about that. "I've never told anyone about that."

"But maybe you needed to tell someone."

"You're not going to tell anyone, are you?"

"I'm going to tell your lawyer."

"No, I don't want him to know that."

"Tommy, this may be the thing that saves your life. He needs to know."

"But I don't want anyone to know about it."

"Look, your life is on the line. If I were you, I'd want to tell anything I could about myself that might keep me from being put to death."

"But I wouldn't want that to get out in the open."

"You talk to your lawyer about that."

There were a few moments of silence, then the doctor said, "You want to ask me any questions?"

Tommy shook his head. "I don't guess so."

The doctor stood up and walked out the door. He summoned the jailer over to tell him that he had completed his examination. The jailer handcuffed Tommy and led him back to his cell.

I'd been pacing like an expectant father in the hallway, occasionally peeping through the glass windows to see what was taking place. I walked over to where the doctor was standing. I looked at him without saying anything. The doctor stared back.

"So, what do you think?" I asked.

"I taped the session, so I'll send you a written transcript."

"Is there anything you can tell me now?" I was anxious to hear.

"Yes, let's go over here and sit down for a moment."

We went out into the hallway and sat next to each other on a bench.

The doctor asked me if I knew the meaning of homophobia.

"Not really," I replied, but to be more truthful, I'd never heard of it.

"Some people have hatred for homosexuals. It can be

caused from some conservative churches who preach that it's a sin. It can be caused from an unpleasant encounter with a homosexual. But it can also be caused from people who try to hide their own feelings of being homosexual."

"You think Tommy might be homosexual?" That really surprised me.

"I don't know that. But you're aware, I guess, that no one is completely homosexual or completely heterosexual? A person may have a preference for a member of the opposite sex, but that doesn't mean they don't harbor some feelings or notions or fascinations about having sex with a member of their own sex. They may never actually commit the act. But that doesn't mean that a man or a woman doesn't sometimes imagine what it might be like to have a homosexual experience."

"I don't think I've ever had that notion," I said.

"How old are you?"

"27."

"Well, who knows, later on you might. I'm not saying that you'd actually have sex with a man, but you might at least think about it."

I shrugged my shoulders.

"What I'm saying is that when a person experiences those feelings, they may hate that about themselves, because it's repugnant to them. So, they lash out at anyone who is homosexual, because they're not able to accept that about themselves."

"You know, I've never really thought about that," I said.

"So, what are your feelings about Tommy?"

"You do know that he has had a homosexual experience?"

"What? He didn't tell me that!"

"That's no surprise. But he was sexually abused by his shop teacher when he was fifteen."

"Good Lord! No, I didn't know that."

"He still has repressed hostility caused from that experience, which could've contributed to what he did. If he doesn't get the death penalty, he really needs some counseling to help him."

"Yes. I'm sure he does," I agreed. "But Doctor, I want to know if I can prove that he was temporarily insane when he committed the act. Had he lost all sense of reasoning?"

"Perhaps," he responded. "I do think he acted instinctively from the guilt he had from his past traumatic experience with the shop teacher."

"He told me he didn't remember killing Calvin," I said.

"That may very well be true from his conscious mind, but subconsciously, he remembered it under hypnosis."

The doctor stood up. "I'm sorry. It's getting late. I've got to drive back home. I'll send you my report."

"Thank you, Doctor. I really appreciate you taking the time to come down here and conduct the interview."

"Sure. I understand your need for it."

"Don't forget. We go to trial on Monday," I said. "Do I need to send you a subpoena?"

"No, I'll make arrangements to be here when you need me. Just call me and let me know as close as possible to the time you want me, so I don't have to sit around the courthouse waiting."

"I'll do my best."

"I'll have you the report by Friday," he said.

"Thanks, Doctor." We shook hands. "I hope you have a safe trip back to Savannah."

Tom Dennard

Wednesday
December 4, 1973

I arrived at the office a little later than normal and noticed several people sitting in the reception area. Bailey followed me back to my office and closed the door.

"There's a lady out front who said she needs to see you, but she doesn't have an appointment. What do you want me to do?"

"Who is she?"

"She said her name was Mrs. Roger Smith. I checked, and she's not a client."

"Do you know what she wants?"

"No, I don't."

"OK. I guess I'll see her. But tell her it has to be brief."

"I'll show her back."

I was standing behind my desk when she walked in. "Yes ma'am, how're you today?"

A short lady, dressed in plain clothes with her hair in a bun stood before me with a dejected expression. She sat down, not saying a word, a real faux pas of large proportions. Southern ladies are most always polite and talkative.

I sat down, and, in my usual jovial nature with clients, asked, "What can I do for you?"

She looked directly into my eyes for what seemed like a long time, then handed me a manila envelope.

I opened it and began pulling out pictures of what appeared to be a shy, blond-haired boy at different stages of life – most seemed to be school pictures from each year.

"Who is this?"

But she still didn't respond. Instead, she handed me a second envelope.

"Is he your son?" I asked before opening the other one.

Suddenly, a wave of horror overcame me as I thumbed through the second envelope with pictures of the same boy's

216

bloody, brutalized body.

I realized she had given a different name to get in to see me. "Are you...?"

She interrupted and uttered her first words, "Yes, he's my son, and you're the man who's trying to get the boy who murdered him set free."

I immediately went on the defensive. "I believe it's a conflict of interest for me to be talking to you, Mrs. Livingston."

"Yes, I know that!" She began to cry.

I handed her a few tissues, kept on hand for teary-eyed clients.

Shaken from those horrific pictures and in an effort to defend myself, I explained that I'd been appointed by the court to represent my client. "When I receive an assignment, I don't have a choice. I've got to accept it."

"Calvin was my only child," she pleaded, her voice rising with each word. "You gotta understand, he was my everything! Now he's gone. And for what reason? Can anyone tell me why? Is it because he was different?"

I knew there was no satisfactory response, but I blurted out, "I have children, too, Mrs. Livingston. I know how you must feel, and I'm truly sorry."

"No, you DON'T know how I feel!" She shot back with indignation. She stared into my eyes. "My husband is cruel. He beats me. He beat Calvin. Now I have no one to turn to."

I tried to console her.

She continued. "My husband ran him out of the house when he was just seventeen. He claimed it wasn't right for Christians to have someone like him living in our house. I realize it's a sin to be what he was, but it ain't no cause to kill somebody," she broke down and began sobbing uncontrollably.

I remained quiet until she stopped.

She used more tissues to wipe her eyes. "He was just beginning to get on his feet. Working two jobs. Bought his first car. It's the only time he seemed to be excited about life," she wiped her eyes again. "Now he's gone!" She shook her head, staring at the floor. "And for what? Why? It's not right. I have nowhere to turn."

I don't think I'd ever experienced the sensation of not being able to speak. I usually have a way with words. But this stumped me. Finally, I came up with, "Do you go to church? Maybe your minister could help."

She shook her head, "Not anymore. I quit going. The preacher lied about my son. He's a hypocrite. I hate him."

I thought for a moment. "Would you be willing to go to counseling?"

"I don't have the money for that. Calvin went to one in Jacksonville, and it cost him $50 an hour. I don't have that kind of money," she paused for a moment to again wipe her face. "I've heard of these Christian counselors who can change somebody like him into being a normal person, but I wasn't able to find one before this happened."

"May I ask you where you got these pictures?"

She hesitated, then revealed, "I have a friend in the police department."

I knew I was completely out of line having her in my office but didn't have the heart or the guts to kick her out. Finally, having no other choice, I stood up and said, "I'm really sorry, Mrs. Livingston, but I'm going to have to ask you to leave. I could get in trouble for talking with you."

At first, she seemed insulted at my refusal to lend an ear for her to pour out her heart. She stood up to walk out, then turned back toward me. The look she gave me only lasted a few seconds, but it spoke volumes of grief, pain, suffering and despair. I knew I'd never forget that expression for the rest of my life.

I immediately called my father, the one who'd always been able to set things straight. About the only advice he offered was to let me know that this is what the law practice is all about – people's problems. "You've got to develop a tough skin," he chided.

We discussed certain questions about conducting cross-examination, arguments to the jury and evidentiary matters; then it was on to the library to work the rest of the day preparing for trial.

I arrived home late that night exhausted.

"So, how was it?" Laura asked.

"Don't mention it. I'm beat." I threw my coat on the sofa. "It's chilly outside. Have the children gone to bed?"

"Yeah. They've been asleep for a while. Do you want to eat now?

"You know. I'm really not hungry. Let's sit down and have a beer. OK?"

She grabbed a couple of Pabst Blue Ribbons from the fridge and sat on the sofa next to me. I put my arm around her and told her about the visit from Mrs. Livingston.

"I don't blame her one bit," Laura exclaimed. "If you were the lawyer representing someone who'd murdered Wynn or Miles, I would've clobbered you over the head with a hammer," she half-way kidded, but I knew her well enough to know she was telling the truth.

"A mother is going to protect her son," she said, emphasizing each word, then changed the subject. "You know, I never open a can of PBR that I don't think of the time Hannah popped all the tops on that case of beer of yours." We both laughed.

"Let's talk about you," I said. "How was your day?"

"Good, actually. I got the children to take a nap, and they slept a long time. It gave me a chance to do some writing that I've been wanting to do."

"That's great! What did you write?"

"Oh, nothing, just stuff. I'll let you read it if you'd like."

"Of course, I want to read it."

"You can do it later. Are you ready to eat?"

"I'm tired and feel sort of down," I sighed. "You know what I want more than supper?"

"What?"

"Just to hold you."

"OK," she reached out to me with both arms.

"No. I mean hold you in bed."

"I should've known," she conceded, as we walked down the hall to our bedroom with my arm around her.

Thursday
December 5, 1973

I called my dad again from the office. "What do you think about me trying to get the Magistrate to hold a preliminary hearing?"

"And what do you think that would accomplish?"

"Aren't we entitled to have one?"

"Son, a preliminary hearing is only for the purpose of seeing if there is enough evidence to bind him over for trial in the Superior Court. Your client has admitted killing the boy. Don't you think that's sufficient evidence to bind him over?"

"He doesn't deny killing him," I argued, "but he says he doesn't remember it."

"Yeah, I know, but that's up to the jury to decide," he said.

"I thought maybe a preliminary hearing might get the charge reduced to voluntary manslaughter."

"Well, you can petition the Superior Court Judge for that," he said, "but I can tell you right now, he's not going to grant it."

"Yeah, I guess you're probably right," I conceded.

"Son, you're in the midst of a political squabble. What's that DA's name?"

"Jack Dillinger."

"You got him running against your judge. With all the publicity this case has gotten, both of them will be going for broke to get the death penalty."

"OK. I suppose you're right."

"If you stir the pot too much," he said, "they'll all gang up on you and crucify both you and your client. That's just the way things work."

"Well, OK. I'm just pretty uptight about this case, Dad. I've got this boy's life in my hands."

"I understand son, but you need to calm down a little bit. I know you well enough to know you'll give it 110%. And that's all you can do. Once you've done that, you can't worry about the outcome."

"That's easier said than done."

"I know," he replied. "But just take it easy."

"Thanks, Dad."

"Sure, call me anytime."

With no appointments scheduled, I decided to go to the jail. The second floor seemed darker than normal. The unpleasant stench always permeated the air, along with voices of females arguing. Tommy seemed dejected and depressed. We greeted each other, and he pulled his chair over to the metal bars next to me without my asking.

"What's going on with you, Tommy?"

"Not good," he mumbled.

"What's troubling you?"

"Oh, I don't know. I've just been thinking a lot."

"About what?"

He hesitated for a moment, then said, "A preacher came around to visit and left a little Bible." He reached through the bars and handed it to me.

"Yeah, this is a book with the Psalms and Proverbs," I said. "It's donated by the Gideon Society."

"What's that?"

"The only thing I know is that it's a group of people who distribute Bibles free of charge all over the world. It's been around for a long time."

"I've been reading it a lot," Tommy said. "Because I want to know what it's like to die."

I thought for a moment. "Well, I don't know any more about dying than anyone else, but I've read about people who've died and have been brought back to life. They describe it like going through a tunnel with a light on the other side where everything is peaceful and calm and pleasant."

"They taught us in boot camp that Marines sometimes

die in combat, but the Marine Corps will live forever, and that means all Marines will live forever," he paused for a few moments. "I've never had so much time alone just to sit around and think. I'm only eighteen. I've never married, never had kids." Then he looked into my eyes with a serious expression. "Do you believe in God?"

"Yes. I do."

"If God is good, do you think He wants me to die because of what I did. I read in the Bible that God forgives. What do you think?"

"Of course. I believe that."

"You've probably never had to really think about these things – like dying. I didn't mind going to Vietnam. I don't mind dying for the Marine Corps, but this is different. I think God would forgive me for killing an enemy in battle, but how is He going to judge me for killing Calvin?" He paused. "You don't have to answer that. I know you don't know."

"Tommy, the only thing I can say about that is you got to have faith."

"I do have faith, but I know if they're going to put me to death, I've got to be ready for it."

"Well, even if the jury finds you guilty, they're not going to put you to death immediately. We can stall it by appealing, and that can delay it for a good while."

"Yeah. I understand. But I still got to get ready," Tommy stared at me with a longing expression. "Do you think after I die, I'll know people who've died?"

"I don't know. I think we will. That's what I believe."

A long moment of silence followed, then Tommy spoke up, "Do you think I'll meet Calvin?"

This knocked me off guard. "I don't know. Maybe."

"What am I going to say to him? Should I say, 'I'm sorry? I didn't mean to kill you'."

I leaned back in my chair and thought for a minute. "I guess so. What would you want to say?"

I could see a tear forming in each eye as he spoke. "I'd tell him I don't know what came over me. Maybe too much to drink. I didn't want to kill him. I'll ask him to forgive me. But that night when he put his hand on me, it triggered something inside me."

"Like what your shop teacher did to you?"

"How did you know that?" He popped back. "I guess that psychiatrist told you, didn't he? I've never told anyone about that!"

"Tommy, you've got to understand that you need to tell me all these things about yourself. I have to know everything, because there may be something I can use at the trial in your favor."

Tommy didn't say anything for a while. He seemed miffed that I knew the secret he'd kept locked in a closet deep down inside him. It must be physically and emotionally painful to unlock the chains and let the monster out. I thought for a moment. "Would you like for me to get a preacher to visit you? Maybe he can answer some of your questions."

"Yeah," he said. "I think I'd like to talk to one," he paused for a moment then said, "If they're going to put me to death, I don't want to go to hell. I need some help to get God to forgive me."

"I understand. I'll try to find someone to talk with you."

Back at the office, I called my minister at St. Mark's Episcopal Church in Brunswick, an older man, not necessarily in touch with the modern world of the day, but at least he was known for his kindness and benevolence. I chuckled when I thought about what Davis had said about him – that he was the only person he knew who could always make you feel worse after talking with him.

Nevertheless, he agreed to visit Tommy and pray with him to try to alleviate some of his fears. That temporarily relieved my mind.

I walked out to chat with Bailey and Bonds. Bailey spoke up, "You had an anonymous phone call. A man said you needed to ask the police about some pictures they found in Calvin's room."

"What? You don't know who called?"

"He wouldn't give his name," Bailey replied.

"And that's all he said?" I asked.

"Yeah, that was about it."

I took off immediately to the county police station. A guy named Jesse, who I'd dealt with in other criminal cases was sitting behind his desk with his feet propped up, smoking a cigarette. After greeting each other, I asked him if they'd searched Calvin's room after the murder.

"Yep, we shore did," he took his feet off the desk and turned to me.

"What'd you find?" I asked.

He walked back to the vault where evidence was stored, brought out a cardboard box, and placed it on the table, "You'll probably get your rocks off looking at these," he laughed.

I began pulling out a number of pictures of naked men, some with erections. After thumbing through them, I asked him what they intended to do with them.

"I don't know. I'll just turn them over to the DA and let him decide."

"What else did you find besides these pictures?"

"That's about it. Just a bunch of his personal stuff. He didn't have much."

I came away thinking what a colossal waste of time. I couldn't figure out why they would want to use those pictures in evidence. It seemed they'd help my case more than the State's. I hadn't been able to get the DA to talk with me, so I had no idea what they had in mind.

I arrived home exhausted about 9:00 that evening. The children were in bed and so was Laura. I snacked out of the refrigerator, undressed, fell in bed and was sound asleep in less than a minute.

About 3:00 a.m. Laura heard Miles crying. She got up to check on him. He couldn't find his pacifier. She picked it off the floor, wiped it off and put it back in his mouth. That was all he needed.

She came back and noticed I was not in bed. The light

was on in the living room. She found me sitting in my underwear with a bottle of bourbon on the table.

"What are you doing in here at this time of night?"

"I can't sleep."

She leaned over the table. "Please come back to bed honey," she said. "It's cold in here."

I shook my head.

"You've got to get some sleep. Why are you in here drinking?"

"I kept trying to go back to sleep and couldn't."

"Please, honey, come back and get in bed with me," she pleaded. "I need you to keep me warm."

I followed her down the hallway carrying the bottle of bourbon in my hand. She got in bed and quickly covered up. I took a slug from the bottle and joined her under the covers."

"You can't keep going on like this, Tyler. You're killing yourself."

"I've told you, honey, I have a boy's life in my hands. The trial starts in three days."

"That's all you think about. The trial, trial, trial. It has consumed you. I can't understand why you're trying so hard to save a Marine who killed somebody. He's a murderer!"

"Can't you see? It was not just him. It was all of us."

She sat up in bed. "What are you talking about?"

I raised up, too. "Our whole country killed Calvin. Not just Tommy!"

"Are you drunk?"

"Our country takes young boys and trains them to be killers to send halfway around the world for what? Tommy was just an ordinary young boy graduating from high school with hopes and dreams like every other kid. He wanted to get a job, find a girl to marry, have a family just like we all did – The American Dream. But our country is in a war we never should've gotten into, and young boys like Tommy are the victims. Don't get me wrong, I'm for a strong military to defend our country, but not to go on the other side of the world to fight a war we can't win."

"But Tommy killed Calvin," she raised her voice. "What are we supposed to do about that?"

"And I blame that on our society with its prejudice against homosexuals. Can't you see? We're all to blame for this murder," I exclaimed.

Laura put her head back down on the pillow, reached out and pulled me in closer. "I don't always understand you, Tyler, but I still love you."

"Love you, too," after a long silence I admitted, "honey, I'm scared."

"What do you mean?"

"I've never tried a murder case, and I'm afraid I don't know how to do it right."

She put her hand on my cheek. "You'll be fine."

"But when I have something really important like this, I get stage fright."

"Stage fright? You? I've never seen you get stage fright. You've always been cool and calm."

"But I do. I can remember sometimes being called on in law school to discuss a case, and I'd be terrified. I could hardly speak. My voice would quiver. My mouth would get dry. It was awful."

Shocked by this revelation, "You're telling me something I never knew about you."

"I still get scared when I get up before the public to speak. I'm really worried about how I'll do in the trial."

"But, honey, you've tried cases before."

"Yeah, but I still get nervous, and right now the only thing I can think about is I've got three days to get ready."

She pulled me close to her. "Don't stress out, honey. You'll do fine."

After a long pause, I brought up something I'd never told her. "Do you think I have a big ego?"

"Why do you ask that?"

"I've been told I need to concentrate on separating my

ego from this trial and do what I feel is the right thing to do."

"Where is that coming from?"

I told her for the first time about the old man confronting me while sitting in a pew at Notre Dame.

"How did he know you were going to have this experience? That was five years ago."

"You tell me. I don't have any idea."

She pulled me closer and hugged me. "You're a mess. What can I do to help you?"

"Just love me," I sighed.

Friday
December 6, 1973

When I arrived at the office that morning, Bailey handed me a special delivery package from Dr. Underwood. I took it to my office and began skimming over the first two paragraphs describing the setting of the interview, the subject, his background and upbringing, the reason for the interview, and his placing the subject in a state of hypnosis.

Among other things, the report repeated how his experience with the shop teacher resulted in anger, anxiety and shame and then proceeded to explain homophobia:

> *Hostility and discrimination against homosexuals are well-established facts. These negative attitudes can lead to verbal and physical acts against homosexuals with little, if any, motivation. In fact, more than 90% of homosexual men and women report being targets of verbal abuse or threats, and more than one-third report being survivors of violence. Negative attitudes toward homosexuals have been assumed to be associated with rigid moralistic beliefs, sexual ignorance, and fear of homosexuality. Homophobia has been defined as the dread of being in close quarters with homosexuals as well as an irrational fear, hatred, and intolerance. It's considered to be an anxiety-based phenomenon that has its roots in the anxiety of being or becoming a homosexual, or from repressed homosexual urges, a form of latent homosexuality, which the individual may be unaware of. When placed in a situation that excites their own unwanted homosexual thoughts, they overreact with panic or anger. There have been studies that indicate that individuals who score in the homophobic range and admit having negative feelings toward homosexuals, demonstrate significant sexual arousal to male homosexual erotic stimuli. However, most of these men are either unaware of or deny their*

homosexual urges.

I was baffled by my ignorance of this subject. It's something that had never occurred to me. Being around Tommy never gave me any indication that he may have repressed homosexual tendencies. I decided to go to the jail to talk with him, knowing he'd probably deny it even if it were true.

"Bonds, I'm going to run down to the jail for a while." I grabbed my coat and walked out the door.

At Tommy's jail cell, I, as usual, pulled my folding chair next to the metal bars, and Tommy moved his chair beside me. We shook hands.

"How's it going with you, Tommy?"

"I'm getting scareder by the minute," he admitted.

I didn't want to let him know my feelings were the same. I knew I had to feign confidence in front of my client and not reveal my restless nights.

"How do you think it's going?" Tommy asked.

"I'm doing my best to get prepared."

"I got a Bible from another preacher who came around last night."

"Oh yeah?"

"He handed me his card and told me to have the jailer call him if I ever needed to talk with him some more about dying."

"Let me see."

Tommy pulled the card out of his pocket.

I read it aloud. "Zebedee McKinney, Pastor of the United Pentecostal Church of Brunswick. Hmm. I don't believe I've heard of him."

"He told me to ask God to forgive me, so I could go to heaven."

"And did you?"

"Yeah, he held my hand, while I prayed."

I leaned back in my chair. "Well, that's good. Did the minister from St. Marks come to see you?"

"Yeah, he talked to me."

"And?"

"He said a couple of things that made me think."

After a brief silence, I asked him, "Are you willing to talk to me about some very private things in your life?"

Tommy gave me a curious expression, "Like what?"

"Sexual things."

Tommy let out a deep sigh as if he were tired of talking about this subject. "Like what?" he asked.

"I know this is not a subject that guys like to talk about with each other, but it's crucial in this case."

Tommy shook his head. "What do you want to know?"

"I want you to know it's just as uncomfortable for me to ask you about these things as it is for you to answer."

"Well, you can ask me," Tommy said.

"All right. Can we start with masturbation? How old were you when you started?"

Tommy squirmed in his chair acting disgusted by my question then responded, "I don't remember. Maybe fourteen."

"And how old were you when you had the experience with your shop teacher."

Tommy stared at the floor. After a few moments, he blurted out, "Fifteen."

"How did you react to that experience?"

After trying to collect his thoughts, he spoke in a soft voice, "I was so ashamed of myself for letting it happen."

"Yeah. And what else?"

Tommy looked at me intensely. "I hated his guts."

"Did you ever at any time look upon those events as being pleasurable?"

"No!" Then he raised his voice. "Hell no!"

"That was only three years ago. Would you say you think

about it often?"

Tommy hesitated for a moment, then admitted, "Yeah. I do."

"How often?"

"Probably every day."

I continued. "OK. Your uncle took you to the whorehouse last May after your graduation. Is that the only time you've had sex with another person?"

"So the doctor told you that, too?" Tommy asked, then answered, "Yeah."

"This may sound crazy, but did you find that experience at the whorehouse pleasurable?"

Tommy looked around and stared at the side of the jail cell and shrugged his shoulders.

"Does that mean 'yes'?"

"Yeah. I guess so."

"Did you have an orgasm?"

He nodded.

"Is it an experience you'd like to repeat again?"

"No," he said emphatically.

"You had a girlfriend in high school, right?"

"Yeah."

"Was she pretty?"

Tommy's eyes began to lighten up. "Yeah. She was pretty."

"Did you ever have sex with her?"

He thought for a minute. "It depends on what you call sex?"

"OK. Fair enough. How about penetration of your penis in her vagina?"

"No. We never went that far."

"Why didn't you?"

He paused briefly. "She had religious beliefs that it was wrong before marriage."

That was a response I could identify with, but I didn't say anything, just continued my questions. "And what about your beliefs?"

"Yeah. I mean. I guess I believe the same."

"But if she would've let you, would you have had sex with her?"

"Yeah. I'm sure I would've."

I leaned back in my chair. "Thanks for being honest with me. Now let me ask you a couple of more questions. You still masturbate, I suppose."

"Why are you asking me all this stuff?" Tommy seemed aggravated, disgusted and angered by the question. "It's really none of your business," he said emphatically. "Are you some kind of pervert?"

That inappropriate remark hit me like an arrow in my heart. "Let me tell you something, Tommy Jennings! I don't really give a damn about your sex life or anybody else's sex life for that matter! But I need you to understand that I'm doing my dead-level best to try to save your ass from being fried!"

After that hostile exchange, there was a prolonged silence.

Tommy tried to recover his composure. "OK. I'm sorry, Tyler," he seemed disgusted and distraught. "Yes, I masturbate," then added, "You have to understand, this is something I don't like to talk about to anybody."

"I understand that. It's hard for me to even ask you the question. Now I need to ask you something very important, and you need to be honest with me. What do you think about when you masturbate?"

Tommy gave me a sneer as if to say, "Now you've gone too far."

"Would you tell me?" I asked.

"I don't know. Just things," he answered, still irritated.

"Like what kind of things? Do you have an imaginary lover?"

Tommy thought for a minute, then said, "Yeah, I guess

so. I think about having sex."

"Who with?"

"Nobody in particular."

"Is it always girls, or do you ever think about boys?"

"Are you calling me queer?" He spoke loud enough for the other inmates on the floor to hear.

"I'm not calling you anything. I'm asking you."

"Hell no, I'm not queer! I'm a Marine. I went through six months of boot camp with hundreds of other guys! No!" he yelled out. "I never wanted to have sex with any of them or with any other male! God only knows how many naked guys I've seen in the showers, and, believe me, I never saw one I wanted to have sex with!"

"OK. Tommy, you can calm down. These are things I need to know," after a pause to let him calm down, I asked, "Have you ever heard of homophobia?"

"No."

"Do you know what it means?"

"No. I never heard of it."

"Well, basically it means that the thing you hate most in others is the thing you hate most about yourself."

Tommy tried to soak that one up and didn't respond, as if he didn't quite understand.

"You said you hated your shop teacher because he molested you, right? Would you have killed him?"

Tommy thought for a minute then began welling with anger, "If I saw him right now, which I can't, because he's dead, but if he was standing here right now, I'd definitely try to put a hurt on him."

"OK."

"He took advantage of me. I was a young kid, pretty shy, and he threatened to hurt my mama if I didn't give in. It was wrong. Yeah, I'd like to work him over."

"But would you want to kill him?"

A long silence ensued. Eventually, Tommy whispered, "I might."

I thought for a minute before hitting him with next question, then blurted out, "How about Calvin. Did you hate him?"

There was no response. Tommy stared at the floor for such a long time, I decided he didn't intend to answer.

"Well, what about it? Did you hate Calvin?"

"No. I didn't hate him. I hardly knew him. We'd only been together a couple of hours," he paused for a few moments, then said, "But what he did to me made me go crazy. I don't remember what all I did, but I didn't mean to kill him."

I took another approach. "Tommy, you told me you were wearing your full-dress Marine uniform when you left home, so it would be easier to get rides, right?"

"Yeah."

"So, you were wearing your uniform when Calvin picked you up and took you to his place, right?"

"Yeah."

I pulled my chair in a little closer so our faces were no more than two feet apart. "Could you tell me why no blood was found on your uniform?"

Tommy took a deep breath and sighed, then after a few moments said, "I don't know."

"Why don't you know?"

"I told you I don't remember," he protested.

"Tommy, you smashed a lamp over Calvin's head and punctured his jugular vein, and there was blood all over the place – on him, on the sofa and all over. Why didn't any of it get on your uniform?"

"I just told you," he demanded. "I don't know!"

"Is it possible you didn't have your uniform on?"

That startled him. He seemed fidgety. "I'm sure I must've."

"But is it possible you didn't?" I edged in a little closer. "Do you think you might've taken it off?"

"No," he acted nervous. "I wouldn't have done that," he insisted.

"Just how drunk were you?" I pressed him.

"I told you," he acted anxious with this line of questioning. "We drank a bottle of wine, and a couple of beers at his place."

"Is that enough to make you not know what you were doing?"

"Look, I told you I don't know!" He raised his voice. "I don't remember!"

"OK," I leaned back in my chair. "What did you and Calvin talk about after he picked you up?"

"Nothing," he shrugged. "Just small talk."

"Like what?"

Tommy seemed more nervous. "I told him a little about boot camp. He told me a little about what he was doing. Nothing really."

I leaned forward in my chair so that my face was pressed against the bars. "When you and Calvin were riding from Jacksonville to Brunswick, did it ever occur to you that Calvin was kind of effeminate?"

He thought for a moment and raised his shoulders slightly. "Yeah. Sort of."

Then I came in with my fastball. "Tommy, did you have any suspicion at all that Calvin might've been homosexual before you agreed to go with him to his place?"

Tommy took long, protracted breaths and swallowed hard as if he were in deep thought. I stared at him in his state of confusion. He didn't say a word for a long time. Then finally he looked into my eyes as if he were a little lamb that had been cornered by its predator. He mumbled under his breath, "Yeah. I guess so."

The Trial
December 9, 1973

"Order in the court!" The sheriff shouted to a packed courtroom. "Hear ye! Hear ye! Hear ye! The December Term of the Superior Court of Glynn County is now in session! Judge Cuthbert Fletcher presiding. All rise!"

With that pronouncement, the sheriff flung open the door behind the judge's bench, and Judge Fletcher, with his usual pomp and circumstance, adorned in a flowing black robe, ascended the bench, while everyone in the courtroom stood.

After he sat down, he said, "You may be seated," then banged the gavel so hard, it reverberated throughout the courtroom like the peal of a bell. "I call the case of the State of Georgia versus Thomas Smith Jennings," he yelled out, then turned to the District Attorney, "Are you ready for the State?"

The DA barked, "We are, Your Honor."

This was the first time the Judge and the DA had spoken words to each other since the announcement a few weeks previously that he'd planned to run against him in the next election.

"Are you ready for the defendant," the judge stared at me, paralyzed with stage fright. The judge got his first glimpse of Tommy, who sat next to me in his full-dress uniform, spit shined shoes, all clean shaven and a fresh haircut I'd arranged for him.

I sprang to my feet and, with as much confidence as I could muster, "Yes, Your Honor, we're ready for the defendant."

The judge then turned to the sea of anxious faces in the audience that contained the jurors and spectators, including, not only Tommy's parents, but also Duck, Bonnie Sue and Preacher Wraggs.

"You may be seated," the judge bellowed, then continued, "The clerk will call the first forty-two names on the list of jurors. The first twelve will sit in the jury box to my left. The next twelve will sit in the jury box to my right. And the rest of you jurors will take your places in the front rows of the courtroom.

The old courthouse occupied a full city block, surrounded by a grove of live oak trees, draped in Spanish moss. Reputedly, in the old days, the square provided a pasture for grazing livestock. The parcel was purchased in 1905 for one dollar from the City. The building, a neoclassical revival style, revered for its exceptional beauty, was designed by Charles Alling Gifford, a member of a New York architectural firm. He became known locally, since in the latter part of the nineteenth century, he had designed a few of the millionaire's homes on Jekyll Island, as well as the Jekyll Island Clubhouse. Adorned with a clock tower that chimed on the hour, the cornerstone of the courthouse was laid in 1906, and the square, upon completion, became the most photographed site in all of Brunswick.

The old courtroom could've easily served as the site for Atticus Finch's defense in the Tom Robinson murder trial. It had that same *To Kill a Mockingbird* flavor: a balcony for black spectators, an old, gray-haired septuagenarian bailiff manning the only entrance door, four huge chandeliers hanging from the vaulted ceiling, and a cast of jurors, all-white, some women but mostly middle-aged and elderly men.

The sheriff, a likable old man, was known for spinning yarns of his fiftysomething years working in law enforcement. In my conversations with him, I got the impression that he maintained a simple lifestyle and struggled to adapt to a changing world where senseless greed and corruption seemed to have become the norm.

After the sheriff had called the names of the jurors and they'd taken their respective places, the judge spoke, "I'm addressing this question to all of you prospective jurors here in the courtroom. Are any of your number related by blood or marriage to the defendant in this case, Thomas Jennings? If so, please indicate by raising your right hand." No one did. "All right. Are any of your number opposed to capital punishment? If so, please raise your right hand."

An elderly lady, dressed in black, sitting on the back row, held her hand in the air.

"What's your name ma'am?"

She spoke just above a whisper, "Lora Belle McKinney."

"I can't hear you ma'am. Would you stand? You're going to have to speak louder," the judge's voice was strong and resonant.

As she stood, she said with a slightly louder volume, "Lora Belle McKinney." She seemed shy and nervous and put off by having to be there.

"Mrs. McKinney, are you opposed to capital punishment?" The judge spoke with an accusatory tone that made her feel guilty.

"Yes sir," she answered nervously.

"Now, Mrs. McKinney, if the State proved beyond a reasonable doubt that the defendant was guilty of murder, could you not return a verdict of guilty if you thought the defendant would be sentenced to death?"

Tommy squirmed in his chair and looked toward me for reassurance. I didn't want to divert my attention from the judge's questions and ignored his glances.

After some moments, Mrs. McKinney said, "No."

"So, you couldn't find a murderer guilty?"

This question offended her even more and gave her the nerve to speak her mind. "Judge, he may be guilty in the eyes of man, but Jesus says we are not to pass judgment on our fellow man."

"Even if he killed somebody?" the judge snapped back.

"I don't believe we have the right to put anyone to death," she spoke more boldly.

"Do you work outside the home, Mrs. McKinney?" The judge asked.

"I'm a housewife and a mother," she said proudly.

"And what does your husband do?"

"He's a preacher."

"A preacher? What church?"

"The United Pentecostal Church of Brunswick," she said with piety.

"What's your husband's name?"

"Zebedee McKinney," she responded.

Tommy looked at me, but I was trying to remain serious and stone-faced.

"I don't usually like to do this, Mrs. McKinney," the judge said, "but under the circumstances, I'm going to excuse you. You may stand down." Then he turned to the clerk, "Mr. Clerk, would you call another juror to replace Mrs. McKinney."

The clerk called the name, "Lester O'Malley." For the first time of the day, I cracked a smile. Lester, a good-ol' boy, originally from Brantley County, operated the liquor store where I buy my beer. I'd seen the judge frequent his establishment, as well. Lester had already told me a few days previously that he'd been called for the jury, and he didn't want to be on it. I watched closely as Lester took his seat in the jury box.

The judge began his preliminary examination by asking the prospective jurors questions to ensure that they were legally qualified to serve on the jury and that jury service would not cause them undue hardship.

"Are any of your number not citizens of the United States?"

The judge looked around at all the jurors, but no one responded.

"Are all of you over the age of 18?"

It was pretty obvious that every prospective juror was an adult.

"Are there any of you who reside outside of Glynn County, Georgia?"

None of them raised their hands.

"Are any of you not physically fit to sit through a relatively long trial that might last for several days?"

No one responded.

"Have any of you heard anything about this case or read anything about this case that might cause you to be prejudiced toward one side or the other or that might prevent you from being an impartial juror?"

The judge noticed that Mr. O'Malley squirmed in his seat. But he went ahead and proceeded with the next question.

The judge raised his voice. "Are there any of your number who could not return a verdict of guilty if the State carried its burden of proof that this man," he pointed his finger directly at Tommy, "that this man," he repeated, "is guilty of murder beyond any reasonable doubt?"

The DA turned around in his chair and scanned each juror. He noticed Lester continued shifting nervously in his seat. The judge observed that, too.

"How about you, Mr. O'Malley?" the judge asked.

"Well, I'll tell you Judge."

The judge interrupted him, "Would you please stand, Mr. O'Malley?"

He stood up and addressed the judge, "I tell you the truth Judge, I don't know if I could or not," he spoke with a decidedly Southern accent.

"And why not, Mr. O'Malley?"

"Well, I'm not sure if one of our fine, red-blooded American boys, who is willing to go to war and fight for our country, should be tried for murder for killing a queer, who tried to put the make on him," he answered in a slow drawl. "Please excuse my language Judge. But it just turns my stomach to even think about it."

The DA sat up straight in his chair. Some of the spectators in the courtroom murmured to each other.

The judge rapped his gavel. "Mr. O'Malley, you're excused. Please step down. Mr. Clerk, would you call another juror into the box?"

The clerk called a different juror and the judge went through the same routine of questions as he did previously to the entire panel of jurors. Afterwards, he announced, "It appears that all the jurors are qualified."

The judge then turned it over to the DA for his questioning. Jack Dillinger had been a trial attorney for many years before running for the office of District Attorney. He didn't have the respect of most lawyers who had to work with him. In fact, most of them referred to him as a "son of a bitch."

To me, he appeared old and worn out; a man who hated his job and constantly had a sour expression on his face that made him appear unhappy. I really never had much to do with him, if I could help it.

He stood up, straightened his coat, combed his fingers through his hair, then in his resounding voice asked, "Ladies and gentlemen of the jury panels, I want to know how many of you have heard or read anything about this case?"

Every juror raised a hand.

"I see," he murmured, then proceeded, "From what you know about this case, are there any of you who have developed a bias or prejudice about this case that would prevent you from finding the defendant guilty if the State proves its case that the Marine over there is, in fact, guilty?"

No one raised a hand.

"Are there any of you who have had an experience in your life that might cause you to favor either the State's case or the defense?"

One man raised his hand.

"Your name sir?"

He stood up. "Joe Henderson," he replied.

"And what can you tell us, Mr. Henderson?"

"Well, when I was in the army, a queer tried to put the make on me, and I whipped his ass. Please pardon my language." He scanned the other jurors to detect their reaction to his statement and then turned back to look up at the judge. When I turned around toward him, it appeared to me that he was a man who could probably whip the ass of most people in the courtroom.

The DA spoke quickly, "Judge, I believe that the Court should strike Mr. Henderson for cause."

"I agree with you," he then turned to the juror, "Mr. Henderson, you may be excused. Mr. Clerk, would you call the name of another juror to replace Mr. Henderson."

The DA finished his questioning of the panels as a whole, then the judge called on me. I picked up my legal pad from the table and walked to the podium next to the jury box to keep them from seeing my knees shaking. My questions were numbered and neatly written. Fumbling with the pad for a moment, I began, "Ladies and gentlemen of the jury, my name is Tyler Tucker. I'm with the law firm of Green and Parker here in Brunswick. I've been appointed by the court to represent the defendant, Tommy Jennings, who has been accused of murder." I pointed to Tommy, who sat tall in his chair with an erect spine, just as I'd instructed him. He was a good-looking boy, wearing his full-dress uniform, and made a fine appearance to the people in the courtroom.

"Your Honor," the DA jumped to his feet. "Mr. Tucker is not supposed to be making any kind of statements to the jury. He should be asking them questions. Would you please instruct him to get on with it?"

"Mr. Tucker," the judge spoke to me in a kind and conciliatory manner, "Go ahead and ask your questions of the jurors. I'll give you ample time to make your opening statement."

Embarrassed that it may appear to the jurors I didn't know what I was doing, I tried to collect my thoughts, then proceeded with the questions. "Have any of you heard anything about this case?"

The DA jumped up again, seeming as edgy as a race horse in the starting gate. "Judge, I've already asked that question, and every one of the jurors raised their hands."

"I'm sorry, Your Honor," before the judge had time to make a ruling I said, "I'll withdraw that question and ask another one."

"All right, Mr. Tucker," the judge said, "just move along."

"Yes sir Judge, thank you," I turned back to the jurors. "From what you have heard about this case, have any of you formed an opinion about the guilt or innocence of the accused, Private First Class Jennings?"

None of the jurors made a move.

"Did any of you know the victim, Calvin Livingston?" I spoke his name softly with as much reverence as possible.

Six of them raised their hand.

I questioned each one of them individually about how

they knew him. Five of them had known him as the delivery boy for the Downtown Pharmacy, who'd brought prescriptions to their homes. The sixth one was a close friend of Mr. Bunkley, the owner of the pharmacy, and had met Calvin there.

I asked if their knowledge of Calvin would prevent them from making an impartial judgment regarding the guilt or innocence of Tommy. I deliberately used his first name to make him seem more personable and likable.

All of them said it would make no difference. I wrote down their names on my pad.

The sixth juror was a member of the Arco Church of God where Calvin and his parents once attended.

"Your name, please ma'am?"

"Ida Doster," she replied. She was short, stout, and her round face contained what appeared to be a permanent smile. She wore a dress that emphasized her protruding stomach, but it didn't appear to bother her at all.

"Mrs. Doster, could you tell us how well you knew Calvin?"

When she started to answer, I quickly realized I'd made a huge mistake asking that question.

"He was the sweetest boy," she sighed in a deep audible breath and with a glitter of tears in her eyes. "And when he grew into a teenager, he was such a good-looking boy, too. His parents were wonderful people."

As she proceeded to heap praise on Calvin, I tried to figure out how to politely shut her up. When she got to the end of a sentence, I quickly spoke up, "Thank you, Mrs. Doster."

The DA jumped to his feet. "Judge, he cut the lady off. Ask him to let her finish," he demanded.

Before the judge had time to respond, I told a little white lie, "Judge, I'm sorry. I thought she'd finished."

The judge then said, "Mrs. Doster, did you have anything further you wanted to say about the victim?"

"No, Your Honor, except to say that Calvin was such a

nice, sweet boy and what a shame it is that he's gone."

I quickly spoke up to stop her from saying anything else, knowing she'd be a sure strike, but felt compelled to ask her this question, "Would your knowledge of Calvin prejudice your mind to the extent that you could not be an impartial juror?"

I remembered being told by older, wiser and experienced trial lawyers that no one ever wants to admit in public that he or she is prejudiced. And she proved them right when she answered, "No."

I proceeded with my questions. "Are any of you related by blood or marriage to Calvin Livingston?"

One hand went up.

"What is your name sir?"

"Jack Coley," a tall thin man, who wore work clothes similar to what a man who worked at the mill would wear.

"Mr. Coley are you related ..."

He cut me off before the question was finished. "I think I might be distantly kin to his mama."

I looked up to the judge for help.

"You need to establish the relationship, Mr. Tucker," the judge urged.

Mr. Coley spoke up, "Judge, I don't know. It just seems like to me I've heard my mama talk about a Mrs. Livingston being somehow kin to her."

"Judge," I said. "I think Mr. Coley should be stricken from the jury."

The judge asked Mr. Coley, "Would you be as close as a first cousin?"

"Oh, no sir," he responded. "It'd be a whole lot more distant than that."

"Maybe third or fourth cousin?" The judge tried to help him.

"It'd probably be further off than that," he replied.

"Would this relationship prevent you from being impartial in this case?" The judge asked in a stern tone of voice.

"Oh, no sir. It wouldn't affect me one bit," he responded.

"Go ahead with your questioning, Mr. Tucker," the judge instructed. "I will not disqualify him."

"I don't have any more questions," I said. Then before the judge could say anything, I jumped up. "Judge, excuse me. I do have one more question."

"All right, Mr. Tucker, go ahead."

"Besides Mrs. Doster, are any of you members of the Arco Church of God?"

No one gave any indication, so I walked back over to counsel table, laid my pad down and said in a soft voice, "Thank you Judge. That's all I have."

The judge spoke up, "It seems that all of the jurors remaining are legally qualified. Mr. Clerk, would you call each name from your jury list, and, as your name is called, you will stand, give your name, address, occupation and your spouse's occupation, if you have a spouse. "All right, he looked down at the clerk. "Would you call the first name?"

"Annie Bell Goodman," the clerk announced.

A thin, little lady on the front row stood up. She wore thick glasses that indicated a severe sight problem.

"I'm Annie Bell Goodman. I live at 1120 Scranton Road, Brunswick, Georgia. I'm a housewife and my husband is a shrimper."

The DA said, "Mrs. Goodman, what do you know about this case?"

"I just read about it in the papers," she said, then added, "I've heard some talk about it."

"The State excuses the juror," the DA said in a quieter voice.

The judge then spoke loudly, "Mrs. Goodman, you may be excused." She got up and walked out of the courtroom.

The judge then said, "Mr. Clerk, call the next juror."

"Kerry Pennington," the clerk announced.

He stood and looked around, nervously to see if others were staring at him. He spoke softly when he told his name and address. He appeared to be what some might call a "nervous Nellie." His eyes twitched when he announced, "I'm a veterinarian." He responded to the same questions asked by the DA of Mrs. Goodman and replied that he'd only seen a piece in the newspaper about the incident.

The DA then asked, "Have you formed an opinion about this case from what you know, Mr. Pennington?"

"No sir," he said in almost a whisper.

"So, if the State proved to you beyond any reasonable doubt that this fellow over here in the uniform," he pointed to Tommy, "murdered Calvin Livingston, would you have any problem in returning a verdict of guilty, Mr. Pennington?"

"No sir. I wouldn't," he said in an unconvincing tone.

"Thank you, Mr. Pennington for being honest and forthright with me," the DA said. After a moment of silence, the DA spoke up louder, "Juror, look upon the prisoner. Prisoner look upon the juror."

From previous criminal cases I'd tried, I learned that this was the DA's manner of accepting the juror.

"Mr. Tucker, you may ask your questions of the juror," the judge said.

"Mr. Pennington, you say you have not formed an opinion about this case?"

"I have not."

"Do you believe there may be extenuating circumstances that may justify someone killing another person?"

"Well, it all depends."

"Depends on what?"

"Depends on a lot of things," he said. "Like if some man was breaking into my house, and I thought he was gonna' kill me, I'd shoot him. I think I'd have the right to shoot him, don't you?"

"So, you believe self-defense, justifies killing another? What else?"

"Well, I don't know," he responded.

"What if someone made improper sexual advances toward you? What would you do?"

"I'd probably run."

Some of the other jurors giggled.

"What if a man grabbed you and touched you in a private place?"

"Well, I don't know about that," he answered. "I'd probably fight him."

"What if you had the capacity to kill him, would you try?"

"I guess if there was no way to escape, I might try."

I moved closer to the juror. "Mr. Pennington, if I was able to prove to you that this young man," he gestured toward Tommy, "is a good boy, never been in any trouble, but was so provoked by the obscene gestures of the victim that it caused something to snap in his head; and if, as a result of his Marine training and in an effort to repel these advances, he inflicted bodily harm on the victim causing him to die, if I could prove that to you, could you find that this man is not guilty of murder?"

The DA quickly leapt to his feet. "Judge, it seems like to me, Mr. Tucker is trying his whole case in one question," he smirked.

"It is a lengthy question," the judge agreed, "but I'm going to let him ask it," then he turned to the juror, "Mr. Pennington, did you understand the question?

"Yes sir. I understood the question. I just don't know how to answer it."

"Well, just answer it the best way you know how," the judge instructed.

"I don't know if I could find him guilty or not. I would have to hear all the evidence first."

I pursued him further. "But after you've heard all the evidence, if I could prove all those things I just said, could you possibly find him not guilty?"

"I don't know if I could or not. I'd just have to see."

The judge interceded. "I think he's answered the question as best he can, Mr. Tucker. Go on to your next question, if you have one," he said sternly.

"Were you ever in the military, Mr. Pennington?"

"No. I was too young to fight in World War II and got a

deferment for the Korean War because of my bad eyes," he said, as he adjusted his glasses on his nose.

The arduous questioning of the jurors absorbed the remainder of the day, with the continual quibbling back and forth between the DA and me. Finally at 5:30 the jury had been selected. The judge seemed exhausted, as well as the rest of the court personnel.

As for the 42 jurors, by law the defendant gets twenty strikes and the State gets ten. The DA had used all his strikes to eliminate the females from the jury, so we wound up with a group of twelve white men, all over the age of 50.

The jurors seemed uneasy. Some looked frightened and squirmed about in their seats as they awaited the next move. Before excusing the jurors for the evening, the judge turned to them, "I instruct you not to discuss this case among yourselves or with anyone else, and that includes your wife and other members of your family. If anyone tries to talk with you about this case, you must tell them immediately that you cannot discuss it, because you're a juror. It they persist in talking with you about the case, then you must report it to me tomorrow when you return to court.

The judge then pounded the gavel loudly and said, "Court is in recess until 9:00 a.m. tomorrow morning." When he stood up, the sheriff announced in a loud voice, "All rise!"

Everyone stood until the judge left the courtroom, at which time, the sheriff walked over to Tommy, grabbed both his arms and placed the handcuffs around his wrists. When he locked the handcuffs, the loud clicking sound reverberated throughout the courtroom causing Agnes to choke up and begin crying uncontrollably. Wes tried to console her.

Then as everyone stood, the sheriff led Tommy by the arm toward the door, his pistol conspicuously hanging from the holster. And, as if she were going under water for the third and last time, Agnes wailed a mournful cry, "Tommy!"

He turned his head toward her, and their eyes met only for a split second.

The sheriff fired back, "Order in the court!" he shouted. As the bailiff held the door open, the sheriff and Tommy walked out. Before shutting the door, still clutching Tommy by the arm, he then led him into the "courthouse holding pen," a cell next to the courtroom where prisoners were kept during their trial. About six feet wide and eight feet long, it contained nothing inside except a bench and a toilet with no seat and no privacy.

I walked out of the courtroom and over to the holding pen, being the only one allowed to go there to visit my client. Tommy was sitting on the bench inside the small cell.

I noticed tears forming in Tommy's eyes. I'd seen the eye contact between him and his mother. It reminded me of an old Agatha Christie quote: "A mother's love for her son is like nothing else in the world. It knows no law, no pity. It dares all things and crushes down remorselessly all that stands in its path."

"I'm sorry," Tommy said, as if he were ashamed of shedding a few tears.

"You don't need to apologize," I attempted to console him. "I understand. As soon as everyone leaves the courthouse, they'll be taking you back over to the jail."

"OK," Tommy slumped then looked into my eyes, "That was harder than I expected, but it's probably going to get worse, right?"

"Yeah, Tommy. I'm afraid it will."

Monday night
December 9, 1973

As I left the courtroom, I saw the DA walking down the steps toward the rotunda. I couldn't help but resent his bullying tactics during the striking of the jury. It seemed an attempt to make me appear incompetent. I resolved right then and there it wouldn't happen again.

Wes, Agnes, Duck, Bonnie Sue and Preacher Wraggs were standing outside waiting for me. Not wanting to deal with all the melodrama, I chose to exit from the back door and walk back to my office in the dark. It'd be a good chance to think my thoughts and check out the Christmas lights in the homes and stores.

James and Davis, had waited around for me. "What are you doing here so late?" I asked.

"We want to hear what happened," Davis said. "Thought we might walk down to the Office for a drink."

The Office, a local watering hole about a block away, provided a place to congregate after work. When we walked in, I spotted a couple leaving a table. Davis told the bartender, "Bring us three Johnny Walkers on the rocks."

"I could use a drink right now," I said.

We clinked our glasses together and took a sip.

"Well, how'd it go?" James asked.

"I think it went OK. I was pretty nervous to start with. That damn Dillinger kept jumping up and objecting to everything I did. It really got to me."

"That's a good thing," James said. "That'd probably help you get over your stage fright."

"Yeah. For sure, it did that. I admit he got my dander up."

"That's just the way Jack operates," Davis said. "So, how about your jury?"

"I think they're all right. All men. Of course, Dillinger struck all the women."

"I guess that's to be expected," James said. "He probably

thinks women might be reluctant to give the death penalty."

"They should've had my wife up there. She wouldn't have any problem sticking it to him," Davis laughed.

Neither James nor I even cracked a smile. We knew what he said was true, and it would also be true with my wife, as well.

"Do you know any of the jurors?" James asked.

"Oh yeah. I forgot to tell you. I got Luther Rooks. He's one of your clients, isn't he?

Davis laughed. "Yeah, he is, and I can tell you that redneck would never find a Marine guilty of killing a queer. You did a good job getting him on there."

We had another round and talked for about a half hour or so. I'd told Laura to leave my supper in the oven, since I had no idea what time I'd get home.

I decided to swing by Lester O'Malley's place to pick up a six-pack in case I got nervous during the night and couldn't sleep. I chided Lester for his tactics in getting off the jury. "What do you mean telling the judge you're prejudiced?" I kidded. "I needed you on my jury."

Lester sat on a stool behind the counter blowing smoke rings from a cigarette. "I didn't want to be up there listening to that crap," he chuckled. "I've got better things to do than that."

We chit-chatted for a few minutes. As I was leaving, he said, "Don't worry, Tyler. You're gonna win your case."

Laura met me at the door with a hug and a kiss. "What do I smell on your breath?" she asked.

I explained about going to the Office with Davis and James.

"I guess you needed it," she said. "The kids went to bed early tonight and your dinner is probably cold and hard as a rock by now. I didn't think you'd be this late."

"Don't worry. I'm hungry enough to eat rocks."

"Oh, by the way," Laura said. "Your father called. He wants to know how your first day went. You probably should call him before you eat."

I grabbed the phone on the wall in the kitchen.

"So, how did it go?" he asked.

"About the way I expected," I said. "The DA struck all the women."

"That's no surprise. All DA's feel that women are more reluctant to give the death penalty."

"I suppose so," I smiled, thinking of Davis' wife and mine, too. "The DA also tried to badger me and push me around."

"Don't let him do that."

"But how do I stop him?"

"Exude confidence. The jury likes a lawyer who acts like he knows what he's doing."

"But what if I don't have confidence?"

"Then just pretend you do. Write at the top of your legal pad in all caps the words, 'EXUDE CONFIDENCE.' Just focus on it, and act like you know what you're doing whether you do or not. The jury has to feel that you're doing your very best to defend your client. If you appear lackluster, then they will think you don't really care. They pick up on things like that."

"I'll try to remember it."

"And don't forget there's a lot of difference in being confident and being cocky. Jurors don't like cocky lawyers."

I laughed. "I don't think you have to worry about that with me."

We talked a little longer about small stuff. I had nothing but love and respect for my father, and he loved me, too. I'll never forget him telling me one time, "Don't you ever refer to me as your old man." He meant it, and I never did.

When I hung up, Laura asked, "Have you talked about this case with your brother?"

"No."

"Do you think your father has mentioned it to him?"

"I don't know. I can't worry about that right now. I'll just have to explain to him that I had no choice. I can't turn the judge's appointment down because it might upset my brother."

After dinner, Laura put her hand on my shoulder, "You look exhausted."

"You're right. I am."

I'd noticed when I walked in that Laura was wearing a good dose of Shalimar cologne, her favorite, and mine, too. That was always a good sign.

"Let's get in bed, and I'll give you a back and neck massage," she said.

"I certainly wouldn't turn that down," I smiled.

Tuesday
December 10, 1973

"Gentlemen of the jury, you have been empaneled to hear the case of the State of Georgia versus Thomas Jennings. I ask that you pay special attention to all the evidence presented in this case in order to obtain a true and just verdict. The State has the burden of proof that the murder was committed by the defendant beyond a reasonable doubt. It will be up to you to find the defendant either guilty or not guilty of murder. In your deliberation, you will have the authority, if you so choose, to reduce the charge from murder to voluntary or involuntary manslaughter. You will also have the authority to recommend to the court the imposition of the sentence, whether it be death, a life sentence or anything less. But your verdict must be unanimous. In other words, all twelve of you must agree on the charge and the recommendation of the sentence.

"You will also be asked to determine if Thomas Jennings committed the crime of theft of a vehicle. If you find him guilty of that charge, you will have the authority to recommend to the court the imposition of the sentence.

"All right, the District Attorney will now make his opening statement to the jury. Are you ready, Mr. Dillinger?"

The DA stood up and said, "Your Honor, I'd like to make a motion that all witnesses be sequestered."

"What do you have to say, Mr. Tucker?"

"I agree they should be sequestered."

"Have both of you given your list of witnesses to the clerk?" The judge asked.

The clerk spoke up, "Yes Judge. They've both given them to me."

"All right, Mr. Sheriff, would you get the list from the clerk and call the names of all the witnesses and make sure that they remain outside the courtroom during the entire trial?"

The sheriff did as he was told.

The judge turned toward the DA. "Go ahead and make

your opening statement to the jury."

Dressed in his usual baggy, navy-blue suit and red bow tie, Dillinger stood up and said, "Yes, Your Honor." He swaggered over to the jury box and, without any notes, told them how he expected to prove all the evidence beyond any reasonable doubt that Tommy Jennings was guilty of cold-blooded murder and theft of the victim's vehicle. He went on to say that Tommy had confessed to killing Calvin and taking his vehicle unlawfully, so there was no doubt about his guilt.

"We have pictures to show you just how brutal this murder was. That Marine over there," he pointed directly at Tommy, "broke a lamp over Calvin's head that cut his jugular vein, and while he was in the process of bleeding to death, that Marine beat his body to a pulp. His counsel will be asking you to give Mr. Jennings mercy, even though he showed none for Calvin. After that vicious and savage attack on Calvin's body, that Marine over there didn't feel one ounce of compassion or sympathy or sorrow. He left him there dying, the same fellow who had befriended him a few hours earlier by giving him a ride from Jacksonville to Brunswick. So, what did Jennings do after he'd killed him? And did he do anything for the dying man? No. He then committed another crime by stealing Calvin's car. He took off in it, thinking that no one would ever find him. But our good police force here in Brunswick caught him for speeding while he was trying to get out of town as fast as possible. That's when he knew the jig was up. When the police booked him for speeding and DUI and took him back to the station, he confessed what he'd done. Now he has got the gall to come up here to this courthouse before you fine, upstanding, law-abiding citizens of the community and ask you to let him off for what he did."

The DA started shaking his head back and forth a number of times in disbelief. "I hope you'll give him what he deserves. He didn't spare poor Calvin's life that night, so why should you spare his?"

There's no doubt Dillinger knew how to sway a jury. I could only wish I had half of his ability to do that.

He walked back and forth in front of the jury box strutting like a rooster. He put his hands on the railing in front of the jury box and dramatically leaned over, staring at each one of them, one at a time, and spoke softly, "I'm going to ask you not only to find Jennings guilty of murder, but to give him the same thing he gave Calvin Livingston" – he yelled out, "DEATH!" It scared the jurors so much, they all jumped back in their seats. He continued in a loud voice, "I want you to give him death in the electric chair, so this killer you see sitting over there at that table, disguised as a Marine, will never again have the opportunity to brutally kill another person. The world will then be a safer place without him."

He paced up and back before the jury and then wheeled around toward them. "I want you to listen carefully to all the evidence that I'm going to present on behalf of the State, and at the end of the trial, I want you to get rid of this killer, once and for all," he ended on a crescendo, being an actor through and through. It was as if he'd just finished singing the national anthem.

Tommy held his head down, staring at the floor. He appeared to be totally battered and shaken by the piercing words of the DA. A scary, empty feeling came over me, knowing that my task would be to overcome those harsh words.

The judge looked down at me, "All right, Mr. Tucker, you may make your opening statement now."

I straightened my tie, buttoned my coat and looked down at the words I'd written at the top of my legal pad: "EXUDE CONFIDENCE." When I picked up my pad to walk to the podium in front of the jury, my mouth felt as dry as cotton. Again, I introduced myself, the name of our firm and that I'd been appointed by the court to represent Tommy. I tried to speak forcefully to keep my voice from quivering.

I told the jury that in order to lure Tommy into his scheme, Calvin knew it would be necessary to get him intoxicated to lower his resistance. They drank an entire bottle of wine, and then he coaxed Tommy to his room for some beers and to rest overnight before continuing his journey back to Camp Lejeune. I pointed over to Tommy, who looked at the jury for the first time. "This eighteen-year-old boy grew up in a fine Christian home, never missed going to church and never got into any kind of trouble."

I finally worked up my confidence to escape from behind the podium and walk in front of the jury as the DA had. "I'm going to show to you during this trial what it's like to go through boot camp and to train a young boy to become 'combat-ready' and how to fight the enemy over in Vietnam and to kill the enemy, even with his bare hands, so as to prevent the spread of Communism and to keep us living in a free society. We should take off our hats to boys like Tommy, who are willing to sacrifice their lives for our country."

Imitating my opponent, I walked back and forth in front of the jury box. "I intend to show you that this homosexual man, two years older than Tommy, got him so drunk that he really didn't know what he was doing. Tommy, only six months ago, tasted his first alcohol when he drank a beer."

Pausing for a moment, I then said in a louder voice, "When Mr. Livingston felt he'd gotten the young Marine drunk enough, he tried to take advantage of him sexually. He made advances toward Private Jennings that provoked him. Like an instant reflex, it caused something in Tommy's head to snap and to feel he needed to defend himself from the enemy and do what he'd been trained to do by the Marine Corps."

I turned back and looked toward Tommy once again in hopes that the jury would follow suit. "Once you've heard all the evidence, I hope you'll treat this young man as if he were your son or your grandson or your nephew or your cousin and find that what he did, while extreme, was justifiable under the circumstances."

When I turned to walk back toward counsel's table, Tommy's eyes met mine, signaling his approval of my statement.

The judge pounded his gavel and said, "The court will be in recess for 30 minutes before we proceed any further."

The sheriff walked over, put the handcuffs on Tommy and led him to the holding cell for a break. Afterwards, when he returned to the courtroom, I looked at him. He appeared pale and clammy.

"Are you OK?" I asked.

"I feel nauseated. Like I might throw up," he said.

"Don't feel like the Lone Ranger. I do, too."

Not only did Tommy appear like he might pass out, I could detect a smell that could only be identified as an odor of fear.

The judge then returned to the bench. The sheriff yelled out, "Order in the Court."

"Mr. DA, you may proceed for the State," the judge said.

I stood up. "Your honor, before we proceed, I'd like to make a motion."

"Go ahead, Mr. Tucker."

I read from my notes: "As attorney for the defendant, I request that this case be heard and tried after clearing the courtroom of all the audience except the necessary court personnel needed to assist the court. This request is made pursuant to Georgia Code Annotated 81-1006, because certain parts of the evidence which we expect to be brought out in the trial of this case are of an obscene and vulgar nature, relating to improper acts of the sexes which would tend to debauch the morals of the young and embarrass the family and friends of the deceased victim. On behalf of the defendant, we hereby waive his constitutional rights to an open and public trial."

I looked up at the judge. He turned to the DA, "What do you have to say about this?"

The DA, always more than willing to make political hay out of any situation spoke with true diplomacy, "Judge, there are many people who are adults who have come here to watch this trial, and they should have the right to see it and hear it."

The judge, sizing up what was going on in the DA's head, said, "All right, I'm going to ask anyone under 21 years old to leave the courtroom."

Tommy looked at me with an expression that read, "Does he mean me?"

I couldn't help but chuckle, which broke my spell of nervousness.

No one left the courtroom.

The judge continued, "Now ladies and gentlemen, in the trial of this case it may be necessary at times to use language that may seem vulgar and obscene. So, I would like for all of you to have the opportunity to leave the courtroom if you feel this would embarrass you or make you feel uncomfortable.

One lady grabbed her pocketbook and walked out.

The judge then called for a brief recess.

When everyone returned to the courtroom, the judge looked over at the DA, "All right, you may proceed."

The DA sounded off in his bombastic way, "I call Deputy Jones to the stand."

A stocky, tall man with long legs and a sharp face, with his upper lip protruding over his bottom one. He ambled over to the witness stand. The clerk told him to place his right hand on the Bible, "And repeat after me. Do you swear to tell the truth, the whole truth, and nothing but the truth, so help you God?"

"I do," he mumbled.

"You may be seated," the clerk said.

The DA wasted no time in firing off questions. "State your name for the jury."

"T. A. Jones," he responded in a nasally tone of voice, wearing his law enforcement uniform and feeling his importance.

"Where are you employed, Mr. Jones?"

"The Glynn County Sheriff's Department," he said.

"On the night of Thanksgiving, which I believe was the 28th of November, but this was after midnight, so it would've been in the early morning hours of Friday, November 29th, did anything unusual happen?"

"Well sir, yes it did. Me and Deputy Jackson was out there patrolling on Highway 17 just north of Brunswick, and we seen this car coming toward us, and it was a'weavin' across the center line," he paused for a moment to clear his throat.

"Go on," The DA urged him.

"Well sir, I wheeled around and turned on my flashing

lights and the siren, and he pulled his car off the road on the right shoulder."

"Then what happened?"

"Well sir, I went up to the driver's side of the car and told him to let his window down. And he did. And I told him to get out of the car. And he did."

"How was he dressed?"

"Well sir,"

The DA interrupted, obviously annoyed, and scolded him. "It's not necessary to say 'Well sir' each time you answer a question."

"Yes sir," he said apologetically. "Now let's see. Where was I?"

"I had asked you, 'How was he dressed?'"

"Well sir," he caught himself. "Oh, I'm sorry. I didn't go to say that again."

"That's all right. Just answer the question."

"He had his pants on. They was his Marine pants. His shirt was hanging out of his pants. He had his shoes on with no socks and his shoes was untied. He looked like he'd got dressed real quick like and didn't have enough time to put his clothes on right."

"Did you see any blood on him?"

"No, I didn't see no blood on him."

"Was there anything unusual about him besides the way he was dressed?"

"Well, he was pretty drunk, if you ask me."

"What about the car he was driving?"

"I seen he had Georgia plates on his car with a Glynn County tag. I figured I might've knowed him, but he was new to me. I never seen him before. But then again, he was just a young boy."

"Did you know that he'd stolen the vehicle?"

I jumped up. "I object, Your Honor. He's leading the witness."

The judge said, "Rephrase your question, Mr. DA."

"I'll withdraw that question," the DA said. "Then what happened, Deputy?"

"I got his driver's license from him and seen he was from Florida. It made me wonder why his car had a Glynn County tag on it."

"Did he say anything to you?"

"Well, he was pretty snockered. I was gonna book him for DUI. We throwed him in the back of the police car; and when we was driving him to the station, he spoke up and said, 'I think I might've killed somebody.' I turned around 'cause I wasn't sure I heard him right. I said, 'What'd you say?' Then he said it again. 'I think I might've killed somebody.' I asked him, 'where did you kill somebody?' He said, 'The Holiday Inn.' So, we drove over there and the night clerk let us in the room where he said it took place. Well sir, we saw the body laying there on the sofa. He'd been beat up something awful. There was blood all over him. It was an ugly sight. When the night clerk saw it, he almost had a conniption fit. I thought we was gonna have to take him to the emergency room."

The DA asked, "And then what happened?"

"We hauled him on down to the station."

"When you got him to the station, did you give him the Miranda warning?"

"Oh, yes siree," he said. "We been doing that ever since that thing came out. I believe it was about seven or eight year' ago, wasn't it? I always read it off the card the sheriff give us. He told us we had to read it to everybody."

"So, did he sign the waiver of his rights to an attorney?"

"He shore did. He said he didn't want no lawyer from here. If he had to have a lawyer, he wanted it to be a Marine lawyer."

"But he did sign the waiver?"

"Yes sir."

"Did he confess to the murder of Calvin Livingston?"

"Yes sir, he shore did."

The DA said curtly. "Did you take any pictures?"

"Yes sir. We took a bunch of 'em."

"Are you the one who took the pictures?"

"Yes sir, I was the one."

"Have you had them in your possession and control since you took them?"

"That's right."

"Do they accurately represent what you saw out there on that early morning of Friday, November 29th, 1973?"

"That's right."

The DA turned to the judge, "Judge, they have already been marked as State's exhibits one through twelve, and we would like to have them tendered into evidence."

The judge looked at me. "Any objections, Mr. Tucker?"

I stood up. "Judge, we feel the pictures are so offensive that the use of them in this trial is only designed to inflame and prejudice the minds of the jurors. We're not denying that my client killed Mr. Livingston, so these pictures are totally unnecessary."

"Overruled," the judge said. "Mr. DA, you can go ahead and enter them into evidence."

The DA, standing next to the bench, said, "Judge, would you like to see the pictures before I hand them to the jury?"

"That's not necessary," he said.

The DA handed them to the juror sitting at the left end of the front row, who sneered as if he were reluctant to touch them. He hurriedly flipped through them, then handed them to the man seated next to him. This man winced as he viewed each one. The DA intently watched the other jurors shuffle through the pictures and cracked a smile as if he relished in their disgust. After all jurors had seen them, the judge turned toward the panel, "Would the jury like a brief recess?"

They all nodded immediately.

The judge banged his gavel. "Court is recessed for ten minutes."

Since they didn't take Tommy out to the holding cell, we

had a few minutes to chat in an attempt to calm each other. I turned to the spectators and saw Tommy's family. Duck shot me a thumbs-up.

When the jury returned, the DA continued his questioning of Deputy Jones. "All right, Deputy, when you arrived on the scene of the crime, did you determine that Mr. Livingston was already dead?"

"Oh, yes. He was definitely dead when we got there. His body was done cold. We called up Leggett's Funeral Home to come pick him up. They got there in about fifteen minutes, and they said he'd been dead around two hours."

The DA continued. "I'm going to show you the written confession that Jennings signed." He handed it to the deputy. "Did you see Jennings sign this?"

"Yes sir."

"And did he sign it freely and voluntarily?"

"Oh, yes sir, he shore did."

The DA turned to the judge. "Judge, we'd like to enter this confession into evidence."

"Mr. Tucker?" The judge looked down at me.

"No objection, Your Honor."

"Let the confession be marked by the Clerk and entered into evidence," the judge said. "Mr. DA, do you have further questions of the deputy?"

The DA reviewed his legal pad, then asked his last question: "Deputy Jones, did all of these events you just related take place right here in Glynn County, Georgia?"

"Yes sir. They did."

"No further questions."

The judge looked at me. "Your witness, Mr. Tucker."

I decided to stand behind the counsel table to conduct my cross-examination. "Deputy Jones, you said when you stopped Private Jennings in the car, it appeared he'd been drinking? Is that correct?"

"Well, I tell you. I seen a whole bunch a drunks in my life, and I'd say he was more than just drunk. He was acting kinda crazy."

"Did you do a breathalyzer test or a blood test on Private Jennings to check his alcohol content?"

"No, we never done nothing like that. We weren't interested in that after we found out he'd murdered somebody."

"You said he was acting kind of crazy. Did it occur to you to ask him or check him out to see if Calvin Livingston might've slipped some kind of drug in his drink?"

"No sir, we never done no such thing like that."

"Did you see any bottles of any kind in the car when you stopped Private Jennings?"

"No sir. I shore didn't."

"Did he tell you while the two of them were sitting on the sofa, that Mr. Livingston put his hand on Private Jennings' private parts?"

"Yes sir. I believe he did say something like that."

"And after you picked him up, did he cooperate fully with you and Deputy Jackson?"

"Yes sir."

"He didn't try to give you any trouble?"

"No sir," he shook his head. "He didn't give us no trouble."

I looked at the judge. "No further questions, Your Honor."

The judge then turned toward the DA. "Do you have any redirect?"

"Just one Judge," he turned toward the Deputy, "Is there any doubt in your mind that Tommy Jennings killed Calvin Livingston?"

"No sir. There ain't no doubt in my mind," he said, then pointed toward Tommy, "And there ain't no doubt in his mind either."

The judge leaned forward and looked at the DA and me. "Do either of you have any further questions of Deputy Jones?"

We both indicated in the negative.

The judge banged his gavel, "It's time for a lunch break. Let's see. It's about a quarter of twelve. I direct you jurors to be back in your seats shortly before 1:00 p.m. Court is in recess."

I ran out to the car to grab the tuna fish sandwich Laura had made. The temperature in the car was about the same as outside – cold. I started the car, turned on the heater and sat there for probably a half hour eating and collecting my thoughts about my role in the midst of the most intense trial I'd ever experienced.

Everyone was back in their seats well before 1:00. The judge ascended the bench about ten minutes afterwards. He banged the gavel and said to the DA, "All right. Call your next witness."

"The State calls Deputy Jackson," the DA announced. He appeared to be about ten years younger than Jones, and both had worked in the sheriff's office for over fifteen years. He took the stand, was sworn in by the clerk and essentially gave the same testimony as Jones. I declined to ask him any questions.

The DA then called Michael F. Manutti. After being sworn by the clerk, he gave his full name to the jury. Instead of a uniform, he wore a black suit, red tie and his head appeared to have been shaved. You would certainly pick him out of a line-up as being a law enforcement officer.

The district attorney began, "Where are you employed, Mr. Manutti, and for how long have you been employed there?"

"I'm a special agent with the Georgia Bureau of Investigation, where I've worked for approximately seven years," Manutti answered in a clear, calm voice that made him appear much more professional than the previous two witnesses. He then told of his duties as a special agent and that he had been called by the sheriff's office in Glynn County to assist in the investigation of this murder.

The DA continued. "And after your thorough investigation, have you made a determination who murdered Calvin Livingston?"

I stood up to object. "Your Honor. We've admitted that

my client killed Mr. Livingston."

The judge said, "I'll let him answer it."

The DA asked his witness again to identify the murderer.

Manutti answered, "Yes. Thomas Jennings. The Marine in the uniform sitting over there." He pointed to Tommy.

The DA turned toward me. "Your witness."

I stood up before the judge had a chance to speak. "No questions, Your Honor."

"Call your next witness," the judge told the DA.

"The State calls Dr. James B. Briley."

Dr. Briley, an older man with a head of gray hair and a wrinkled face, walked to the witness stand, dressed in all-black, and was sworn. After giving his name, he stated that he was a pathologist for the state crime lab. When the DA began to qualify him as an expert witness, I stipulated that Dr. Briley was an expert in his field and there were no objections to having him qualified as such.

The doctor described the autopsy, and that, in his opinion, Calvin's death occurred from bleeding by the laceration of his jugular vein caused by the breaking of a lamp over his head. His testimony continued much too long, a real test of my patience. The DA was trying to saturate the jurors with the horrifying pictures of the victim's body. Each time I objected to the DA's attempts to inflame the jury, the judge overruled me.

At the end of the doctor's testimony, I stood up. "No questions, Your Honor." I felt the jury had heard enough of the brutality of the crime.

The judge turned to the DA, "Call your next witness."

"Your Honor, that completes our witnesses for the State."

"Do you rest?" the judge asked.

"I believe that's all we have at this time Judge, but we reserve our right to rebuttal."

"Gentlemen," the judge spoke to the DA and me, "I think we will recess for the day and start the defendant's case tomorrow." He then turned to the jury, "Gentlemen of the jury, I instruct you not to discuss this case with anyone whosoever, not even your wife, your children, or any member of your family or your friends, nor should you discuss this case with each other. If anyone approaches you or phones you or tries to communicate with you in any respect having to do with this case, then you must report it to the sheriff or me when you return to court in the morning. Also, if you see anything in the newspaper, or hear anything on the radio, or see anything on TV about this case, I instruct you not to read it, hear it or see it. In other words, you must be silent, blind and deaf with regard to anything that might relate to this case, except what you hear in this courtroom. Is that understood?"

They nodded in unison.

"All right. I hereby excuse the jury until 9:00 a.m. tomorrow morning. The court is in recess," he banged the gavel.

The sheriff yelled, "All rise!"

The judge exited the bench and out the door to his chambers.

"Everyone remain in your place until the prisoner is removed from the courtroom!" the sheriff shouted, as he walked toward Tommy with the handcuffs and led him out of the courtroom with one handcuff around Tommy's wrist and the other around his.

I watched the faces of each juror as they filed by, wondering what they were thinking.

I walked out to the holding cell. "I'm tired as hell," I told Tommy. "If you don't need to talk with me, I think I'll go home early and try to get a good night's sleep before we kick off in the morning."

"That's fine," Tommy said, standing up straighter.

As I walked down the steps to the rotunda, Preacher Wraggs met me with a serious expression. "Tyler, I'd like to know how you thought things went today."

"Pretty much as expected," I said with a shrug, hoping he wouldn't settle in for a long conversation as he was prone to do. "They didn't pull any surprises."

"Do you feel like you have a good case?"

"I plan to give it everything we've got. That's about all I

can say."

"You know Tommy's parents are really having a tough time during this trial," he said. "I wish I could be in there to try to comfort them."

"I understand. But when the witnesses are sequestered, you're not allowed to come into the courtroom until it's time for you to testify."

"At this point, we just have to roll the dice and see what happens." I walked down one step below him, pretending to be in a hurry to leave.

Preacher Wraggs extended his bottom lip and looked down at me underneath his glasses with an expression that made me feel he was unsatisfied with my response. He placed his palms together underneath his nose. "We'll be praying for you."

"Thank you, Preacher. We'll need all the prayers we can get."

"I hope you'll do everything you can."

"If I can put up the best argument I've ever made in my life and plead for mercy, the judge has the authority to give him a life sentence."

"What's the likelihood of that?"

"Voters don't like judges being too lenient on criminals. Next summer is an election, and the DA is running against the judge, so both of them need to appear tough on crime."

"Yes, I understand."

"This case has gotten a lot of publicity in the newspapers and TV, and it would be a minor miracle to get the judge, with a guilty verdict in his face, to reduce the penalty to life in prison. But if he did, Tommy would be eligible for parole in seven years."

After those remarks, the preacher had a more conciliatory attitude. "Well, Tyler, we know you're doing your best. Is there anything you need from us?"

"Yes. In your testimony tomorrow, I'm expecting you to be the best character witness for Tommy you can possibly be."

We talked for a few minutes, and I reviewed some of the questions I planned to ask him. After briefing him, I told him that he'd be my first witness.

"I'll do my best," he smiled and added, "Please tell Tommy I have a prayer chain back home praying daily for him," he paused, "you know, Tyler, with God, all things are possible."

"I do believe that, Preacher."

We shook hands, and I took off down the steps and back to the office. Everyone had left, so I checked my phone messages. There were none I cared to return. Clients may be upset with me, but I had nothing left for them after a long day of trial.

At home, Hannah and Wynn met me at the door. Each one grabbed a leg and demanded to be picked up and hugged, saying, "Daddy! Daddy!" This was the best medicine I knew to relieve the tension from my body.

Laura walked out of the kitchen, wiping her hands with a dish cloth. "How did it go?"

"About the way I figured," I said, as I leaned down to kiss her. "How was your day?"

"Miles screamed all day, but other than that," she said, making a face.

"What was wrong with him?"

"I don't know. I finally got him down a while ago. He was exhausted, and I was, too."

"Well, what do you think?"

"I'm not sure. I came close to taking him to Dr. Waddell. It seemed to me that his stomach was hurting. I don't know what it was, but I finally got him calmed down enough to go to sleep. I hope he doesn't scream tonight. I know you probably need to get some rest."

"Yeah. I'm pretty exhausted right now."

"I figured you would be. Hannah and Wynn have eaten. So, if you can get them to sleep, then you and I might could have a little one on one."

"That'd be nice," I smiled for the first time today.

I checked on Miles. He was sound asleep. I leaned down and kissed him on the forehead. Miles took a deep breath and, even though he remained asleep, he cracked a little smile. My heart melted. This little boy loved his dad, and his dad loved him.

I helped Wynn with his blue flannel pajamas while Hannah put on her pink gown, covered with images of little lambs. I grabbed my ukulele, and the three of us snuggled up in Wynn's bed.

"OK. What song do we want to hear tonight?"

"Sing *500 Miles*, Daddy," Hannah begged.

"No, sing *Baa Baa Black Sheep*," Wynn insisted.

"How 'bout I do both? OK?"

I sang softly with a soothing voice to get them in the mood for sleep. After ten or fifteen minutes, they both drifted off. I kissed Wynn then slipped down toward the end of the bed to get up. I lifted Hannah in my arms and placed her in her bed. I covered her with the sheet, a spread and blanket and kissed her goodnight.

The temperature outside had dropped to the high thirties. While the house was heated with central heat, Laura preferred for the house to be cool at night. That's how she was raised. She had told me that her father always made her keep the window open next to her bed, no matter how cold it was outside.

I went into the kitchen. Laura was stirring a pot of vegetable soup.

"Are you hungry?" she asked.

"Yeah, I guess. This day wiped me out."

"You know I'm worried about you," she placed her hand on my shoulder.

"What are you worried about, honey?"

"I can see how this trial is taking a toll on you."

I shook my head and took a deep breath. "Yeah, I guess you're right."

"I don't think you realize how conflicted you are. You internalize things, and you need to get them out on the table and deal with them."

"What do you mean?"

"Tyler, I know you well enough to know that you don't have prejudices. You always treat people with respect, no matter what color they are or what their sexual preference may be," she took a deep sigh. "I've seen how tolerant you are with your brother. And I know he loves you and respects you very much, because you have accepted him for who he is."

"OK. And what is your point?"

"You are a good moral person, one of the most progressive, open-minded men I know of. My problem is if you knowingly and willingly appeal to the prejudice of the jury, just how moral is that?"

Before I had a chance to respond, she got up and opened two cans of beer and handed one to me. I pressed the cold can to my forehead.

"Thanks, I need this," I took a big gulp. "honey, I can't help it if people are prejudiced."

"Tyler, don't you feel like justice should prevail?"

"Of course, I do. Justice should prevail. But, as a lawyer, I have to be an advocate for my client. It's like being a boxer. Someone hires me to get into the boxing ring and do my best to knock the other guy out. That's what being a lawyer is. I'm not a judge to determine right and wrong. I'm a hired slugger. I don't jump into the ring and say to myself that this guy I'm boxing is a nice guy so I shouldn't hit him. You have to start slugging away at the other guy because that's what you've been hired to do."

Laura placed both her hands on me and said, "This twenty-year-old kid. Think about him. Did he deserve to be killed because he wanted to have sex with another guy?"

"Look, honey, it's more complicated than that," I took a large swallow of beer. "Tommy was sexually abused by his teacher when he was just a young teenager. He suppressed those horrible, traumatic experiences for all these years. I never had anything like that happen to me, but I can only imagine how it would affect a kid. He joined the Marines and knocked himself out to be the best Marine he could possibly be. They drilled him and taught him to become a killer, not just with a gun, but with his bare hands. He was combat ready. They had him prepared to go to Vietnam and be, not just a fighter, but a killer."

"I would not want that for Wynn and Miles," she said. "I don't want them to be fighters and killers."

"Of course we don't want that for them," I said, trying to defuse her. "But they'll have to make their own decisions. It's up to them to be whoever they are."

"Let's don't talk about this anymore," Laura sighed. "It makes me upset."

"Yeah, me too," I said.

I later broke the moments of silence with what turned out to be a bomb shell. "Did I ever tell you about what happened to me one night when I was leaving a pub in London?"

"No. You didn't."

"I was walking out of a pub near my hotel and noticed a guy coming up behind me. He caught up with me and asked me if I'd like to go to his flat."

"And what did you say?"

"I told him I was tired and wanted to go back to my hotel."

"And then what?"

"He said I might be missing out on the best time of my life."

"And what did you say?" Laura seemed surprised.

"I didn't say anything. I just shrugged my shoulders."

"Yeah. And what else did he say?"

"He said he'd guarantee that I'd get the best blow job I'd ever had."

Laura seemed angered. "Why have you never told me this?"

"What's there to tell? It's no big deal. I didn't go with him. I just said 'No.'" I laughed. "I didn't have the guts to tell him it would have to be the best one I'd ever had, because I'd never had one."

She didn't even smile and remained sullen. "Well, maybe you should've taken him up on it."

"Laura, I can't believe you said that!"

"So, what did you do?"

"Nothing. I just walked on back to my hotel."

She stood up with her hands on her hips. "I just wonder, Tyler Tucker, if you can hear what you're saying."

"What?"

"He propositioned you. How many years ago?"

"'68 –'73. Five years."

"You're saying that a guy tried to have sex with you, and it was such an insignificant thing that you didn't even mention it to your wife for five years?"

"Yeah. So, what's the big deal?"

"Why didn't you kill him?" she asked with a large dose of sarcasm.

I didn't answer; only took a deep breath.

"How much bigger were you?"

"He probably came up to my shoulders."

"Why didn't you beat him up and stomp him in the ground?" she asked with even more anger and derision in her tone of voice.

"Laura, please. I get your drift. Let's let it go."

"All I want from you, Tyler Tucker, is to listen to what you just told me."

I didn't answer. She'd made her point. "Let's go ahead and eat. I want to go to bed."

She leaned back, took a long, deep breath and didn't speak for a moment. "OK. It's ready," she said.

I smiled and leaned over to kiss her. "You know I love you, don't you?"

"Yes," Laura sighed and began to cave in. "And I love you, too."

"You know what I just thought about?" I asked her, as I put my hand on her shoulder.

"What are you going to tell me now?"

"I'm going to tell you that you're the one in this family who should've been the lawyer."

Wednesday
December 11, 1973

Judge Fletcher ascended the bench, straightened his robe, and pounded his gavel, signaling the start of a new day of trial.

"Mr. Tucker, are you ready to proceed for the defendant?" The judge looked at me and asked.

I leapt to my feet. "Yes sir, Your Honor, we're ready."

"Call your first witness," the judge directed.

"The defendant calls Reverend Ashley Wraggs to the stand."

When the clerk administered the oath to him, "Do you swear to tell the truth, the whole truth and nothing but the truth so help you God," the minister retorted, "I do not swear."

The clerk asked, "Then do you affirm?"

"Yes sir, I do."

I inquired into his background, how he came to be a minister, what churches he'd served as pastor, and how he became the preacher at the Palatka Baptist Church. I sized him up as a likable enough fellow even though his refusal to swear gave him an air of being incurably pious and self-righteous; a malady typical of a lot of clergymen I'd encountered.

"Are you familiar with the Jennings family?"

"Oh, yes. Miss Agnes Jennings is one of the cornerstones of my church. She's there anytime the church doors are open," he said with a smile.

"Is she the mother of Tommy Jennings, the defendant in this trial?"

"Yes sir, she is," he said.

"And how about Tommy Jennings? How long have you known him?"

"My goodness. I've known him since he was a little boy."

I then popped off the three required statutory questions

of a character witness. "From your knowledge of the defendant, have you had an occasion to observe his conduct and to know his reputation in the community?"

"I certainly have."

"Is it good or bad?"

"It's not only good, it's excellent. He has been a faithful member of my church, never missed a Sunday, and he's a fine young man in our community."

"Would you believe him under oath?"

"Of course I would. I've never known Tommy to ever be in any trouble whatsoever until now, and this is just a terrible shock for me and for his family and even the whole community. Yes, he would tell the truth. I'd believe anything he told me. I've never known the boy to lie, and I know him pretty well. I've eaten many times in the Jennings home, and Tommy was always the type of boy that any parent would like to have."

"Have you ever known Tommy to get in any trouble or have a fight with anyone?"

"Absolutely not. Tommy is not that type of boy. As I've said, he's just about the nicest boy you'd ever come across. No, he's never been in any kind of trouble, and, believe me, I would certainly know it if he had, because Miss Agnes would've sent him straight to me if he'd ever gotten into any kind of mischief."

I looked up at the judge, who then asked me, "Have you completed your questions of this witness, Mr. Tucker?"

"Yes sir."

"All right," he turned toward the DA. "Do you wish to cross examine this witness?"

The DA thought for a few moments. I knew he would be reluctant to cross examine a man of the cloth. Preachers know how to persuade a crowd, so it didn't surprise me when he replied, "No sir."

The judge raised his voice. "Call your next witness, Mr. Tucker."

"The defendant calls Dr. John Underwood."

The sheriff went out and brought the doctor in to take the stand. As he stood, the clerk swore him in, and he sat down. A tall, imposing figure, probably in his late fifties, who'd testified in many trials, both civil and criminal, and he had a confident air about him.

"State your name, profession and where you live."

"Dr. John Underwood. I'm a psychiatrist, and I practice my profession in Savannah, Georgia."

I then proceeded with the necessary questions to qualify the doctor as an expert. However, the DA interrupted my questions, "Judge, I'm familiar with this doctor, and I'm willing to stipulate that he is an expert in his field of psychiatry."

I began my direct examination. "Doctor, did you examine the defendant in this case, Tommy Jennings?"

"Yes, I did."

"And when did you do your examination?"

"Tuesday night, December third, just last week."

"Would you tell the jury the method you used to elicit information from Tommy?"

"Yes. I often use hypnosis in my practice, especially in criminal cases. This way I know the information I'm receiving from the patient is generally true. It would be rare for a patient under hypnosis to tell a lie."

I cleared my throat. "Please tell the jury what information you received from this patient."

"Well, since this case involved sexuality, I felt it necessary to get the patient to tell me about his sexual history."

"Yes. Go on."

"When I asked him if he'd ever had sex with a female, he answered in the affirmative. It seems his uncle took Tommy and a friend to a house of prostitution in Jacksonville on the night of their high school graduation."

Agnes wheeled around and gave Duck the dirtiest look she'd ever given him. Wes couldn't help but snicker.

The doctor continued. "He indicated that this was his only sexual encounter with a female other than the usual amount of petting with his girlfriend when they were in high school."

He turned toward the jury. "I then asked him if he'd ever had a sexual experience with a male. When I asked this question, he became very agitated. He started squirming in his chair. He even moaned as if he were in pain. He then revealed that his shop teacher had forcibly performed fellatio on Tommy – in other words, oral sex, when he was a freshman in high school. This teacher threatened him by telling him that he'd give him a failing grade if he didn't participate and furthermore would do harm to his mother if he refused to allow him to do what he wanted."

Duck looked over at Wes with an expression of rage and disbelief. Wes clinched his jaw. Tommy leaned over and put his face down on his arms. The jurors seemed shocked. A few looked over toward Tommy.

The doctor went on to say, "This was a horrible and traumatic experience for him. He admitted he'd never told anyone about what happened."

"Please continue."

"Tommy revealed that he'd heard from his best friend the night of Thanksgiving a couple of weeks ago that his shop teacher, Mr. Lawson, had been killed in a motorcycle accident. Tommy never told his friend what'd happened, but when he dropped him off, Tommy went home and got his father's shotgun, and then went to the cemetery and used up a box of shells shooting at Mr. Lawson's grave."

Some of the jurors squirmed in their seats and looked around at each other.

The doctor continued, "That was the same night he began hitching back to Camp Lejeune, North Carolina, and was picked up by Calvin Livingston."

"Please tell the jury what he told you about what happened after meeting Calvin."

"He said they drank a bottle of wine, and when they arrived in Brunswick, Calvin asked him to go with him to his room at the Holiday Inn to get some sleep and then continue hitching to Camp Lejeune the next morning. When they got to Calvin's room, they drank some beers. Tommy was talking about being shipped off to Vietnam and that he might never come back. Calvin then leaned over like he wanted to hug him, but Tommy pushed him back. Then Calvin put his hand on Tommy's crotch, and he went crazy. He said that was the same thing that Mr. Lawson had done to him. He grabbed the lamp from the table and broke it over Calvin's head. Calvin was apparently knocked unconscious. Blood was gushing from his mouth. Tommy got scared. He jumped up, took Calvin's car keys and took off in his car. Apparently, he was speeding and was stopped by the police a few blocks away."

"Did he tell you anything else?"

"Yes. Tommy began crying, saying he didn't mean to do it. He didn't mean to kill him, but something just snapped in his head."

The DA had kept unusually quiet, not objecting to any of the doctor's testimony.

I continued questioning the doctor. "Do you feel that the defendant was temporarily insane at the moment he committed the murder?"

"I object," the DA spoke up. "He's leading the witness, and furthermore, he has not laid the proper groundwork for alleging temporary insanity."

"Judge," I pleaded, "The doctor, who is an expert, testified to the psychological trauma that the defendant had endured which caused him to lose his ability to determine right from wrong."

"He didn't say any such thing!" The DA insisted.

The judge interrupted. "I'm going to send the jury out. They don't need to be a party to this legal argument." He turned to the sheriff. "Sheriff, would you take the jury to the jury room."

The sheriff walked over to the jury box and led them out.

The judge turned to the DA, "Now tell me, what is your complaint?"

"Judge, Mr. Tucker is implying that the defendant has some type of psychiatric illness or medical condition that has rendered him insane so that he was unable to know right from wrong at the time he committed the crime. They have not proved that the defendant suffered from any kind of mental illness."

The judge turned back to me and asked, "What do you have to say to that, Mr. Tucker?"

"Judge, we contend that the psychological trauma he'd experienced with his shop teacher prevented him from controlling his actions, even though he understood that what he did was wrong. It was an irresistible impulse. I can cite law regarding this."

The judge seemed to be uncertain as to what to do, but then straightened his back, "I'm going to sustain the DA's objection."

I slumped in my seat. The judge noticed my reaction, and added, "Mr. Tucker, the jury heard the testimony of the psychiatrist. They can draw their own conclusions about what he said."

"Yes, Your Honor. I have no further questions of this witness."

When the DA stood up, the judge said in a loud voice, "I think we should have a lunch break. Court will be in recess until 1:00 o'clock."

At that point, food didn't interest me, so I went back to the office to call my father. He'd tried many criminal cases as a judge.

"The judge overruled my attempt at temporary insanity," I told him.

"That's no surprise. It's difficult to prove without some showing of a previous mental condition," he said. I could hear the sympathy in his voice and knew how much he wanted to help me.

"What do you think about whether I should put Tommy on the stand?"

"That's a tough one. It could help the jury to see his demeanor and especially his regret about what happened, but you certainly don't want to swear him."

The laws of Georgia at the time allowed a defendant in a criminal case to make an unsworn statement to the jury. If it was unsworn, the DA would not be allowed to cross examine him. If he was sworn in as a witness, the DA could go after him. It was a tough call, because the DA can argue that what a defendant says in an unsworn statement may or may not be true, because they haven't put their hand on the Bible and sworn to tell the truth.

I told my dad I wasn't sure what to do. "I'm thinking of not putting him up at all."

"Really?" he sounded surprised. "Why?"

"Anything he would say would be repetitive, because the psychiatrist told the whole story of what happened."

"It's your call, Tyler. You have to go with your gut, but usually a jury likes to hear from the defendant, study his demeanor and see his reactions."

"OK. I'll think about it, but I just wanted to hear what you had to say."

"I'm confident you'll do the right thing son."

After a bit of small talk about the family, we said goodbye.

I also talked with James and Davis to get their opinion, but they, pretty much, said the same thing as my father.

On arriving at court, I learned there'd been some disturbance between Tommy's family and Calvin's mother, including a few of the fellows from the community, who'd been sitting with her to support her during the trial. They all apparently got into a shouting match in the rotunda of the courthouse. Thankfully, no one took a swing at the other, but I cautioned Tommy's family to ignore anything said by those who are supporting Calvin.

Newspaper and TV reporters swarmed me as I walked up the stairs, all wanting to hear what I thought about how the trial was going. I really wanted to tell them my version of the case but then I thought better and gave them the usual, "No comment."

The judge banged the gavel to begin the afternoon session.

"Mr. DA," the judge announced. "Do you wish to cross examine Dr. Underwood?"

"Yes, Your Honor."

The judge then cautioned the doctor, "Remember you have been sworn as a witness, and you're still under oath."

"Yes sir," he responded.

"Doctor," the DA began, "I'm sure you're aware that I've cross examined you several times before in other cases?"

"Yes, you have," the doctor cracked a smile. "I remember them very well."

The DA asked, "I believe you said this morning under direct examination that people under hypnosis always tell the truth?"

"No. I didn't say that," the doctor argued. "Most of the time they do. But I listen for tonal modulations if I suspect someone may be lying. I listen for often-used words or phrases that are said in a slightly different way. It's like when you suspect your child has misbehaved, and when you ask him what he's been doing, and he says, 'nothing.' The 'nothing' may sound higher, squeakier and go up in tone at the end, almost as if it's a question. This is a good example of the discomfort of a person under hypnosis revealing a particular thing that can send a subconscious signal to me that something is wrong."

"And you're able to detect that from the tone of their voice?"

"Yes, but, furthermore, I study their body language. This tells a lot about whether or not a person is lying."

The DA continued. "And you can tell that from the way they may squirm around?"

"Yes, and sometimes patients under hypnosis will say, 'I'm tired. Can we talk about this later?' That's a real sign they may be lying."

"I see. So, did you suspect the prisoner over there might be lying to you?"

"No sir. I never saw any sign at all that he might've been lying."

I tried to hide my pleasure at the doctor's answer.

"So, doctor, do you think that Marine over there was so

stupid that he didn't suspect that he was being set up when asked by Mr. Livingston to go to his room with him late at night while both of them were under the influence of alcohol?"

"My assessment of Private Jennings is that he was very naïve. He had a girlfriend in high school. He had a sexual experience with a prostitute the night of his high school graduation, and he'd been forced to have a homosexual experience with his shop teacher when he was only fifteen. While I certainly can't say for a certainty, it's my opinion that Private Jennings did not have enough experience to suspect that Mr. Livingston had ulterior motives in asking him to go to his room. I believe Private Jennings was the type who would believe on the surface what a person said without any ulterior motives."

"But after he got to his room, didn't the bright young Marine have sense enough to figure out what was happening?"

"Again, it's only speculation on my part, but Private Jennings not only had very little experience with sex, but he also was a neophyte when it came to drinking alcohol."

The DA looked around at the jurors to get their reaction, but they were stone-faced. He continued further into his cross-examination. "Then what happened?"

"After the two of them drank a bottle of wine, and then began drinking beer in the room, I frankly think Private Jennings was well under the influence of alcohol. I don't know about Mr. Livingston. Perhaps he was, too. But I do know that alcohol lowers your inhibitions."

"But, Doctor, you know better than that. Drunkenness is no legal excuse for committing a crime. You can't get out of killing somebody by saying, 'Oh, I was drunk. So, it was not my fault.'"

"I understand sir. However, a gullible young man could've been encouraged into drinking more than he normally would have by someone who had a motive to weaken his resistance and allow him to have his way with the intoxicated young man."

"Doctor, you said that a few hours earlier, on the evening of the murder, the prisoner had just learned of the death of his shop teacher. Is that correct?"

"That's what he said."

"And you testified that he was so irate with him, he went to the cemetery where the teacher had been buried and used up a box of shells blasting away at his grave. Is that correct?"

"That's what he told me."

"You'd have to be pretty enraged to do something like that, wouldn't you?"

"I suppose you would."

"What do you mean 'suppose'? That person would have to be pretty angry, don't you think?"

"Yes, he would."

"Then later on that evening, this mad man, who'd been sexually assaulted by his teacher, was hitchhiking back to his base in North Carolina and got picked up by a queer, isn't that what you said?"

"I didn't use that word."

"I know you didn't. But you know what I mean, don't you?"

"Of course."

"Don't you think the defendant had a heart filled with hatred and venom for homosexuals? When he met Calvin, he might've thought, 'Here's my chance to rid the world of another queer.'"

"That doesn't sound like something this young man would've thought."

"How do you know that? How do you know what he thought?"

"I don't. That's just my expert opinion."

"So, for all you know, this murder could've been premeditated, right?"

"I don't think so."

"But you don't know, do you?"

"No, I don't know. It's just my belief."

"He could've gone to Livingston's apartment with the

intent to kill him, right?"

"I told you I don't think so."

"But you also said you don't know, so it is possible, isn't it?"

"Yes, I suppose anything's possible."

I wanted to jump up from my seat and say, "Amen."

The DA calmly said, "No further questions, Your Honor."

I felt as if I was about to tee off with a partner who'd just hit a hole in one. "What do I do now?" I thought. Then looking down at my pad again and seeing the words of my father, 'EXUDE CONFIDENCE,' I knew what I had to do.

I stood up, pulled my shoulders back and walked up in front of the doctor, still sitting on the stand, and asked him quietly and politely, "Doctor, as you just said, anything is possible, isn't it?"

"Yes, I suppose most anything is possible," he said.

"Especially in human behavior, right?"

"Absolutely."

"It's possible that Private Jennings passed out, and someone else came in the room and killed Mr. Livingston, right?"

"Yes, that's possible."

"It's also possible that Mr. Livingston killed himself, isn't it?"

"Anything is possible," he repeated.

"I could go on and on about possibilities, but we're not dealing with possibilities. We're dealing with probabilities, right?"

"Yes. That's certainly my understanding."

"We have to look at what is logical – not what is possible."

"Yes."

"And you testified that what Private Jennings told you is not only possible but also probable and logical. Is that correct?"

"Yes. That is correct."

"No further questions, Your Honor."

The judge turned toward the DA. "Do you have any redirect?"

"No Judge. We do not."

"May this witness be excused?" The judge asked the attorneys.

We both nodded in agreement.

"You may be excused, Doctor," the judge said.

Both of us sat down with a sigh of relief.

"Let's have a ten-minute break," the judge announced.

"All rise," the sheriff yelled.

The judge walked out and everyone stood in the courtroom and remained standing to stretch themselves. The jury went to their room for a bathroom break.

When the judge returned, and, before he even sat down, he said, "Call your next witness, Mr. Tucker."

"Judge, I'd like to call Staff Sergeant McDonald."

The sheriff walked out of the courtroom and shouted, "Staff Sergeant McDonald, Staff Sergeant McDonald, Staff Sergeant McDonald." The sheriff walked back into the courtroom. "He doesn't answer Judge."

I felt my heartbeat accelerate. "Judge, he was supposed to have been here by noon today."

"Where did he have to come from?" the judge asked.

"From Camp Lejeune, North Carolina."

"Who are your other witnesses?" The judge asked.

"Just the defendant."

"Well, Mr. Tucker, we have no choice but to go ahead with the defendant," the judge insisted.

"Judge I really don't want to take them out of order. I want to have the defendant's statement last."

"Mr. Tucker, I can't hold up the court's time waiting for a witness who isn't here. You'll have to proceed with something."

I tried to think of a stalling tactic. "Judge, he may be in the rest room. Could you ask the sheriff to check, please?"

The sheriff returned in two or three minutes and announced. "He's not in the rest room Judge."

"Mr. Tucker," the judge insisted. "You have no choice. You either put up the defendant or you rest."

"All right Judge," I sat down and began talking to Tommy in a low voice that no one else could hear. I hadn't completely made up my mind whether or not I really wanted to put him on the stand.

The judge became impatient. "Mr. Tucker, you must move forward."

"Judge. I call Private First Class Thomas Jennings to the stand."

Tommy stood up as if he were standing at attention. His dress uniform and good looks made him appear captivating, even to an all-male jury. As he walked toward the stand, the judge asked, "Is he to be sworn, Mr. Tucker?"

"No, Your Honor."

"All right," the judge turned toward the jury. "The defendant is going to make an unsworn statement."

At that moment, the courtroom door flung open, and there he stood, as if he'd descended from outer space. Just as Tommy had described him, he was a sawed-off, stumpy fellow who looked like he could eat nails. In full dress uniform, short flattop and sparkling black shoes he appeared to be a classic Marine drill instructor, the type you might see on billboards encouraging boys to join the Marines. For the first time during the trial, Tommy beamed with delight when he caught a glimpse of the sergeant, an indication to the entire courtroom of the admiration he felt for him.

My body became limp with relief. I raised my voice. "If Your Honor please, I have never met the sergeant, and I would like to have a few minutes with him."

"All right, Mr. Tucker. Court will be in recess for fifteen minutes."

After the judge exited the courtroom, the sergeant came over to counsel table. Tommy jumped up and stood at attention, saluted then shook his hand. The sergeant appeared to be all business, no smiles, no back-slapping, and remained stone-faced as one might expect. He apologized for being late. "There had been a wreck on Highway 17 between Brunswick and Savannah that held up traffic for over an hour," he said.

We walked out of the courtroom to talk for a moment about his testimony. When he excused himself to go to the restroom, I heard the judge bang the gavel, so I hurried back to counsel's table where Tommy was sitting.

"Mr. Tucker, you can call your next witness," the judge said.

The sheriff went out the door and called for him. The bravado with which the sergeant marched into the courtroom and swaggered toward the stand was downright intimidating – enough to make the hairs stand straight up on the back of your neck. It was as if you could hear the "Star-Spangled Banner" being played by the Marine Corps Band. The jurors appeared to be in awe, as if they were in the presence of a genuine war hero. In fact, the entire courtroom seemed to be filled with an electrical current.

"Swear the witness, Mr. Clerk," the judge ordered.

After the sergeant was sworn and answered the usual questions of name, rank, duty station and other personal information, I asked Sergeant McDonald's opinion of Tommy.

"Jennings was one of my finest recruits," his voice resonated throughout the courtroom.

"Tell us what you mean by that?"

"Yes sir, I will. He shot expert on the rifle range and made private first class as soon as he was eligible. By the time he finished boot camp, I felt confident that Jennings would be a recruit who could be molded into a genuine Marine. And that's about the ultimate compliment I would ever give anybody. Once a Marine, always a Marine!" He raised his voice in a machismo manner as if he were lecturing a group of recruits.

"Sergeant, would you tell the jury something about what Private Jennings went through in boot camp?"

"Sir, we get these young boys from the farms, from the city streets, and all types of places. Most of them think they're smart, because they're usually about eighteen years old and think they know everything there is to know. We have to knock that smart attitude out of them. If we can reduce them to where they feel they're nothing, then we can mold them into being a Marine. We want them to take pride in themselves. We try to harden them. As a drill instructor, I do my best to train these boys into becoming the finest Marines they can be, not only for the corps, but for the good of our country," he paused.

"Go on, Sergeant," I said.

"The body these boys come in with isn't good enough for the Marine Corps. We set out to build them a new body by doing push-ups, sit-ups, leg races, bends and thrusts, as many pull-ups as they can do, one-mile runs at full speed, then we go to two-mile runs, then later three-mile runs. They have to learn stamina and endurance if they're going to make it as Marines. We try to separate the men from the boys."

He paused and gazed at Tommy, whose expression was one of reverence for Sergeant McDonald.

"And what else, Sergeant?" I asked.

"Boot camp challenges not only the body but the mind," he said. "They have an abundance of classroom hours of instruction. There's at least two hundred years of Marine Corps history for them to learn. We run them through the regimental confidence course and train them to fight with bayonets and with their hands. They get a pretty heavy dose of combat training, because they either learn to kill or be killed. Being a Marine is the toughest club they'll ever join. We keep our standards high and our ranks small. We look for quality, not quantity, and for men who seek a challenge and are not afraid of tough physical training. We teach them to serve their country proudly," he emphasized the word 'proudly' in a bold manner.

As he paused, I urged him to keep going.

The sergeant pointed at Tommy, "What I've been talking about is what that Marine sitting over there has been through, and he has passed with flying colors. We've made him ready for combat and to fight for our freedom and democracy in Vietnam, as well as in any other country he's called on to fight in. You might wonder why we teach our boys to fight to kill, but when you have an enemy wanting to conquer you, then you're proud to have boys like him who know how to fight to kill. We tell them in the beginning, There are no compromises, no short cuts and no promises except one, and that is that you will be a Marine. I have never in my life seen a Marine who was not proud to be one."

"Sergeant, please continue."

"Once that Marine, sitting over there at the table, went through boot camp, experienced the firing range, water survival training, the tear gas chamber, learning how to throw a hand grenade, the live infiltration course, then he was tougher than he ever thought he could be. He may have thought he couldn't do things like that, but he did. When you look at that Marine, you better know that it was tough to earn that uniform. It's the finest uniform that any soldier can wear. Private Jennings came into the Marine Corps as a boy, and he finished boot camp as a man. That makes me want to sing, but since I'm not a good singer, I'll just say it,

"From the Halls of Montezuma
To the shores of Tripoli;
We fight our country's battles
In the air, on land, and sea;"

"That makes goose bumps pop up all over me," the sergeant continued, "because I know Private Jennings over there inside and out. I can hear him now saying those words I taught him so well, 'I WILL NEVER SURRENDER!' I can tell by looking at him that even though he has been through all this trouble he has gotten himself into, he hasn't lost his pride, because he has learned a pride that nothing nor anybody can ever take away from him."

Tears filled Tommy's eyes, and he kept trying to wipe them away with the back of his hand so no one would see.

The sergeant continued. "To be a Marine, you have to

believe in yourself, your corps, your country and your God. Private Jennings is a man of dignity. If he's given the opportunity, he will serve his country proudly and courageously. I took a vow when I was made a drill instructor that I would have each one of my men ready to go to war, because the very survival of this country could someday depend on one Marine. When I look at the uniform Private Jennings is wearing, I see two hundred years of pride, spirit, strength, courage, honor, valor and tradition. The title that he will wear forever inside him until he goes to his grave is that he is a United States Marine."

He ended with such intensity, I could imagine hearing the kettledrums rolling, clashing cymbals, bands playing in the background and the American flag being raised on Iwo Jima. Even some of the jurors had tears in their eyes. They all sat in stunned silence as the echoes of the sergeant's last words dissipated like smoke from a smoldering fire.

Once the spell was broken, and everyone in the courtroom sat in stunned silence, even the judge appeared to have the need to compose himself. He leaned forward and cleared his throat. "Mr. District Attorney, do you wish to cross exam the sergeant?"

For the first time during the trial, the DA's voice seemed frail and feeble. "No, Your Honor," he muttered as he shook his head.

As a fellow lawyer, I could almost feel sympathy for him, but not quite.

As the sergeant left the room, he stopped at defendant's counsel table and stuck out his hand. Tommy jumped up as if he'd been called to attention. They shook hands, and the sergeant began marching out.

I asked the judge, "May Sergeant McDonald be excused, Your Honor?"

The judge turned toward the DA. "Do you wish to retain him?"

"No, Your Honor."

The sergeant waited by the door until the judge said, "Sergeant, you're dismissed."

As I watched the sergeant leave, it was like Roy Rogers riding on the back of Trigger off into the sunset.

I stood up. "Judge, we'd like to put the defendant on the stand for an unsworn statement."

"Go ahead," the judge said.

Tommy looked dashing in his dress uniform. His shoes glistened like mirrors. His short GI haircut and close shaven face gave him the appearance of a clean-cut, believable young man.

We had rehearsed his statement several times, and he'd memorized what he was going to say. Instead, he sat there on the stand twisting his hands on his lap without speaking, obviously terrified. Even some of the jurors and spectators began squirming in their seats with discomfort. I kept staring at him, urging him along with my hands and body-motion. Then all of a sudden, he began speaking in a low tone of voice.

"My name is Tommy Jennings. I was born and lived all my life in Palatka, Florida. I graduated from high school this past June and joined the Marines."

I had told him to look at the jurors while talking, but Tommy found it difficult to do, which gave him the appearance of being shy. Before he continued, he gazed out into the courtroom and made eye contact with his mother. The sight of her seemed to give him an unsettling sense of shame. He could only imagine what kind of hell he must be putting her through.

"My mother is sitting out there in the courtroom," he paused, because he got choked up. I stared at him, because everything he'd said thus far had not been part of the script.

Then he continued, "My mother taught me good values and took me to church every Sunday. I always made an A or a B in every subject in school and graduated in the top 10% of my class. I never drank any alcohol until after I graduated. I never did any kind of drugs. I joined the Marines and went to Parris Island, South Carolina. Like Sergeant McDonald said, it was tough. It was the hardest thing I've ever done in my life, but now I'm a Marine. I was supposed to be shipped out to Vietnam just a couple of days after this thing happened. Like the sergeant said, a Marine has to have a killer instinct if he expects to survive in combat. If you hesitate for one second, you'll be a dead Marine."

Tommy paused and looked toward the jury for the first time. He'd lost some of his stage fright. "I'd been given leave to go home for Thanksgiving, and I spent the night before and the day with my family. The night of Thanksgiving, I decided to hitch back to my base at Camp Lejeune, North Carolina. It was probably after midnight when I got picked up by this guy in Jacksonville. He had a bottle of wine that we drank on the way. When we got to Brunswick, he asked me to go to his place and get a little sleep, then start out fresh the next morning. I was pretty tired and felt a little woozy from the wine. He worked as a night clerk for the Holiday Inn. He had a room there. When we got to his room, we drank a couple of beers. He didn't have anywhere for us to sit except a small sofa. While we were sitting there next to each other, he made a pass at me and put his hand on my crotch. I don't know what happened. I guess something must've snapped in my head. The policemen said I hit him over the head with a lamp, but I don't remember it. I don't remember anything that happened after that, until I was riding to the jail in the back of a police car. I told him that I thought I might've killed somebody. I don't remember doing it, but if I did, I'm really sorry, and I hope God will forgive me."

Tommy looked at me. I nodded my approval. He'd passed the test. His words were sincere and believable. He stepped down from the stand and walked toward counsel table, his shoulders back, his head high.

"Do you have anything further, Mr. Tucker?" The judge asked.

"We would like to introduce some pictures that are in the hands of the District Attorney that we've never seen. I asked him to let me see them, but he refused."

The DA jumped up. "Judge, the pictures he's talking about are totally irrelevant and immaterial."

"Don't you think that's up to me to decide?" the judge responded, then added, "We'll need to take up this argument back in my chambers. I don't know how long this will take, but it's getting late in the day. I think I'll excuse the jury until 9:00 a.m. tomorrow morning." He then gave them the usual instructions that they should not discuss this case with anyone.

The sheriff yelled out, "Court is in recess. All rise."

The judge walked to his chambers. The DA and I followed. The judge took off his robe, hung it on a nearby hat rack and sat behind his desk. "You gentlemen have a seat," he said. "All right. What do we have here?"

I spoke up, "Judge, the police searched Calvin Livingston's room and confiscated a cardboard box that had pictures of nude males and some magazines showing provocative pictures of men. We would like to introduce them into evidence."

"Why?" The judge popped back.

"Well, It's evidence that will show his homosexual nature," I said.

"I believe that's unrefuted, isn't it? Has anyone in the trial of this case tried to deny that the boy was homosexual?" the judge asked.

"No sir," I said. "But it will help to support our case."

The DA jumped into the conversation. "Judge, all he wants to do is to prejudice the minds of the jurors against Calvin Livingston."

I then raised my voice. "Judge, I can't believe he said that after he introduced those horrible pictures of Calvin's dead body, bloodied all over."

The judge reared back in his chair and lit a cigar. "Well, let me look in the box to see what all is in there."

The DA said, "Judge, it'll take a little while for me to get a couple of deputies to bring the trunk over here."

"Where is it?" The judge asked.

"It's in the sheriff's office."

The judge picked up the phone, dialed the sheriff and asked him to deliver the box to his office. As they waited, the judge asked, "How much longer do you fellows think you'll take before we can give this case to the jury?"

"We've completed the defendant's evidence Judge," I answered.

"I'm not sure," the DA said. "I may have something on re-direct, but it shouldn't take too long."

"With your arguments to the jury and my charge, we should be able to give the case to the jury after lunch tomorrow, don't you think?"

We both agreed.

After a bit of small talk among us, two deputies brought the trunk in for the judge to inspect. They opened it, and the judge began picking up pictures of naked men. "Damn!" the judge exclaimed. "These pictures sure do make me feel inferior."

We all laughed. The judge glanced at a few of the magazines, then turned to me. "How are these things going to help your case?"

"Judge, it will show the jury what was on his mind."

"But that's not in dispute, is it?"

"I think the jury has the right to look at them," I insisted.

"The boy is dead. He was killed by your client. None of that is in dispute," the judge said with emphasis. The DA kept quiet to let the judge carry the argument for him.

"But Judge," I pleaded. "We are saying that my client was provoked into doing what he did. These pictures might help show that, and, besides, you let the DA introduce those awful pictures of the dead body."

The judge turned to the DA, "You got anything to say about this?"

"I don't see any reason to show those pictures to that group of men on the jury. It doesn't accomplish a damn thing. We are not denying that Calvin Livingston was a queer."

The judge turned back to me, "I'm going to overrule your motion and sustain the District Attorney's objection."

When I went back to my office, I was in a state of anger. James saw me when I walked in. "What's wrong, Tyler?"

"I'm mad as hell." I stormed back to my office, picked up

the phone and called my father. "Don't you think the judge committed reversible error? If my client is convicted, do you think the appellate court would send it back for a new trial?"

"Calm down son. The judge may have erred, but it's not reversible error."

After our conversation, Bailey and Bonds brought out the morning newspapers from Jacksonville and Savannah. Both had front-page articles about the trial. One headline read, "SORDID TALE TOLD IN MURDER TRIAL." The other read, "JENNINGS CASE MAY GO TO THE JURY TOMORROW."

I picked up the papers and read the articles. One of the articles said, "Tyler Tucker, the defense attorney, claims justifiable homicide, because the victim picked up the Marine, who was hitchhiking, took him to his place in Brunswick and tried to perform unnatural sex acts with him." I took the papers to my desk to finish reading. I couldn't help feeling an ego boost, because my name had never before appeared in the Jacksonville Times Union and the Savannah Morning News.

It was after 5:00, when I started to leave the office. Everyone else had gone. I heard the phone ring and couldn't decide whether or not I should answer it. I certainly didn't want to get stuck with some long-winded client, but then again, I thought it could be Laura.

"Hello."

"When in the hell you gonna finish that trial? We miss you."

"Red!" I recognized his voice as one of my basketball teammates. "Man, I know. I want to get back out there on the hardwood so bad, I can't even tell you how much."

"We've been losing games. We need to get you back out here hitting that jump shot."

"Man I miss you guys. I'd love to be dribbling a basketball right now."

"Come on, man, we need you," he insisted.

"It looks like we should finish this trial tomorrow night. When is the next game?"

"Not 'til next week."

"Well, I'll definitely be there with you guys next week."

"Man that's good to hear," Red said.

"Thanks for calling buddy. You just brightened my whole day."

Wednesday night
December 11, 1973

When Duck and Bonnie Sue first arrived in Brunswick, she'd given him permission to drive her Cadillac. But then an immediate awkwardness occurred. Should they get separate rooms at the motel? Agnes, so wrought up and distressed about the predicament of her son, divorced herself entirely from worrying or caring about the two of them. So, Duck, in his most humble manner, asked Bonnie if she'd mind sharing a room. She hesitated at first, but then consented, provided he slept on the sofa. Gradually, after a few nights of sleeping separately, Bonnie invited Duck to move from the sofa to the bed. Things between them functioned very well after that, especially since he agreed to any and everything she asked for and more. Furthermore, she found Duck much more pleasurable in bed than her rich, married boyfriend.

The second night in Brunswick, they'd wandered around town looking for a billiard parlor and found Sonny Hall's pool room on Gloucester Street. They'd not missed a night going there since. Shooting pool had been Duck's favorite pasttime, other than drinking beer and chasing women.

Bonnie had played a little pool in her earlier years and had also drunk her share of beer. But since she'd "found the Lord," she'd abandoned her sinful ways and hadn't picked up a cue stick nor touched a drop of alcohol.

Not only had they discovered a good place to hang out, but it had the added attraction of serving the best chili in that part of the country. They'd eaten a bowl every night and, afterwards, shot a few games.

That particular Wednesday night all the tables had been taken so Duck and Bonnie sat at the bar. In glancing around the room, Duck recognized one of the fellows on table number three as being a juror on Tommy's case. He pointed him out to Bonnie, who agreed that, indeed, he definitely was one of the members of the jury.

Duck had drunk enough beer to embolden him, so, with somewhat of a swagger as if he were a regular, sauntered over to the table where the juror was shooting with an older man, placed a quarter on the side of their table and then walked back to the bar.

"What'd you do that for?" Bonnie asked. "He may not win."

"Yeah, but if he does, I'd like to shoot a game with him," he said, as he leaned back on the barstool to eye the quality of his game. "He shoots pretty good," Duck smiled.

"But not as good as you, right?" she laughed.

"We'll see."

"You think he might have seen us at the trial?" Bonnie asked.

"I doubt it. We've been sitting so far back, and the courtroom has been full of people. I don't think we stand out. Do you?"

"Probably not."

When the two men finished the game, the juror won, so Duck wandered over to the table, stuck his hand out and introduced himself. "They call me Duck."

The juror, being about Duck's age, said, "I'm Luther Rooks."

"Good to meet you, Luther. Just traveling through town with my girlfriend, and this looked like a good place to hang out."

"Yeah, it is. I come down here every Wednesday night to eat some chili and shoot a little pool. That's my night out."

"Wife give you a kitchen pass, huh?" Duck laughed.

"Yeah. You're right about that. You wanna shoot a game?"

"Sure," Duck said. "I'll rack 'em," He gathered the balls from the slot underneath the table and placed the triangular rack around them, pushing the balls from behind with both thumbs in order to give his opponent a good, tight rack. "OK, Luther, you bust 'em."

Luther thrust the cue forward with such force, it sent the white ball straight into the rack of balls, sending them scurrying in every direction. One striped ball, the ten, found the side pocket and the twelve-ball slammed into the corner pocket.

"Nice," Duck commented. "Looks like you got the big balls."

Luther then proceeded to sink one ball after another until his luck ran out. One of the striped balls, the fourteen, struck the eight ball, causing it to scoot into the side pocket. "I'll be damned!" Luther exclaimed. "Haven't scratched all night."

"It happens to the best of us," Duck said, then patted him on the shoulder, "Here, let me buy you a beer."

"But I lost," Luther said. "I should buy you one."

"Whatever you say, my good man," Duck patted him on the shoulder with a big smile.

They gave up the table and walked over to the bar together on the opposite side of Bonnie. The bartender filled two frosted mugs with Budweiser on tap, and handed one to each of them.

As they stood next to the bar, Duck took a swig and then asked, "So, what do you do for a living, Luther?"

"Work at the mill," he said, not sounding very happy about his job.

"Oh yeah? I caught that stench as soon as we rolled into town. Those paper mills smell like a fart," he laughed.

"Smells like money to me," Luther said with a smirk.

Duck took a large swallow. "Well, what you been up to lately?" Duck asked.

"I'm on a damn jury over at the courthouse – a murder case."

"Oh yeah?" Duck acted innocent. "I've never served on a jury before."

"Well, I've been on a few of 'em, but never a murder case."

"What's it about?" Duck asked in all candor.

"A Marine was hitching up 17, and a queer picked him up. When the queer grabbed his crotch, the Marine killed him."

"No shit?"

"Hell, I don't blame him," Luther added. "If a queer grabbed my crotch, I'd kill him, too."

"Hell yeah," Duck nodded. "I remember one time a queer tried to put the make on me, and I beat the shit out of him."

They both laughed.

"Did you fight in the war?" Luther asked.

"I sure did," Duck replied.

"Yeah, me too," Luther sighed. "There was a queer boy in my unit, and, believe me, he had a hell of a time with the rest of us GI's. I don't know how, but somehow he survived."

"Yeah man, I know what you mean," Duck laughed.

"Well old buddy," Luther said, after gulping down his last swallow. "I better get on to the house. The old lady will be raising hell. Plus, I got to get my ass back up to that courthouse tomorrow morning. I sure hope we can finish that damn thing tomorrow," he pronounced. "I've heard about enough of it."

"Well, good to meet you Luther," Duck said, as they shook hands.

"If you're around next Wednesday night, I'll be back in here. We can shoot another game," Luther said as he turned around and sauntered out the door.

Duck walked back over to Bonnie, nodding his head. "Well, that was worthwhile," he smirked.

"You think so?"

"I know so."

Thursday
December 12, 1973

"Order in the court, all rise," the sheriff called out.

The judge took the bench, banged the gavel and said, "You may be seated."

The DA stood up and said, "We rest, Your Honor."

I stood up and announced, "The defendant rests, Your Honor," and then moved to reduce the charge from murder to voluntary manslaughter.

Without hearing any argument regarding my motion, the judge said, "Motion denied."

I stared at the judge in disbelief, wondering why he wouldn't even allow me to present my argument in support of the motion. I could sense the steamroller turning over and over on its axis moving in our direction. I knew from the beginning it was in the judge's interest, as well as the DA's, to see that my client would be found guilty. But it was beginning to become much too obvious.

The judge then spoke up, "All right gentlemen, are you ready to present your closing arguments to the jury?"

We both answered affirmatively.

The judge turned toward the jury panel. "Gentlemen of the jury, when the defendant places anything into evidence other than the unsworn statement of the defendant, then he loses his right to opening and closing argument. So the State will have the right to open and close."

The judge looked at the DA, "Do you wish to make an opening argument to the jury?"

"No sir. We waive our right to opening argument and reserve the right to close."

"All right then, Mr. Tucker, are you ready to proceed for the defendant?"

"Yes sir, Your Honor."

I stared at my legal pad, which reminded me of my father's advice, "EXUDE CONFIDENCE," then walked over in front of the jury box, took a long, deep breath and began.

"Gentlemen of the jury, I apologize to you that I'm not quite as eloquent as my opponent, the District Attorney. He has a way with words that I don't possess. He does his job well, and I'm just a neophyte – can't hold a candle to him."

Looking into the face of each juror, it hit me that this was my last chance to get in a few licks for Tommy's life. My law professor had emphasized the importance of the closing argument that convinced me that a case could rise or fall on what I had to say to the jury. It was much more difficult for me to shoot from the hip. I'd written my argument on a legal pad but knew how ineffectual it would be if I read it. So, I decided to just wing it, and do the best job possible to remember what was there. I cleared my throat and began.

"I was appointed by this court to represent Tommy Jennings in connection with a murder charge against him. You, the jury, have heard all the evidence that has been presented. In the District Attorney's opening statement, he outlined what he intended to prove, and I did the same. We each put up witnesses to testify as to what they knew about this case. Now it's time for us to argue the case based on the evidence in the most favorable light possible on behalf of our clients. The District Attorney wants you to convict my client of murder and have him put to death in the electric chair. What a waste and what a pity if that were to be done! My argument to you is to set him free, because what he did was justifiable homicide. Homosexual acts are a crime according to the laws of Georgia. They are classified as sodomy, a term that took its name from the Biblical Sodom and Gomorrah. It is a felony in this state, and it is lawful and justifiable to kill a person to prevent the commission of a felony.

"We contend, and I believe the evidence has shown that from the moment Calvin Livingston picked up this Marine sitting over there, he began to plan and scheme and connive to find some way to have sex with this good-looking eighteen-year-old boy. The very first thing he did was to try to lower his inhibitions by the use of alcohol. He had a bottle of wine in order to break down his defenses. After they finished drinking the bottle of wine, like a spider, Calvin could sense he had his prey in the web. He encouraged him to go to his room and once they got there began offering beers for him to drink more. Tommy admittedly was not very experienced when it came to drinking alcohol. He'd never been drunk before and only had his first drink five or six months previously. Calvin felt that if he could get him drunk enough, he could have his way with him. This was all part of Calvin's scheme. When he felt he'd gotten the young boy drunk enough, then it was time for him to make his move.

"Gentleman, I ask you, have any of you ever witnessed a spider when a fly or some insect gets stuck in her web?"

Several of the jurors nodded their head.

"Can't you see, that's exactly what happened here? The spider rushes down the web and secures the insect by wrapping more webbing around the prey, so there can be no escape. Calvin thought he'd finally gotten this handsome, young Marine where he wanted him – unable to defend himself. So, he was prepared to make his move. He reached his hand over and placed it on Tommy's sex organ. But what Calvin didn't know was that Tommy had been sexually abused by his shop teacher when he was only fifteen years old, and this had been the most traumatic, disturbing and painful experience of Tommy's young life. So, Calvin's plan backfired. Even though young Tommy was definitely intoxicated, he still knew right from wrong. And he never ever wanted another male to take advantage of him again.

"Now don't forget that Tommy had just completed the most rigorous training of his life. As a Marine, they had prepared him to be combat-ready. He was to be shipped off to Vietnam in a few days. You heard his training sergeant testify about the painstaking training Tommy had to experience to teach him to be a killer, even with his bare hands. So, when Calvin made this lewd advance on Tommy, something snapped in his head. He came to suddenly and his Marine training took over in order to defend himself. He grabbed the nearest object he could find, which in this case was a lamp, and broke it over Calvin's head, which according to the crime lab, severed the jugular vein in Calvin's neck, causing him to bleed to death.

"Tommy, as he told you on the stand, is very remorseful and sorry that this happened. But I submit to you that Calvin was the author of his own misfortune. His plan backfired. He thought he had his prey subdued and was ready to commit a sexual act upon Tommy. But even in his drunken stupor, Tommy instinctively tried to protect himself from the felonious act being attempted on him.

"Gentlemen, I ask you to put yourself in Tommy's place. If you can imagine yourself being drunk and someone is trying to rape you, what would you do? What force would you use to repel the rapist?

"After the District Attorney completes his argument, the judge will give you the law that you need to know as it relates to this case. The judge will charge you that in a trial for murder, it is necessary and essential that malice, either express or implied, must be shown. Without the existence of malice, the homicide is either justifiable or manslaughter. The burden of proof is on the State to prove malice. I ask you, where is the malice? The dictionary defines malice as being the intention or desire to do evil or ill will toward another. The burden of proof is also on the State to prove intent. Where is the intent?

"The State will try to make you believe that Tommy Jennings plotted to kill Calvin Livingston as some type of revenge that he had against homosexuals and that he killed Calvin Livingston in order to steal his car. That is ludicrous, and all of you know it. This is not what the preponderance of the evidence shows. I believe that all of you are much too intelligent to fall for that scenario. Tommy didn't need a car. He was leaving for Vietnam in a couple of days. If everything had gone according to the plan, Tommy would've slept the night there on the sofa and the next morning walked less than a half-block up to Highway 17 to hitchhike back to Camp Lejeune. Tommy told you he had no knowledge or recollection of even taking the car away. The first thing he remembered was riding in the police car toward the station. Remember that the State is required to prove all elements of the crime beyond a reasonable doubt. If you have any doubt, in your mind, then you can't find the defendant guilty.

"We believe the judge will also charge you that if you find from the evidence that the defendant killed Calvin Livingston while Calvin was committing or attempting to commit an unnatural sex act upon him, which is a felony in the eyes of the law, and that the homicide was committed to prevent the commission of the felony upon him, then the homicide is justifiable. And if the homicide is justifiable, then you must bring back a verdict of not guilty.

"A verdict of not guilty is not intended to establish the fact that the defendant did not commit the act charged. But you can find the defendant not guilty if you feel the homicide was justifiable. And you have heard all the extenuating circumstances and the justification that I have argued to you today.

"I thank you, gentlemen, for your attention in this case. We are into our fourth day, and you have all been extraordinarily patient to listen to our witnesses and our arguments. I hope you will find it in your heart to bring back a verdict for the defendant of not guilty."

As I turned to walk back to counsel table, my shirt was as wet as if it'd been dipped in water.

The DA then stood up, cleared his throat and pranced toward the jury box as pumped up as if he were about to run a hundred-yard-dash.

"I want to tell you gentlemen something," he pointed toward Tommy. "That prisoner over there is guilty of the most brutal and uncalled-for murder in the history of this county. I'm sure you got the drift from the defense attorney. He's trying to divert your attention from his client to the poor boy he killed. Calvin Livingston is not on trial here. That killer sitting over there at the table is the one we're trying. He's confessed to the murder, so you don't have to determine who killed Calvin. He did it! But they want you to believe that what he did was justifiable."

The DA began pacing up and down in front of the jury box and then continued. "Was there any threat whatsoever to that Marine's life? Absolutely not. Calvin was a skinny, frail boy that didn't have a Chinaman's chance against a well-developed athletic man like Jennings, who'd been skilled and trained in the art of killing people. He said so himself. There is no way the defense can insinuate that it was necessary to kill this frail boy in order for the Marine to protect himself. Did he think little Calvin was going to kill him? It was not self-defense, gentlemen. It was NOT kill or be killed. Calvin was not armed with a weapon. What we have here is a match between a strong, trained killer against a fragile boy, who'd probably never been in a fight during his entire life.

"No, my friends, what the defense is trying to tell you is that big bruiser sitting over there was so offended by the sexual advance made to him, that it became necessary to kill him. That is preposterous! Absurd! All that big Marine had to do was to get up and walk out the door, and nothing would've ever happened. All he had to say was, 'No. I'm not into that.' It would've ended it right then and there. He could've even said, 'Hell no!' And then pushed him away. I'm sure the killer Marine over there could've outrun him if he'd wanted to. He certainly could've avoided what he did," he paused for a moment and coughed.

"Is there any one of you twelve men who for one minute believes that this well-trained Marine couldn't have prevented any acts from being committed on his body without hurting Calvin Livingston? Of course not, but they're wanting you to believe that it was necessary to kill the frail boy because of an improper advance. My friends, this is not the Old West where gunslingers kill if somebody looks at them the wrong way. We've come a long way from there. If the killer Marine had wanted to protect his chastity, he didn't have to use extraordinary force to the point of death. Did you see those pictures of Calvin? You'll have them in the jury room with you. I urge you to look at them again, as horrible as they may be, just to see how brutal, how cruel, how unmerciful this killing was. He beat this poor boy to a pulp. Those pictures show me the most brutal, ruthless, vicious and savage slaying of a man I've ever seen in my life.

"Look at that killer over there sitting in his Marine uniform. He shouldn't be allowed to wear the uniform of the brave men who have gone before him. I tell you, that Marine over there has no conscience. Oh yeah, he tried to tell you fine gentlemen what pride the Marines had instilled in him. But let's look at a bit of evidence that the defense never tried to explain. Do you remember Deputy Jones? He was the

State's first witness. Do you remember what he said about the killer over there when he arrested him? He testified that the Marine had on his pants but his shirt was hanging out of his pants. Now why was that? Deputy Jones also said the Marine had his shoes on with no socks and his shoes were untied. Now why was that? He also testified that it looked like he'd gotten dressed in a hurry and didn't have enough time to put his clothes on right. Do you remember that? The defense never attempted to explain that bit of testimony. Why did they avoid that very material piece of evidence? The prisoner says his memory had failed him. He wants you to believe that he had no idea what happened that night. Don't you believe that for one minute! Of course, he knew what he was doing. I don't care how drunk he pretended he was. I submit to you that he was trying to egg poor Calvin on. He wasn't sitting there on the sofa all dressed up in his uniform. Why was his shirt hanging out? Why didn't he have on any socks? Don't you think he might have undressed to tempt Calvin, who we admit had homosexual tendencies? I submit to you that it was all planned and premeditated. He knew he could easily knock this boy off, which he did, then take his car and head on back to Camp Lejeune. But thank God, we have some very skilled and diligent police officers in this county who spotted the car and made a quick arrest. I would've given anything if that killer over there had been brave enough to put up sworn testimony instead of taking the coward's way out. I'd loved to have cross-examined him. He talks about how brave he is, but he lacked the courage to testify like a man. The laws of Georgia permit a defendant to make an unsworn statement, then I don't have any right to ask him any questions. If I could've, I would've asked him questions that would've made him shiver and shake all over.

"Once I complete this closing argument, the judge will charge you the law in this case, and I want you to listen carefully. Once we have proved the homicide beyond any reasonable doubt, which has already been admitted by the defendant, then the burden of proof shifts to the defendant to prove that the murder was justified. I contend there is no way the defense can possibly prove to your satisfaction that it was necessary for the muscle-bound Marine to use that amount of force against a frail young man just because he was repulsed by an inappropriate and improper advance. I submit to you that killer over there with his head hanging down is dangerous. You don't want to turn him loose. He's a menace to society. We don't need his type on the streets. Let's get rid of him once and for all. You can help out this community and all of society by giving him the same medicine he gave to Calvin Livingston. Unfortunately, the law won't allow him to receive the same pain and suffering Calvin must have endured. His death will be painless, but at least he won't be out in the public baiting homosexuals for the purpose of killing them."

Then the DA shouted out, his voice so loud it scared some of the jurors as well as the spectators, "Convict him of murder and sentence him to die in the electric chair!"

The DA turned and walked back to counsel table with his usual fanfare. A dramatic silence fell over the courtroom, interrupted by the judge when he said, "Let's take a fifteen-minute break."

"All rise," the sheriff yelled.

Everyone stood, but the judge didn't leave the bench. He began thumbing through his book of charges to the jury. When the sheriff saw what was taking place, he yelled out "Court is in recess for fifteen minutes! The jury must remain in the box to wait for more instructions from the judge."

At the beginning of the trial, I'd given some suggested charges for the judge to consider. The judge looked down at me standing at counsel table. "Mr. Tucker, I will not give your charge on involuntary intoxication."

"Yes sir," I said. "You don't think that applies?"

"If I did, I'd give it," he snapped back.

I turned away in defeat. It seemed the judge had not been with me at all during this trial. I expected a little bit more cooperation and assistance, but it had not been there. I knew the judge liked me, but I also knew the judge wanted to be re-elected and that would overrule our friendship.

I sat back down beside Tommy, who'd been overwhelmed by the DA's argument to the jury. It frightened him, to say the least. I tried to comfort him and let him know that what was said was typical and not at all unusual. I told him, "It's the DA's responsibility to get a guilty verdict with the greatest penalty possible. It looks good on his record."

The judge's charge to the jury regarding the law that applies in capital cases was long and tedious. I watched the faces of the jurors to see what I could read from their expressions. It became apparent that their minds wandered. Some seemed to nod off. It's not easy for laymen to listen, much less absorb, a long, drawn-out speech in legal language, unfamiliar to them. It went on for more than an hour and didn't finish until half past twelve. Obviously, the jurors had turned it off a good hour before. They appeared tired and probably hungry.

Lawyers and judges consider the charge to the jury extremely important in the trial of any case, whether civil or criminal, but jurors have generally made up their mind one way or the other long before the judge makes his charge.

The judge said to the jury, "You gentlemen, go to the jury room, elect your foreman and begin your deliberation. Before you go, give the sheriff your order for lunch, and he will deliver it to you. The rest of the court is in recess," he added.

The sheriff handcuffed Tommy and led him to the holding cell. When I walked out, I received nasty looks of scorn from the homosexual community as if they wished they could tear me into shreds. I wondered what kind of looks they'd given Tommy when he walked by.

The time had come for the nervous wait. I likened it to the anxiety when my three babies were born. I could only imagine what Tommy was going through, as well as his family. Minutes seemed like hours.

The court reporter, Mrs. Hammond, a nice lady from Jesup, who'd been working trials and depositions for many years, came up to me and congratulated me on the manner in which I handled the trial. "You acted like a pro," she said. I knew that wasn't true, but, like any other lawyer, I liked to have my ego salved.

I heard someone in a soft voice call, "Mr. Tucker?" I turned to see Tommy's mother at the railing that separates the spectators from the rest of the courtroom. I walked over to her. She was dressed nicely in something she'd probably wear to church.

She took my right hand and clasped it between both of her soft hands. "I want to thank you for everything you've done for my son. We were worried in the beginning that you would not be able to handle this case, but we think you did as good as anybody could."

"Well, thank you ma'am."

She continued, "I don't know anything in the world about law even though I've been married to a lawyer for a long time. I've always managed to stay out of the courtroom. I never wanted any part of it. We're praying for the best, but no matter what happens, I want you to know we appreciate what you've done for my Tommy."

"Well, thank you, Mrs. Jennings. I appreciate that. I just hope that everything is going to go all right."

She looked into my eyes. "What do you think will happen?"

"I honestly don't have any idea."

"The preacher and I think we have a good chance," she said.

"You do?"

"You see, we've been praying together at night. We believe in prayer, Mr. Tucker. Through God, all things are possible."

"Yes ma'am, I believe that, too."

As she turned to leave, she added, "Anyway, we just wanted to let you know that we thank you for everything."

"I appreciate it."

Laura had packed a lunch that I'd left in my car, consisting of a ham and cheese sandwich, with crackers and an apple. I gulped it down quickly and hurried back to the courtroom. I needed to be close by in case the jury were to come in with either a verdict or to ask the judge a question, which they frequently do.

I stopped by the restroom. Several men were in there having an argument about the case. When I walked in, they immediately became silent. "You done a good job," one of them spoke up. I thanked him.

I was well aware that there were people in the courtroom who felt scorn and contempt for me, which is sometimes difficult for a lawyer to handle. I'm sure they don't take into consideration that I was appointed by the court, received no money and required by my oath as a lawyer to do the very best job I could for my client. When I was sworn in by my father to become a lawyer, I remember raising my right hand and saying, "I will faithfully discharge the duties of an attorney and counselor at law and represent my client to the best of my abilities."

Back in the courtroom, no one was there except the sheriff. I walked over to him and sat down. He was a colorful old fellow who'd been in the sheriff's office most of his life, and had experienced many things in his day.

"Well, it looks like you hung 'em up, Tyler," he joked.

"You think so?"

The sheriff, who looked as if he could play the part of Santa Claus at Christmas, chewed tobacco and had a Maxwell House coffee can he used for his spittoon.

"You never know about juries," he said. "I've seen many of 'em in my day. A whole lot of times, when It gets late in the evening that usually means they want a meal off the county," he laughed. "I've seen times when you give 'em a meal, and they'll come right back with a verdict."

He snickered, and continued, "I had a jury hung up one time. It was getting on into the night. The judge said, 'Let's get 'em some dinner. Maybe that'll help.' Well, I went and knocked on the door and went in. I asked 'em if they'd like some dinner. The foreman said, 'Yeah, bring us eleven T-bone steaks and one bale of hay.'" I cracked up and the sheriff's fat belly shook as he laughed out loud.

The sheriff had another experience he wanted to tell. He cleared his throat. "Yeah, one time we had a jury that'd been out about six hours, so the judge told me to go and call 'em back to the jury box. I brought 'em back in, and the judge said 'Will the foreman please stand.' Nobody moved. So the judge asked again, 'Who did you elect as your foreman?' Finally one of the men stood up and said, 'Judge, that's what we've been trying to do ever since we've been out.'" This time the sheriff's belly shook even harder as he and I laughed together.

We sat there for a minute in silence, then the sheriff said, "Looks like to me you fooled 'em, Tyler."

"What do you mean by that?"

"You did a damn good job defending the boy," the sheriff replied.

"Well thanks, but what do you mean by I fooled them?"

At that point, the judge entered the courtroom. "Sheriff, go get the District Attorney. I'm going to bring the jury back in. It's four o'clock. They've been out for three-and-a-half hours. Let's see if they're making any progress."

The sheriff called the DA, then led Tommy back into the courtroom. Everyone took their seats, and the spectators outside the courtroom came filing back in.

"Mr. Sheriff, bring the jury in."

After they'd taken their seats, the judge spoke up, "Who is your foreman?"

Mr. Ryals, the haberdasher, stood up. A short man, about five foot six inches, he was well-dressed in a three-piece suit. I was aware that the judge had known him personally for many years since that's where he bought his suits.

"Mr. Ryals, is there anything you all need from me to help you reach a verdict?"

"No sir. I don't think so. There's still one or two who haven't agreed with the rest of us."

"Well, it's getting late," the judge said. "Do you think you can reach a verdict before the day is out, or do you want me to dismiss you and have you come back in tomorrow?"

"No sir. Judge, if you can give us about another hour, I think we might can come to an agreement."

"All right," the judge said. "Mr. Sheriff, take them back to the jury room."

Afterwards, the sheriff came back and took Tommy to the

holding cell.

I walked out to see about him. "Is there anything you need?"

"Yeah," he said. "Get me out of here."

I shook my head. "What's your second choice?"

"I don't know," he shrugged.

"You want anything to eat or drink?"

"Are you kidding? I couldn't put anything on my stomach right now if I had to."

"Yeah, I understand," I agreed. "My stomach's churning, too."

I walked back into the courtroom and watched the minutes on the clock drag by at a snail's pace. At this time of year, just before Christmas, the days are short. The sun goes down shortly after 5:00 p.m.

About 5:30, it was dark. The judge came into the courtroom in a disgusted mood. "Sheriff, get the District Attorney. I'm going to lock the jury up."

When the jury returned, the judge asked the foreman, "Are you making any progress, Mr. Ryals?"

"Yes sir. A little bit. But we're not quite there yet."

"I'm going to lock you up for the night and let you get some sleep. Maybe tomorrow morning you will feel more like deliberating on a verdict." Some of the jurors looked shocked, thinking he was sending them to jail. The judge then allayed their fears by saying, "The sheriff has made arrangements for you to go to the Holiday Inn for the night. The deputies have cars that will take you down there. Each of you will be allowed one telephone call to your family, but no other calls can be made by any of you. I remind you again that you are not to discuss this case with anyone, not even to each other until you return here to the courtroom tomorrow morning at 9:00 o'clock. If anyone tries to talk with you about this case, I want you to notify the sheriff. He will be staying there in the motel with you."

The judge rapped his gavel, and the jury followed behind the sheriff like little ducklings following their mother into the water. I thought it was quite a coincidence that they were going to stay where the murder took place.

I went back to the office before going home. I sat at my desk, unloaded my briefcase, pulled out my legal pad and reviewed some notes I'd scribbled in the courtroom that afternoon while waiting for the jury.

I called my father to let him know the jury was out. His only comment was, "Well, Son, you've done all you can do. It's up to them now."

Friday
December 13, 1973

While I wouldn't call myself superstitious, Tommy was quick to remind me that today was Friday, the thirteenth. The judge sounded his gavel promptly at nine a.m. The jurors were seated in the box and everyone was in his place with fresh faces.

"Gentlemen, I hope all of you had a good night's sleep," the judge commented to the jury in a very folksy tone of voice.

They nodded their heads.

"All right, I want all of you to go to the jury room and resume your deliberations. I implore you to bring a verdict back to me as soon as you can."

Tommy appeared washed out from lack of sleep and his inability to get any food down. I asked Tommy again if he wanted something to eat or drink.

"No, I can't. I'm still nauseated."

The pressure had reached a crescendo with both of us, knowing that very soon a decision would be reached on Tommy's fate. His future existence as a living person lay in the hands of twelve men.

Minutes dragged into hours, as the sheriff sat next to the jury room in a straight chair leaning back against the wall adjacent to the door. I could tell he was listening to their deliberations, because I used to do the same thing when I law-clerked for the judge in Atlanta. I stared at him seeking a clue, but he remained closed-mouth on what he was hearing, and his expression was stone-faced.

After a while, the sheriff motioned to me that he needed to go to the restroom and ordered me not to sit in his chair next to the jury room. As much as I wanted to, I didn't.

When he came back in, he said, "There's some hippie-looking fellow out there – said he wants to see you if you got a minute."

"Who in the hang could that be?" I walked out in the

hallway, and there stood my brother, Vernon. "Hey, what're you doing here?"

"I came to see the famous trial lawyer," he smiled, his brown hair dangling below his shoulders. He appeared to be more physically fit than the last time I'd seen him, as if he'd been working out in a gym.

We shook hands and sat together on a bench just outside the courtroom door.

"What brings you here?" I asked.

"Dad told me about the trial, and I wanted to check it out."

"You're too late," I shrugged. "It's almost over."

"I've been here the last two days, sitting in the balcony," he admitted. "I'm proud of you, Tyler. You did a good job representing your client."

That statement really shocked me. "Why didn't you let me know you were here?"

"I didn't want to throw you off your game," he chuckled.

"So, what's with the long hair?" I needled him.

"I've been letting it grow ever since Woodstock."

"You went to Woodstock?" That really surprised me.

"Yeah man. Went to Atlanta Rock Festival in Byron – went to Charlotte Jam. There's a hell of a lot about me you don't know."

"What did the folks say about that?"

"Dad can't tolerate it, but Mom still loves me." He paused, then added. "You know you and dad are a lot alike. You don't care for people who are different."

"That's not true Vern, and you know it," I shot back, offended by his remark.

He stiffened and glared at me with his eyebrows pulled together. "Then why are you trying to free someone who killed a queer like me?"

"Vern, I don't dislike you. I don't have anything against homosexuals. I'm just trying to do my job the court appointed me to do."

"And you don't think that's wrong? How could you live with yourself if you got him off scot free? Don't you think he needs to be punished?"

I didn't respond, because I didn't know what to say. This trial had taught me a lot about homosexuality I didn't know. As a lawyer, I'd never had the experience of getting someone who committed a crime set free. I honestly didn't know how I'd feel if that were to happen.

He continued to stare at me. "When was the last time you called me?" he asked sarcastically.

"I don't know."

"How 'bout never."

"Vern, I've got a wife and three kids and a law practice. It just takes all my time."

"Bullshit! You don't even know my number or where I live."

"Look. I probably need to get back in the courtroom in case the jury comes back," I said since he was making me more uncomfortable than I already was.

He leaned in toward me, "Tyler, you can't run away from me like that. You know damn well the sheriff will find you when the jury reaches a verdict." Vern shook his head, swishing his hair from side to side. "You've never had anything to do with me since the day I was born. I'm surprised you even recognized me." He then looked at me and snickered, "You know, you're the All-American man, a cookie-cutter out of *Better Homes and Gardens*. As for me, I'm enjoying the hippie life, living in Atlanta, the gay capital of the south – lots of gay bars, restaurants, even gay churches. But you wouldn't know anything about that, would you?"

"It's not the kind of life I want to live, Vern."

"That's OK man. You don't need me in your life, and I don't need you either."

Having this confrontation with my brother was not exactly what I wanted at that particular time. "Vern, look, I'm sorry."

"Sorry for what? I'm happy. You're happy. Let's just leave it at that."

"What can I do to make it up to you?"

"You can't do anything to make it up. You're 27. I'm 24. That means you and I have lost 24 years of getting to know each other. The thing I'd like most is for us to, at least, act like brothers in the future. I'm not a bad person. In fact, I'm a pretty fun-loving guy that you should get to know."

"Yeah, I agree with that," I said. "I'm willing if you're willing."

We shook hands. I slapped him on the back, and said, "I hope you're not doing drugs."

"You sound just like Dad," he laughed. "I smoke a joint or two, but not doing any hard drugs. He paused and put his hand on my shoulder, "You know, Tyler, it's a different time, a new era. Don't let it pass you by brother."

We stood up. "By the way," he said. "I called Laura. She asked me to come stay at your house."

"That's fine," I said.

"Is it OK if I go back into the courtroom with you? He asked.

"Sure, come ahead."

As the noon hour approached, the crowd in the courtroom began to grow larger with newspaper and TV reporters milling about. I thought to myself that this was the nearest thing to public hangings that used to attract mobs of curious onlookers. It made me wonder just how far society had progressed since the legions of blood-thirsty Romans delighted in watching the Christians being ravaged by the hungry lions. Even the balcony of the courtroom, in previous times used only by people of color, began to fill with spectators.

As the large clock on the roof of the courthouse began to gong the noon hour, a loud rapping on the jury room door could be heard throughout the courtroom. This sound always sends chills up the spines of any defense lawyer in a criminal case, as well as the defendant.

The sheriff opened the door and the foreman stuck his head out, sounding words that everyone was anxious to hear, "We have a verdict!"

The sheriff told them to hold up until he called them. He then went to the judge's office to let him know and to the holding cell to collect Tommy. He called the DA, and after everyone was in place, the sheriff brought the jury out.

Everyone anxiously watched them as they filed out of the jury room one by one into the jury box. Their faces had no expression, yet it was hard to conceal the fact that they knew something that everyone else was eager to know. Tommy gritted his teeth with his eyes closed. I wrung my sweaty palms together. The district attorney sat stoically. No noise was audible but a frenzied sensation could be felt by all.

The judge said, "Mr. Foreman, do you have a verdict?"

Mr. Ryals stood up. "Yes sir. We do."

"Would you publish the verdict to the court?"

He held a piece of paper in his hand that he read from. "We, the jury, find the defendant guil…" Before he could complete the word, he started coughing, as if he'd swallowed wrong. He couldn't stop coughing.

I slumped in my seat. Tommy crossed his arms on the table and laid his head down.

The buzz among the spectators in the courtroom was electric.

The judge spoke up, "Mr. Sheriff, could you get a glass of water for the foreman?"

When the sheriff returned, Mr. Ryals drank the water and cleared his throat. "I'm sorry Judge. I must've gotten something tickling my throat."

"That's all right," the judge responded. "Let's try it again."

After clearing his throat, he announced, "We the jury find the defendant guilty on the charge of murder and on the charge of theft of the automobile." He cleared his throat again, "But Judge, we don't wanna give him any time to serve."

The sounds then began emanating from the courtroom like the wind blowing through a pine forest. No one, not even the judge, had a clear understanding what they'd intended to do.

"I don't understand," the judge said. "What do you mean by that?" he asked as if he were a teacher scolding a pupil.

"Well," Mr. Ryals again cleared his throat. "The Marine admitted killing the boy and he admitted taking the boy's car, so he's guilty of doing those things, but we don't want him to serve any time for either one of them. We feel he needs to get on back up to Camp Lejeune and head off for Vietnam to serve our country."

The judge seemed puzzled. "Are you saying that even though the defendant admitted his guilt in the two crimes, the jury feels that he was justified in committing those crimes?"

The DA jumped up. "Judge, I object to this verdict! This is highly improper!"

"I'm trying to get to the bottom of it," the judge replied as if he were reprimanding the DA.

The judge turned back to Mr. Ryals. "If the jury feels he was justified in committing the crimes, then you have to find him not guilty."

Mr. Ryals turned around to the other jurors. "Ain't that what we all wanted to do?" They all nodded their heads.

The DA jumped back up. "Judge, this is completely irregular, and I object."

"Do you want me to send them back to the jury room, Mr. District Attorney?"

"Absolutely," he replied.

The judge then said to the jurors, "I'm going to send you back to the jury room and ask that you come back with a proper verdict."

The sheriff led the jurors to their room and opened the door for them. The elation coming from Tommy and me could not be contained. We were about to explode with joy, high-fiving each other. Agnes and Preacher Wraggs both said aloud in unison, "Praise the Lord!" At which time, the judge rapped his gavel and said, "Order in the court!"

The jury returned shortly with a not guilty verdict bringing cheers and tears from many of the spectators. Tommy grabbed me and gave me a hug. The pent-up emotions: worries, dread, fear and apprehension seemed to dissipate in our embrace. Agnes rushed to Tommy and grabbed him in her arms and audibly wept in sobs of joy repeating, "Thank God, Thank God! Our prayers have been answered."

The DA grabbed his briefcase and stormed out of the courtroom in a huff. Calvin's mother shouted out, "You killed my son. You're a murderer." Some of the members of the community who were there to support Calvin took her arm and escorted her out. A number of the spectators came up to me to offer congratulations. Eventually, Wes, Duck and Bonnie Sue were able to work their way through the crowd to shake my hand. I couldn't help but notice the big smile on Tommy's face, which I'd never seen before. The reporters from the newspapers and television stations swarmed around both of us, asking questions and flashing pictures.

When most of the courtroom cleared out, Duck came up to me and said, "I knew this was gonna happen." But he didn't tell me about the conversation he had with Luther Rooks at the pool hall. I found out about that later.

After all the hullabaloo had calmed down, I grabbed my briefcase. Tommy saw me leaving and came back over. "Tyler, I can't thank you enough for what you've done for me. I really appreciate it so much."

"Of course, Tommy. I wish you the best."

"I'd like to stay in touch with you if that's OK," Tommy said.

"Sure, call me or write me anytime."

I told Vern to go to my house, and I'd get there as soon as I could. Back at the office, I called my father and Laura to tell them the news. James and Davis and Bailey and Bonds all congratulated me on the hard-fought victory, and they were more than pleased to have me back in the office to start working again on something that would produce some income.

As the pressure began to drift away, exhaustion set in. I told Bailey and Bonds I needed to go home and get some rest. They understood.

When I arrived home, Laura was sitting in the living room talking to Vern.

"Hi," I sounded off in good spirits, as I opened the door.

"Hi," she replied, but sat still in her favorite chair and didn't get up to kiss me like always. In a marriage, words are not necessary to convey messages. I read her expression of disappointment as if she'd spoken a thousand words.

"Where are the children?" I tried to change the subject.

"Hannah and Wynn are still at playschool, and Miles is taking a nap."

I pulled my chair up beside her, placing my hand on her knee. "Well, at least it's over."

"You're too good a lawyer," she said sarcastically, removing my hand.

"No, it's not that. I did my best, but I agree with you, the jury verdict was probably based on prejudice and bias."

"That's what I was just talking about with Vern. It bothers me, Tyler. You've now permitted open season on homosexuals. You've made it legal to kill someone who has a different sexual preference, and that's not good."

"Honey, it's not me. It was not my fault. I was appointed by the court to do a job, and I did the best I possibly could. Can't you understand that?"

"But doesn't the verdict bother you?" She raised her voice.

"Laura, you don't understand. I really got to know Tommy pretty well. He's a good kid – never done anything wrong. He joined the Marines, and they trained him to be a killer to go fight this war in Vietnam. He'd been sexually abused by his teacher. He'd repressed this anger deep inside him. When Calvin made a pass at him, he snapped. He was intoxicated. I don't think he really knew what he was doing. It certainly wasn't premeditated. I don't think he has a mean streak in his entire body. It was just a culmination of events, like a perfect storm."

"You don't have to try your whole case in front of me. I've already made up my mind."

"I'm glad you weren't on my jury," I kidded, but wished I'd never said that. It didn't go over very well.

Ignoring my disparaging remark, she continued on her tirade, "I'm sorry, Tyler. It upsets me to see him get off with no punishment."

"Look, I know how you feel honey, and I understand it, but I don't think homophobes are going to go out and start killing homosexuals because of this case."

She didn't respond. She just sat there with the same expression I'd seen so many times before when we'd had arguments. Vern kept conspicuously silent during all of this.

I stood up. "Look, you guys. I'm spent. I gotta get a little rest. I'm going back and take a nap, OK?"

"Sure," she sighed. "I'll try to keep Miles quiet when he wakes up."

When I stretched out on the bed, I fell asleep before my head even hit the pillow. It seemed only minutes had passed when Laura began shaking me.

"What?" I sprung up in fright. "What is it?"

"There's some guy at the door wanting to see you."

"Who is it?"

"I don't know. He said he was a preacher."

"What does he want?"

"How do I know?"

I got up, put on my clothes and walked to the front door all bleary-eyed. There stood Preacher Wraggs.

"I'm sorry to bother you, Tyler, but Tommy wants you to go with us."

"Go with you? Where?" I grimaced.

"To visit Calvin's grave," he said.

"Calvin's grave?"

"Yes. He wants to go. He doesn't want his family to be with him. He only wants you and me."

"Do I have to do this?" I pleaded. "I'm really beat."

"Tyler, he needs to, and he won't go without you."

"You know, Preacher, I'm pretty exhausted."

"I'm sure you are."

"OK," I conceded "give me a minute, and I'll meet you out front." I went back to the bedroom, grabbed my coat and knit hat. When I told Laura what was going on, she asked, "Are you sure you're up to this?"

"No. As a matter of fact, I'm not, but whatever!"

I asked Vern if he'd like to go with me.

"Sure," he said.

I introduced Tommy and Preacher Wraggs to Vern, and the four of us piled in to the preacher's old '59 Buick and drove to Palmetto Cemetery without saying a word. The preacher had been there earlier to find the gravesite, so he knew where to go.

We walked together to the grave without speaking and stood there for a few moments. The inscription on the headstone read, "Calvin Livingston; Born October 2, 1953; Died November 29, 1973."

After standing in silence for a good while, Tommy walked to the granite slab over the grave that the community had purchased for Calvin. Preacher Wraggs, Vern and I stood silently behind, as a cold northeast wind blew across our backs causing us to shiver.

Tommy stood for a moment, then knelt beside the grave. "I didn't mean to kill you. I'm sorry you had to die." Tears began streaming down his face. Finally, he raised his head, wiped the tears on the sleeve of his jacket and stood up. Preacher Wraggs walked to where he was standing, put his arms around him in a bear hug. When he released him, Tommy walked over to me and hugged me again saying, "Thank you for everything you did for me."

Preacher Wraggs spoke up to break the spell, "Let's join our hands in prayer."

I grasped Tommy's hand then Preacher Wraggs' as the four of us stood at the foot of the grave in a small circle.

The preacher sounded off as if he were speaking from the pulpit. "O God, in heaven above, look down upon these two boys – one standing beside me, and one lying in the grave. Bless them Dear God. They both made mistakes, and I ask that You forgive them for all their sins of omission and commission. Take young Calvin into Your Loving Arms, and be with him and his family and friends. He was taken from this earth at such a young age, please find a place for him in Your Heavenly Kingdom."

He then increased the volume. "Almighty God and merciful Lord, please grant to Tommy, absolution and remission for his sins. He has repented, Dear God, and I ask that you have mercy upon him. May the rest of his time here on this earth be pure and holy, so that at the end of his life, you may find a place for him of eternal joy in Your Heavenly Kingdom."

And with an even louder voice, he said, "Glory be to the Father, and to the Son, and to the Holy Spirit. As it was in the beginning is now and ever shall be, World Without End, Amen!"

Driving home, Vern sat in back with Tommy, while I chatted with Preacher Wraggs up front. On arriving home, we all said our goodbyes among handshaking, backslapping and well-wishing. Before they left, Vern reached his hand out to Tommy and with complete sincerity said, "I wish you all the best." I could feel myself getting choked up watching that gesture coming from my brother.

After they drove away, Vern asked, as we walked toward the door, "You know what I'd like to do?"

"What?"

"Let's go over to the island and walk on the beach."

"Are you crazy? With this cold wind and temp in the thirties?"

"What's wrong brother? You can't take it."

I'd never been bullied by my brother, and I wasn't going to let him call my bluff at this late date. I grabbed gloves and scarves, and we each carried our down jackets.

"I've got an extra knit hat for you," I said.

"With all this hair, do you think I need it?" he laughed.

"Take it just in case." I grabbed my favorite Davidson black and red one and gave it to him. I took the scruffy, orange and green one I'd worn since high school.

Vern wanted to drive his old VW van, so we took off over the St. Simons Causeway listening to a Lynyrd Skynyrd cassette at full blast, preventing any semblance of conversation. We arrived at East Beach, next to Gould's Inlet, separating St. Simons Island from Sea Island. No other person could be seen. Vern parked the van next to the huge boulders placed there after Hurricane Dora in 1964, commonly referred to by the locals as the "Johnson Rocks," named for the then sitting President.

Vern reached under the seat and pulled out what appeared to be a shaving kit, the container where he kept his stash. He pulled out a pipe and looked over as if he were daring me, "Wanna take a little toke before we go walking?"

"Good God, Vern. You know it's a felony in Georgia. If I got busted, I'd lose my license to practice law."

He laughed. "Such a backward state we live in. Homosexuality is against the law, too, so, I guess I'm just a common criminal."

He lit the pipe and, throwing caution to the wind, I joined him in smoking a bowl, and chasing it with Vern's bottle of Ripple, the wine of choice for most hippies.

Vern, without speaking, stared for a long time at the ocean rolling in at high tide lashing against the rock wall. The northeaster seemed almost gale force. He took a deep inhale and attempted to blow a smoke ring, then in a soft voice, muttered, "What's it like being married?"

"Best thing I ever did." After saying it, the thought hit me that this was not something I should've said. Hearing echoes of Laura, "Tyler, you've always one-upped him in everything."

"I guess it's something I'll never experience," Vern mused, then continued gazing straight ahead in a daze.

"I'm sorry," I said sincerely.

"You don't have to be sorry," he spoke in a tone as if he were chastising me. "I didn't choose to be what I am. It would've been a whole lot easier to be what society calls normal instead of being called queer. But it's the hand I've been dealt, and I have to play it as best I can."

He immediately stepped out and began walking down the

beach ahead of me. I followed with the wind howling at my back. Clouds blocked the sun, making it even colder. I put on gloves, tugged at my knit hat to cover as much of my head as possible and then picked up the pace to catch up with my brother.

We conversed in small-talk about him and his friends in Atlanta who frequent the gay bars. I talked about my continued love of basketball. We laughed about Mom and Dad's reaction when Vern told them he was homosexual, and she wanted me to try to talk him out of it. We joshed each other about growing up. I called him a "mama's boy," and he called me "a stuck up bastard," we both laughed like we'd never done before. Sand blew behind us along the surface of the beach as if we were being chased by a flock of seagulls, swift enough to sting the back of our legs. As we walked next to the large sand dunes, I interrupted our conversation. "Gotta take a leak."

"Mind if I join you?" he asked.

For whatever reason, that made me laugh. We walked together into the dunes, taller than we were, surrounded by remnants of waving sea oats blowing in the wind.

I snickered as I watched Vern pee a figure in the shape of a peace sign. Being higher up in the dune and about three feet up-wind from him, I began staring at a flock of pelicans flying overhead. It didn't occur to me that my stream would blow in his direction, giving him an unwanted shower. Still looking up in the sky, a force suddenly hit me from behind that threw me onto the sand. Vern had leaped on my back and wrestled me to the ground where we tussled like two little kids in kindergarten.

"You think you can piss on me and get away with it!" He pounded me with his fists, not in a hurtful way, but enough to take out his pent-up aggression that had probably existed since birth. I didn't attempt to fight back, knowing that this was an incident that needed to happen.

Back on the beach both of us, being more relaxed than we'd ever been with each other, discussed various things; mostly our parents, reminisced about growing up together and how we'd missed out on having a good relationship. We vowed to compensate for that in the future, and somehow, I felt I'd just met my new best friend.

We appeared to be walking faster than normal as the wind propelled us further along the beach. The sand, rushing by our legs at breakneck speed, seemed surreal, camouflaging the surface of the beach and making us feel as if we were walking through clouds.

After a brief period with no conversation, I turned to him, "You know, Vern, this trial was the hardest thing I've ever had to do in my life."

"I can believe that," he agreed.

"I want you to know I don't have any prejudice against homosexuals," I said. "It's a free country, and as long as they don't harm anybody, what do I care?"

He gave a short laugh. "But your client did the harm."

"Yeah, but I'm talking in general about homosexuals harming another person."

Vern smiled but didn't comment.

"Look," I said. "You know me well enough to know that I'm a competitor. I've always wanted to succeed in everything I've ever done. Even in basketball, I play my heart out trying to win every game, and I'll admit that my competitive spirit probably had something to do with this trial."

He shrugged his shoulders. "But you'll have to admit winning this case got a murderer free."

I shook my head. "Vern, I swear to you, it never occurred to me that he would get off without any punishment. I thought a victory would be to keep him out of the chair. I didn't want him to die, because I don't believe in capital punishment. I was just as shocked as everyone else with the jury verdict."

He kept walking without responding.

I turned toward him and continued my defense. "I agree with you that he should've received some punishment – just don't put him to death."

He shot back without hesitation. "Oh, he'll be punished all right. He'll torture himself for the rest of his life with guilt, and that'll be worse than any punishment the court could ever give him."

I replayed the wisdom of my brother's comment. It's something I hadn't even considered. Then I said, "I'm sure the first thing he'll want to do is to see if the Marines will take him back."

Vern remained silent, then added, "If they don't, he'll need to get some counseling as soon as possible, or else he'll be suicidal."

I thought for a moment then said, "Let's talk to Dad to see if he can help get Tommy back in the Marines. Dad has friends who are influential."

"Good idea," Vern agreed. "I bet he knows two or three congressmen personally."

After walking for a good while in the wintry breeze without talking, I again broke the silence, "Soooo, what was your impression of Tommy?"

He remained quiet for a good while as if he needed to get his thoughts together before he answered. Like a voyeur, the setting sun peeped through the clouds for the first time, illuminating not only Vern's face, but also the waves rolling onto the white, sandy beach. I can still see his sly grin, and the words he spoke will echo in my mind for the rest of my life.

"You know, Tyler," he smiled in a smug sort of way. "It takes one to know one."

THE PALATKA DAILY NEWS
MAY 4, 1974

The Defense Department notified the family of Private First-Class Thomas Smith Jennings, last year's graduate of Palatka High, and son of Wesley and Agnes Jennings, that he has been awarded the Bronze Star, posthumously. The report goes on to say that his platoon was assaulting a strong enemy position when they began receiving heavy fire from the Viet Cong. Rockets blazed through the jungle, and the sounds of machine guns and other automatic weapons filled the air. His platoon advanced on the enemy and stopped in front of a stream. Jennings, on his own, dashed across the stream in the face of enemy fire. He crawled on his belly as close as he could and began tossing hand grenades into the enemy bunkers. On his way back, he dragged two of his wounded comrades to safety. When he returned in an attempt to save even more, he received fatal wounds from enemy fire. While he died there on the battlefield, many of his fellow Marines were saved because of the heroic actions of Private Jennings. His platoon leader, Sgt. Nicholson, described his encounter with the enemy to be above and beyond the call of duty. Our community should be proud to know that a hero like Jennings was born and raised here in Palatka. The family informed the newspaper that the time of his funeral will be announced as soon as his body is returned. His burial will take place in the Arlington Cemetery in Virginia.

Made in the USA
Columbia, SC
31 July 2018